SWIMMY AND THE VALLEY OF THE LAST SONG

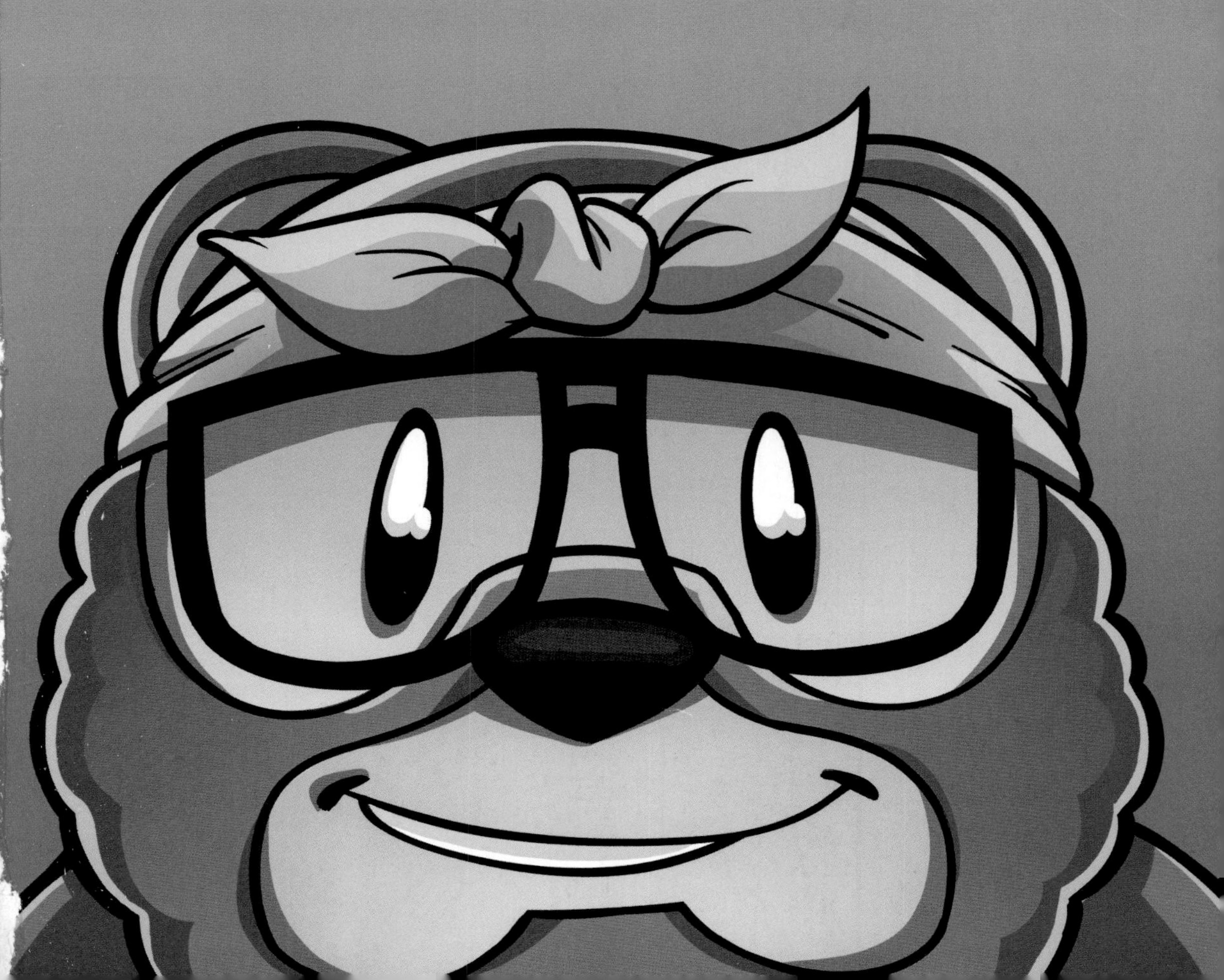

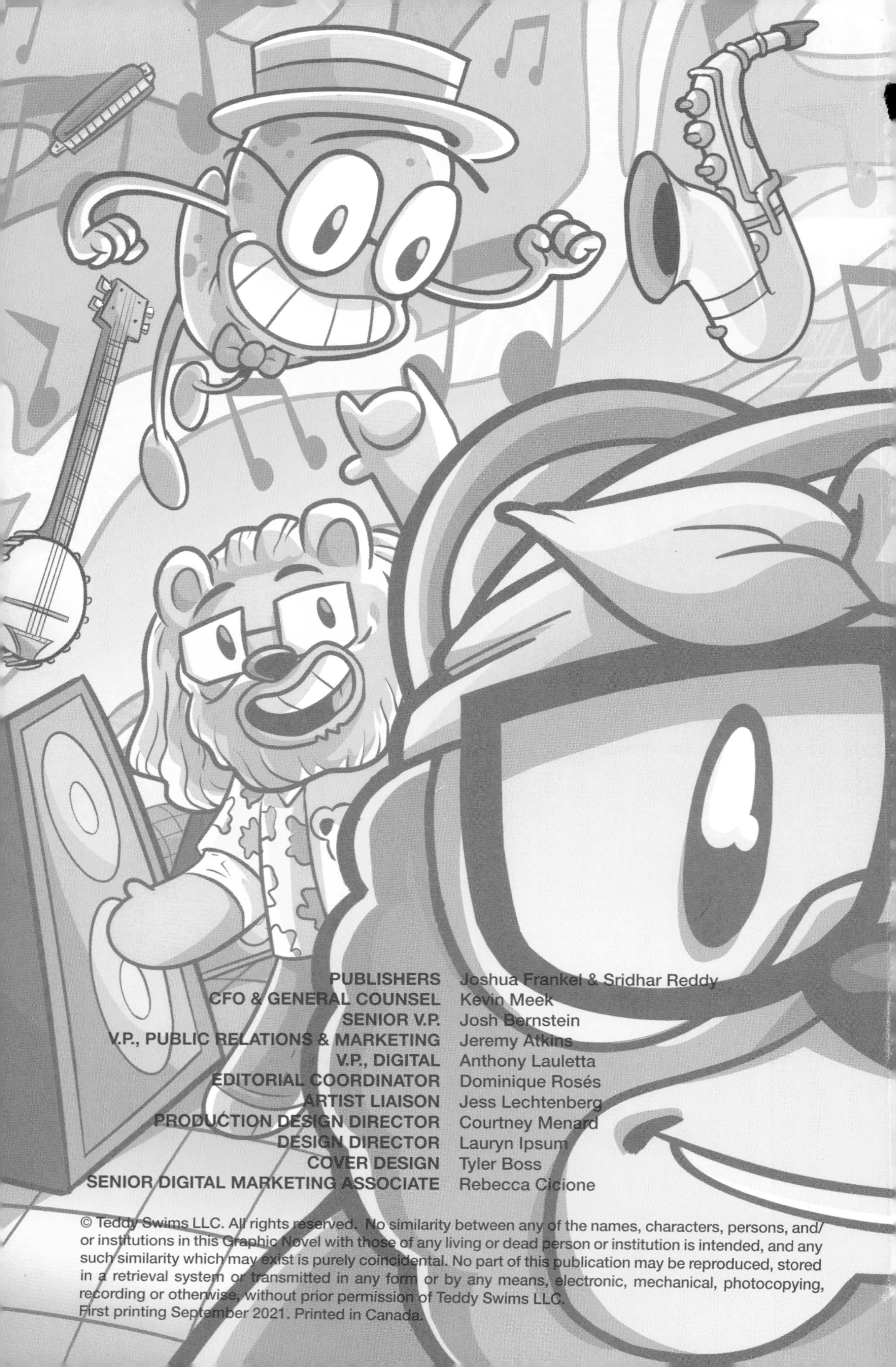

PUBLISHERS	Joshua Frankel & Sridhar Reddy
CFO & GENERAL COUNSEL	Kevin Meek
SENIOR V.P.	Josh Bernstein
V.P., PUBLIC RELATIONS & MARKETING	Jeremy Atkins
V.P., DIGITAL	Anthony Lauletta
EDITORIAL COORDINATOR	Dominique Rosés
ARTIST LIAISON	Jess Lechtenberg
PRODUCTION DESIGN DIRECTOR	Courtney Menard
DESIGN DIRECTOR	Lauryn Ipsum
COVER DESIGN	Tyler Boss
SENIOR DIGITAL MARKETING ASSOCIATE	Rebecca Cicione

First printing September 2021. Printed in Canada.

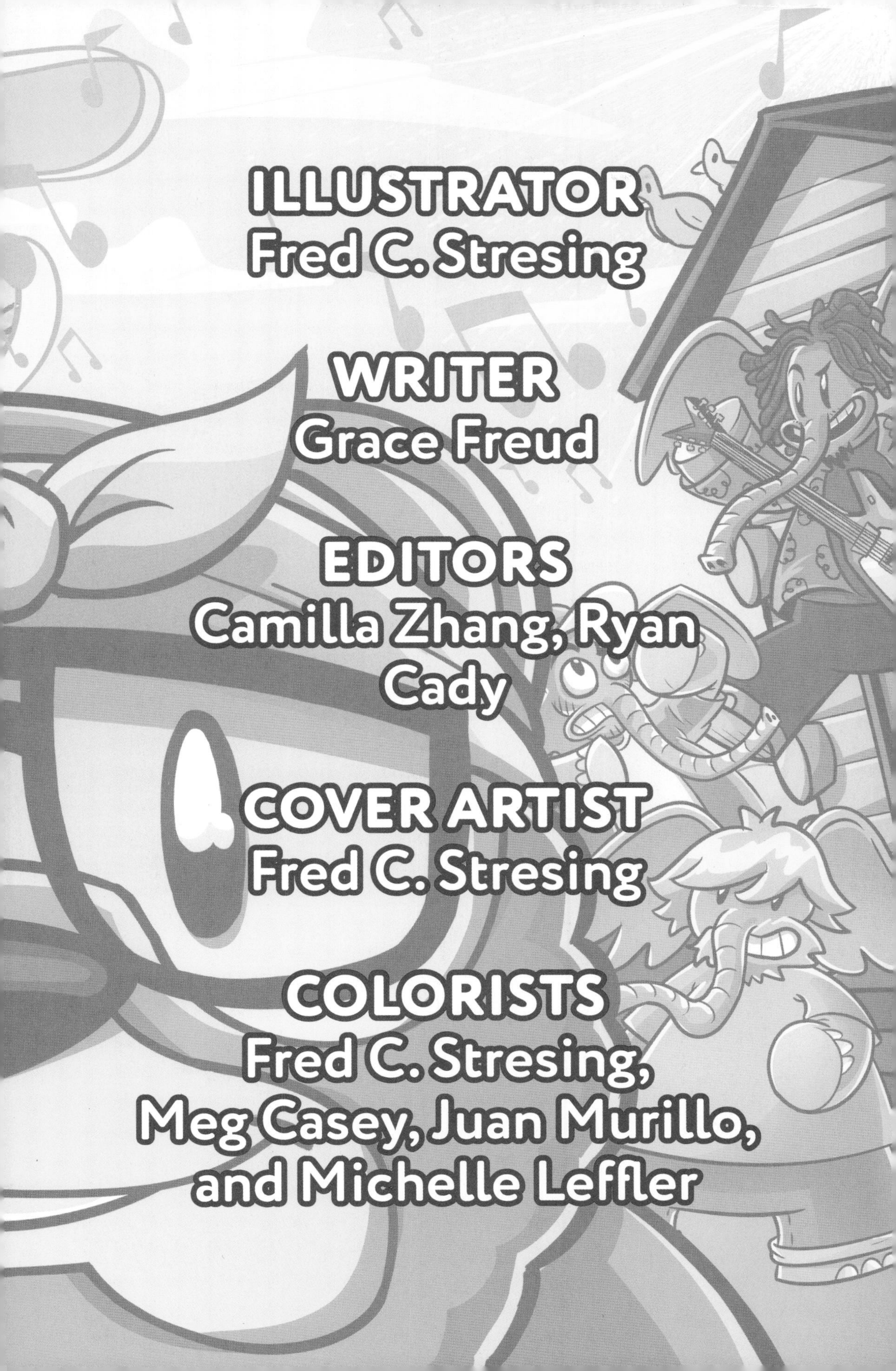

ILLUSTRATOR
Fred C. Stresing

WRITER
Grace Freud

EDITORS
Camilla Zhang, Ryan Cady

COVER ARTIST
Fred C. Stresing

COLORISTS
Fred C. Stresing, Meg Casey, Juan Murillo, and Michelle Leffler

Ever since I was a kid I've dreamed of building my own universe of characters and stories that everyone can enjoy, especially children. I believe so strongly that the job of a musician or anyone with a platform should use it to guide and influence the upcoming generation in a positive way! And for the adults, I always want to do anything I can to preserve that child in all of us because it's the most important part of us! That being said, developing a comic book has always been a dream of mine! I hope you fall in love with Swimmy's adventure as much as I have. Here's to dreaming even bigger and making this a series!

—TEDDY SWIMS

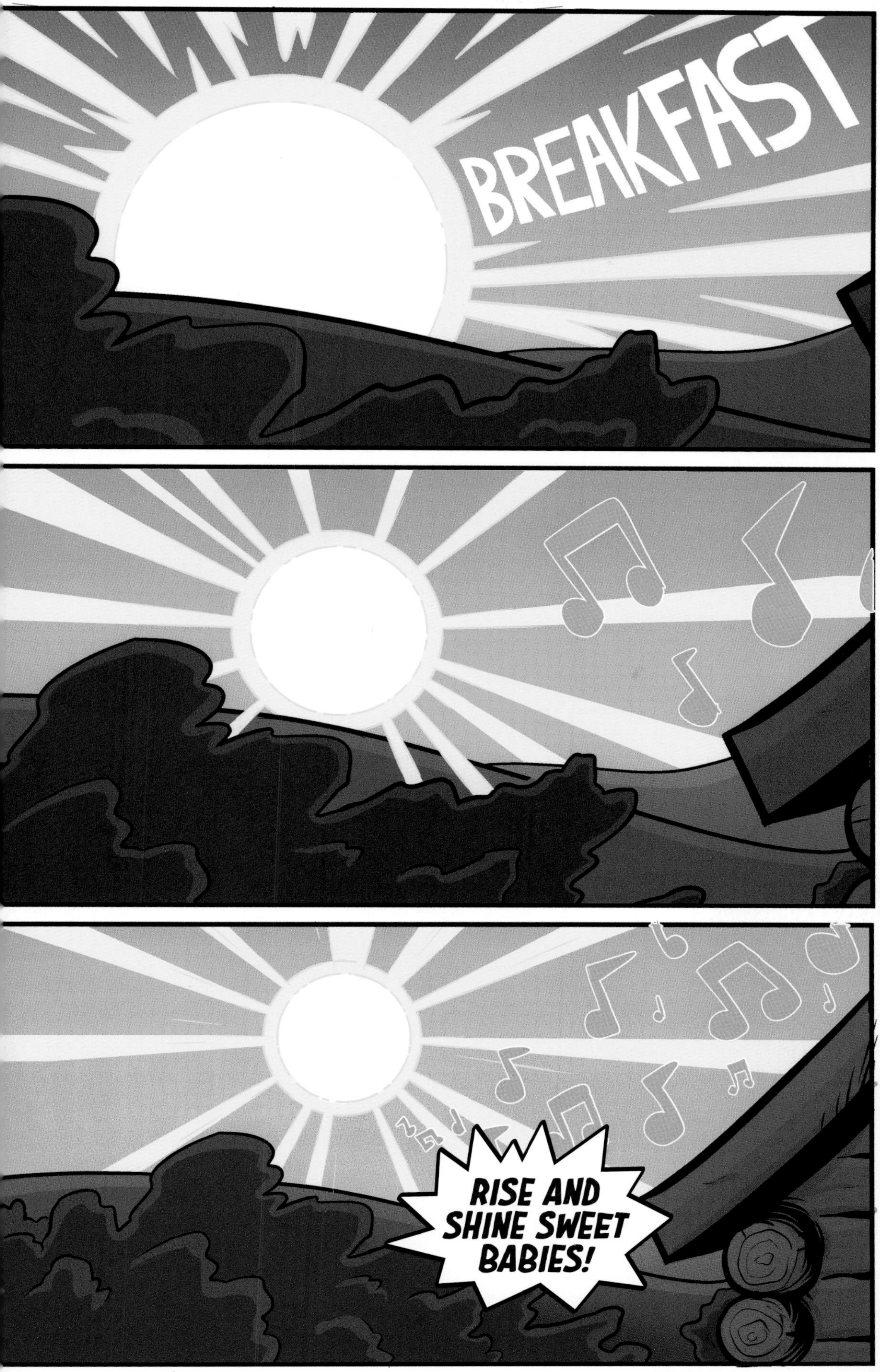
BREAKFAST
RISE AND SHINE SWEET BABIES!

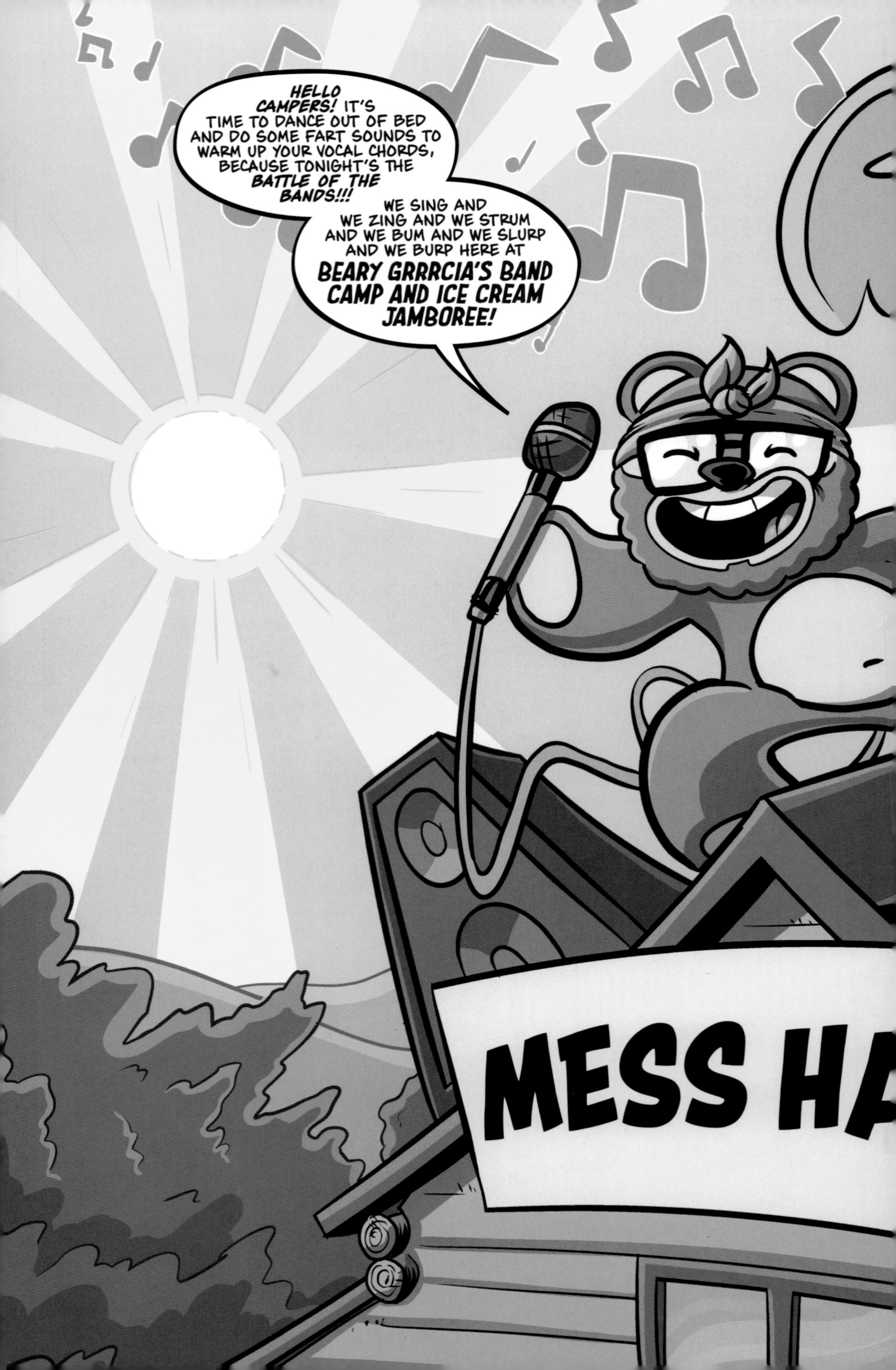
HELLO CAMPERS! IT'S TIME TO DANCE OUT OF BED AND DO SOME FART SOUNDS TO WARM UP YOUR VOCAL CHORDS, BECAUSE TONIGHT'S THE BATTLE OF THE BANDS!!!
WE SING AND WE ZING AND WE STRUM AND WE BUM AND WE SLURP AND WE BURP HERE AT BEARY GRRRCIA'S BAND CAMP AND ICE CREAM JAMBOREE!
MESS HA

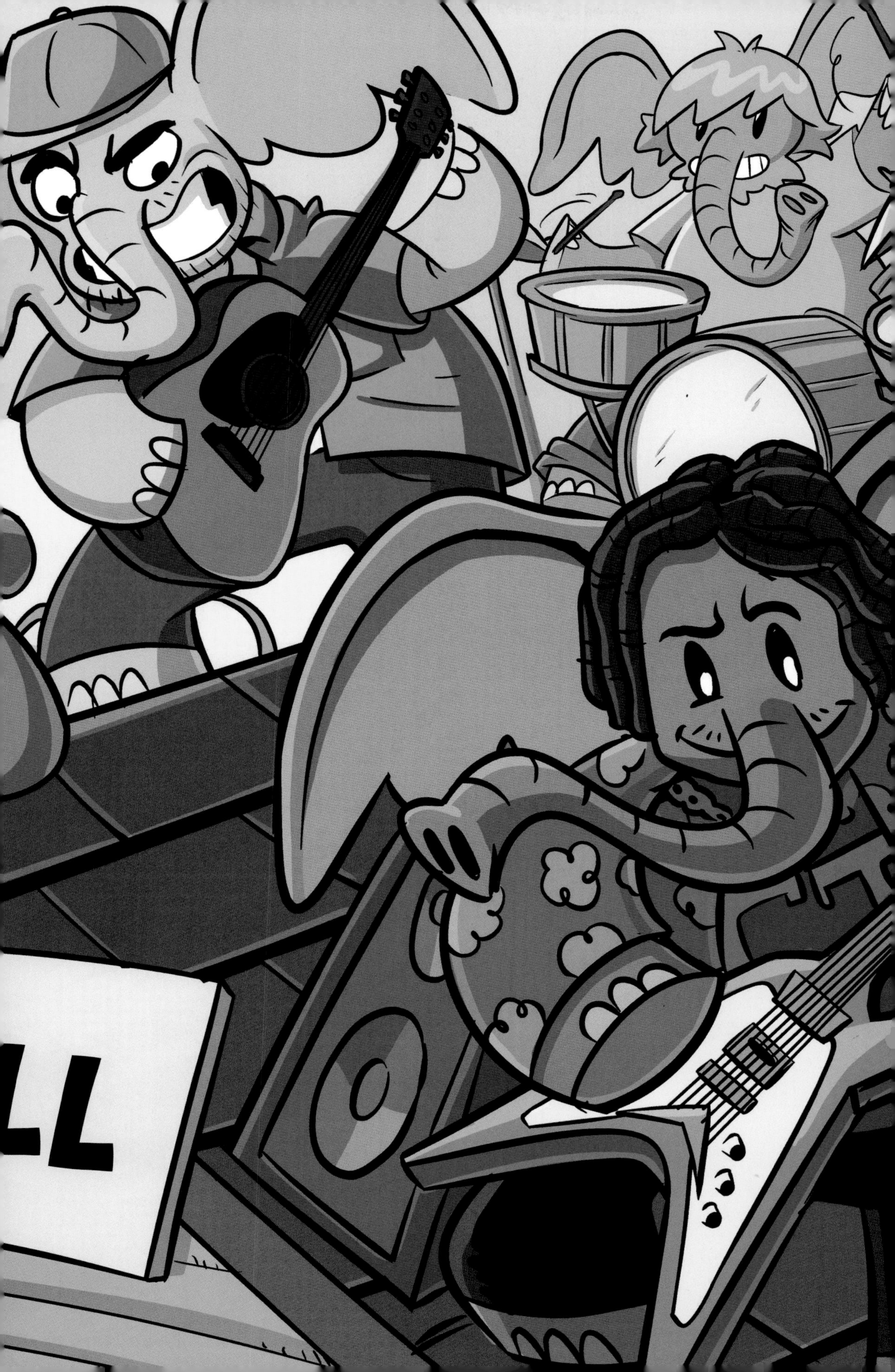
LL

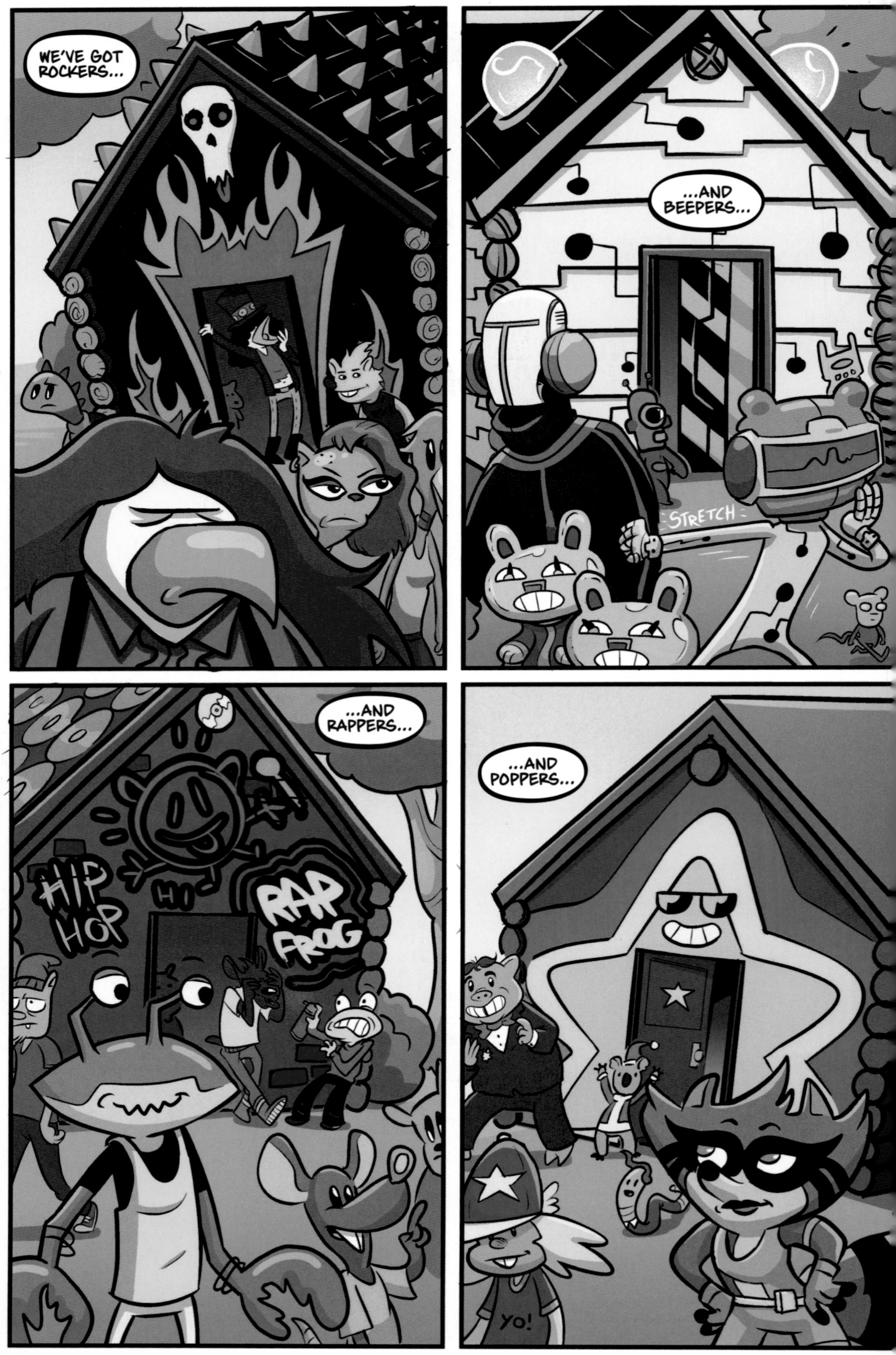
WE'VE GOT ROCKERS...
...AND BEEPERS...
STRETCH
...AND RAPPERS...
HIP HOP
HI
RAP FROG
...AND POPPERS...
YO!

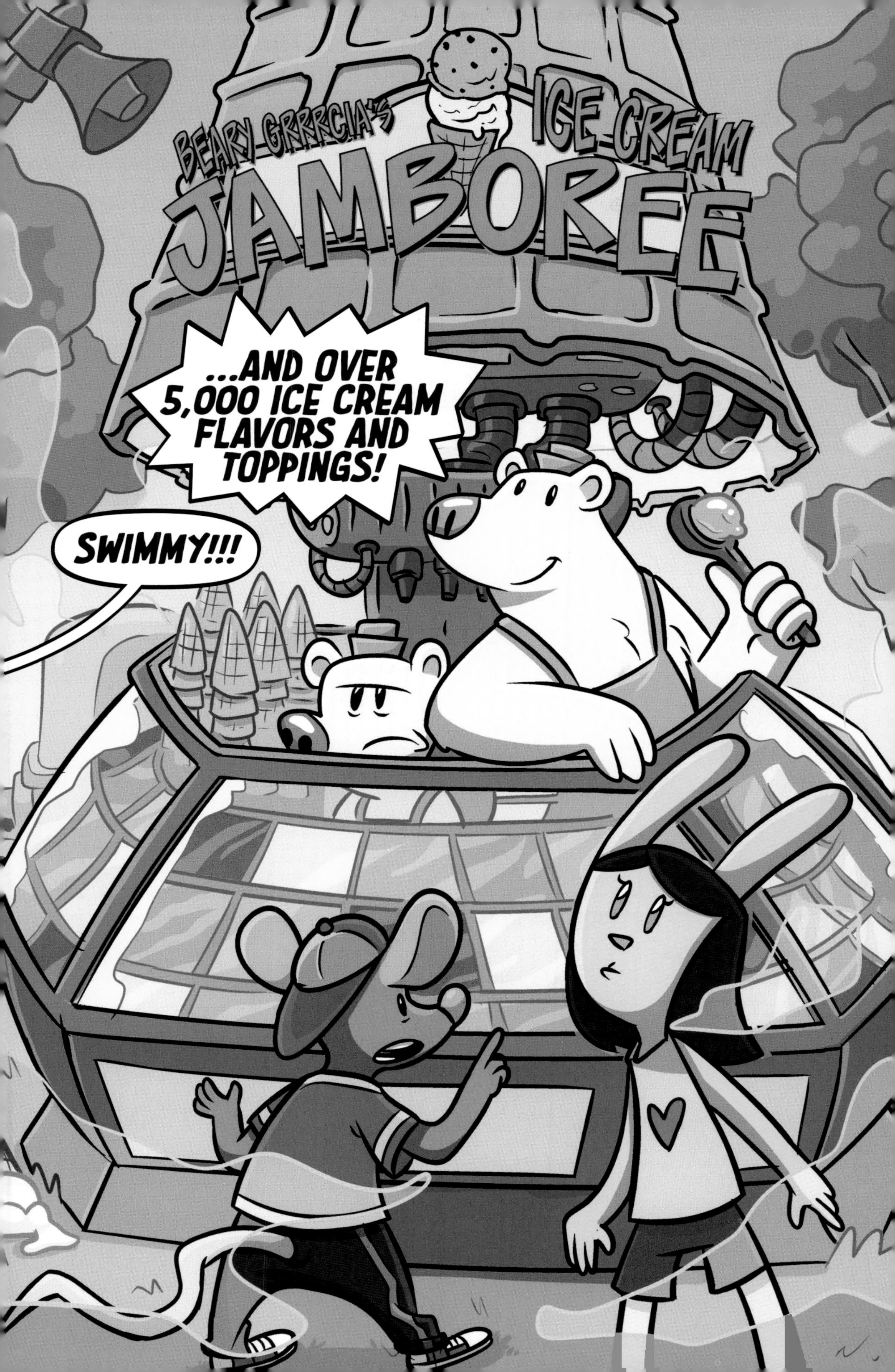
BEARY GRRRCIA'S ICE CREAM
JAMBOREE
...AND OVER 5,000 ICE CREAM FLAVORS AND TOPPINGS!
SWIMMY!!!

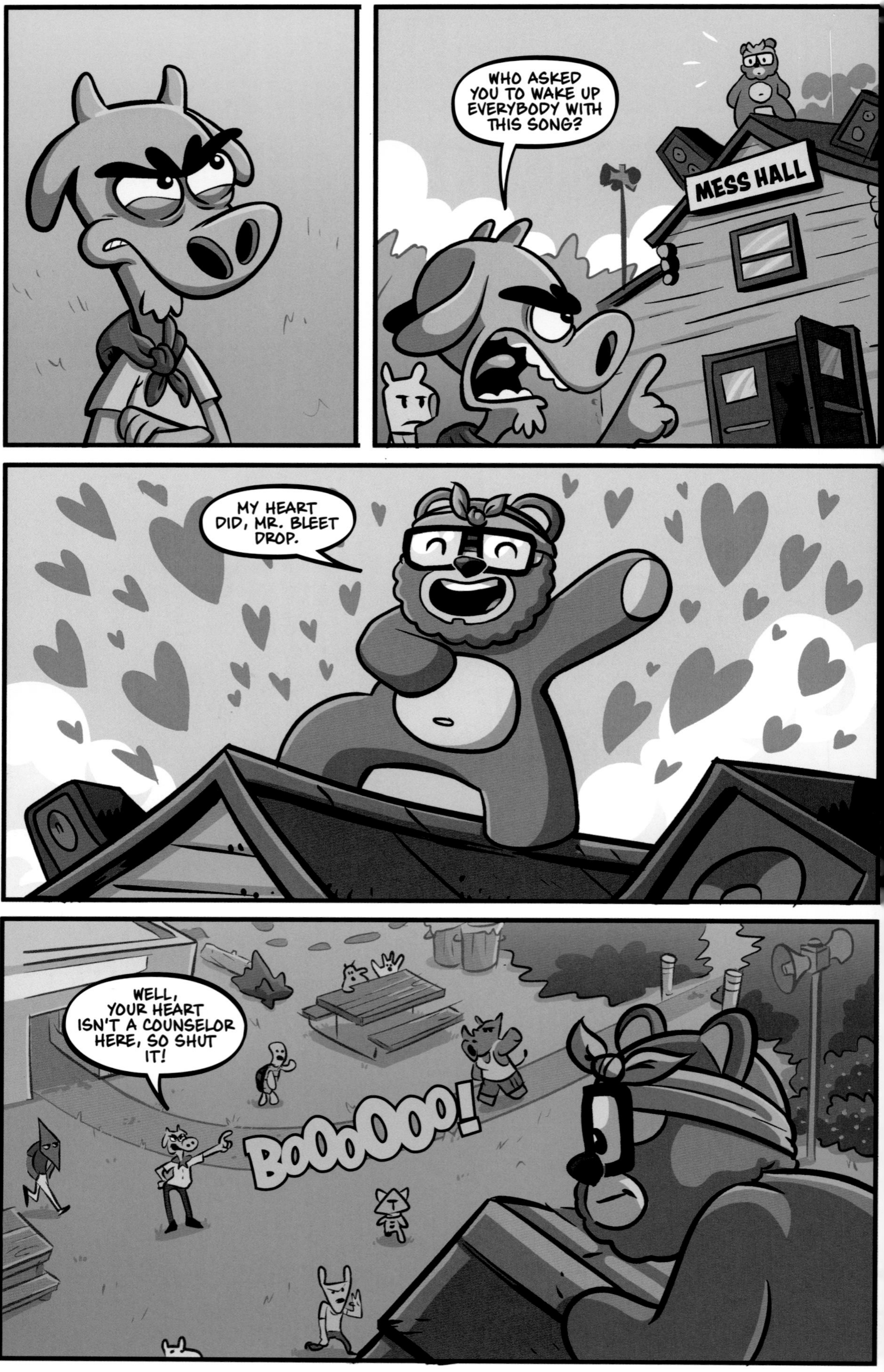
WHO ASKED YOU TO WAKE UP EVERYBODY WITH THIS SONG?
MESS HALL
MY HEART DID, MR. BLEET DROP.
WELL, YOUR HEART ISN'T A COUNSELOR HERE, SO SHUT IT!
BOOoOOO!

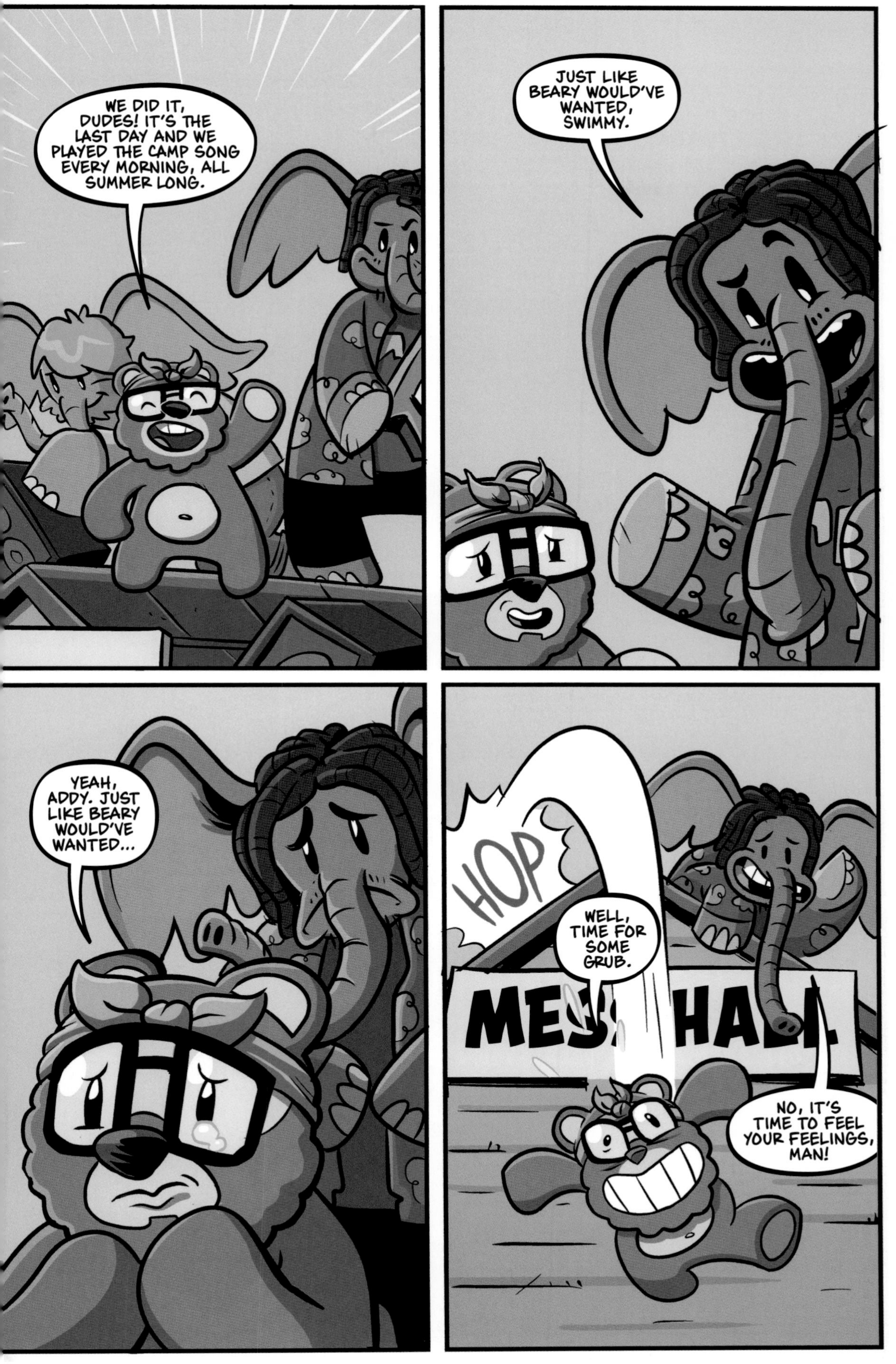
WE DID IT, DUDES! IT'S THE LAST DAY AND WE PLAYED THE CAMP SONG EVERY MORNING, ALL SUMMER LONG.
JUST LIKE BEARY WOULD'VE WANTED, SWIMMY.
YEAH, ADDY. JUST LIKE BEARY WOULD'VE WANTED...
HOP
WELL, TIME FOR SOME GRUB.
MESS HALL
NO, IT'S TIME TO FEEL YOUR FEELINGS, MAN!

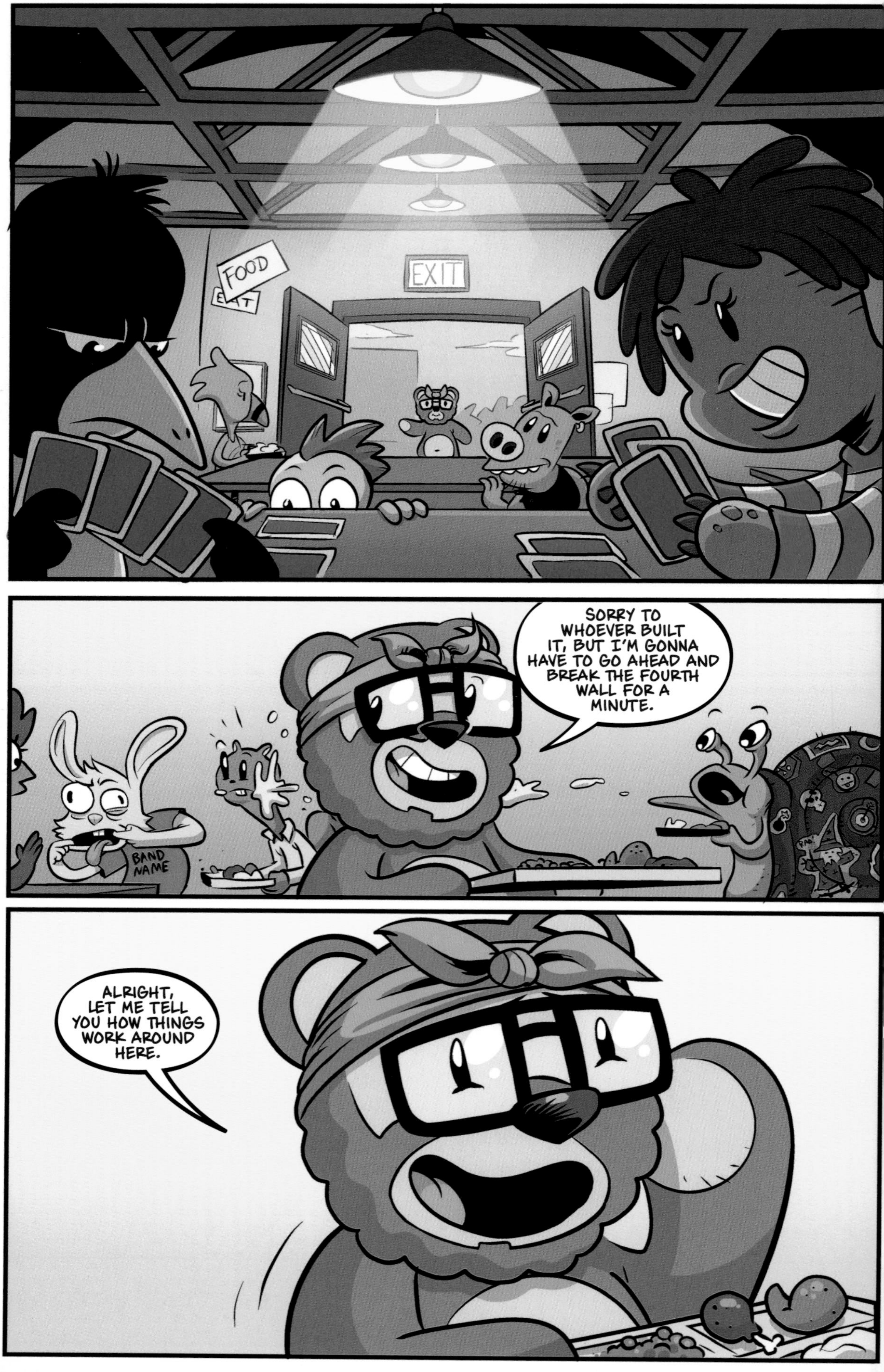
FOOD
EXIT
SORRY TO WHOEVER BUILT IT, BUT I'M GONNA HAVE TO GO AHEAD AND BREAK THE FOURTH WALL FOR A MINUTE.
BAND NAME
ALRIGHT, LET ME TELL YOU HOW THINGS WORK AROUND HERE.

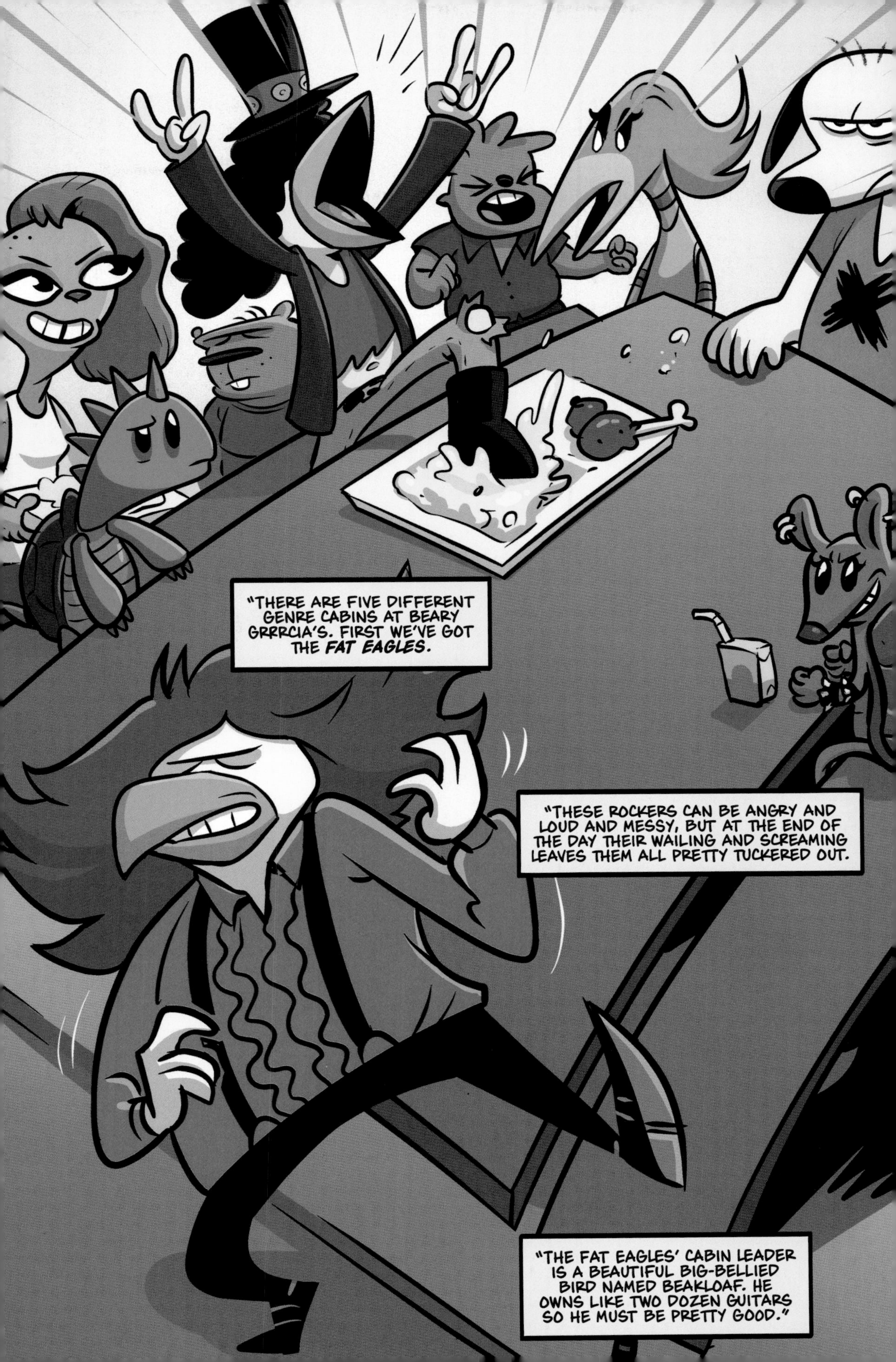
"THERE ARE FIVE DIFFERENT GENRE CABINS AT BEARY GRRRCIA'S. FIRST WE'VE GOT THE *FAT EAGLES*.
"THESE ROCKERS CAN BE ANGRY AND LOUD AND MESSY, BUT AT THE END OF THE DAY THEIR WAILING AND SCREAMING LEAVES THEM ALL PRETTY TUCKERED OUT.
"THE FAT EAGLES' CABIN LEADER IS A BEAUTIFUL BIG-BELLIED BIRD NAMED BEAKLOAF. HE OWNS LIKE TWO DOZEN GUITARS SO HE MUST BE PRETTY GOOD."

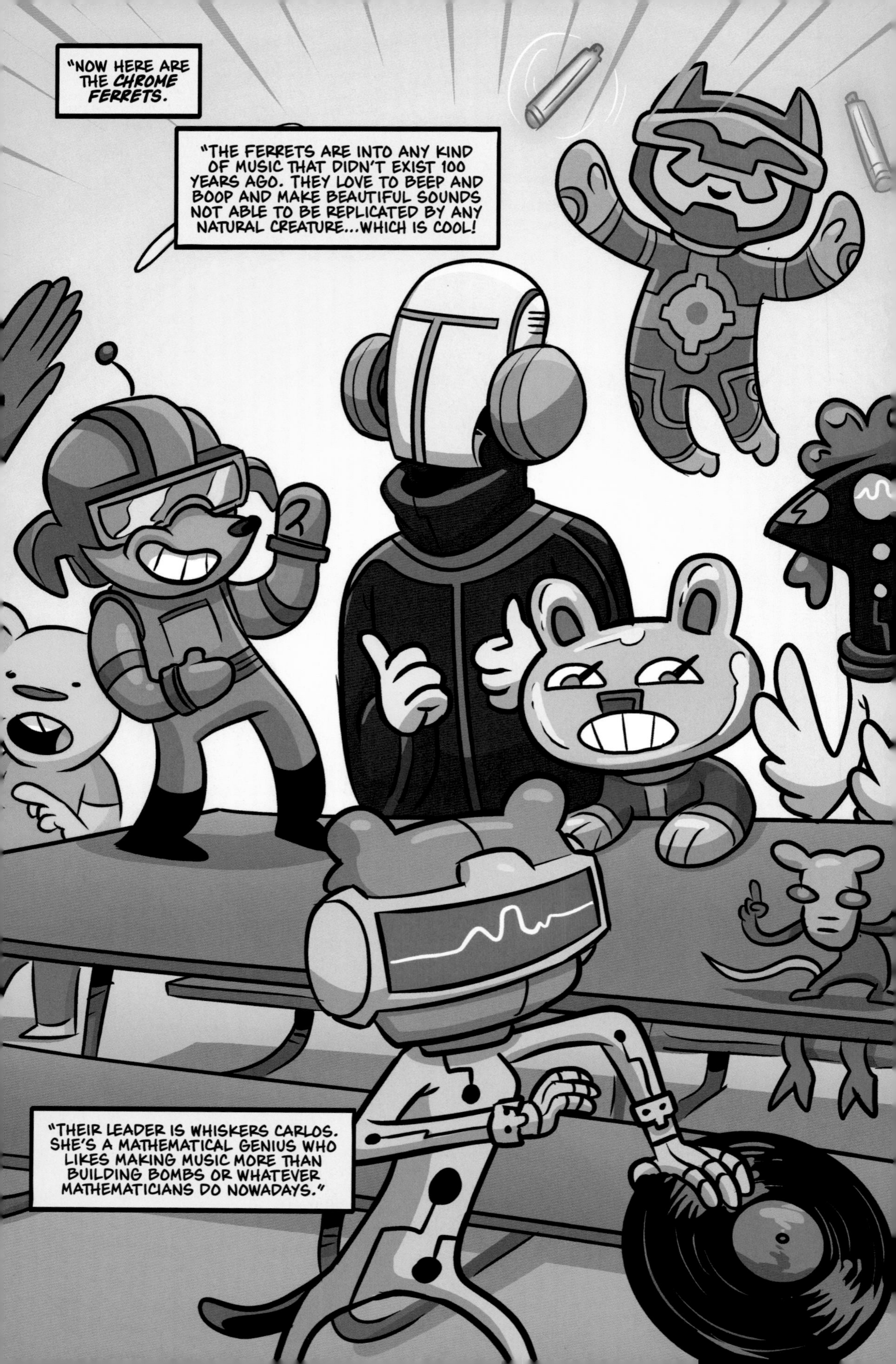
"NOW HERE ARE THE *CHROME FERRETS*.
"THE FERRETS ARE INTO ANY KIND OF MUSIC THAT DIDN'T EXIST 100 YEARS AGO. THEY LOVE TO BEEP AND BOOP AND MAKE BEAUTIFUL SOUNDS NOT ABLE TO BE REPLICATED BY ANY NATURAL CREATURE...WHICH IS COOL!
"THEIR LEADER IS WHISKERS CARLOS. SHE'S A MATHEMATICAL GENIUS WHO LIKES MAKING MUSIC MORE THAN BUILDING BOMBS OR WHATEVER MATHEMATICIANS DO NOWADAYS."

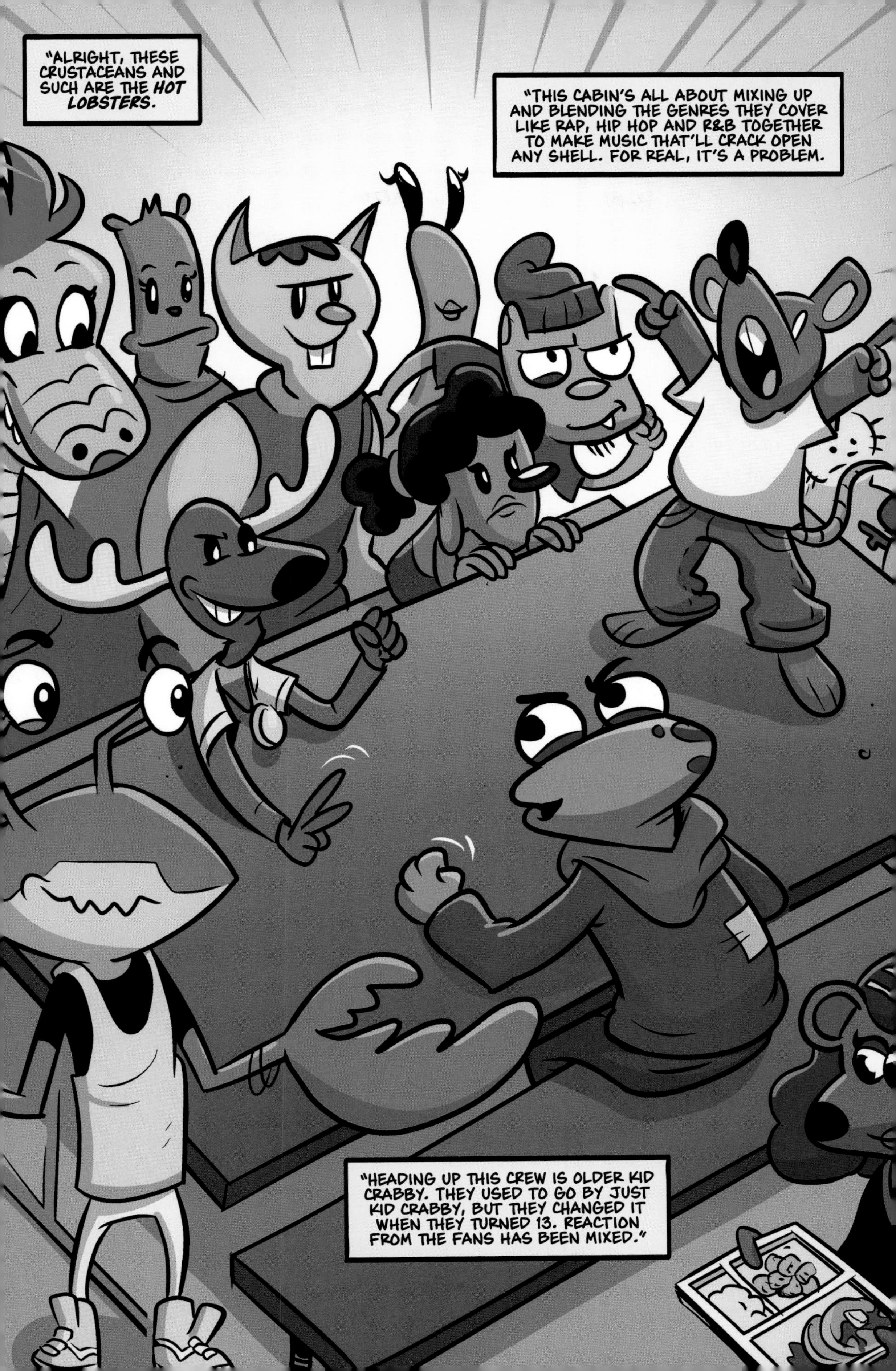
"ALRIGHT, THESE CRUSTACEANS AND SUCH ARE THE *HOT LOBSTERS*.
"THIS CABIN'S ALL ABOUT MIXING UP AND BLENDING THE GENRES THEY COVER LIKE RAP, HIP HOP AND R&B TOGETHER TO MAKE MUSIC THAT'LL CRACK OPEN ANY SHELL. FOR REAL, IT'S A PROBLEM.
"HEADING UP THIS CREW IS OLDER KID CRABBY. THEY USED TO GO BY JUST KID CRABBY, BUT THEY CHANGED IT WHEN THEY TURNED 13. REACTION FROM THE FANS HAS BEEN MIXED."

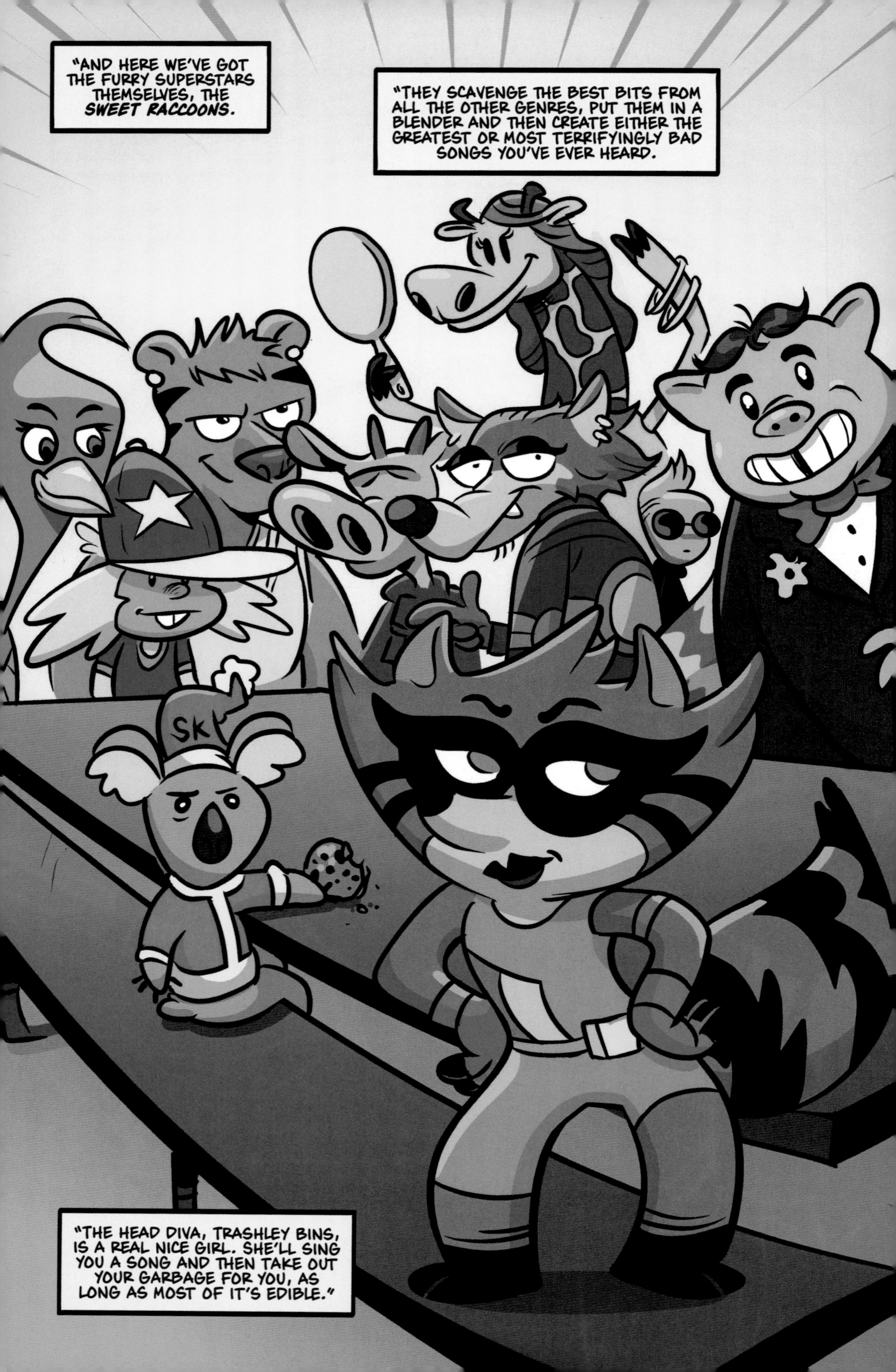
"AND HERE WE'VE GOT THE FURRY SUPERSTARS THEMSELVES, THE *SWEET RACCOONS*.
"THEY SCAVENGE THE BEST BITS FROM ALL THE OTHER GENRES, PUT THEM IN A BLENDER AND THEN CREATE EITHER THE GREATEST OR MOST TERRIFYINGLY BAD SONGS YOU'VE EVER HEARD.
SK
"THE HEAD DIVA, TRASHLEY BINS, IS A REAL NICE GIRL. SHE'LL SING YOU A SONG AND THEN TAKE OUT YOUR GARBAGE FOR YOU, AS LONG AS MOST OF IT'S EDIBLE."

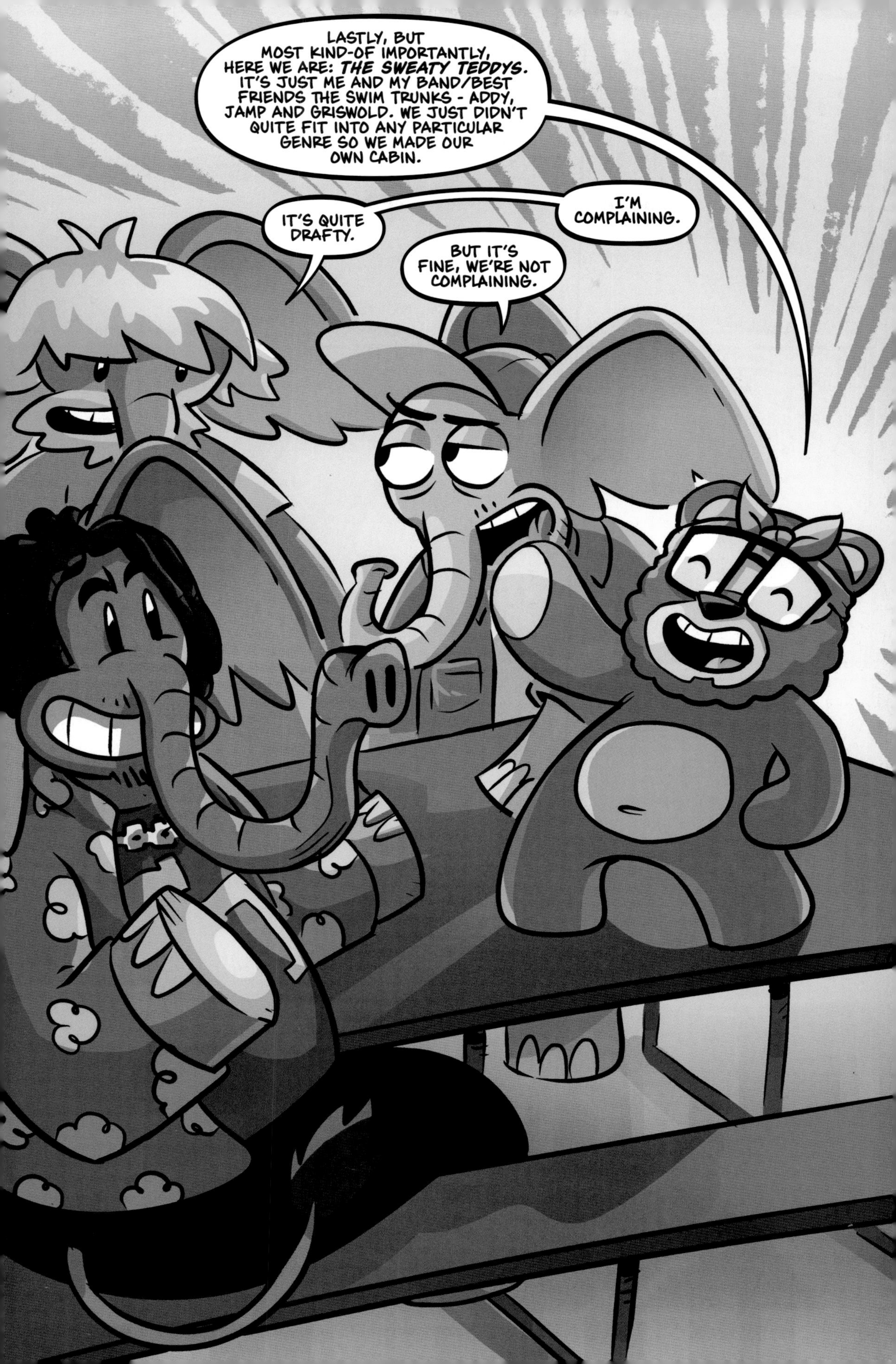
LASTLY, BUT MOST KIND-OF IMPORTANTLY, HERE WE ARE: *THE SWEATY TEDDYS.* IT'S JUST ME AND MY BAND/BEST FRIENDS THE SWIM TRUNKS - ADDY, JAMP AND GRISWOLD. WE JUST DIDN'T QUITE FIT INTO ANY PARTICULAR GENRE SO WE MADE OUR OWN CABIN.
IT'S QUITE DRAFTY.
I'M COMPLAINING.
BUT IT'S FINE, WE'RE NOT COMPLAINING.

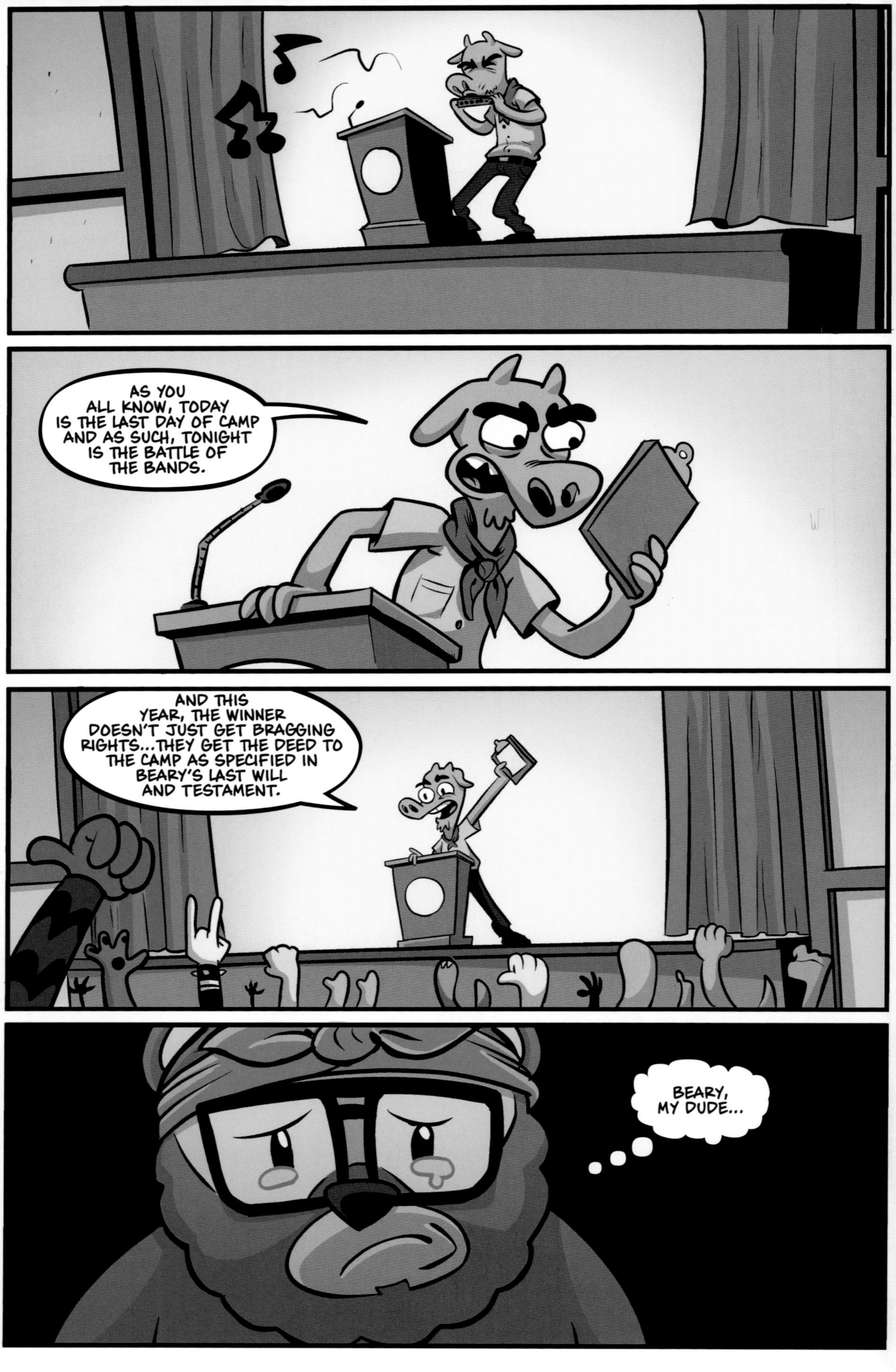
AS YOU ALL KNOW, TODAY IS THE LAST DAY OF CAMP AND AS SUCH, TONIGHT IS THE BATTLE OF THE BANDS.
AND THIS YEAR, THE WINNER DOESN'T JUST GET BRAGGING RIGHTS...THEY GET THE DEED TO THE CAMP AS SPECIFIED IN BEARY'S LAST WILL AND TESTAMENT.
BEARY, MY DUDE...

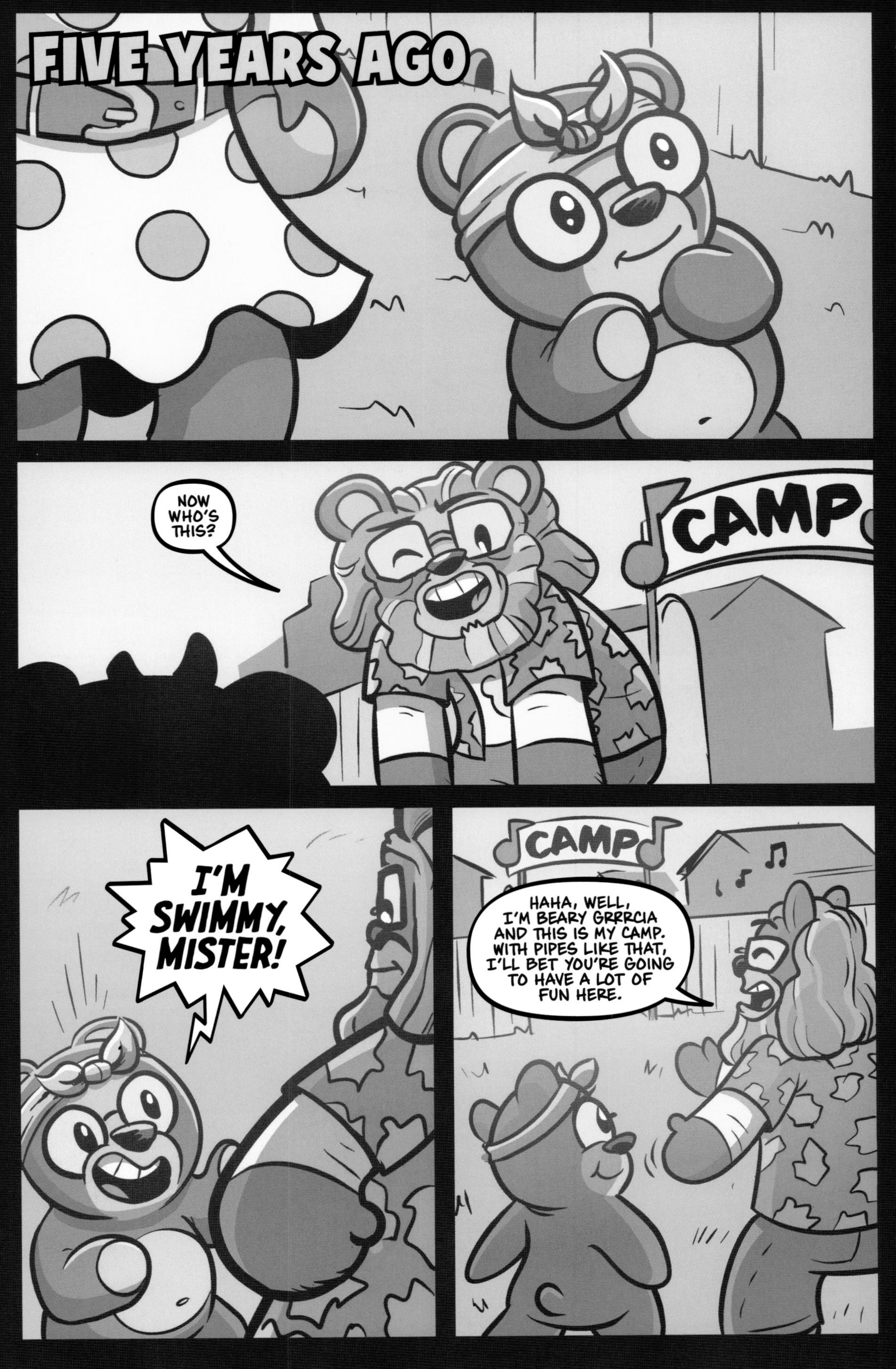
FIVE YEARS AGO
NOW WHO'S THIS?
CAMP
I'M SWIMMY, MISTER!
CAMP
HAHA, WELL, I'M BEARY GRRRCIA AND THIS IS MY CAMP. WITH PIPES LIKE THAT, I'LL BET YOU'RE GOING TO HAVE A LOT OF FUN HERE.

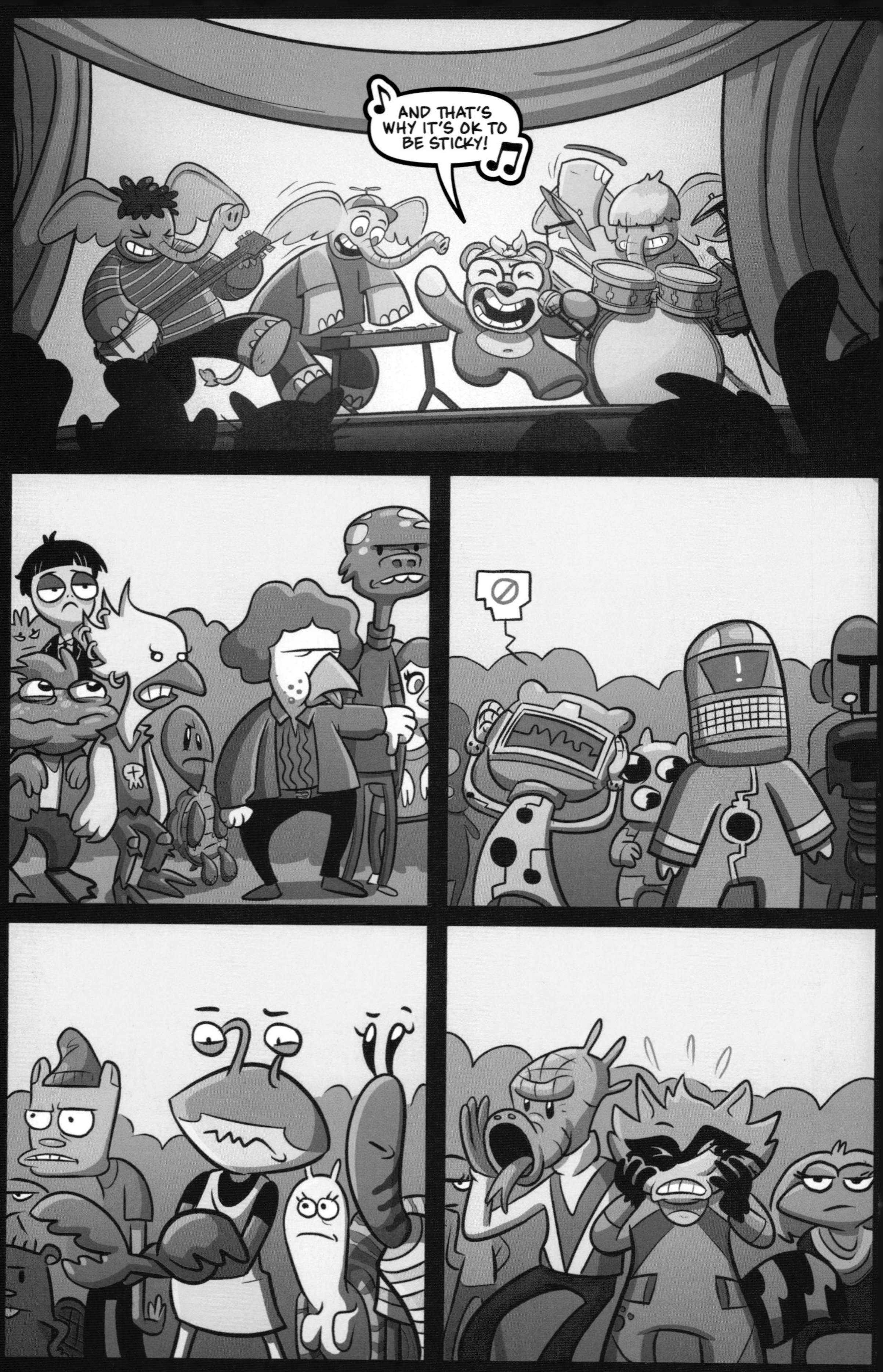
AND THAT'S
WHY IT'S OK TO
BE STICKY!

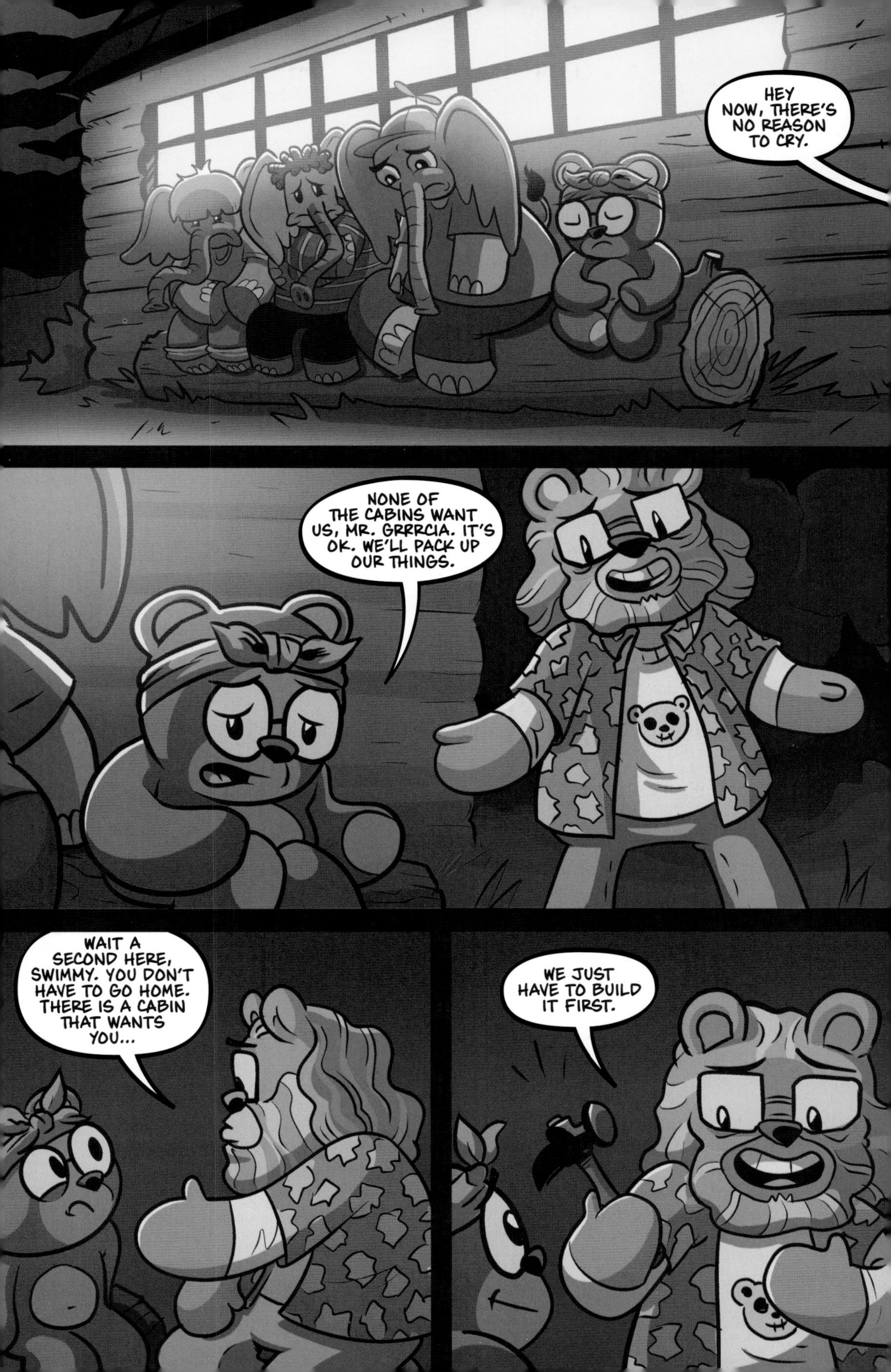
HEY NOW, THERE'S NO REASON TO CRY.
NONE OF THE CABINS WANT US, MR. GRRRCIA. IT'S OK. WE'LL PACK UP OUR THINGS.
WAIT A SECOND HERE, SWIMMY. YOU DON'T HAVE TO GO HOME. THERE IS A CABIN THAT WANTS YOU...
WE JUST HAVE TO BUILD IT FIRST.

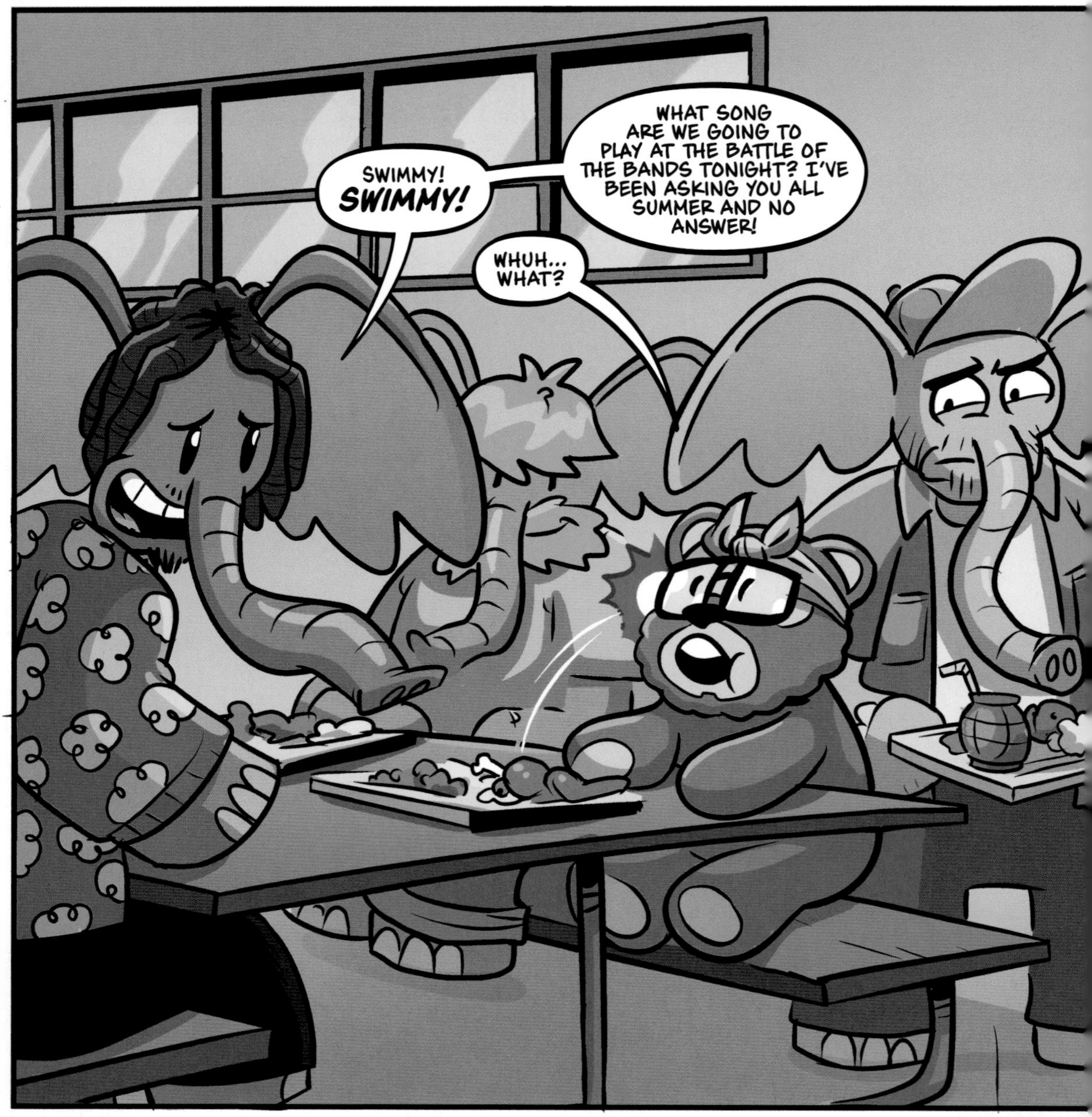
SWIMMY! **SWIMMY!**
WHAT SONG ARE WE GOING TO PLAY AT THE BATTLE OF THE BANDS TONIGHT? I'VE BEEN ASKING YOU ALL SUMMER AND NO ANSWER!
WHUH... WHAT?

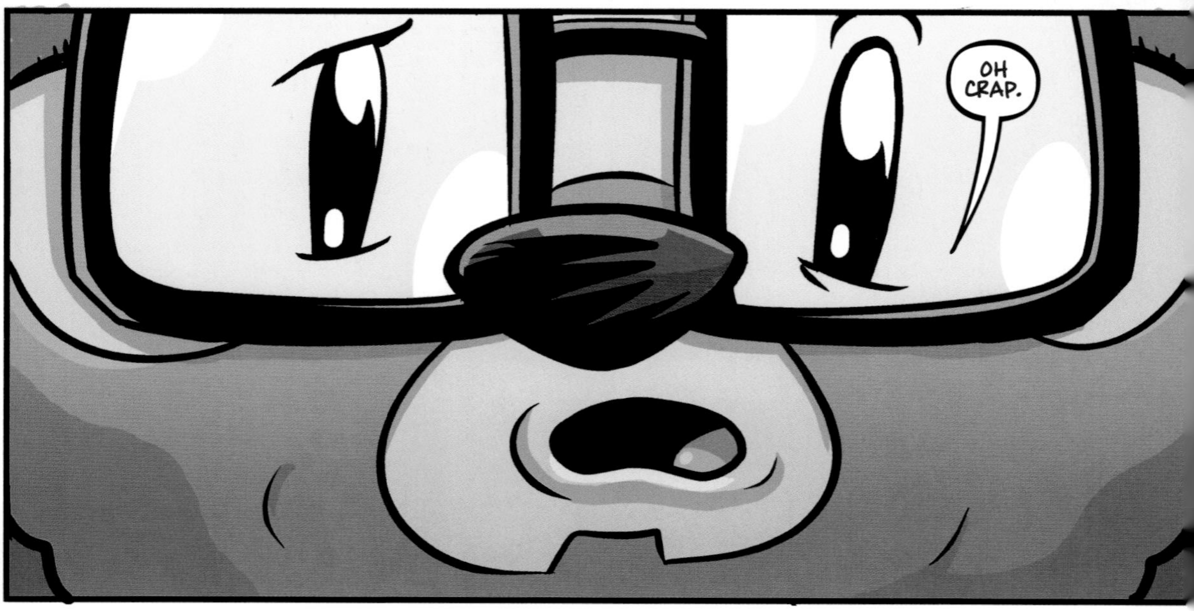
OH CRAP.

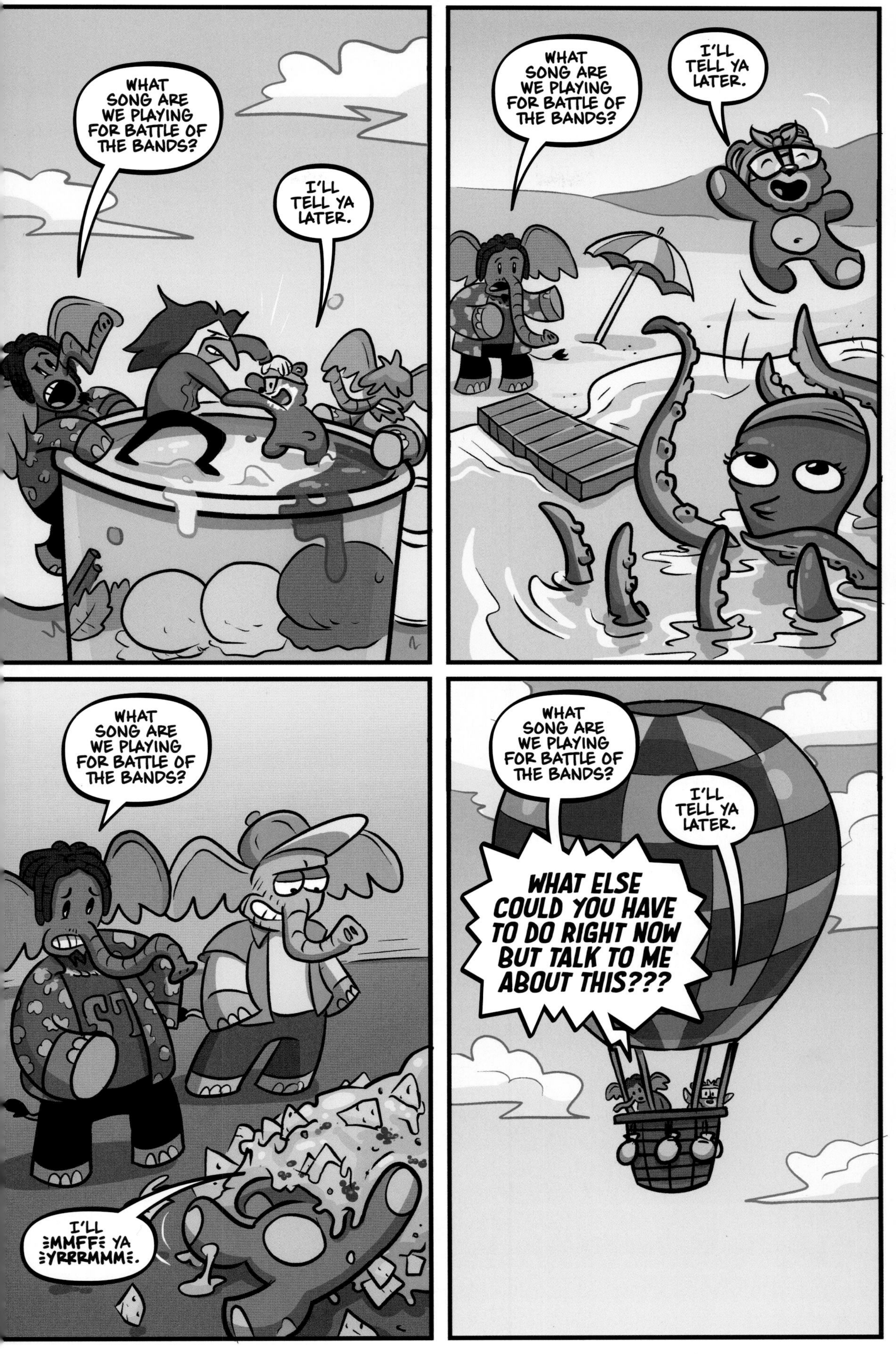
WHAT SONG ARE WE PLAYING FOR BATTLE OF THE BANDS?
I'LL TELL YA LATER.
WHAT SONG ARE WE PLAYING FOR BATTLE OF THE BANDS?
I'LL TELL YA LATER.
WHAT SONG ARE WE PLAYING FOR BATTLE OF THE BANDS?
I'LL MMFF YA YRRRMMM.
WHAT SONG ARE WE PLAYING FOR BATTLE OF THE BANDS?
I'LL TELL YA LATER.
WHAT ELSE COULD YOU HAVE TO DO RIGHT NOW BUT TALK TO ME ABOUT THIS???

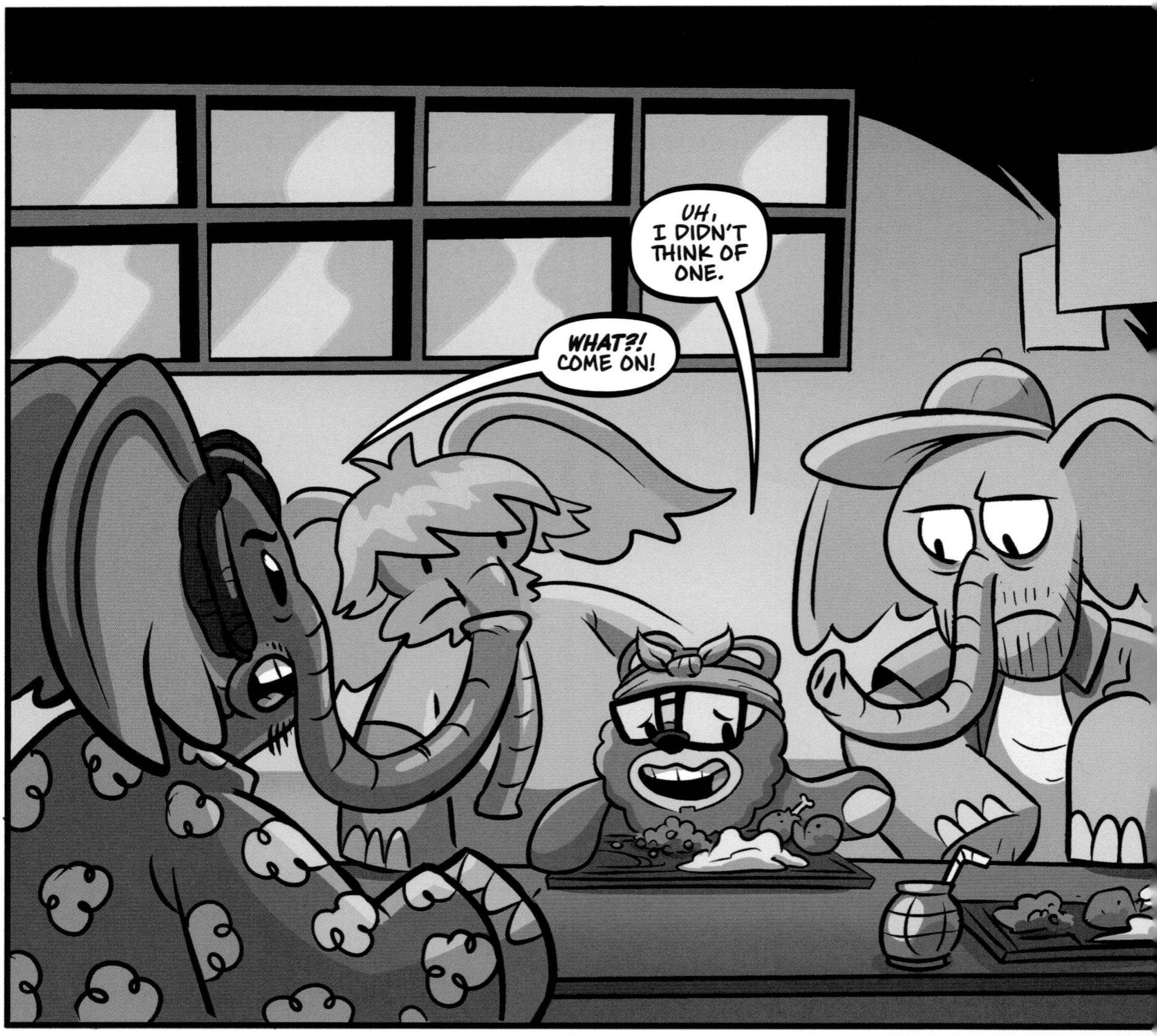
UH, I DIDN'T THINK OF ONE.
WHAT?! COME ON!

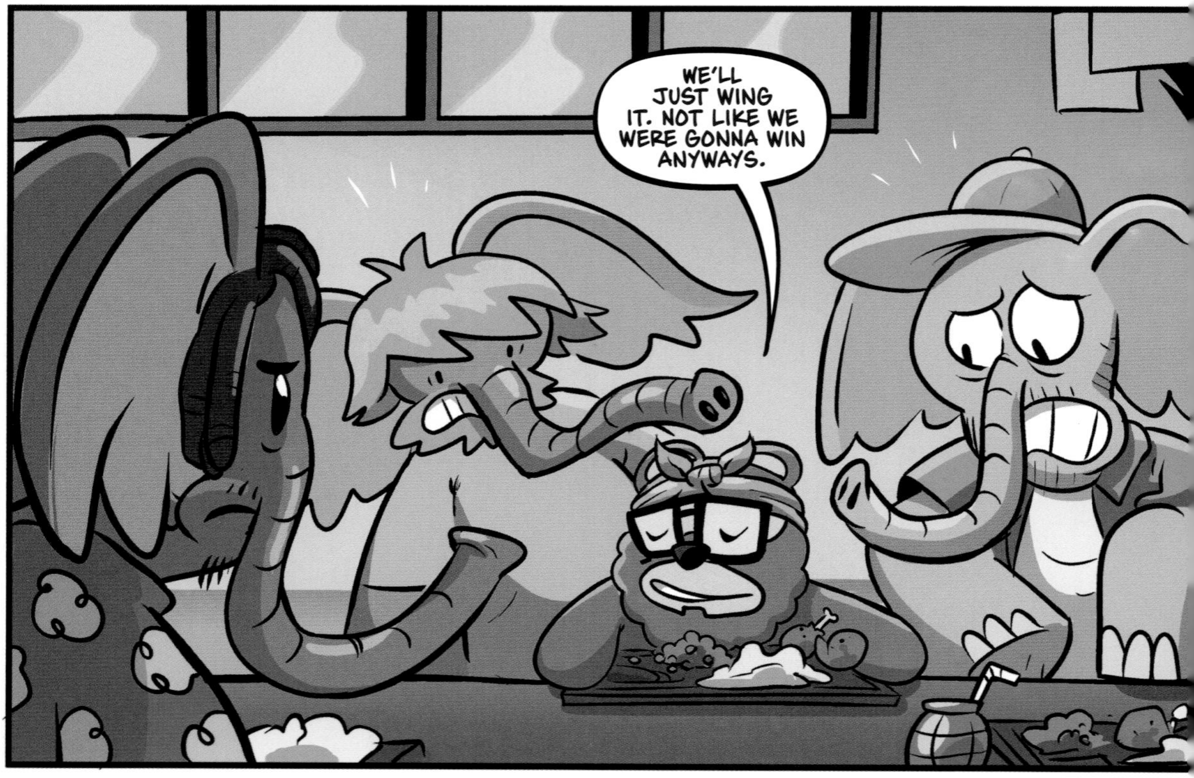
WE'LL JUST WING IT. NOT LIKE WE WERE GONNA WIN ANYWAYS.

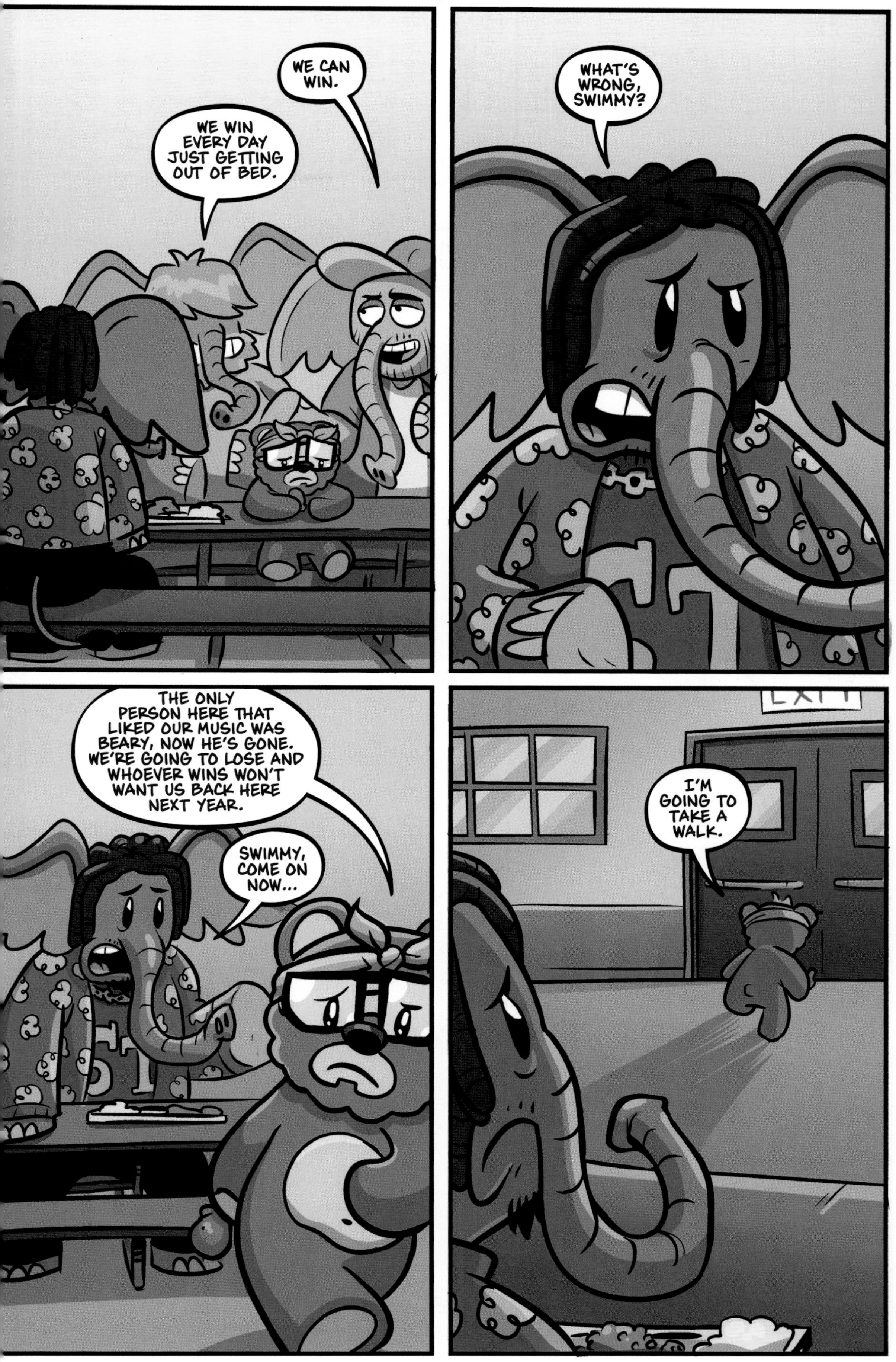
WE CAN WIN.
WE WIN EVERY DAY JUST GETTING OUT OF BED.
WHAT'S WRONG, SWIMMY?
THE ONLY PERSON HERE THAT LIKED OUR MUSIC WAS BEARY, NOW HE'S GONE. WE'RE GOING TO LOSE AND WHOEVER WINS WON'T WANT US BACK HERE NEXT YEAR.
SWIMMY, COME ON NOW...
I'M GOING TO TAKE A WALK.

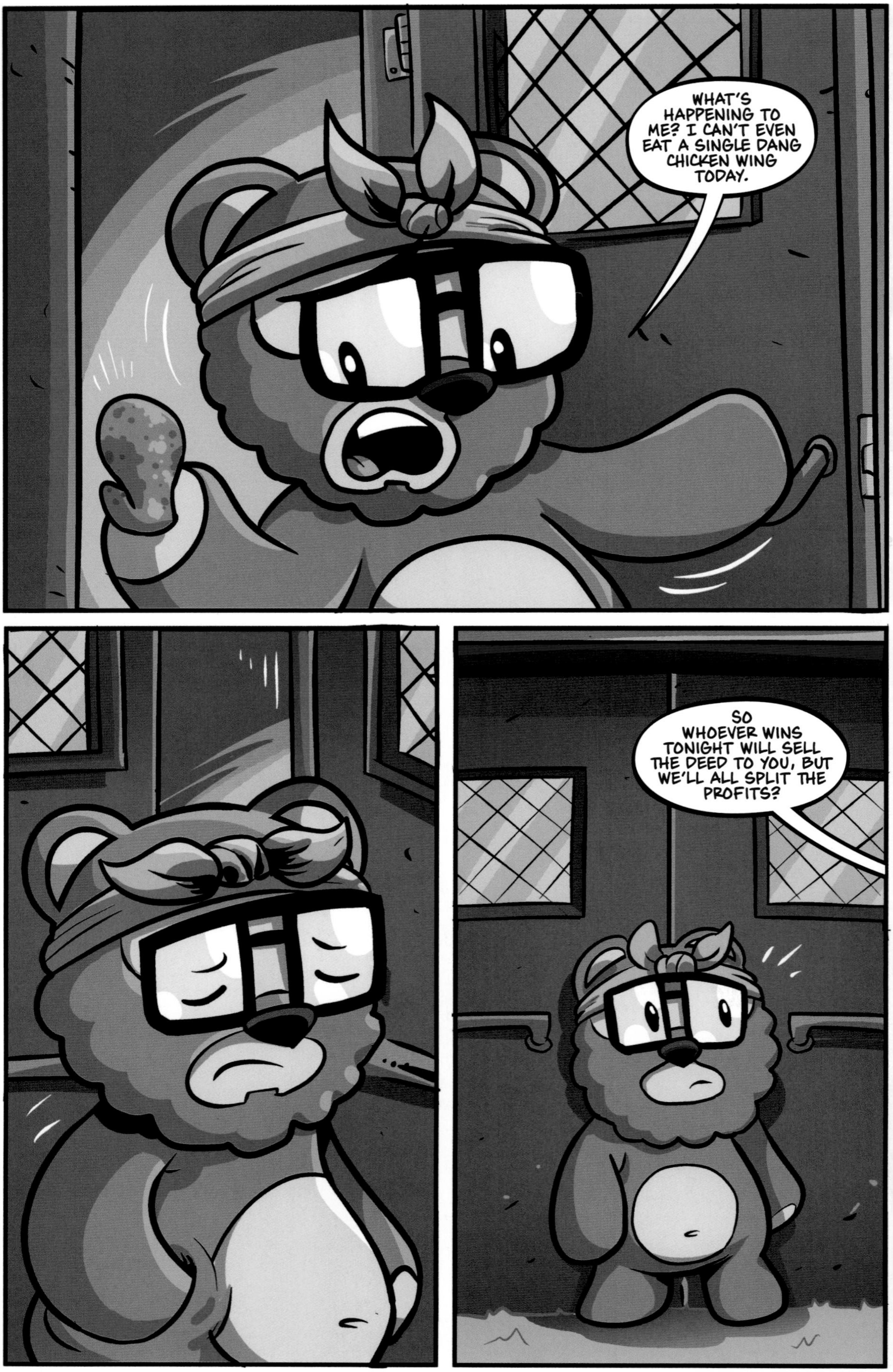
WHAT'S HAPPENING TO ME? I CAN'T EVEN EAT A SINGLE DANG CHICKEN WING TODAY.
SO WHOEVER WINS TONIGHT WILL SELL THE DEED TO YOU, BUT WE'LL ALL SPLIT THE PROFITS?

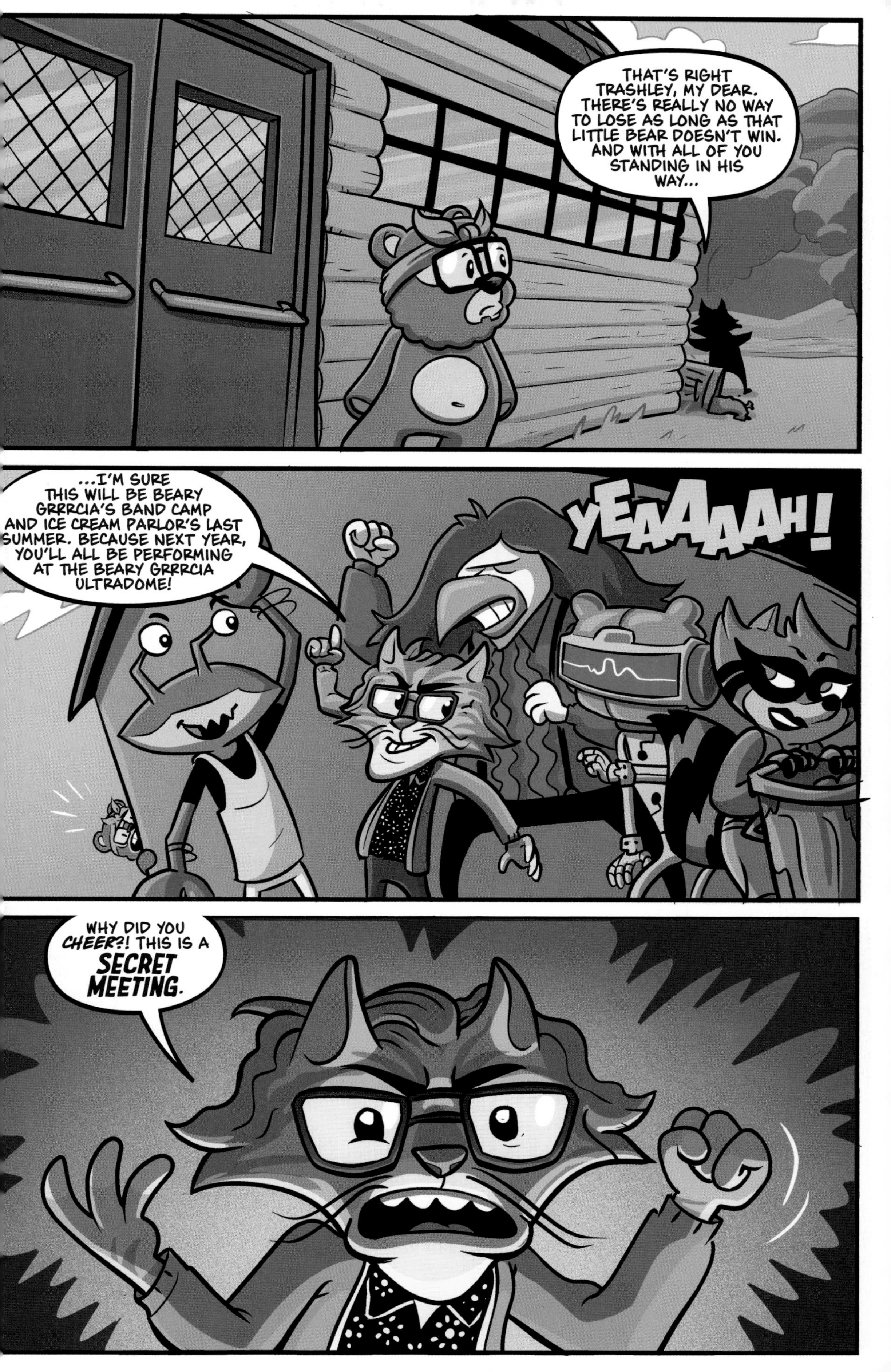
THAT'S RIGHT TRASHLEY, MY DEAR. THERE'S REALLY NO WAY TO LOSE AS LONG AS THAT LITTLE BEAR DOESN'T WIN. AND WITH ALL OF YOU STANDING IN HIS WAY...
...I'M SURE THIS WILL BE BEARY GRRRCIA'S BAND CAMP AND ICE CREAM PARLOR'S LAST SUMMER. BECAUSE NEXT YEAR, YOU'LL ALL BE PERFORMING AT THE BEARY GRRRCIA ULTRADOME!
YEAAAAAH!
WHY DID YOU *CHEER?!* THIS IS A **SECRET MEETING.**

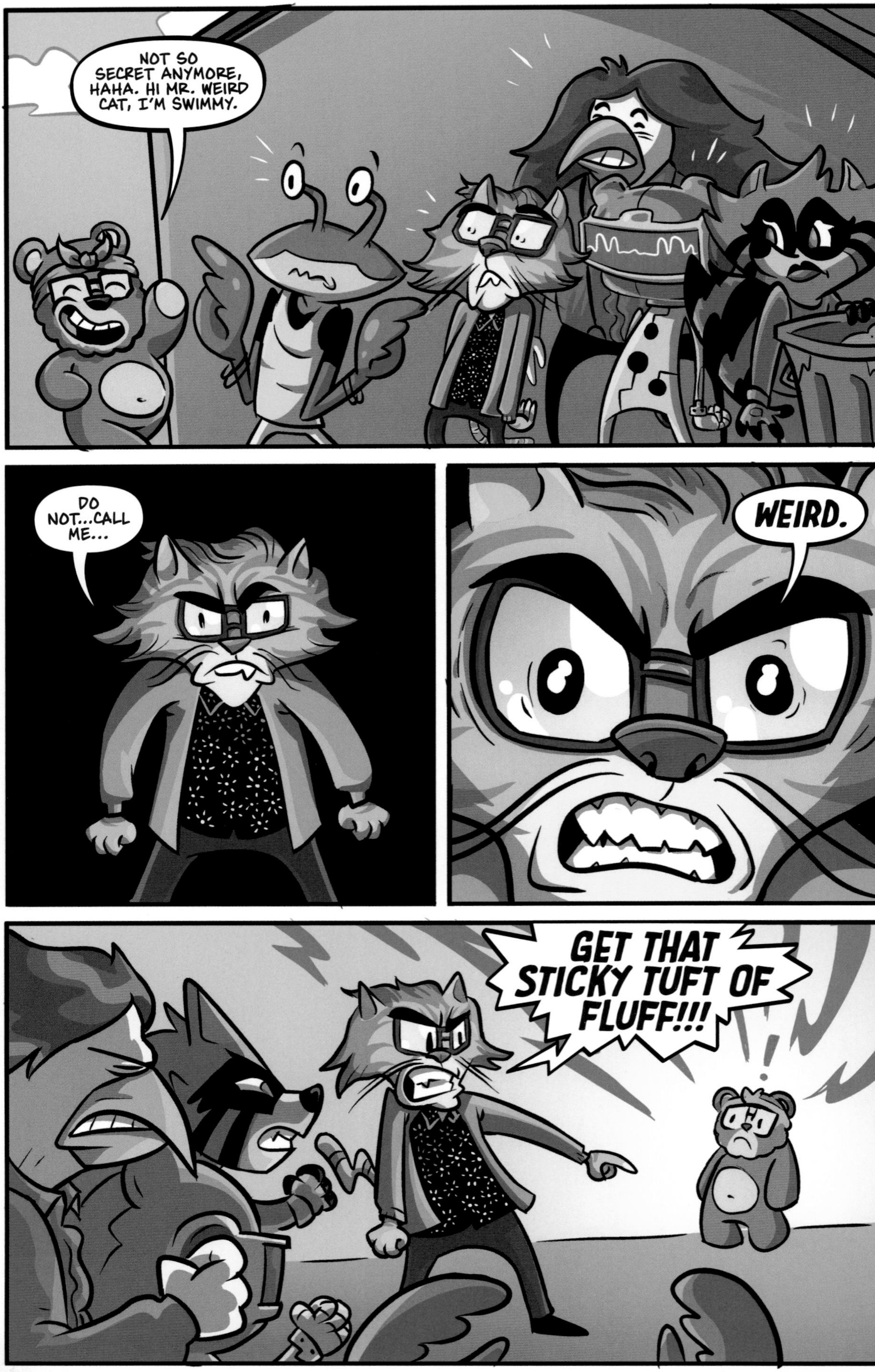

NOT SO SECRET ANYMORE, HAHA. HI MR. WEIRD CAT, I'M SWIMMY.
DO NOT...CALL ME...
WEIRD.
GET THAT STICKY TUFT OF FLUFF!!!

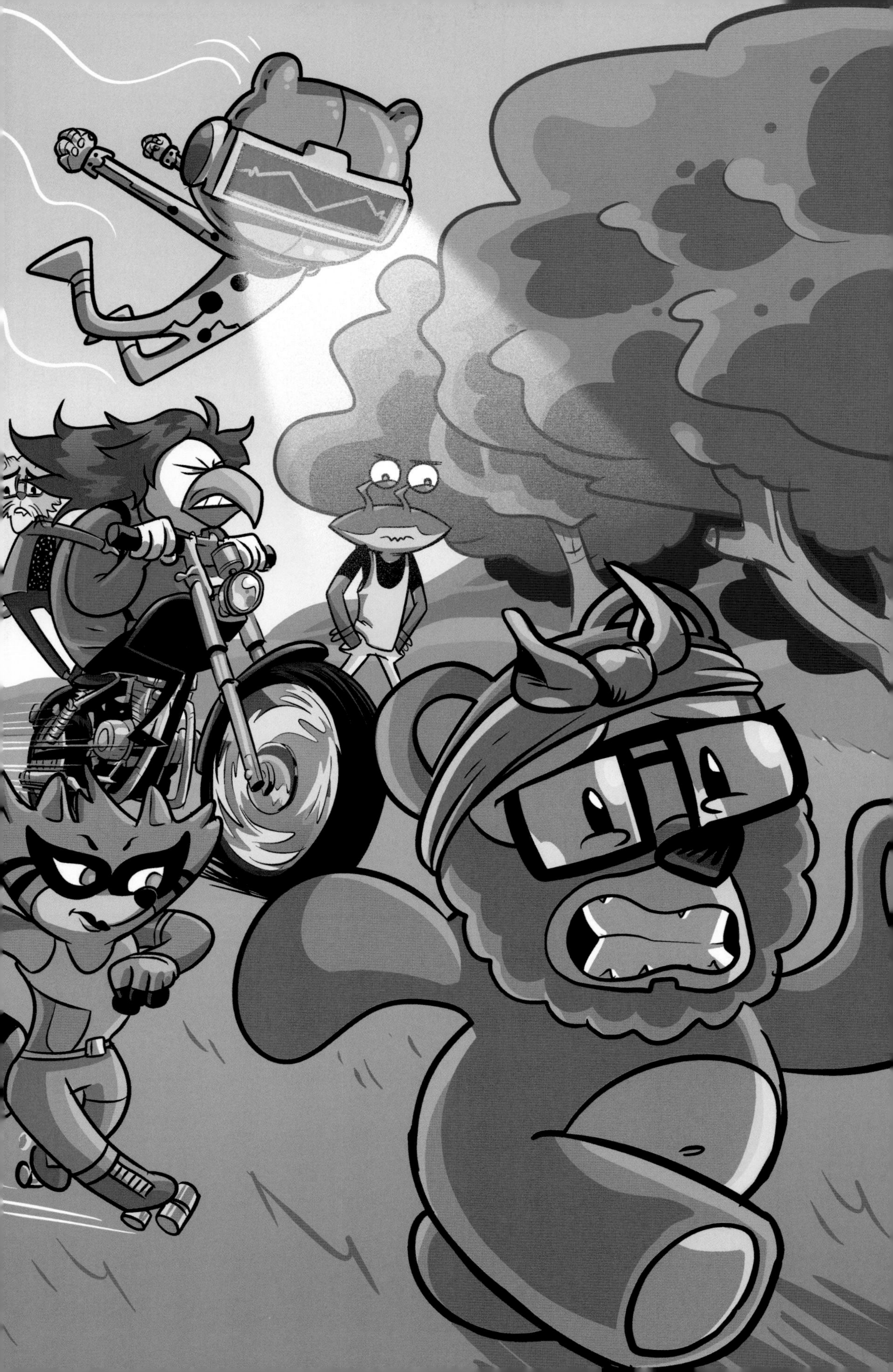

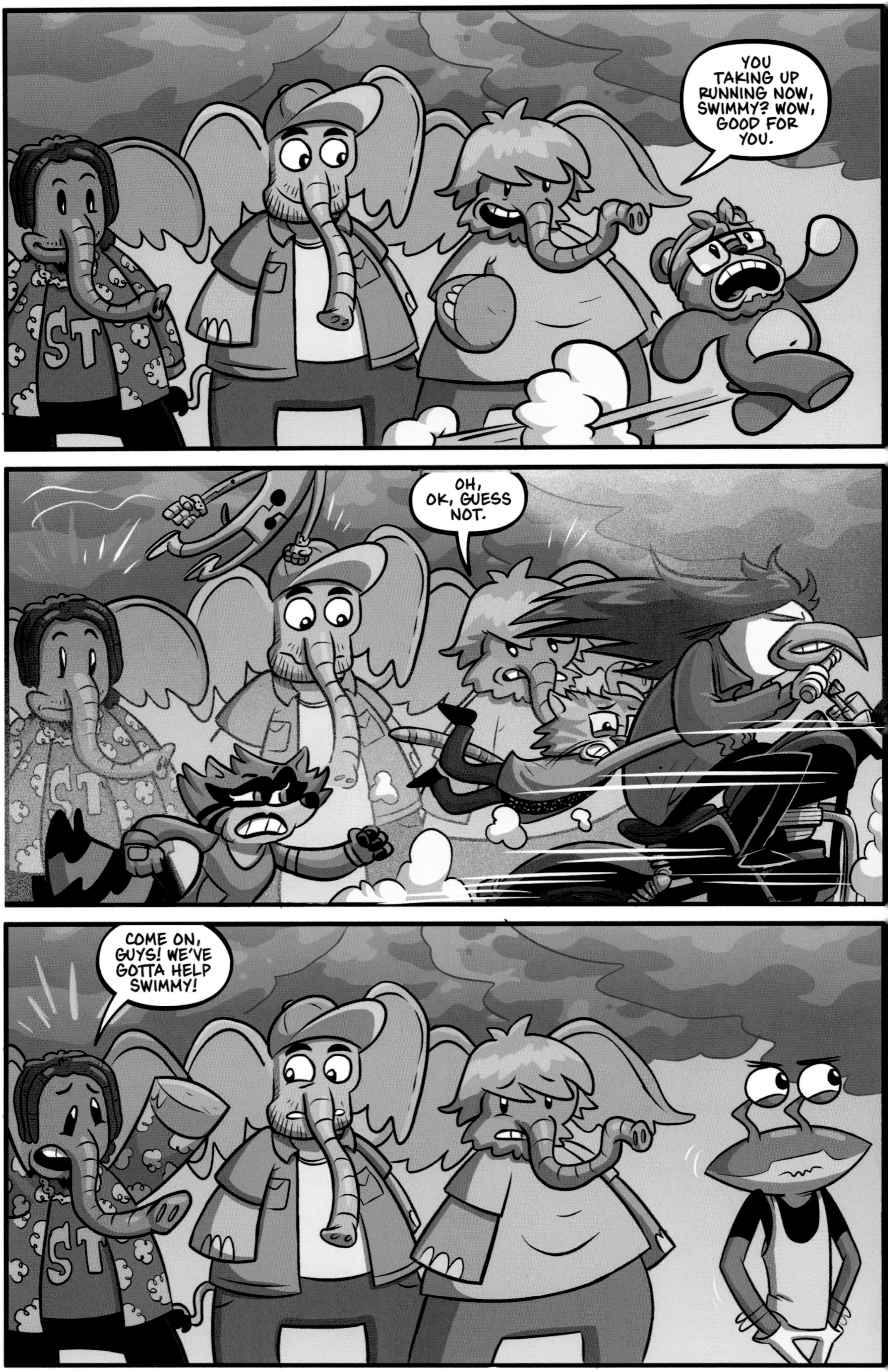
YOU TAKING UP RUNNING NOW, SWIMMY? WOW, GOOD FOR YOU.
OH, OK, GUESS NOT.
COME ON, GUYS! WE'VE GOTTA HELP SWIMMY!

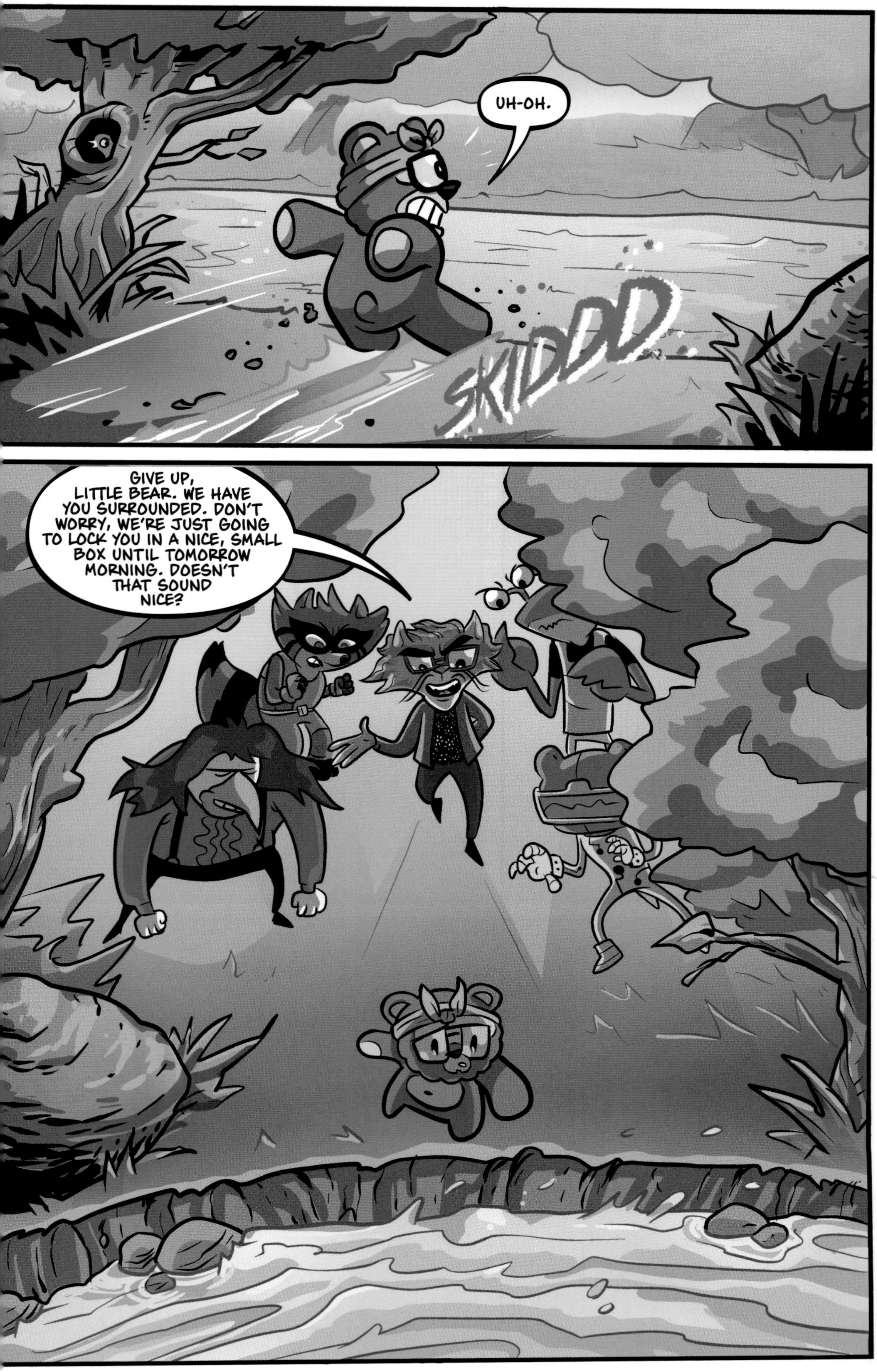
UH-OH.
SKIDDDD
GIVE UP, LITTLE BEAR. WE HAVE YOU SURROUNDED. DON'T WORRY, WE'RE JUST GOING TO LOCK YOU IN A NICE, SMALL BOX UNTIL TOMORROW MORNING. DOESN'T THAT SOUND NICE?

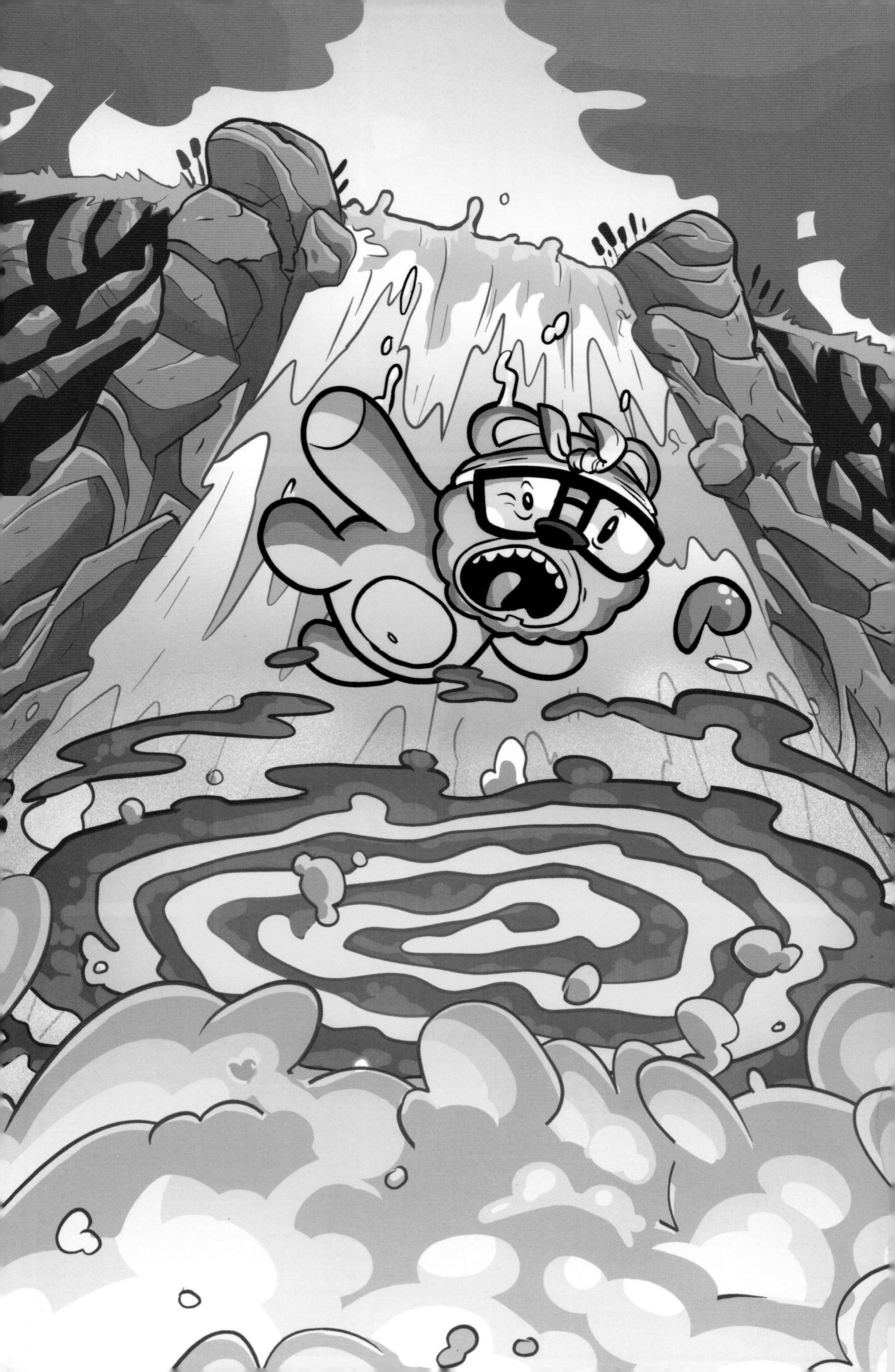

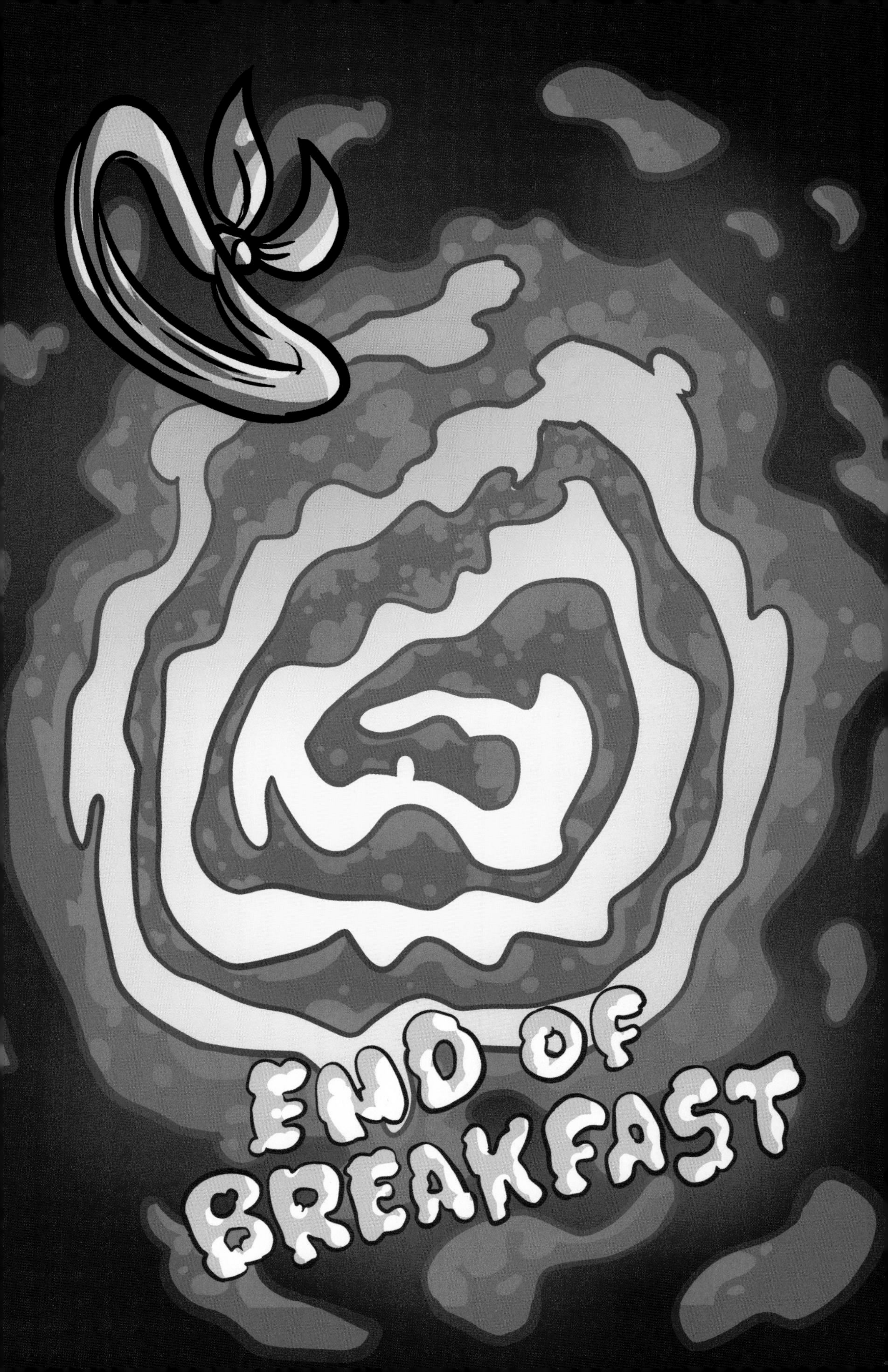
END OF
BREAKFAST

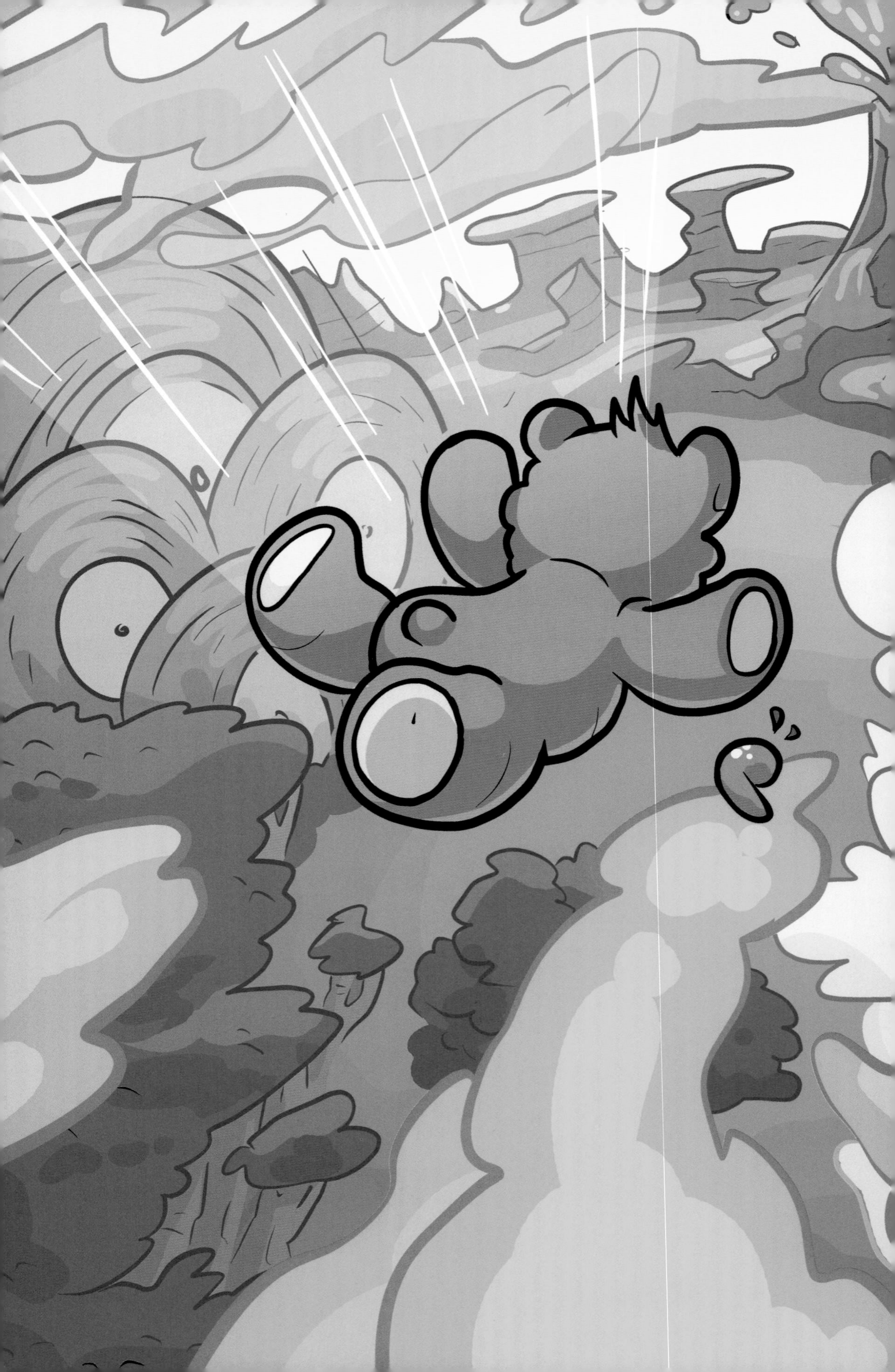

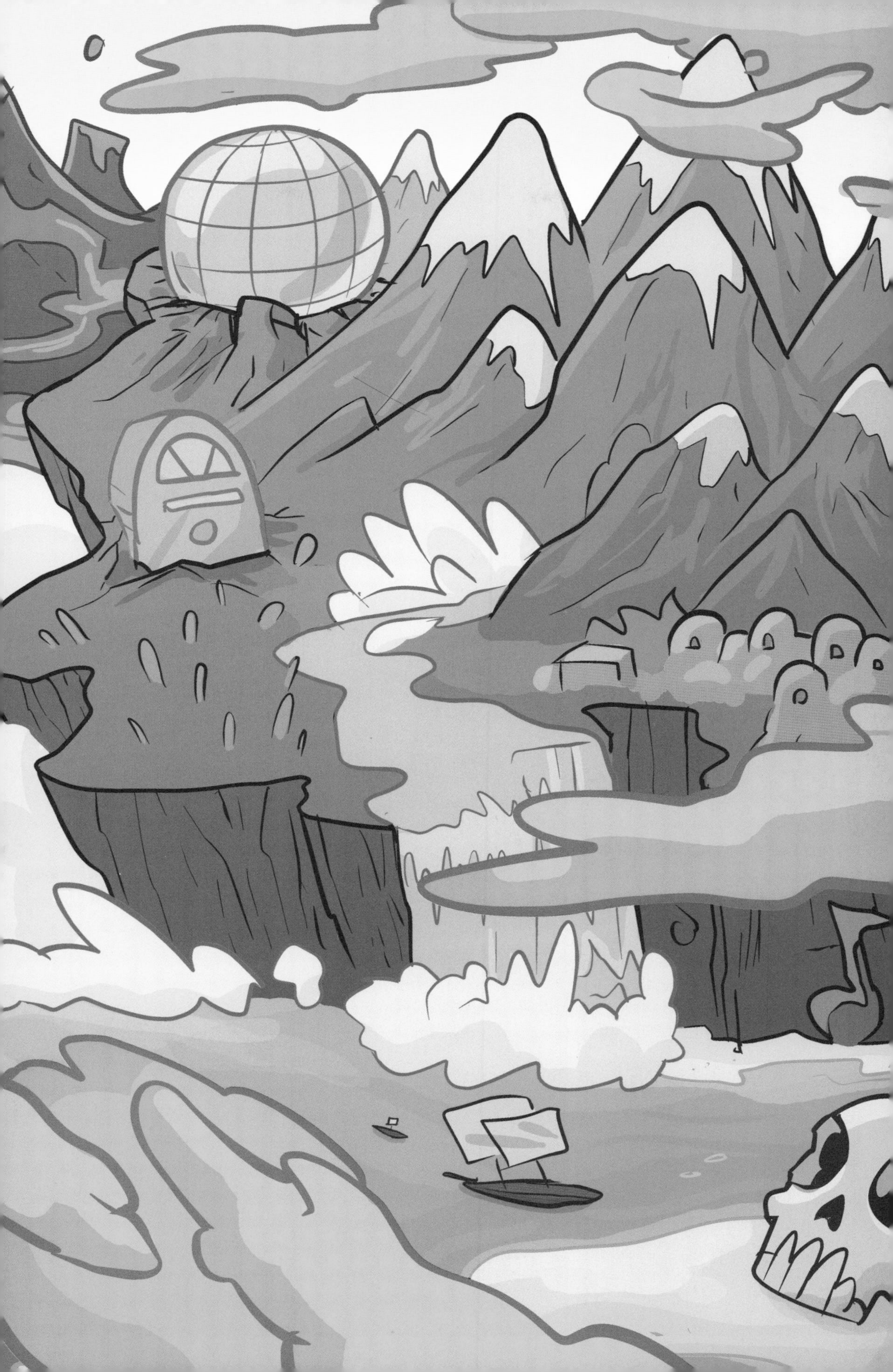

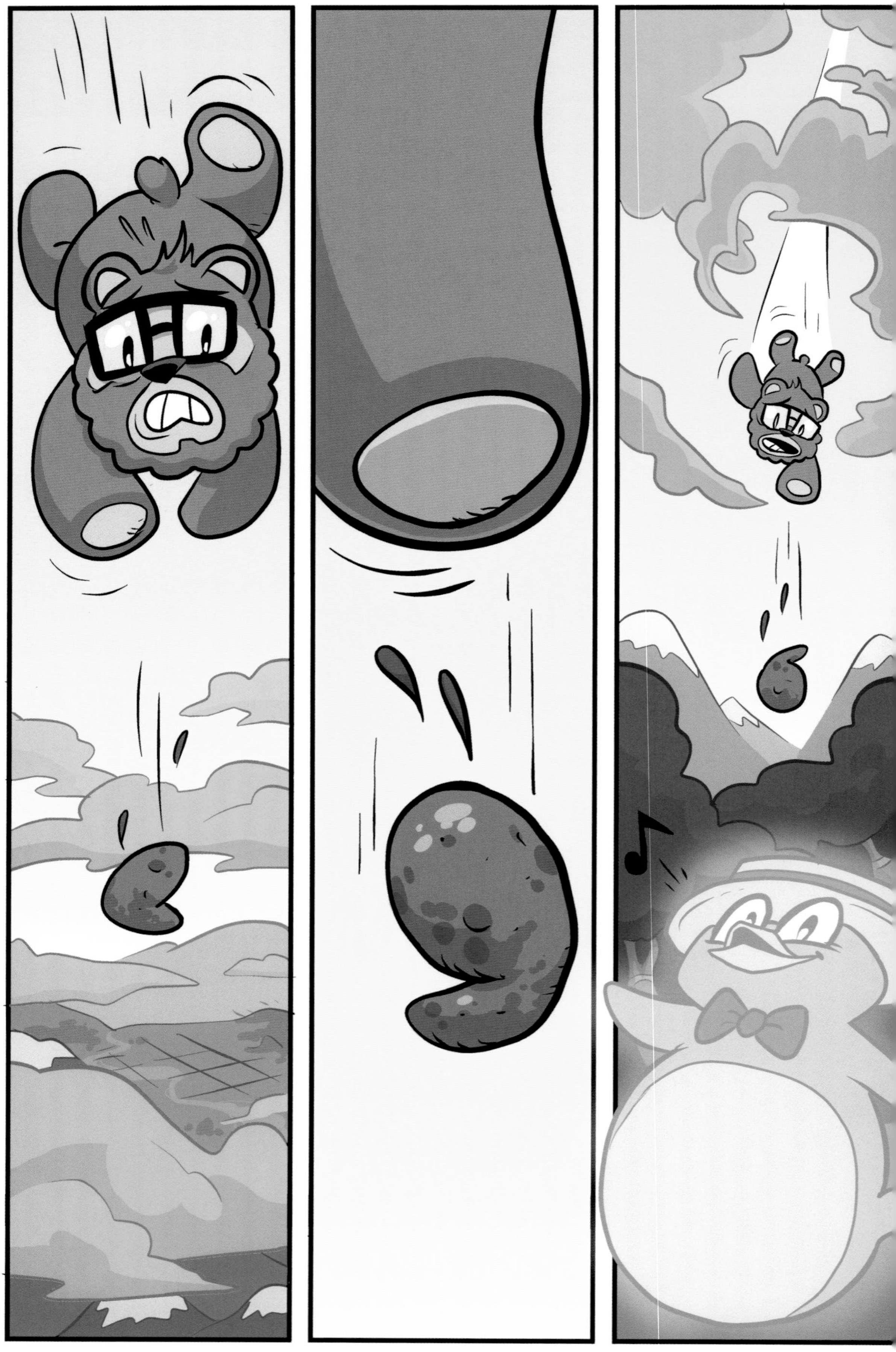

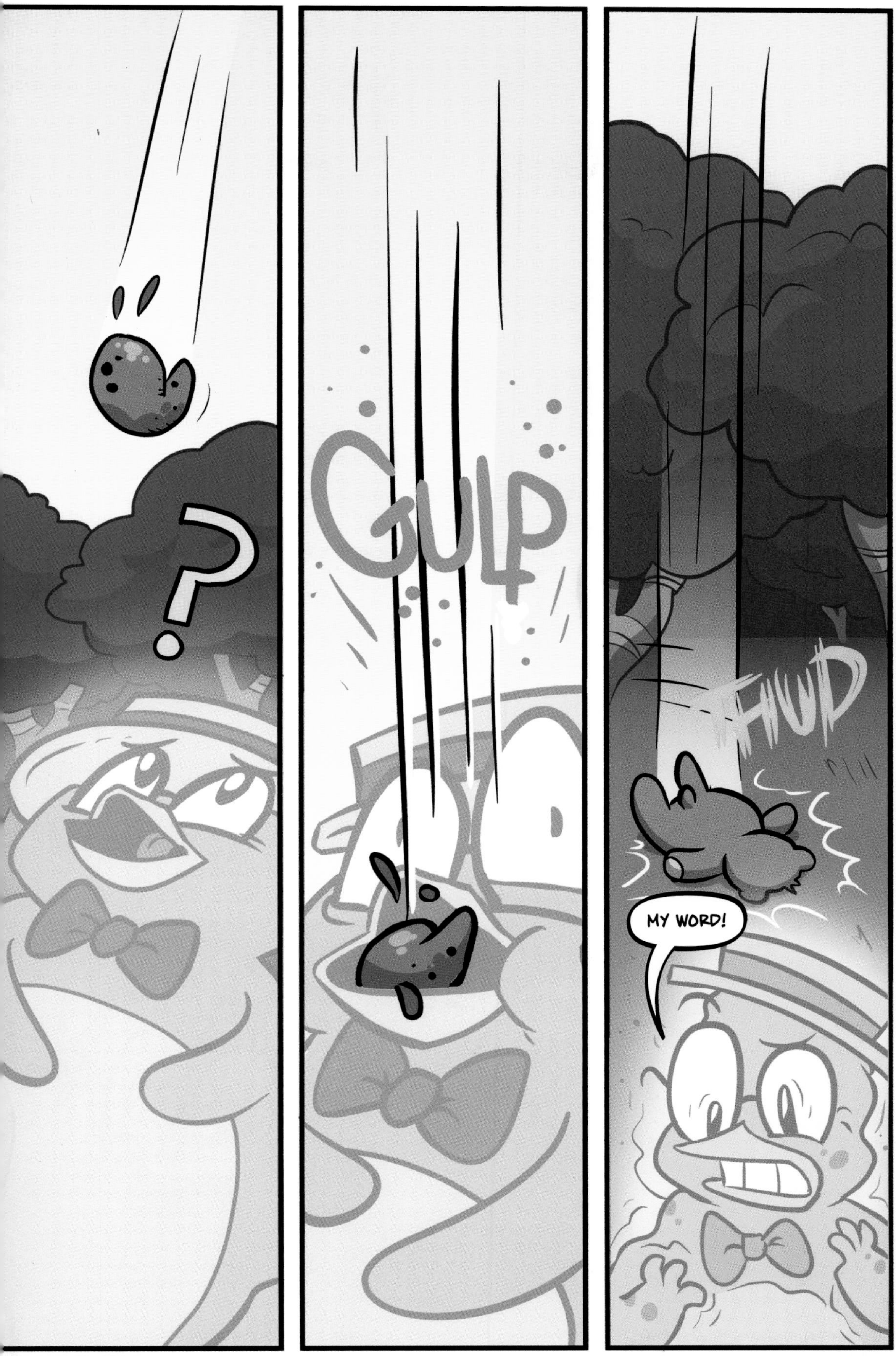
?
GULP
THUD
MY WORD!

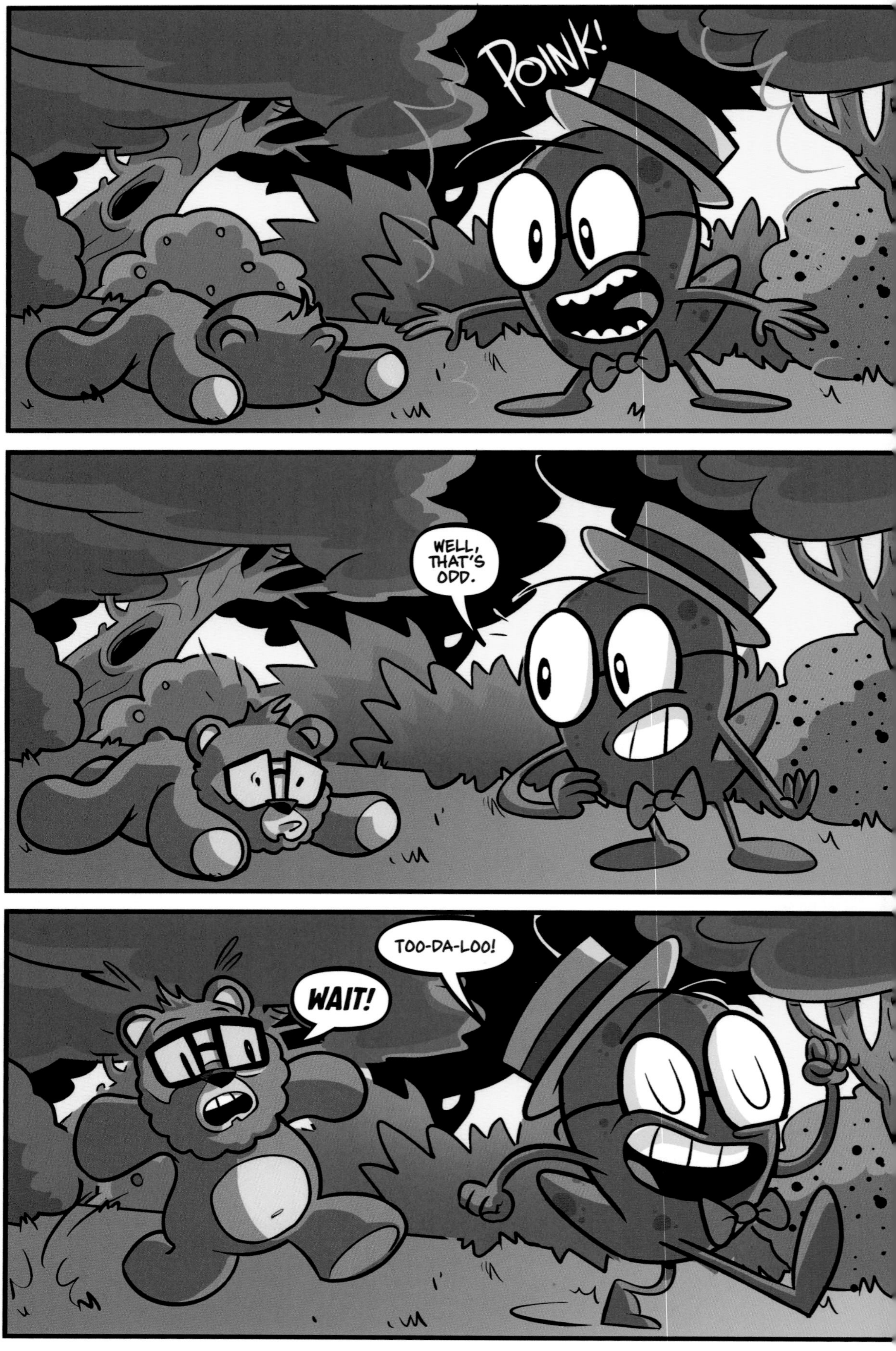
POINK!
WELL, THAT'S ODD.
TOO-DA-LOO!
WAIT!

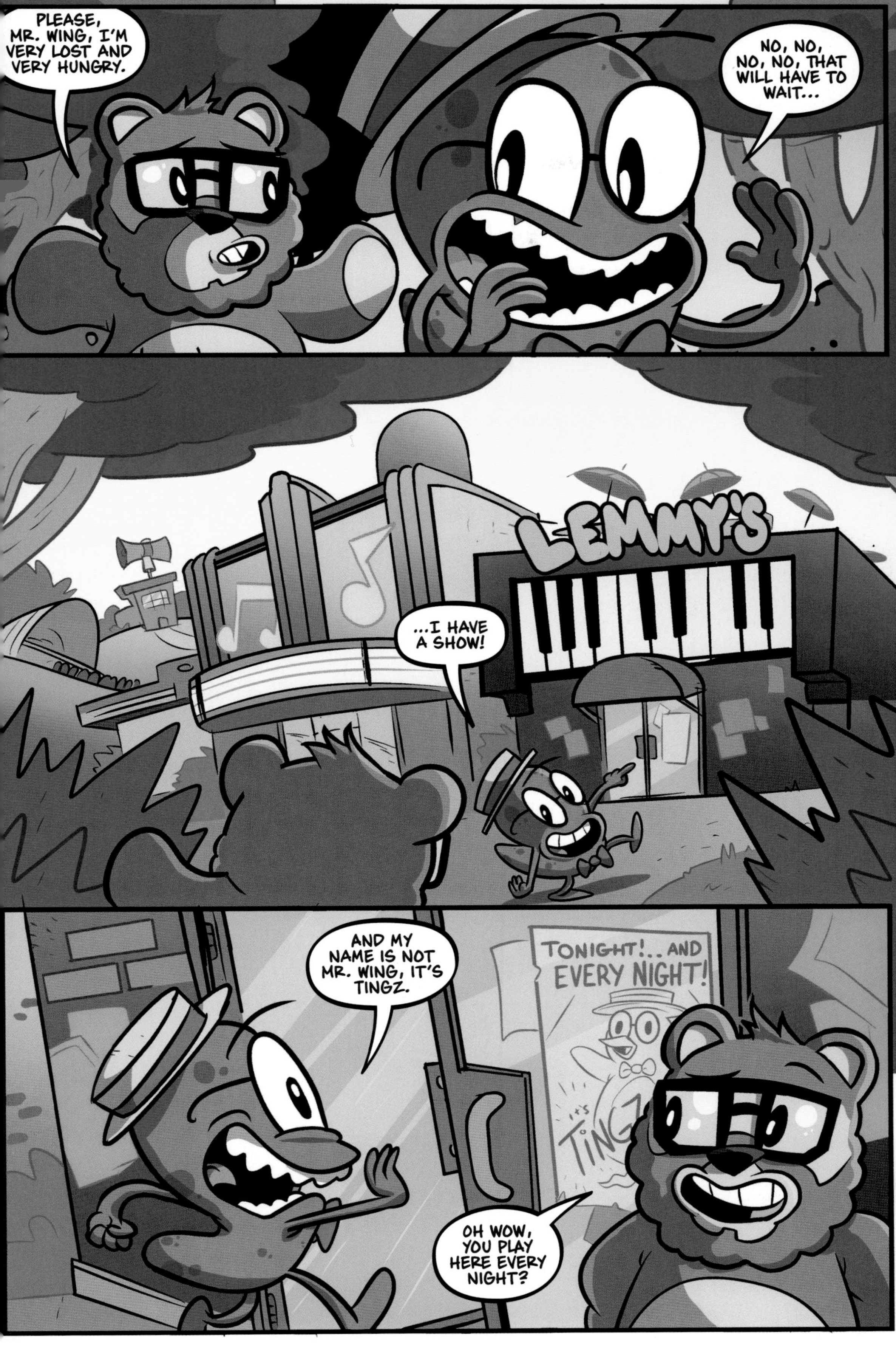
PLEASE, MR. WING, I'M VERY LOST AND VERY HUNGRY.
NO, NO, NO, NO, THAT WILL HAVE TO WAIT...
LEMMY'S
...I HAVE A SHOW!
AND MY NAME IS NOT MR. WING, IT'S TINGZ.
TONIGHT!.. AND EVERY NIGHT!
OH WOW, YOU PLAY HERE EVERY NIGHT?

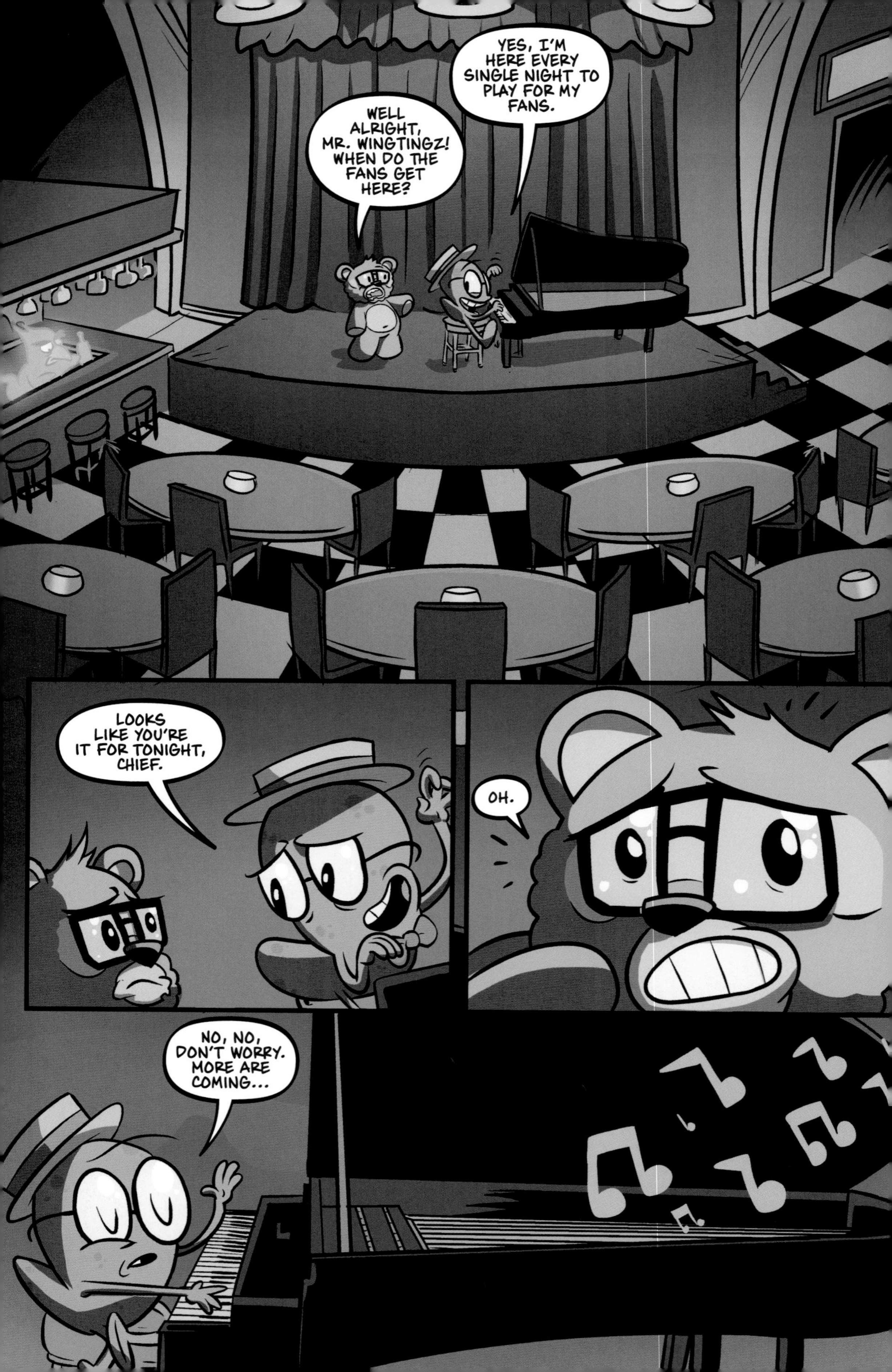
WELL ALRIGHT, MR. WINGTINGZ! WHEN DO THE FANS GET HERE?
YES, I'M HERE EVERY SINGLE NIGHT TO PLAY FOR MY FANS.
LOOKS LIKE YOU'RE IT FOR TONIGHT, CHIEF.
OH.
NO, NO, DON'T WORRY. MORE ARE COMING...

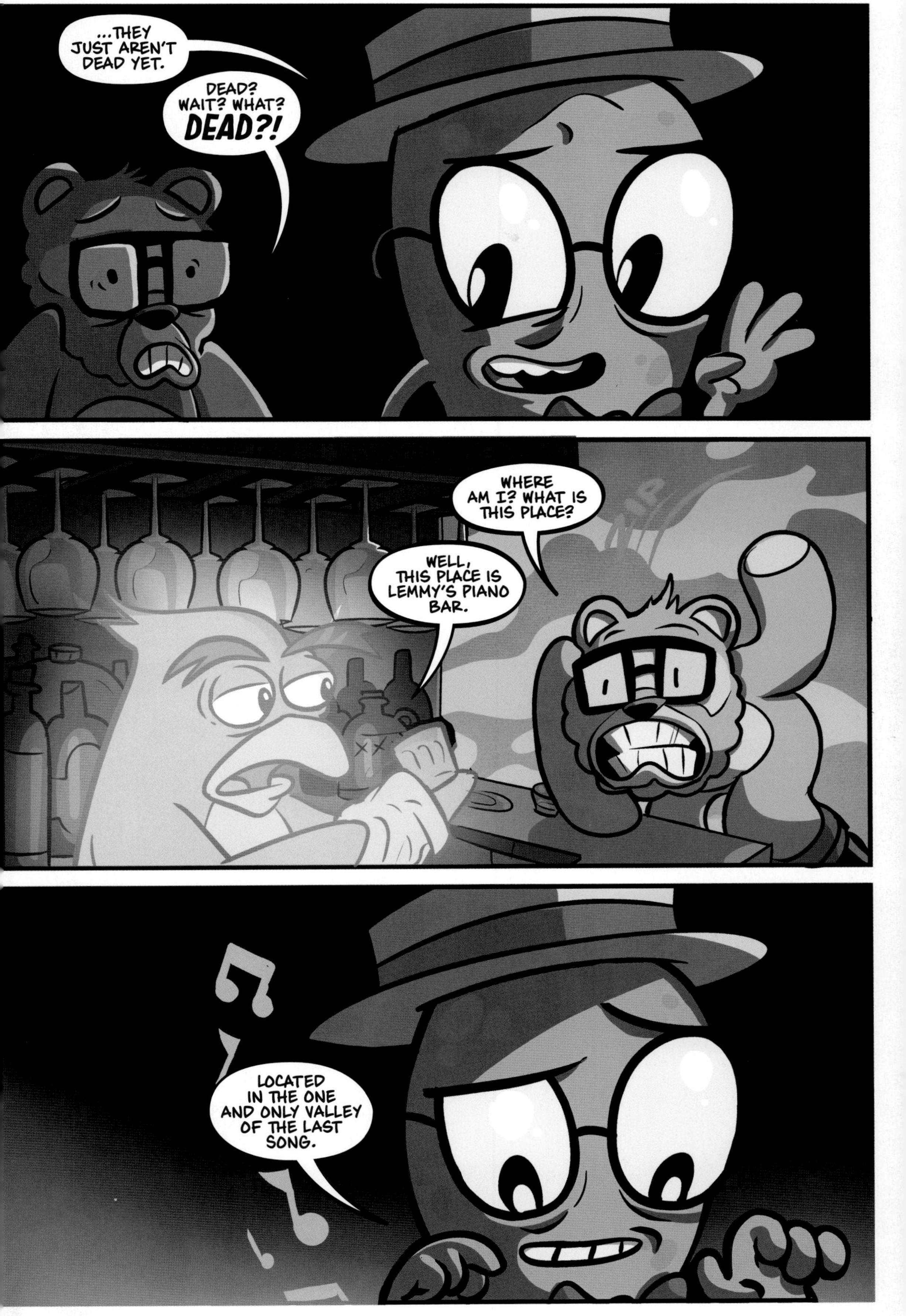
...THEY JUST AREN'T DEAD YET.
DEAD? WAIT? WHAT? DEAD?!
WHERE AM I? WHAT IS THIS PLACE?
WELL, THIS PLACE IS LEMMY'S PIANO BAR.
LOCATED IN THE ONE AND ONLY VALLEY OF THE LAST SONG.

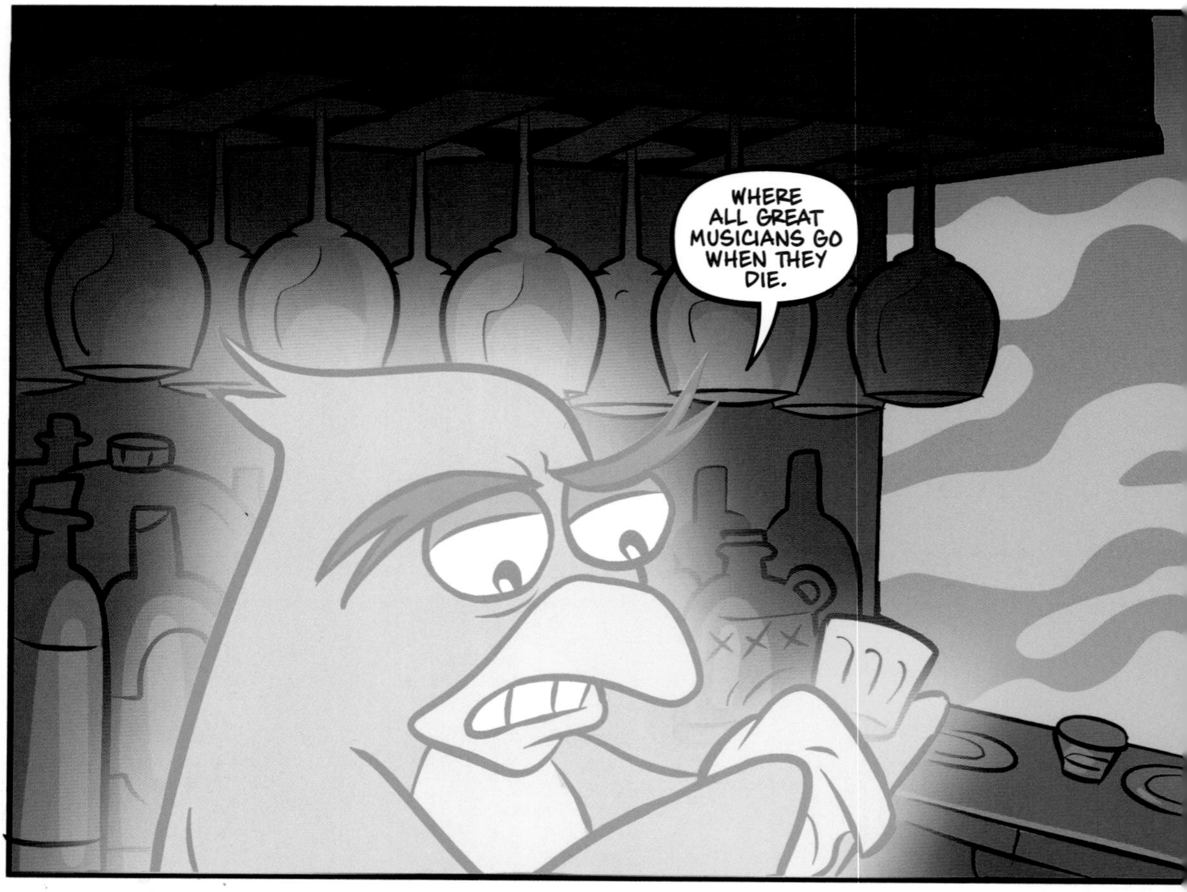
WHERE ALL GREAT MUSICIANS GO WHEN THEY DIE.

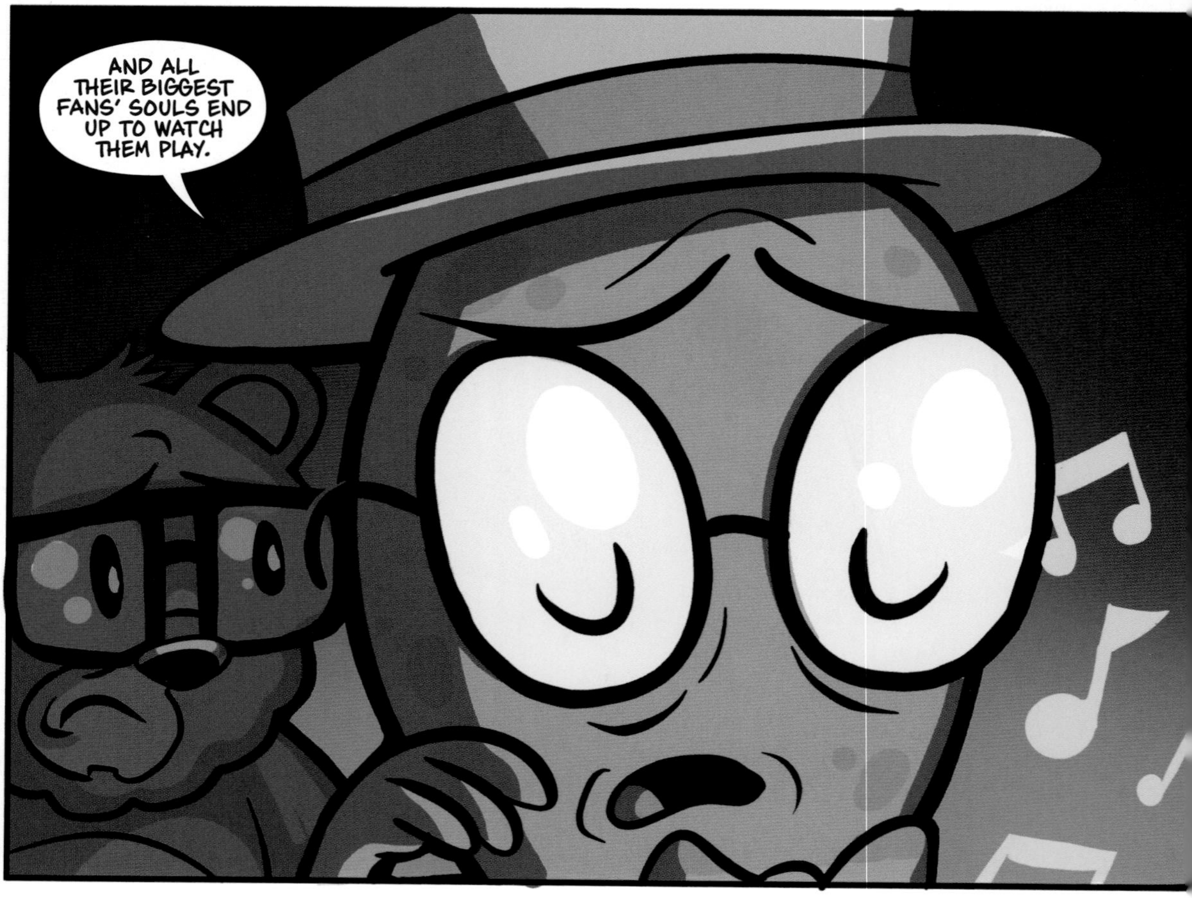
AND ALL THEIR BIGGEST FANS' SOULS END UP TO WATCH THEM PLAY.

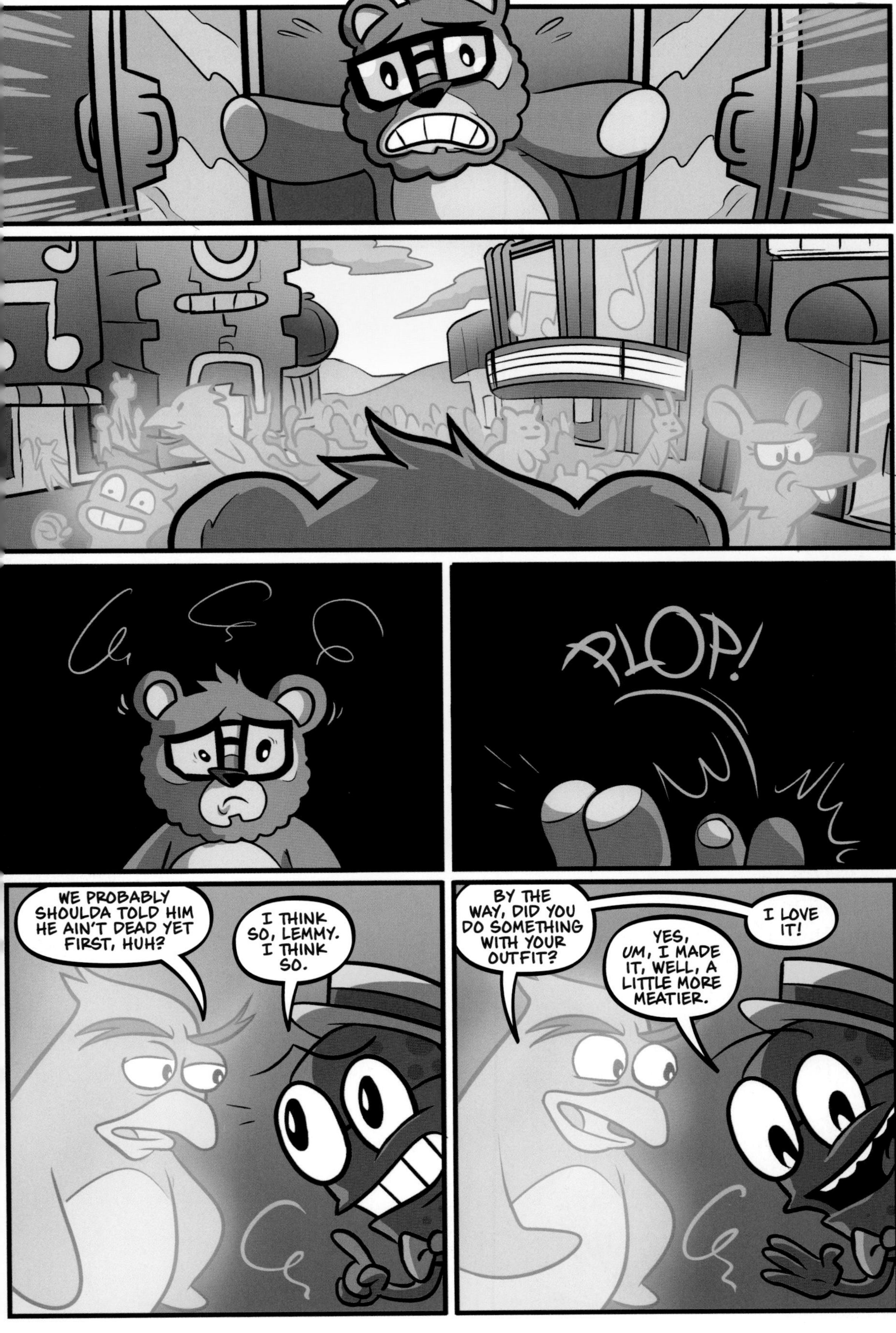
PLOP!
WE PROBABLY SHOULDA TOLD HIM HE AIN'T DEAD YET FIRST, HUH?
I THINK SO, LEMMY. I THINK SO.
BY THE WAY, DID YOU DO SOMETHING WITH YOUR OUTFIT?
I LOVE IT!
YES, UM, I MADE IT, WELL, A LITTLE MORE MEATIER.

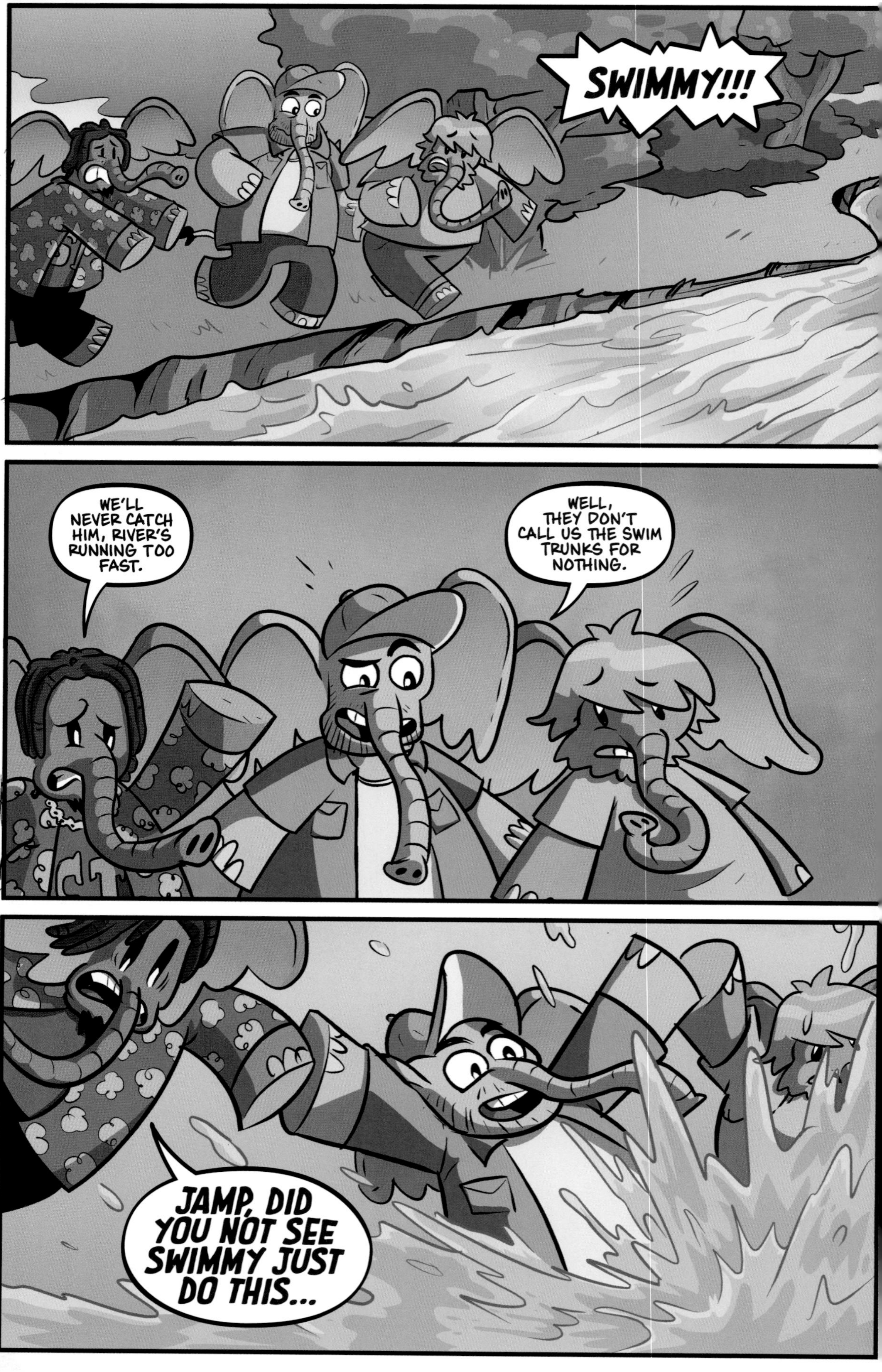
SWIMMY!!!
WE'LL NEVER CATCH HIM, RIVER'S RUNNING TOO FAST.
WELL, THEY DON'T CALL US THE SWIM TRUNKS FOR NOTHING.
JAMP, DID YOU NOT SEE SWIMMY JUST DO THIS...

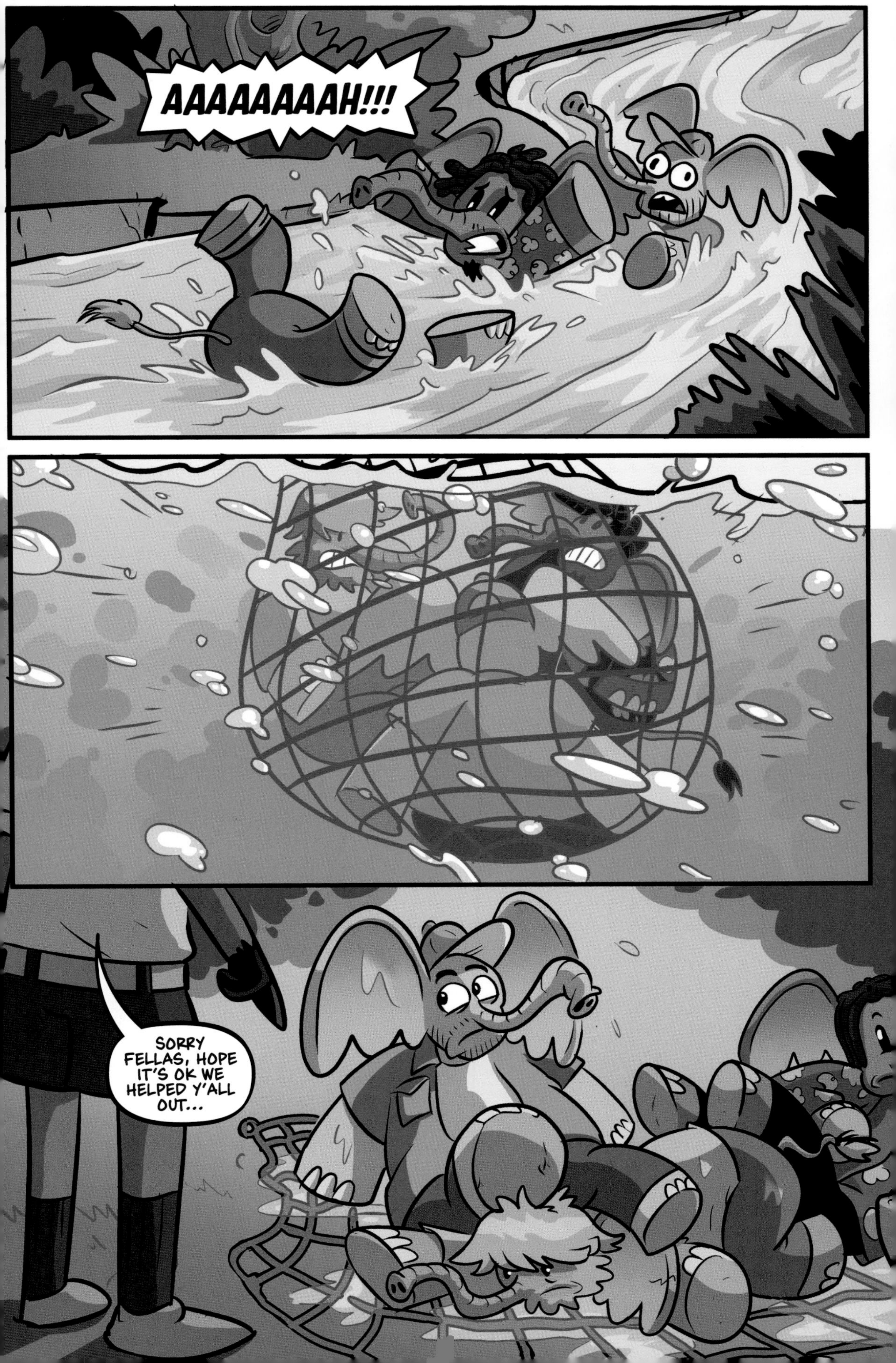
AAAAAAAAH!!!
SORRY FELLAS, HOPE IT'S OK WE HELPED Y'ALL OUT...

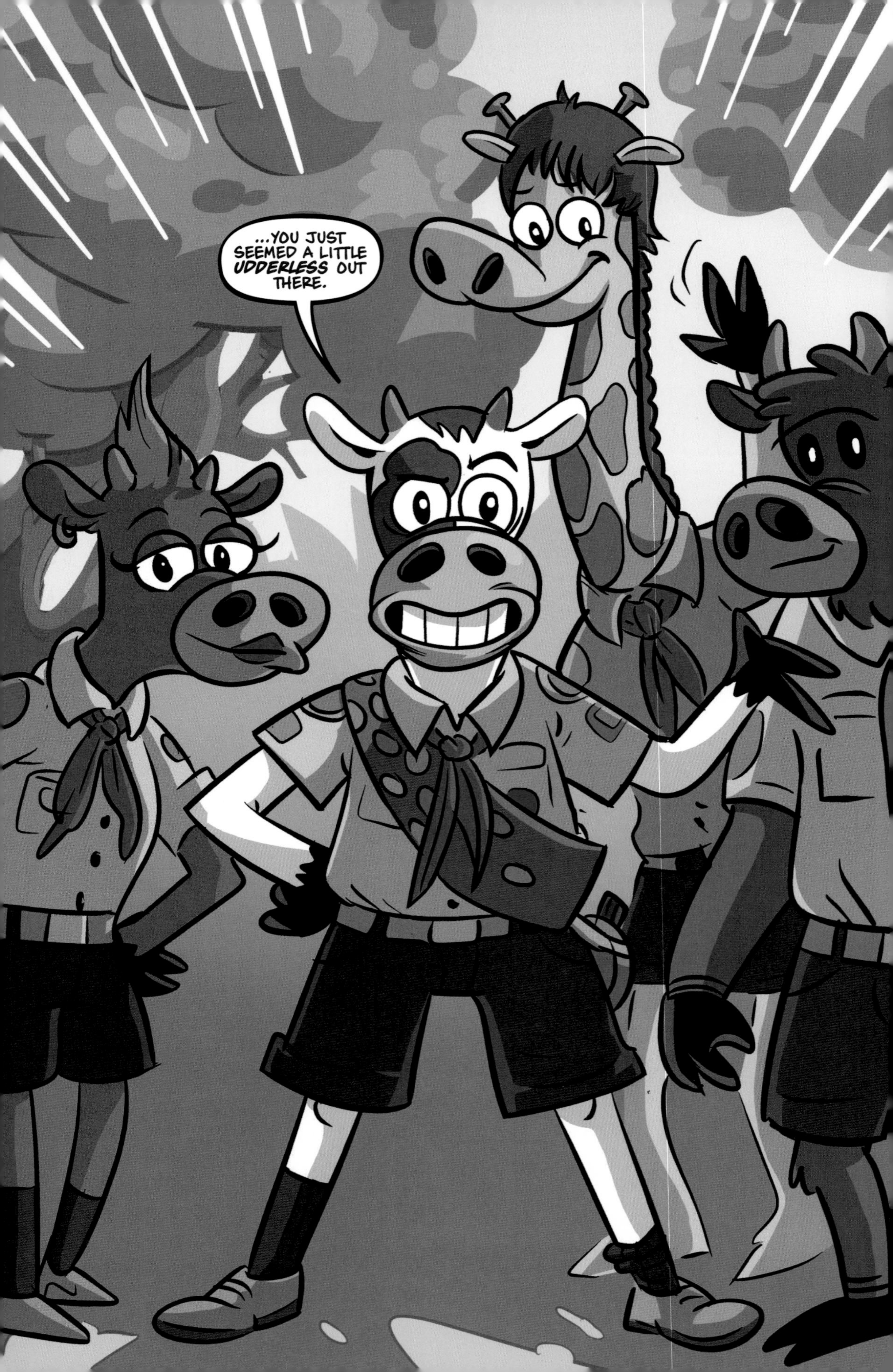
...YOU JUST SEEMED A LITTLE *UDDERLESS* OUT THERE.

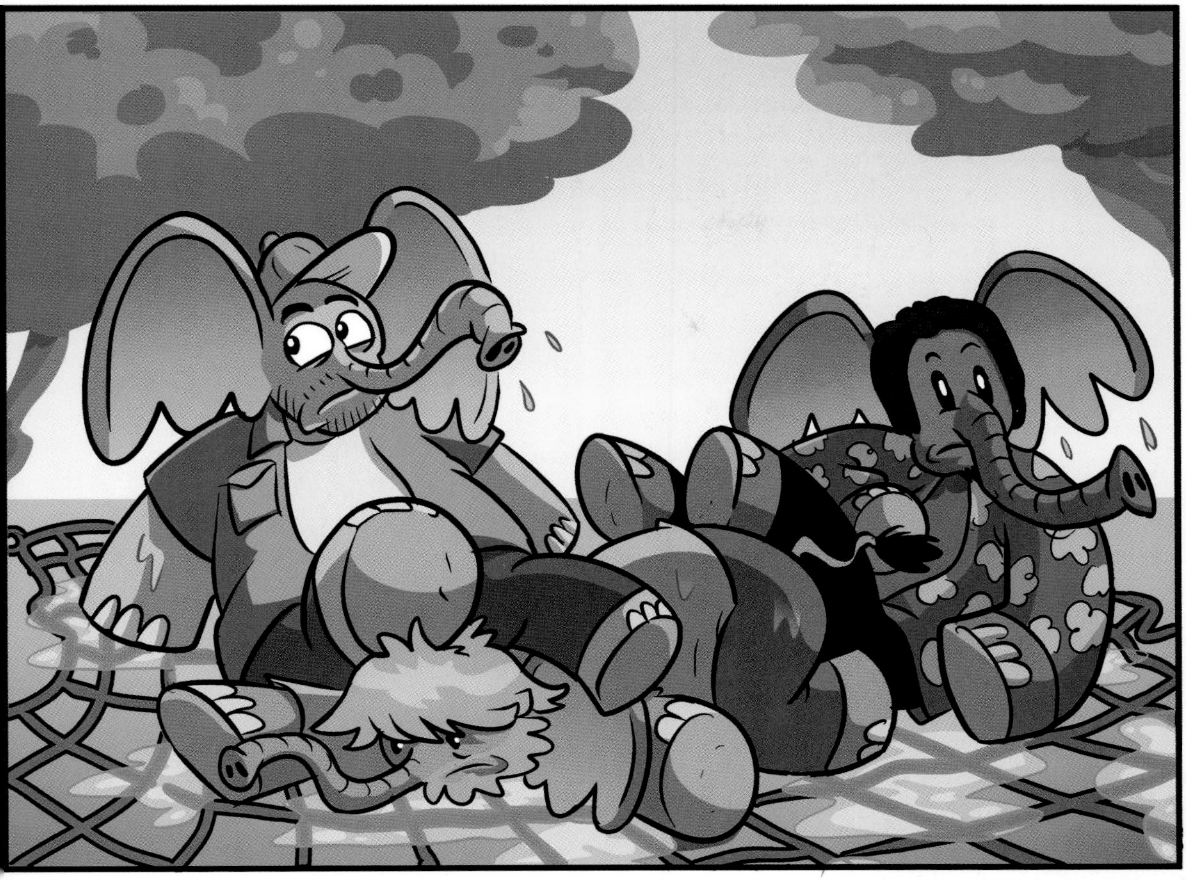

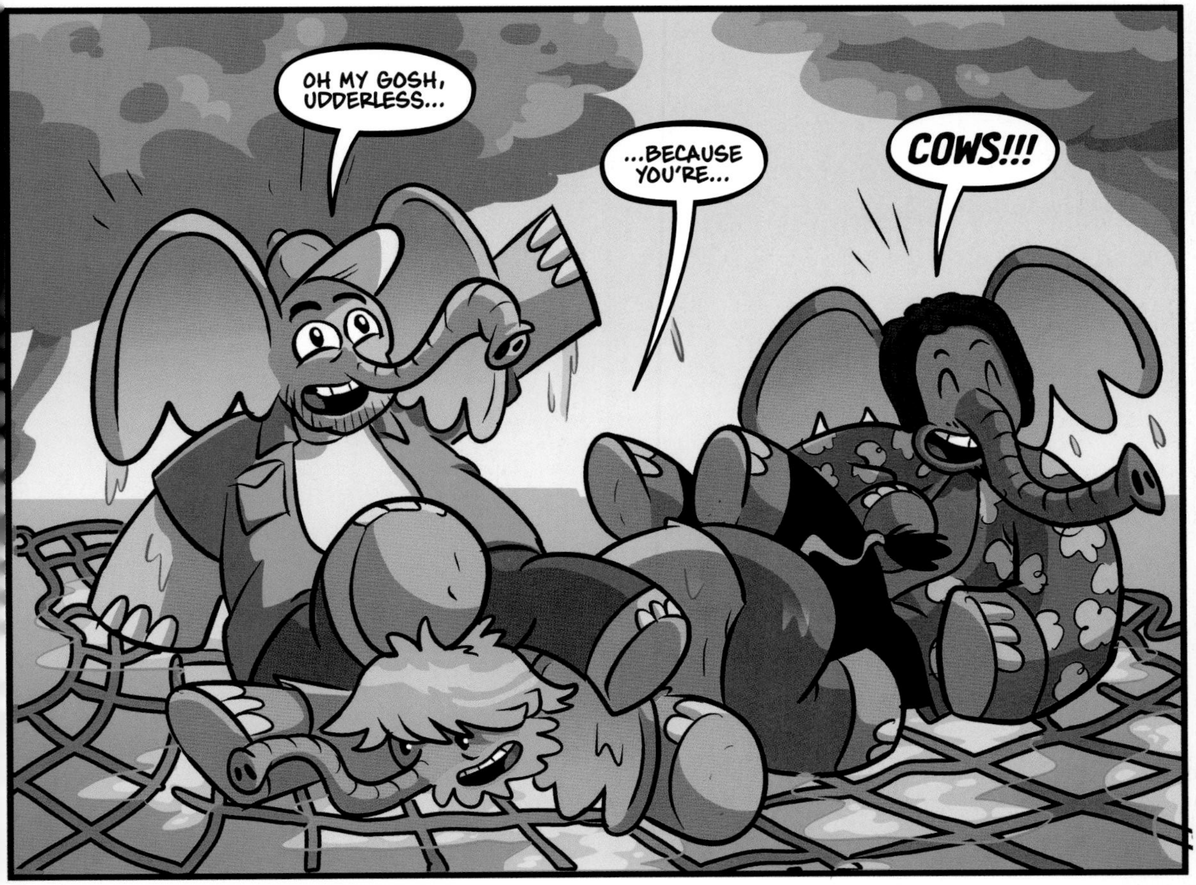
OH MY GOSH, UDDERLESS...
...BECAUSE YOU'RE...
COWS!!!

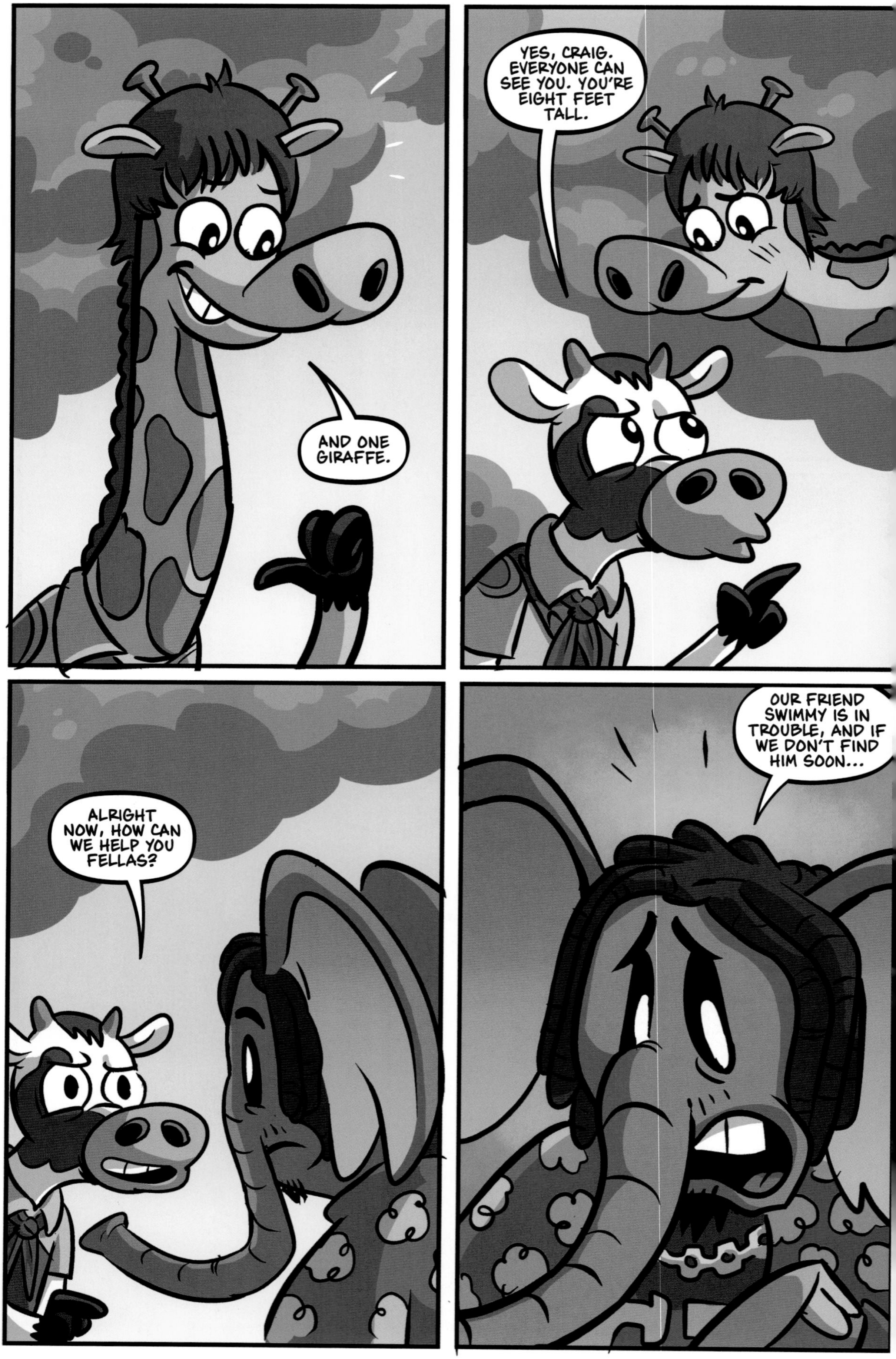
AND ONE GIRAFFE.
YES, CRAIG. EVERYONE CAN SEE YOU. YOU'RE EIGHT FEET TALL.
ALRIGHT NOW, HOW CAN WE HELP YOU FELLAS?
OUR FRIEND SWIMMY IS IN TROUBLE, AND IF WE DON'T FIND HIM SOON...

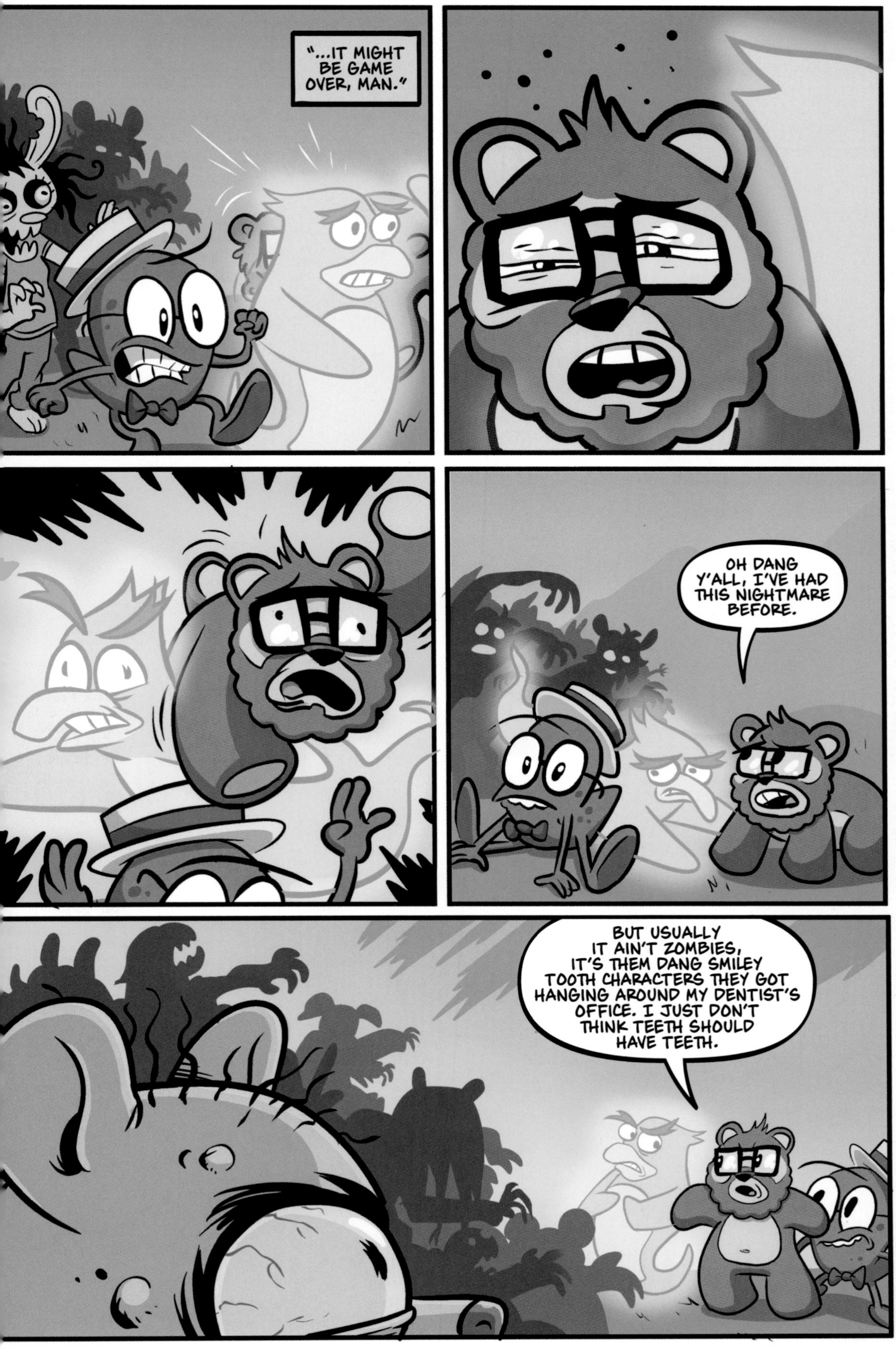
"...IT MIGHT BE GAME OVER, MAN."
OH DANG Y'ALL, I'VE HAD THIS NIGHTMARE BEFORE.
BUT USUALLY IT AIN'T ZOMBIES, IT'S THEM DANG SMILEY TOOTH CHARACTERS THEY GOT HANGING AROUND MY DENTIST'S OFFICE. I JUST DON'T THINK TEETH SHOULD HAVE TEETH.

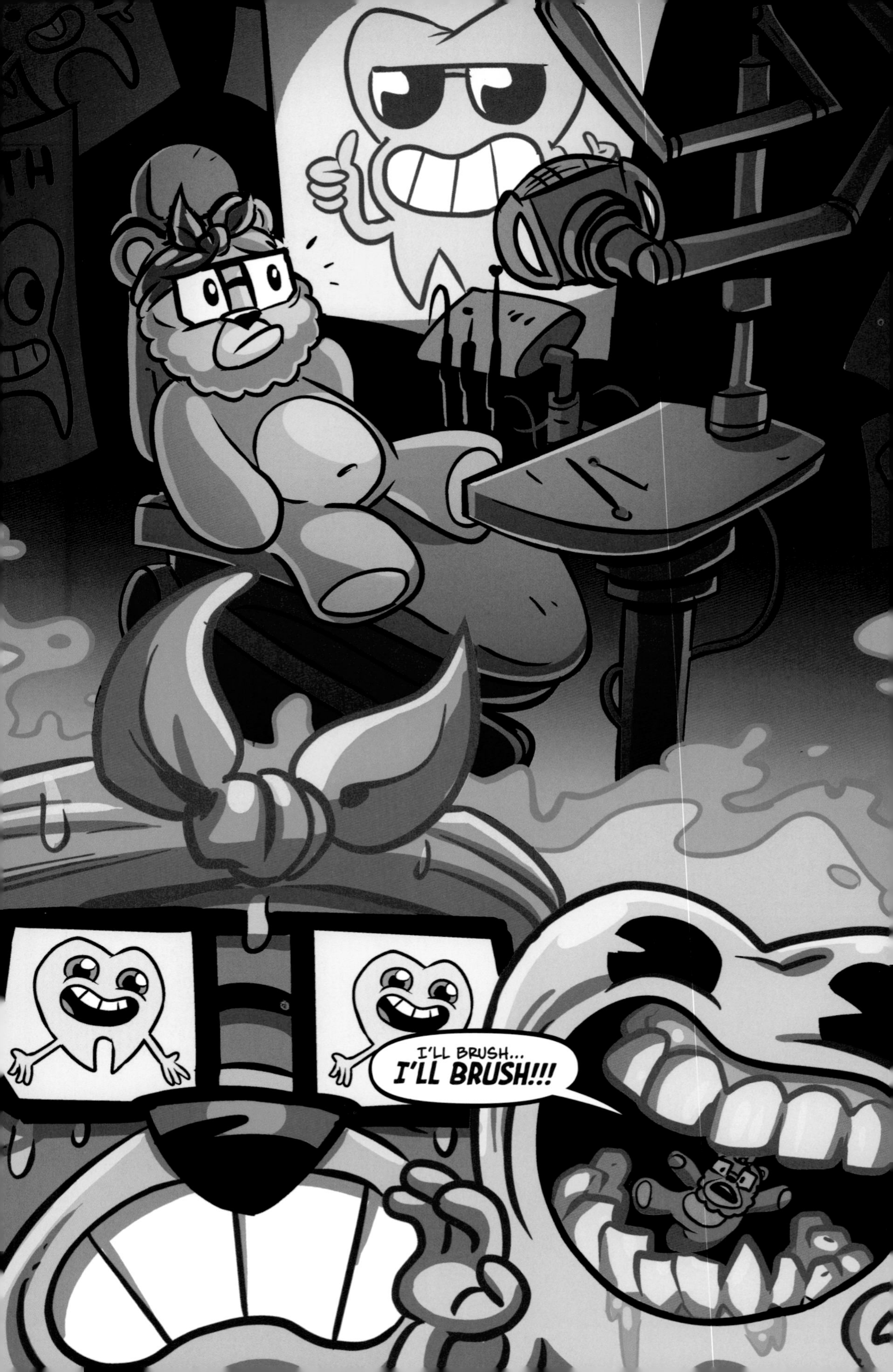
I'LL BRUSH... I'LL BRUSH!!!

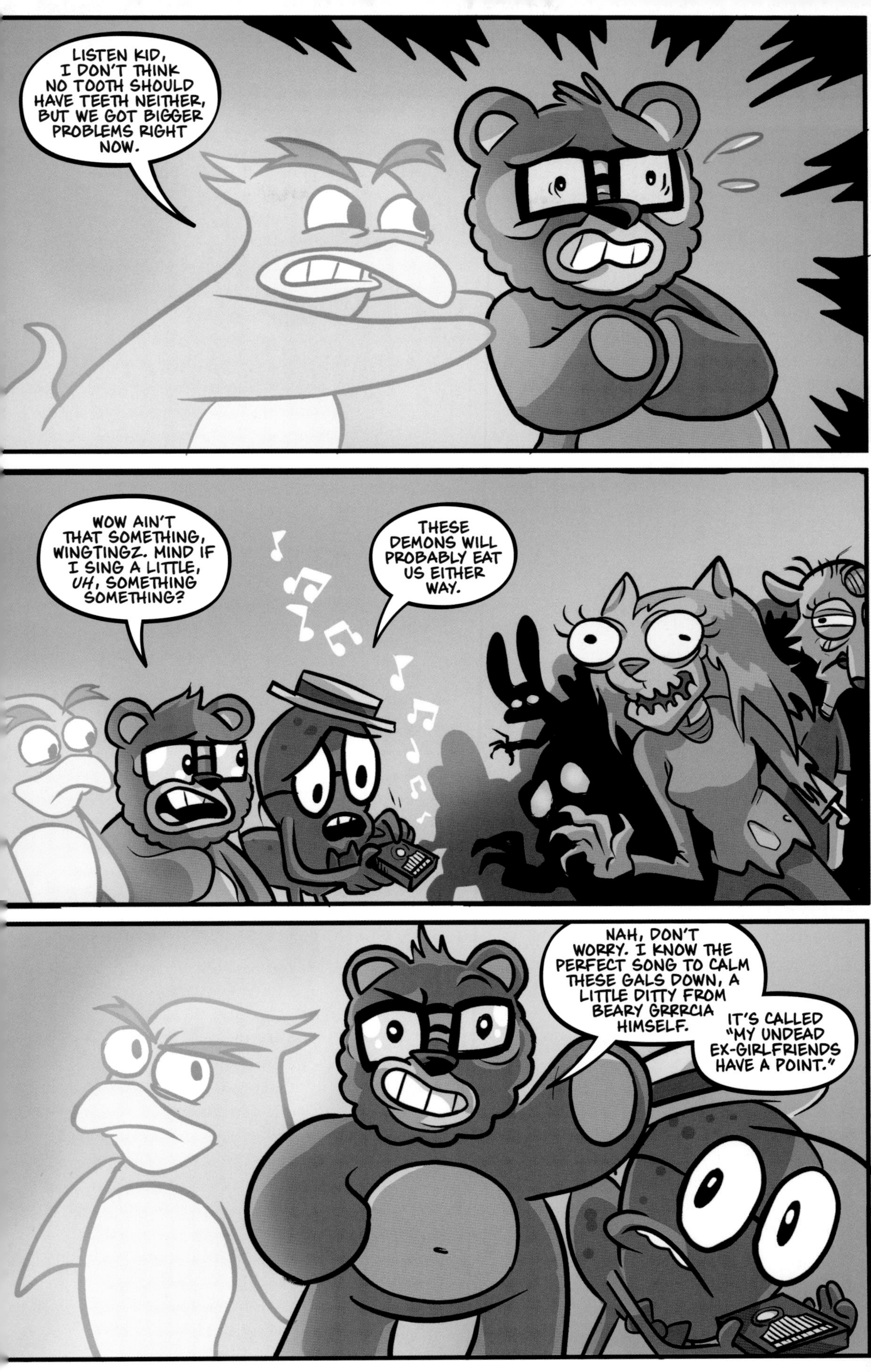
LISTEN KID, I DON'T THINK NO TOOTH SHOULD HAVE TEETH NEITHER, BUT WE GOT BIGGER PROBLEMS RIGHT NOW.
WOW AIN'T THAT SOMETHING, WINGTINGZ. MIND IF I SING A LITTLE, *UH*, SOMETHING SOMETHING?
THESE DEMONS WILL PROBABLY EAT US EITHER WAY.
NAH, DON'T WORRY. I KNOW THE PERFECT SONG TO CALM THESE GALS DOWN, A LITTLE DITTY FROM BEARY GRRRCIA HIMSELF.
IT'S CALLED "MY UNDEAD EX-GIRLFRIENDS HAVE A POINT."

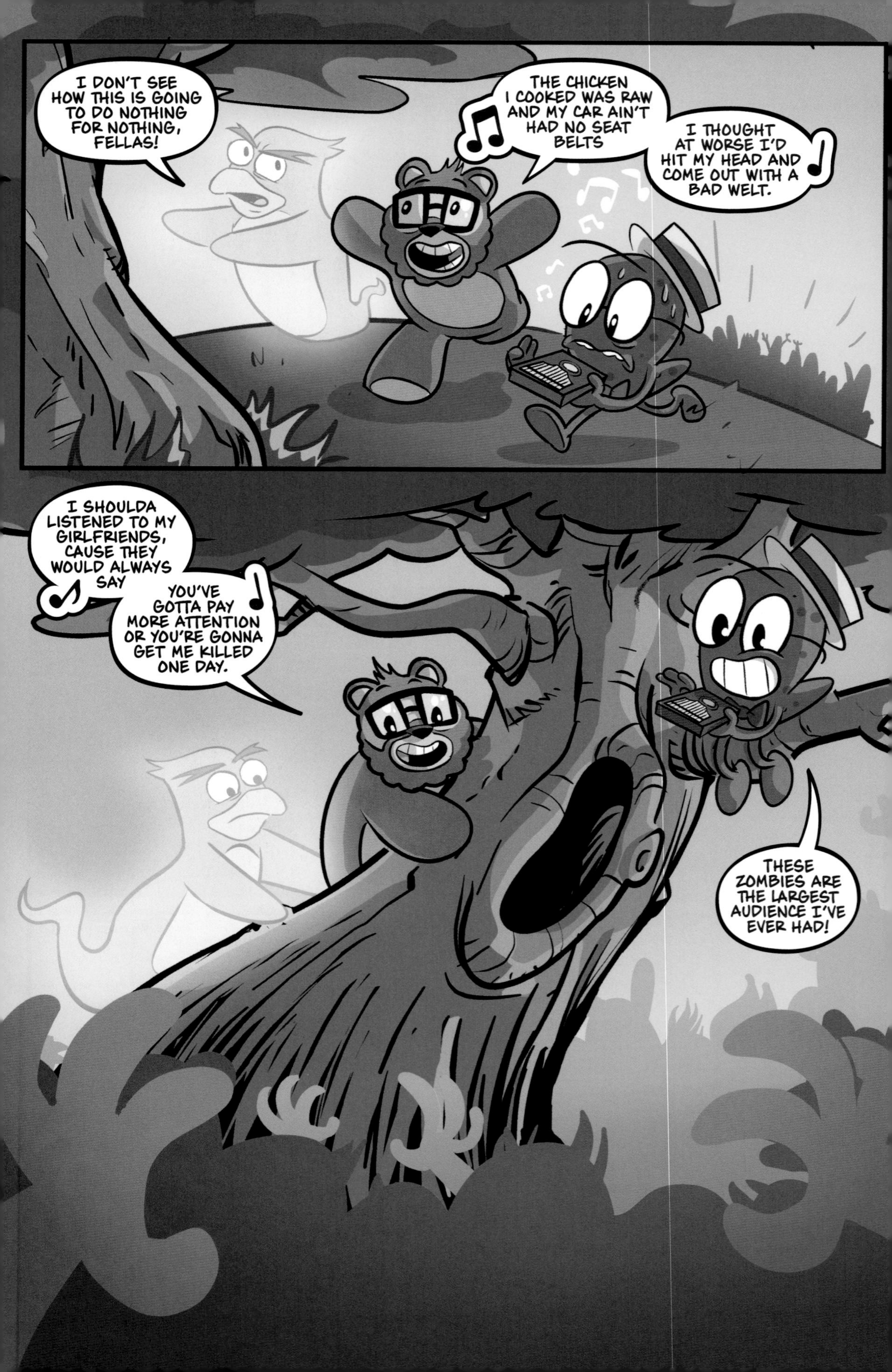
I DON'T SEE HOW THIS IS GOING TO DO NOTHING FOR NOTHING, FELLAS!
THE CHICKEN I COOKED WAS RAW AND MY CAR AIN'T HAD NO SEAT BELTS
I THOUGHT AT WORSE I'D HIT MY HEAD AND COME OUT WITH A BAD WELT.
I SHOULDA LISTENED TO MY GIRLFRIENDS, CAUSE THEY WOULD ALWAYS SAY
YOU'VE GOTTA PAY MORE ATTENTION OR YOU'RE GONNA GET ME KILLED ONE DAY.
THESE ZOMBIES ARE THE LARGEST AUDIENCE I'VE EVER HAD!

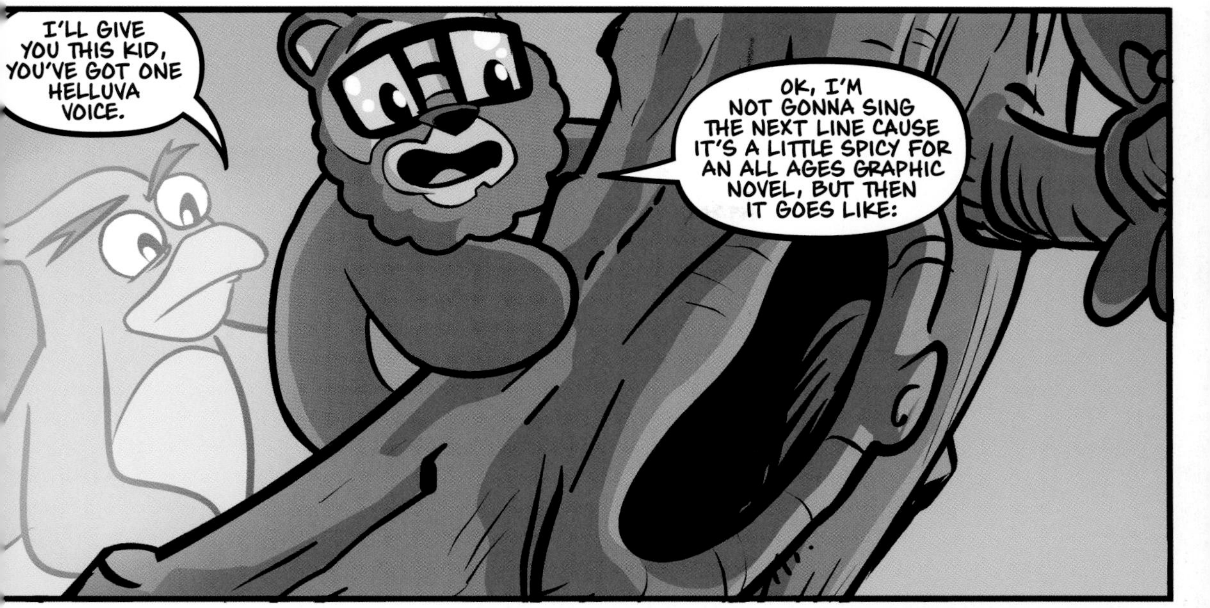
I'LL GIVE YOU THIS KID, YOU'VE GOT ONE HELLUVA VOICE.
OK, I'M NOT GONNA SING THE NEXT LINE CAUSE IT'S A LITTLE SPICY FOR AN ALL AGES GRAPHIC NOVEL, BUT THEN IT GOES LIKE:

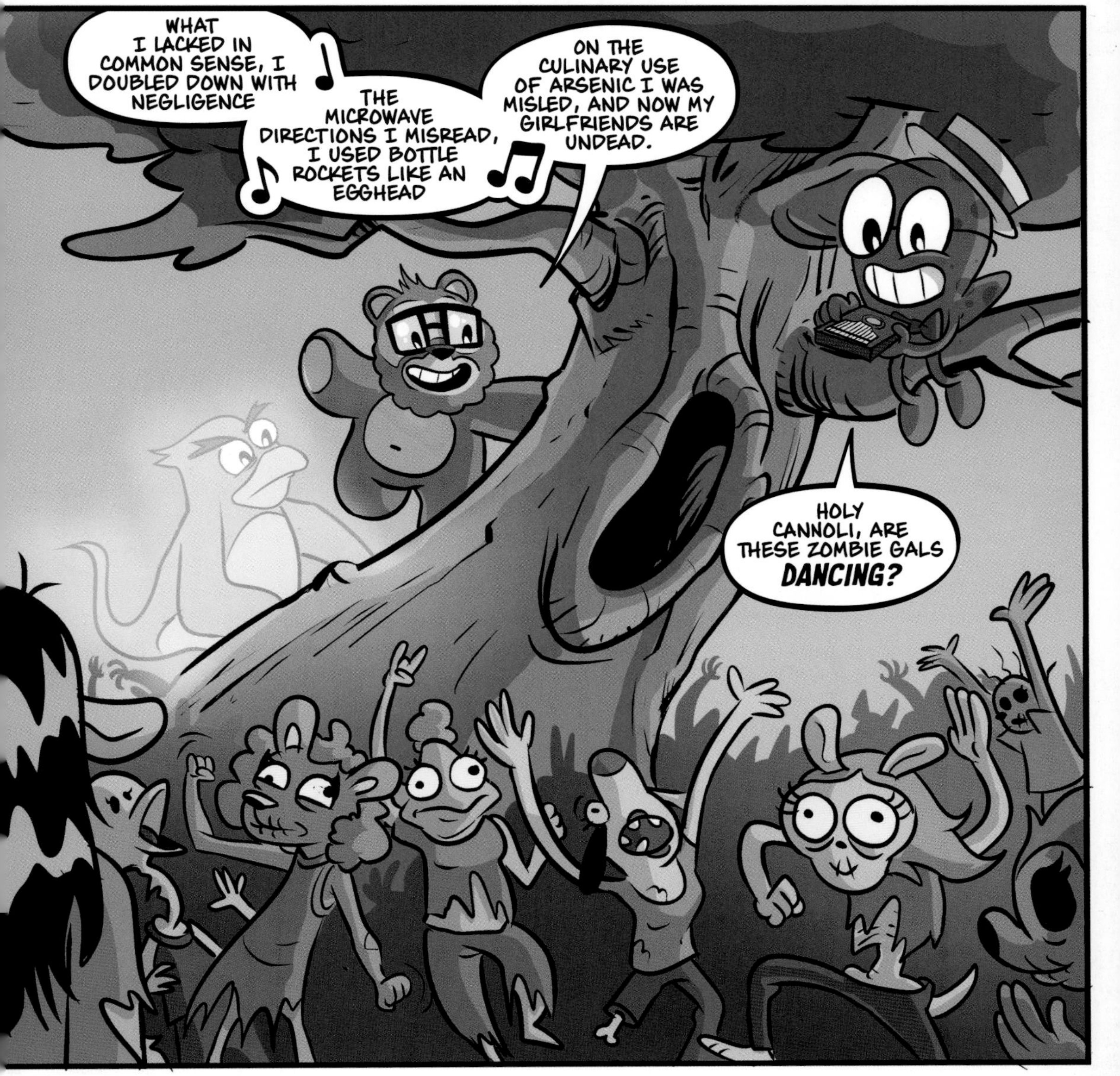
WHAT I LACKED IN COMMON SENSE, I DOUBLED DOWN WITH NEGLIGENCE
THE MICROWAVE DIRECTIONS I MISREAD, I USED BOTTLE ROCKETS LIKE AN EGGHEAD
ON THE CULINARY USE OF ARSENIC I WAS MISLED, AND NOW MY GIRLFRIENDS ARE UNDEAD.
HOLY CANNOLI, ARE THESE ZOMBIE GALS DANCING?

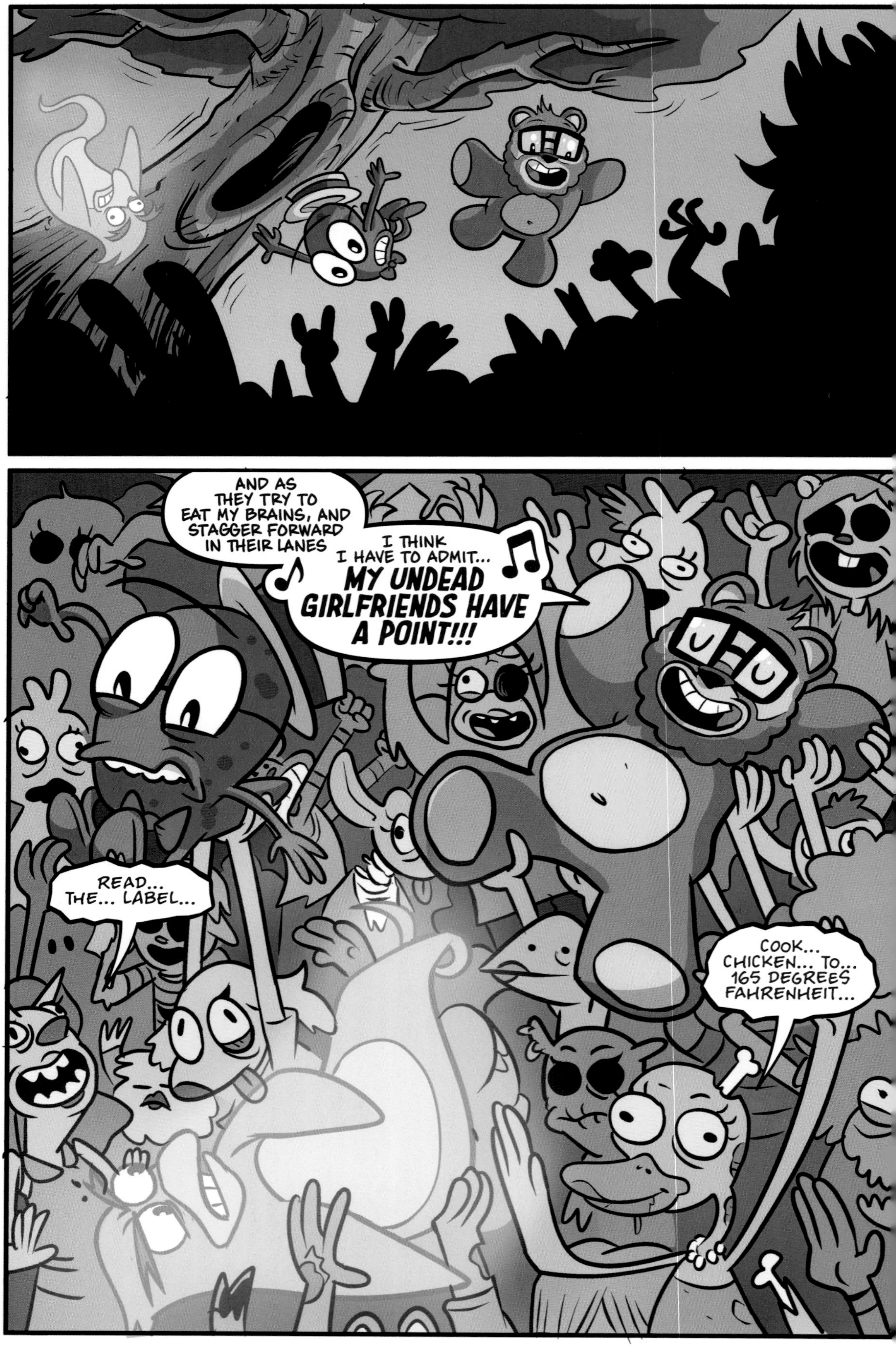
AND AS THEY TRY TO EAT MY BRAINS, AND STAGGER FORWARD IN THEIR LANES
I THINK I HAVE TO ADMIT...
MY UNDEAD GIRLFRIENDS HAVE A POINT!!!
READ... THE... LABEL...
COOK... CHICKEN... TO... 165 DEGREES FAHRENHEIT...

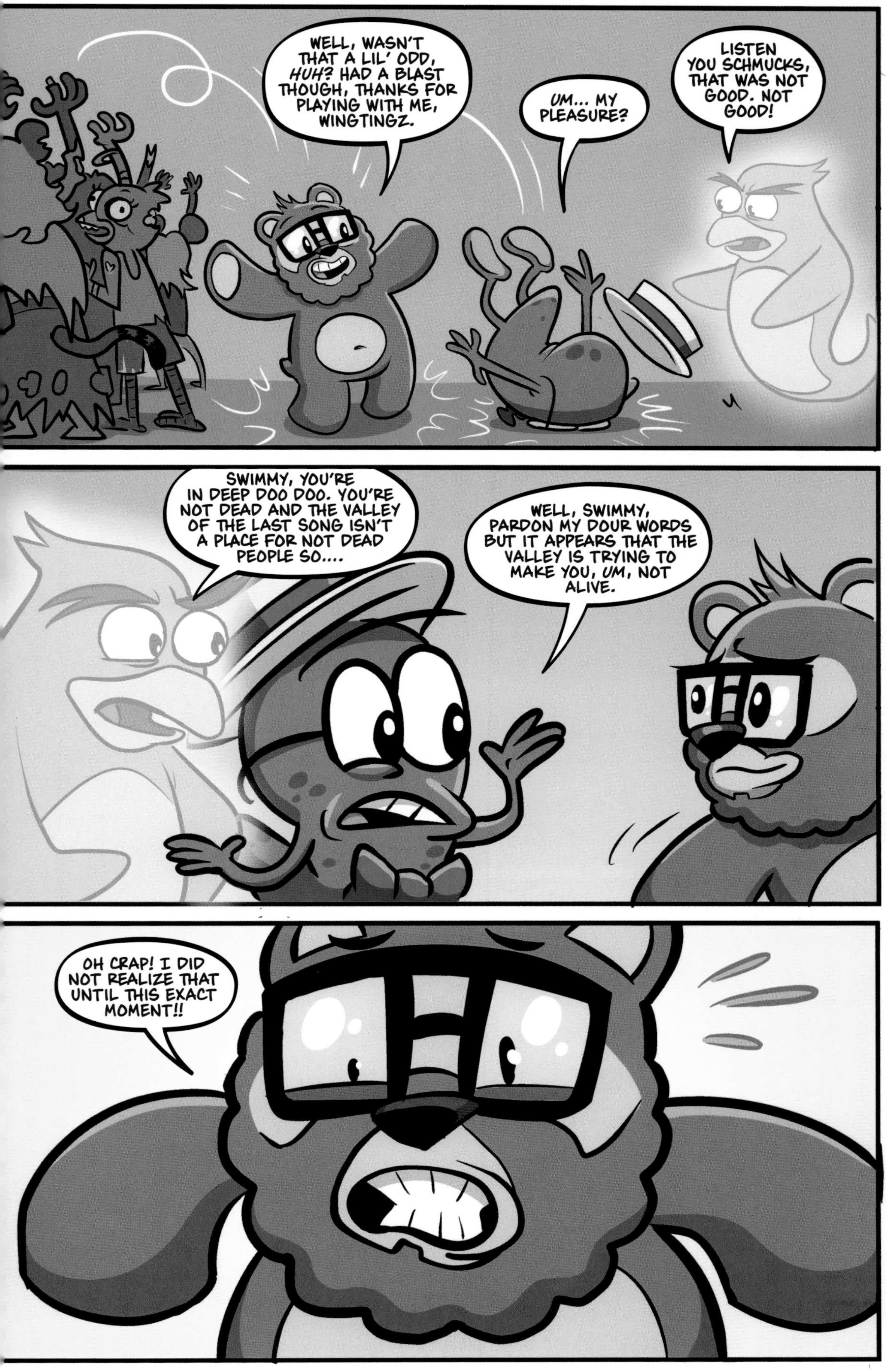
WELL, WASN'T THAT A LIL' ODD, HUH? HAD A BLAST THOUGH, THANKS FOR PLAYING WITH ME, WINGTINGZ.
UM... MY PLEASURE?
LISTEN YOU SCHMUCKS, THAT WAS NOT GOOD. NOT GOOD!
SWIMMY, YOU'RE IN DEEP DOO DOO. YOU'RE NOT DEAD AND THE VALLEY OF THE LAST SONG ISN'T A PLACE FOR NOT DEAD PEOPLE SO....
WELL, SWIMMY, PARDON MY DOUR WORDS BUT IT APPEARS THAT THE VALLEY IS TRYING TO MAKE YOU, UM, NOT ALIVE.
OH CRAP! I DID NOT REALIZE THAT UNTIL THIS EXACT MOMENT!!

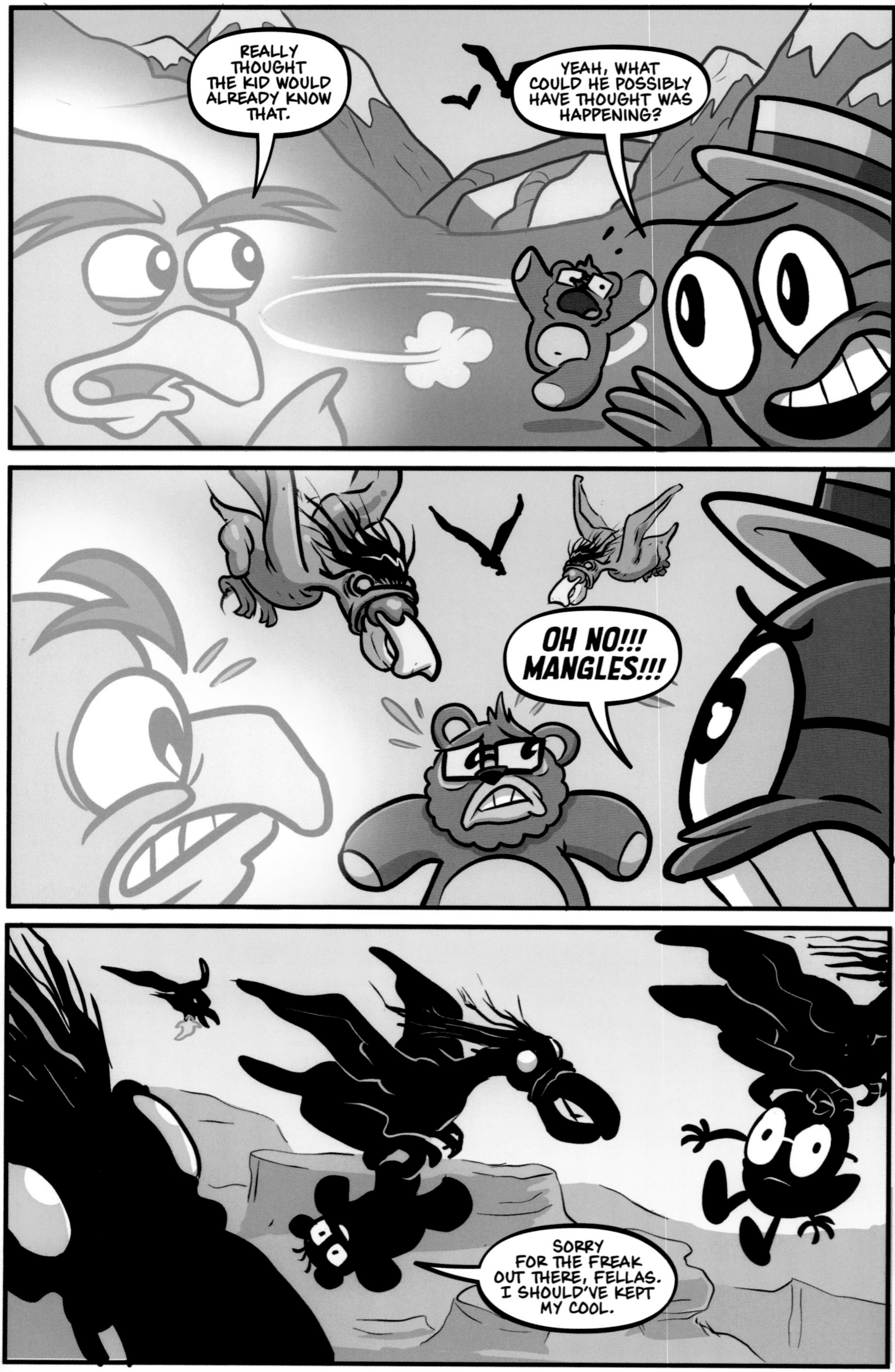
REALLY THOUGHT THE KID WOULD ALREADY KNOW THAT.
YEAH, WHAT COULD HE POSSIBLY HAVE THOUGHT WAS HAPPENING?
OH NO!!! MANGLES!!!
SORRY FOR THE FREAK OUT THERE, FELLAS. I SHOULD'VE KEPT MY COOL.

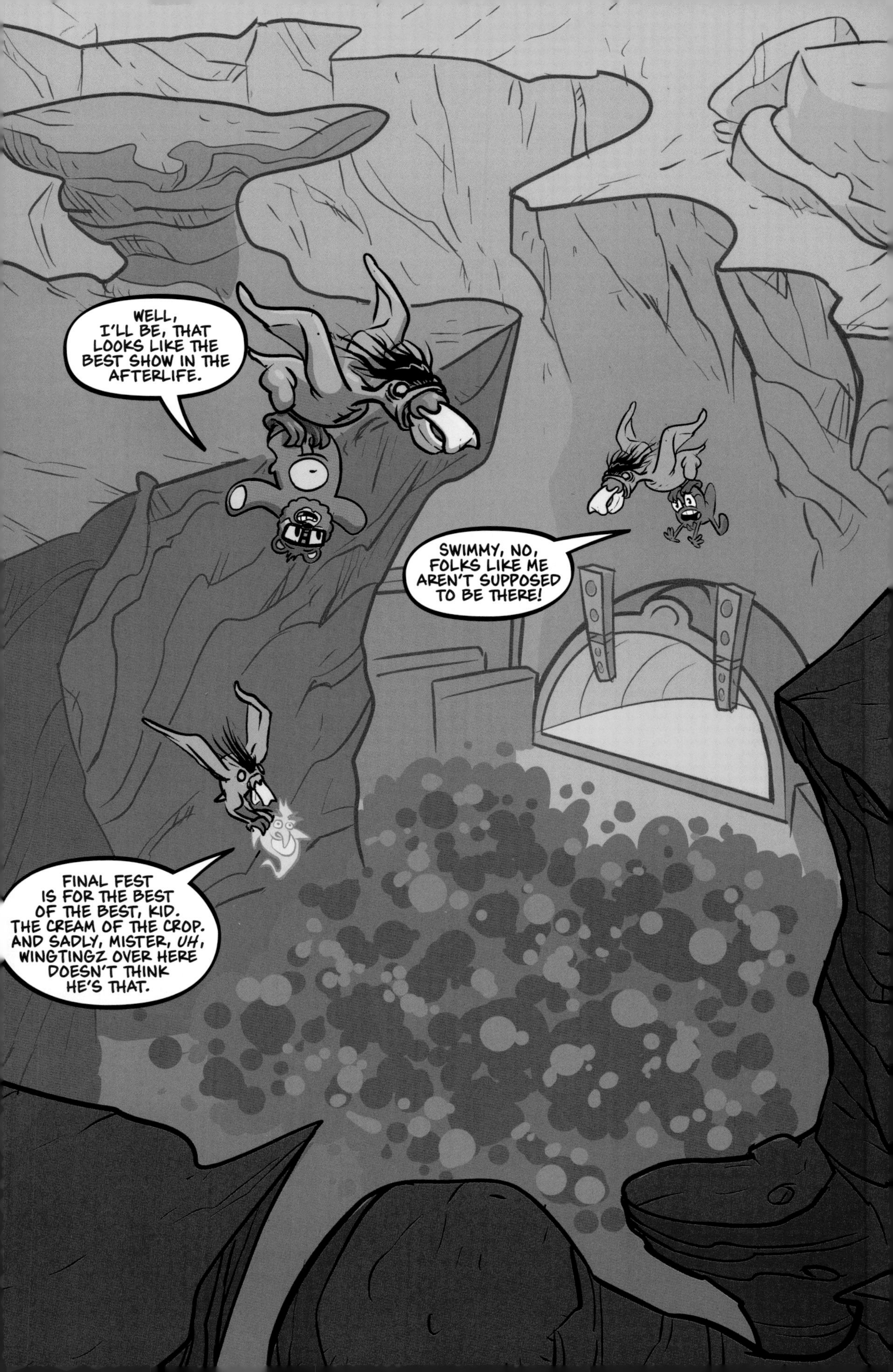
WELL, I'LL BE, THAT LOOKS LIKE THE BEST SHOW IN THE AFTERLIFE.
SWIMMY, NO, FOLKS LIKE ME AREN'T SUPPOSED TO BE THERE!
FINAL FEST IS FOR THE BEST OF THE BEST, KID. THE CREAM OF THE CROP. AND SADLY, MISTER, UH, WINGTINGZ OVER HERE DOESN'T THINK HE'S THAT.

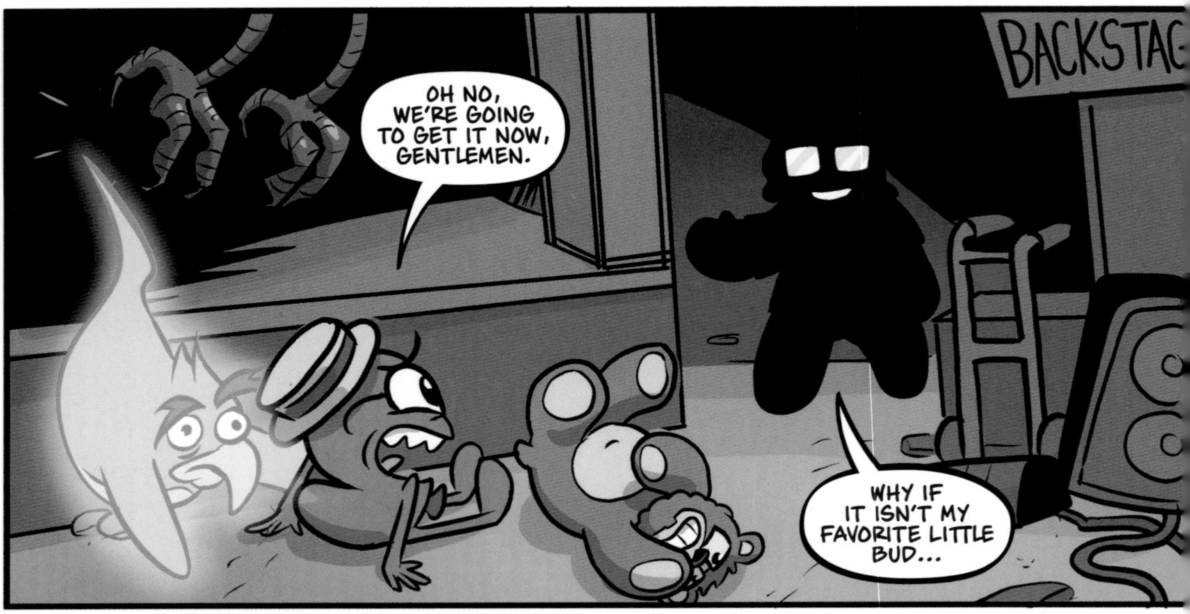
BACKSTAG
OH NO, WE'RE GOING TO GET IT NOW, GENTLEMEN.
WHY IF IT ISN'T MY FAVORITE LITTLE BUD...

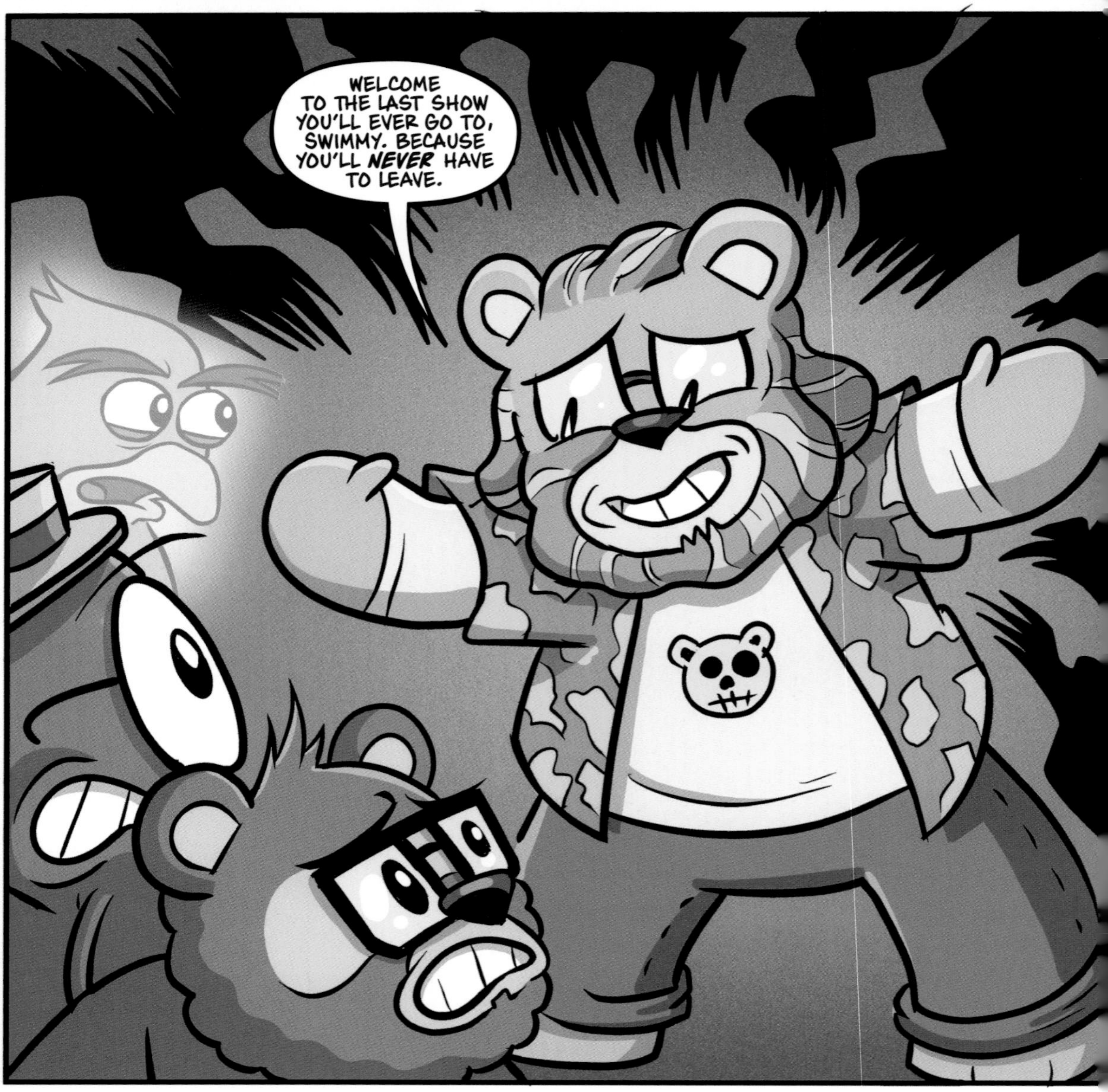
WELCOME TO THE LAST SHOW YOU'LL EVER GO TO, SWIMMY. BECAUSE YOU'LL *NEVER* HAVE TO LEAVE.

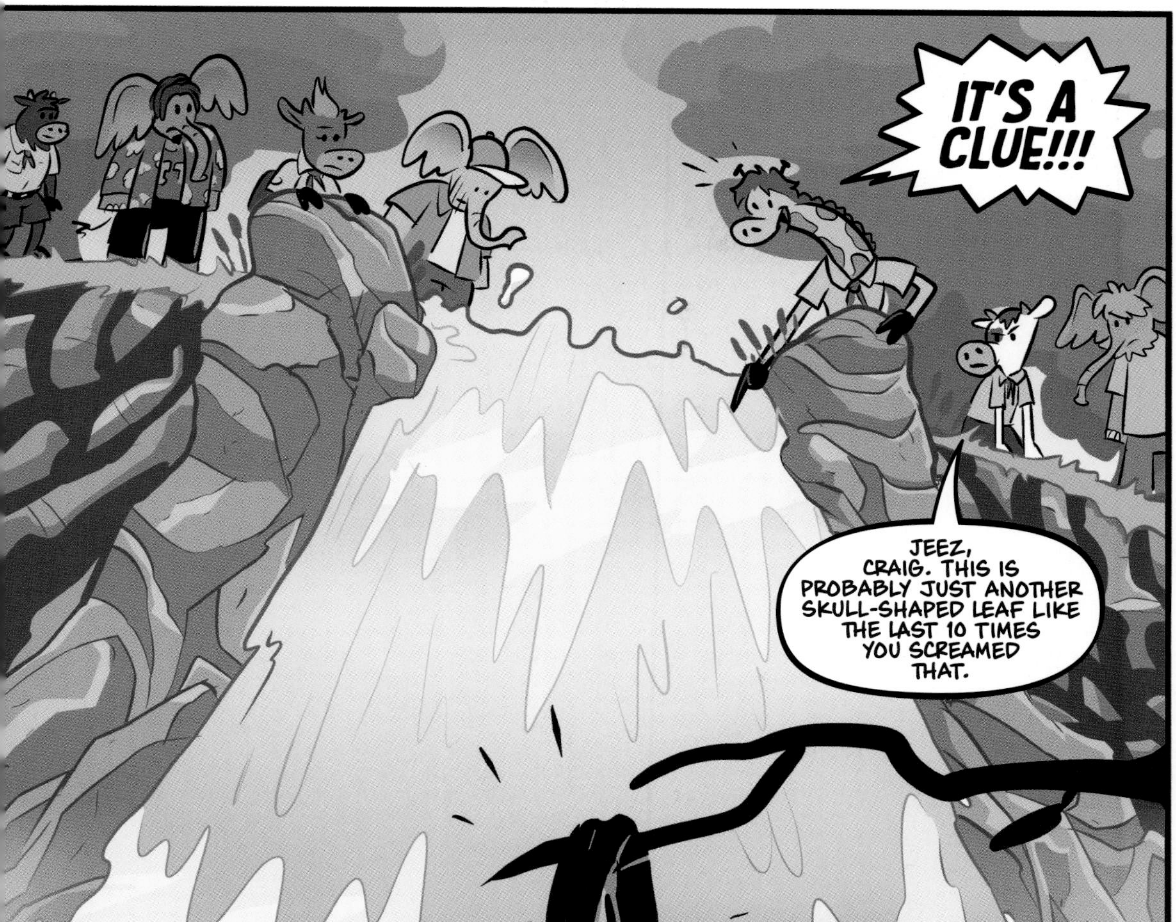
IT'S A CLUE!!!
JEEZ, CRAIG. THIS IS PROBABLY JUST ANOTHER SKULL-SHAPED LEAF LIKE THE LAST 10 TIMES YOU SCREAMED THAT.

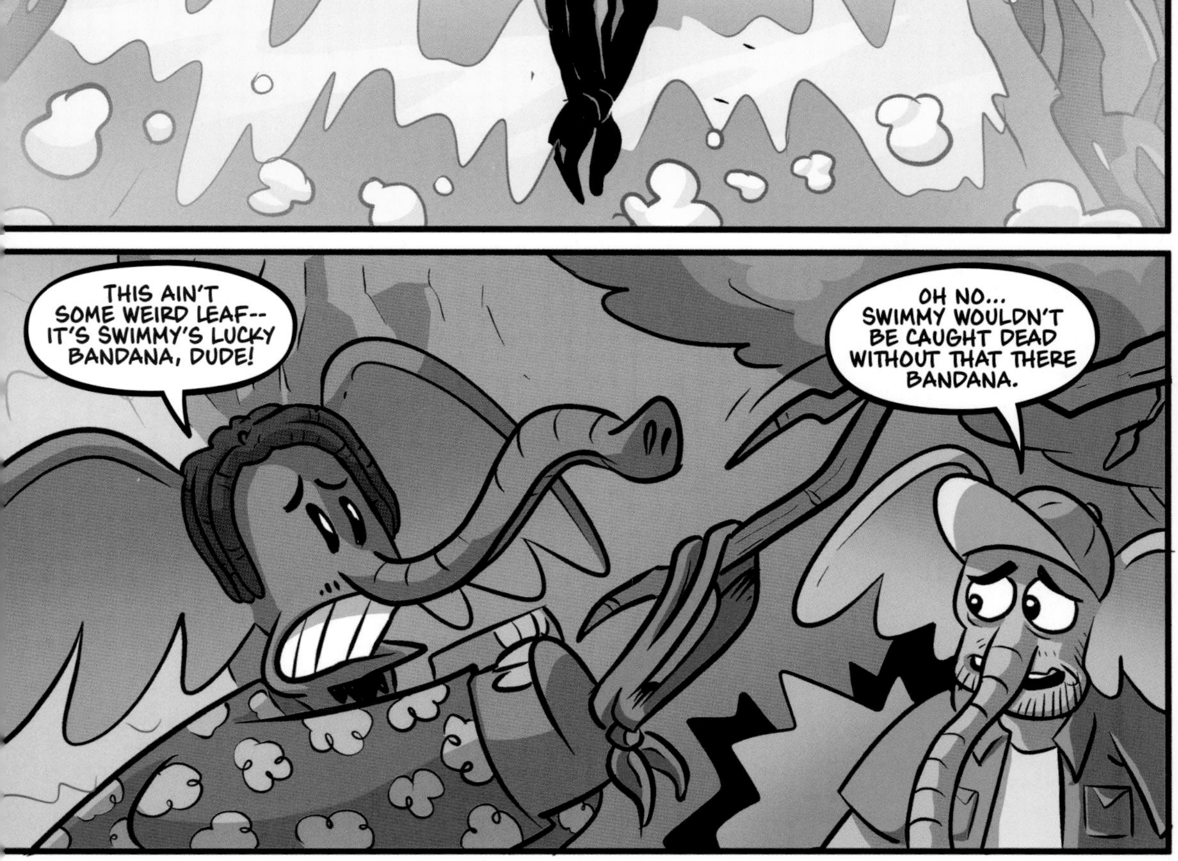
THIS AIN'T SOME WEIRD LEAF-- IT'S SWIMMY'S LUCKY BANDANA, DUDE!
OH NO... SWIMMY WOULDN'T BE CAUGHT DEAD WITHOUT THAT THERE BANDANA.

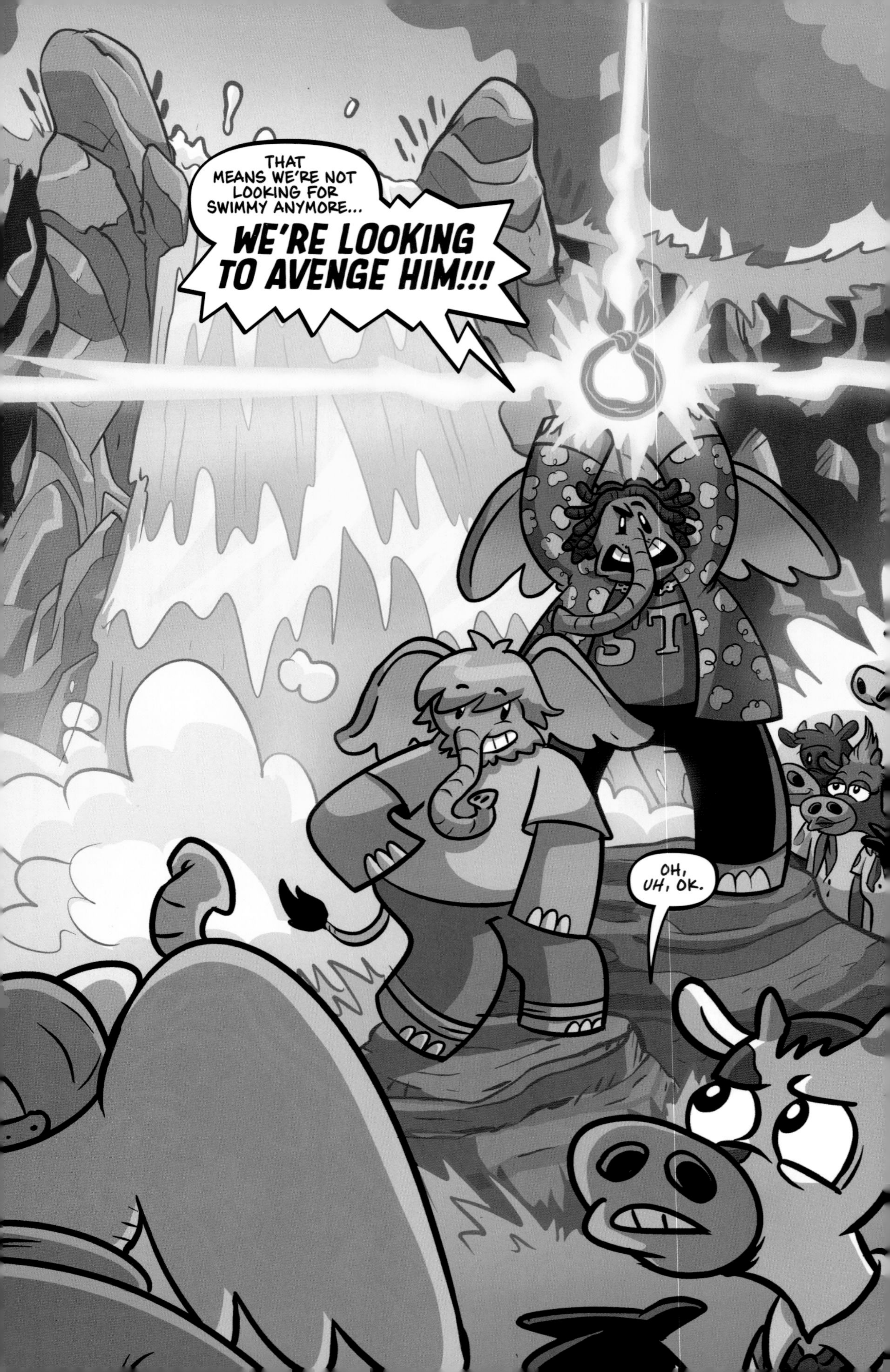
THAT MEANS WE'RE NOT LOOKING FOR SWIMMY ANYMORE...
WE'RE LOOKING TO AVENGE HIM!!!
OH, UH, OK.

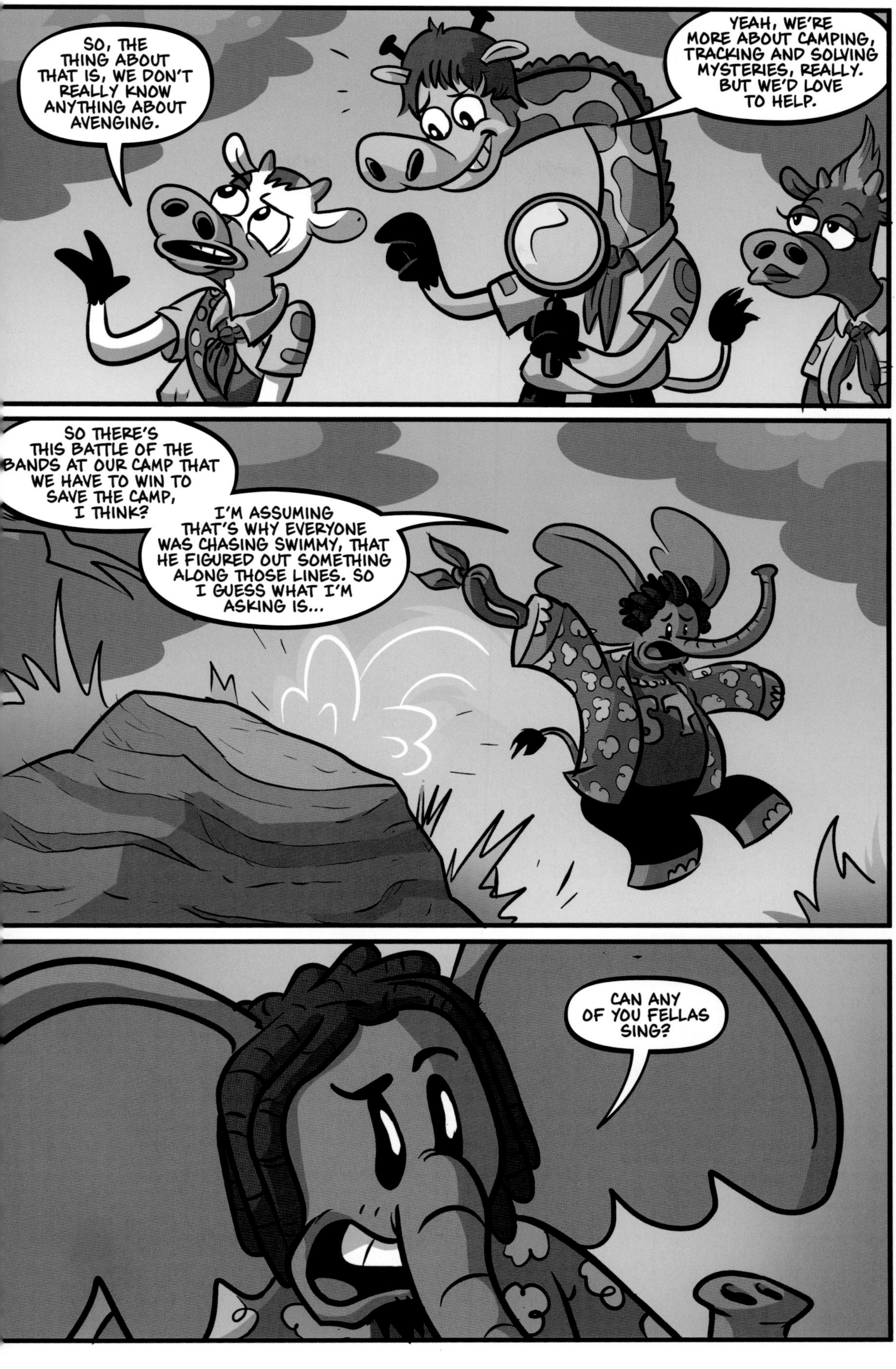
SO, THE THING ABOUT THAT IS, WE DON'T REALLY KNOW ANYTHING ABOUT AVENGING.
YEAH, WE'RE MORE ABOUT CAMPING, TRACKING AND SOLVING MYSTERIES, REALLY. BUT WE'D LOVE TO HELP.
SO THERE'S THIS BATTLE OF THE BANDS AT OUR CAMP THAT WE HAVE TO WIN TO SAVE THE CAMP, I THINK?
I'M ASSUMING THAT'S WHY EVERYONE WAS CHASING SWIMMY, THAT HE FIGURED OUT SOMETHING ALONG THOSE LINES. SO I GUESS WHAT I'M ASKING IS...
CAN ANY OF YOU FELLAS SING?

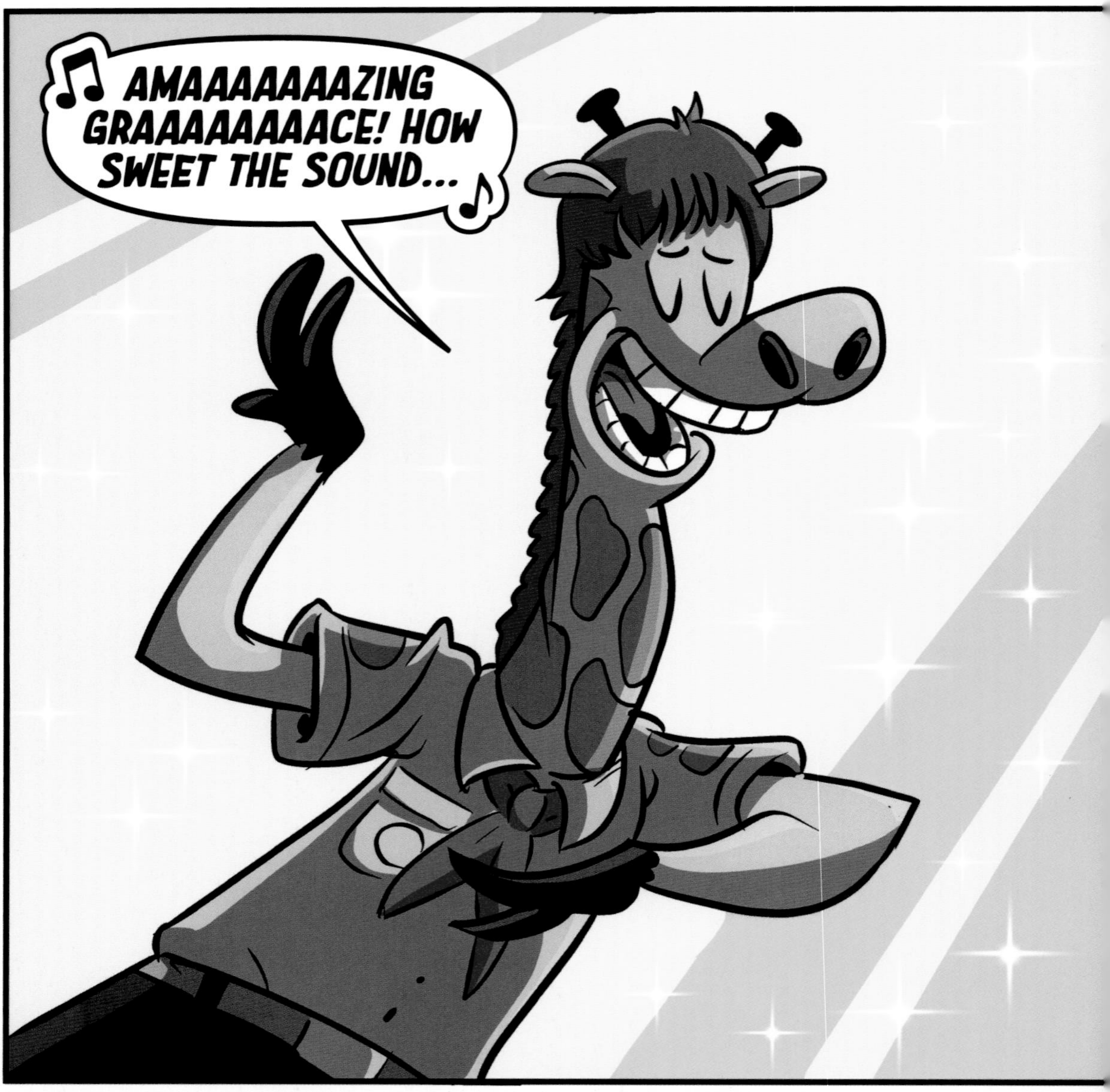
AMAAAAAAAZING GRAAAAAAAACE! HOW SWEET THE SOUND...

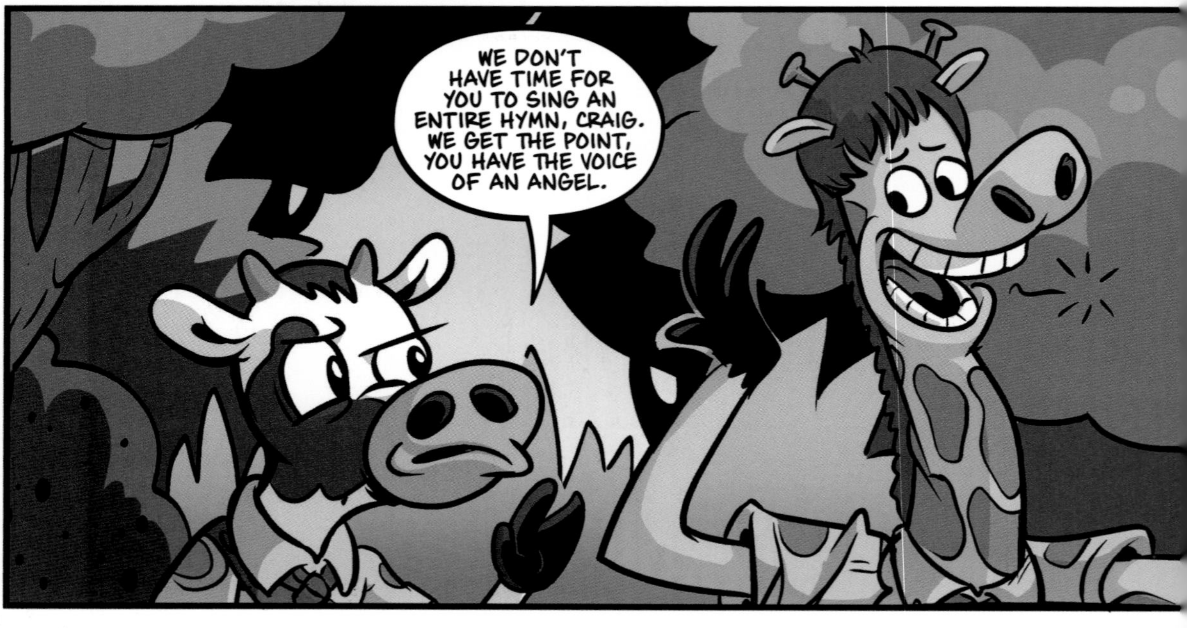
WE DON'T HAVE TIME FOR YOU TO SING AN ENTIRE HYMN, CRAIG. WE GET THE POINT, YOU HAVE THE VOICE OF AN ANGEL.

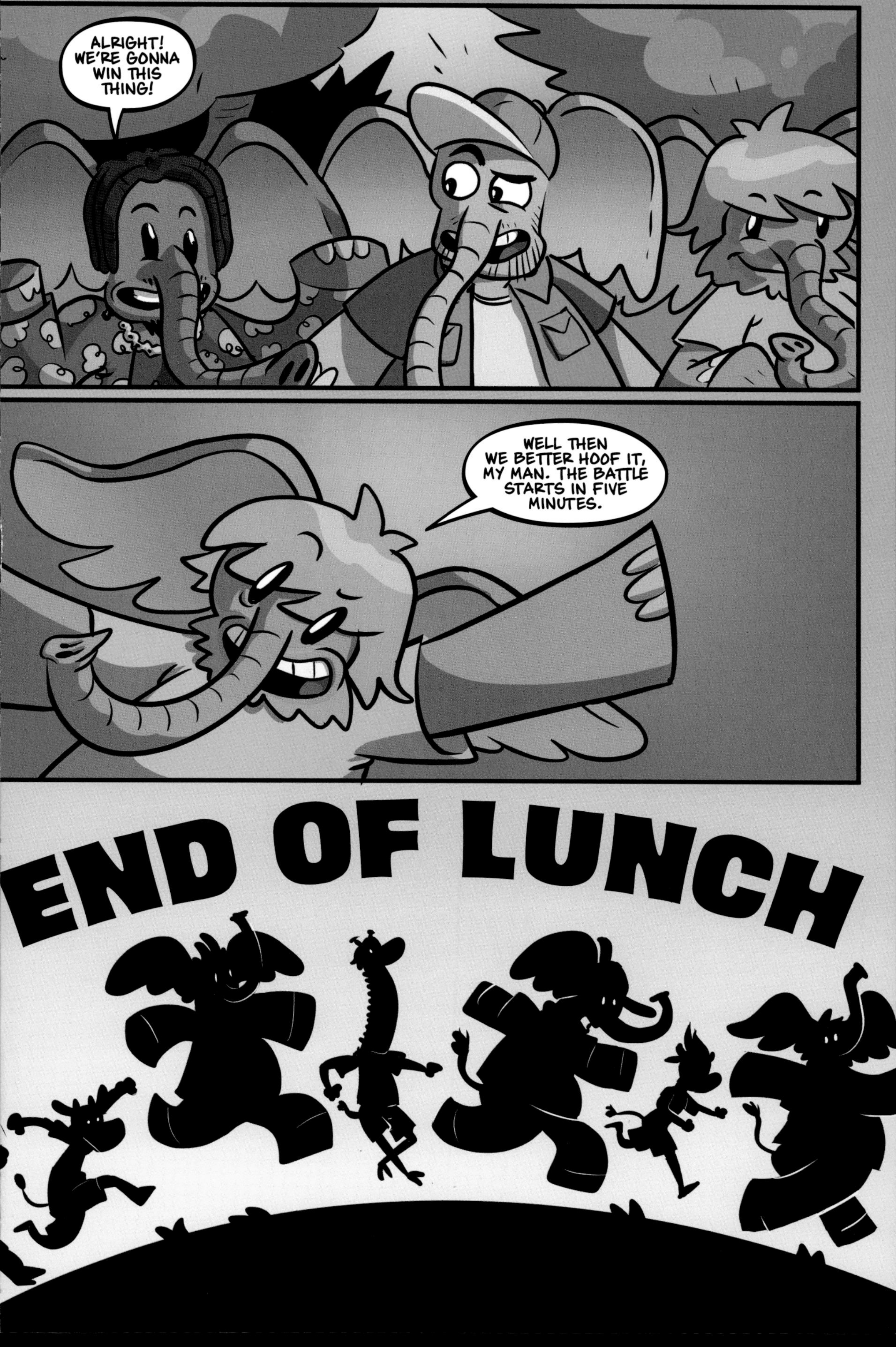
ALRIGHT! WE'RE GONNA WIN THIS THING!
WELL THEN WE BETTER HOOF IT, MY MAN. THE BATTLE STARTS IN FIVE MINUTES.
END OF LUNCH

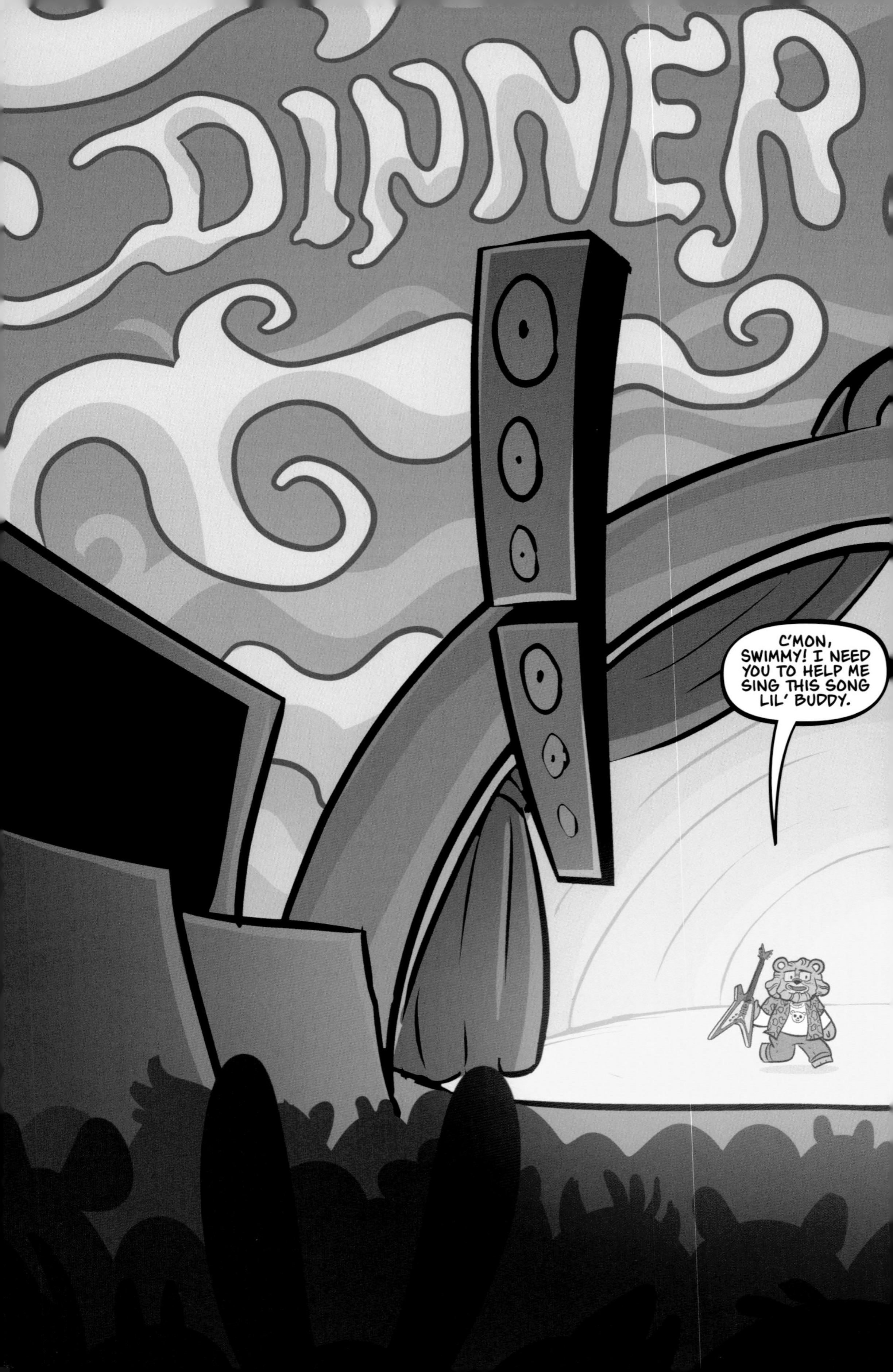
DINNER
C'MON, SWIMMY! I NEED YOU TO HELP ME SING THIS SONG LIL' BUDDY.

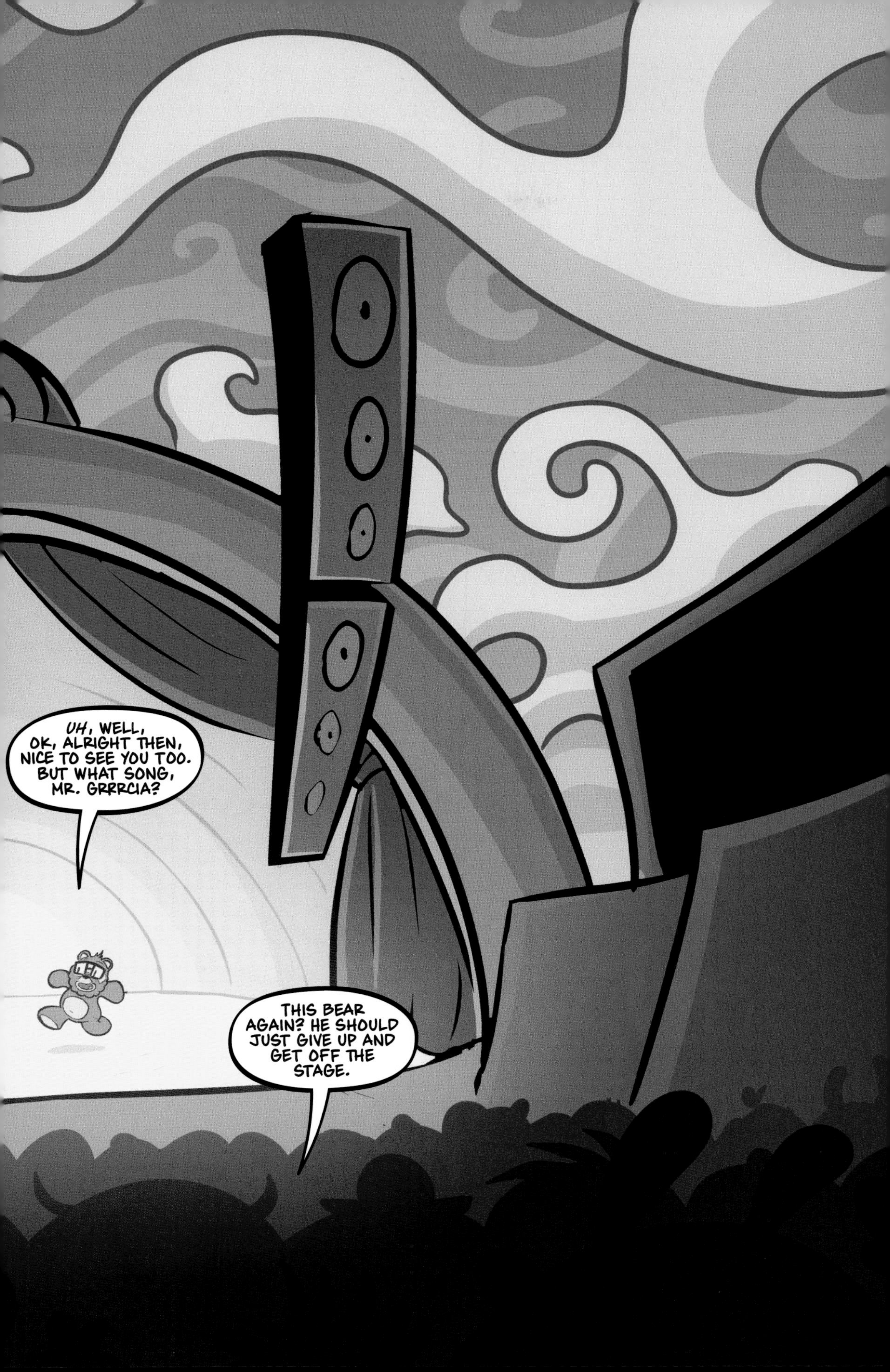
UH, WELL, OK, ALRIGHT THEN, NICE TO SEE YOU TOO. BUT WHAT SONG, MR. GRRRCIA?
THIS BEAR AGAIN? HE SHOULD JUST GIVE UP AND GET OFF THE STAGE.

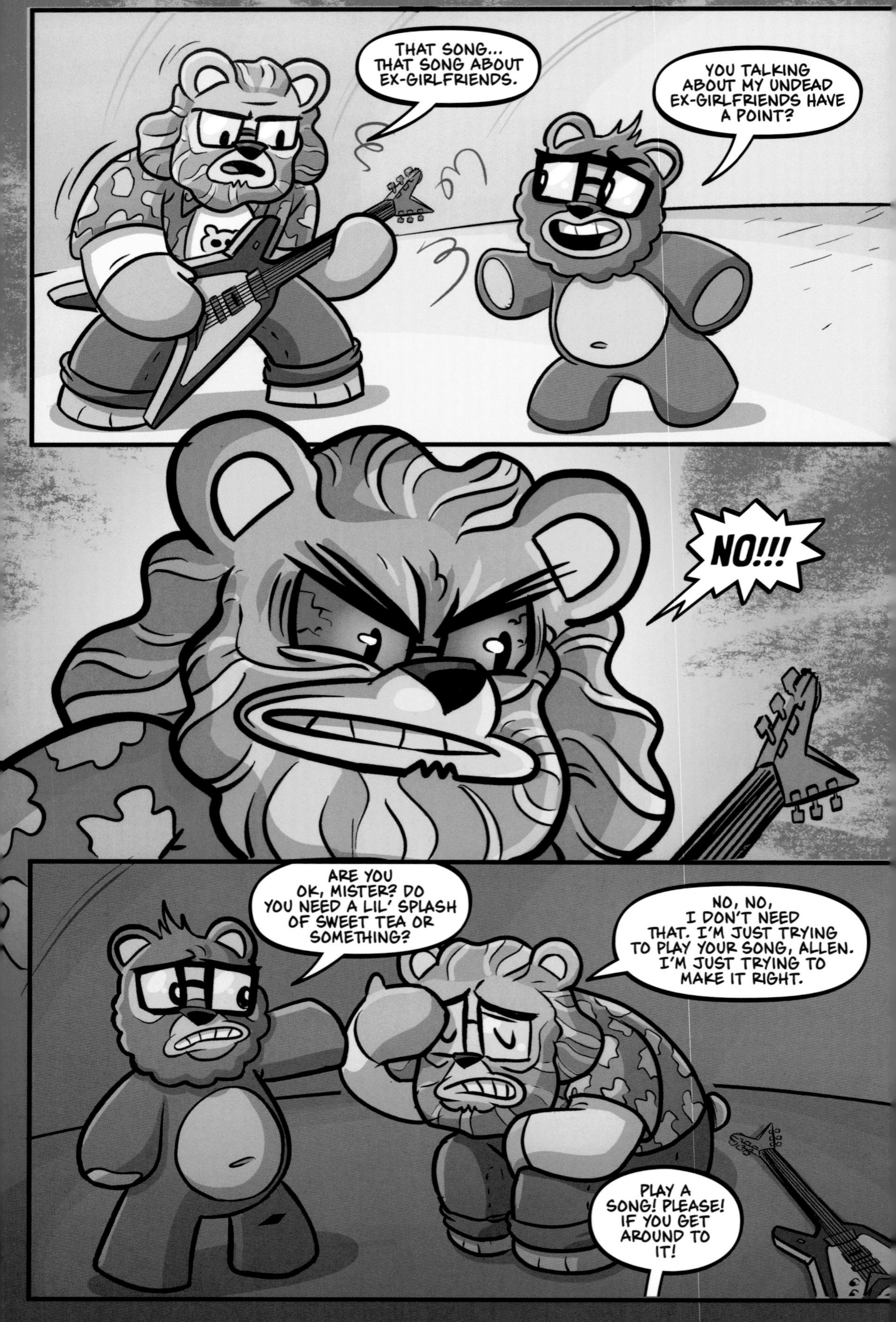
THAT SONG... THAT SONG ABOUT EX-GIRLFRIENDS.
YOU TALKING ABOUT MY UNDEAD EX-GIRLFRIENDS HAVE A POINT?
NO!!!
ARE YOU OK, MISTER? DO YOU NEED A LIL' SPLASH OF SWEET TEA OR SOMETHING?
NO, NO, I DON'T NEED THAT. I'M JUST TRYING TO PLAY YOUR SONG, ALLEN. I'M JUST TRYING TO MAKE IT RIGHT.
PLAY A SONG! PLEASE! IF YOU GET AROUND TO IT!

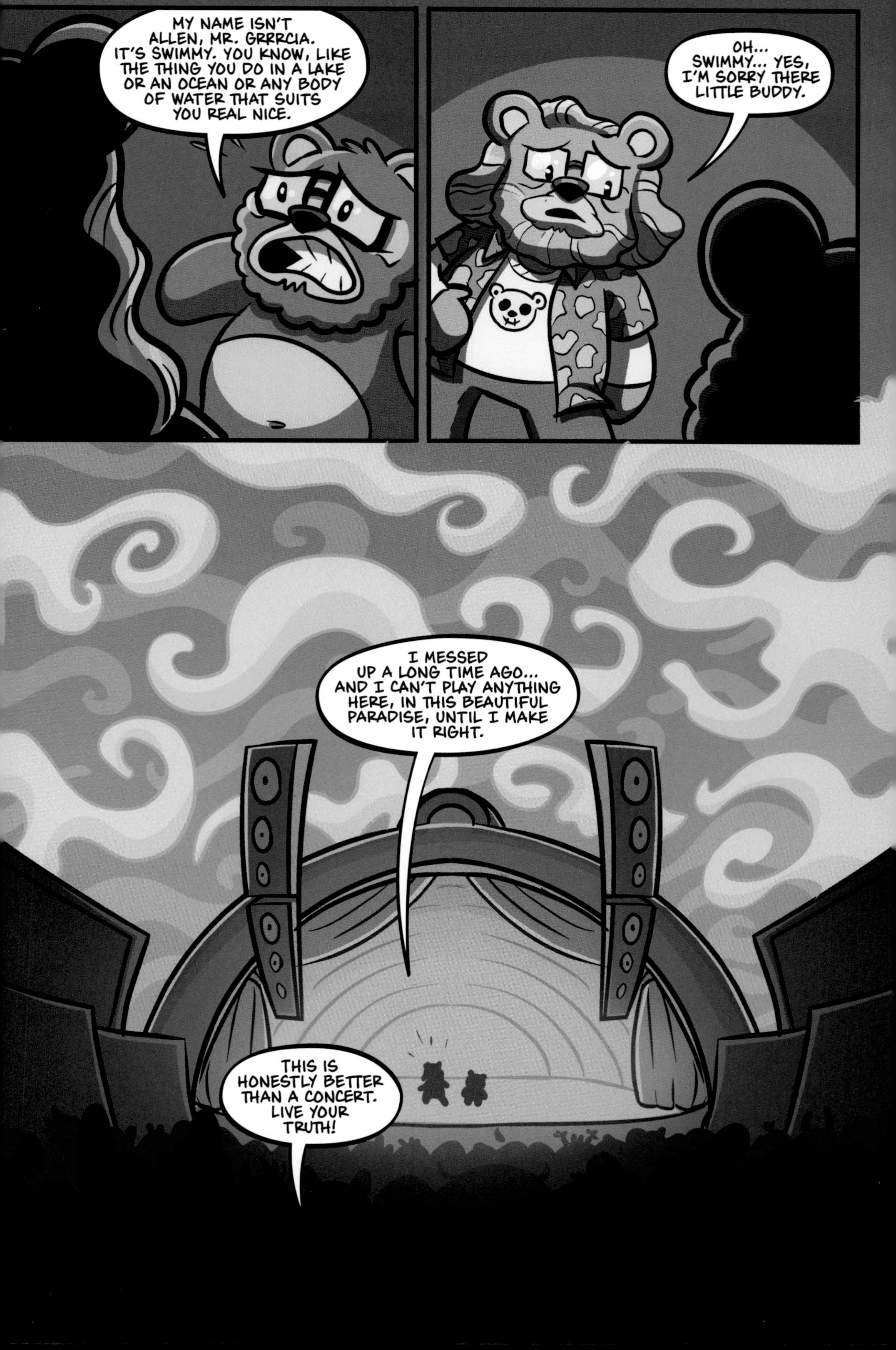
MY NAME ISN'T ALLEN, MR. GRRRCIA. IT'S SWIMMY. YOU KNOW, LIKE THE THING YOU DO IN A LAKE OR AN OCEAN OR ANY BODY OF WATER THAT SUITS YOU REAL NICE.
OH... SWIMMY... YES, I'M SORRY THERE LITTLE BUDDY.
I MESSED UP A LONG TIME AGO... AND I CAN'T PLAY ANYTHING HERE, IN THIS BEAUTIFUL PARADISE, UNTIL I MAKE IT RIGHT.
THIS IS HONESTLY BETTER THAN A CONCERT. LIVE YOUR TRUTH!

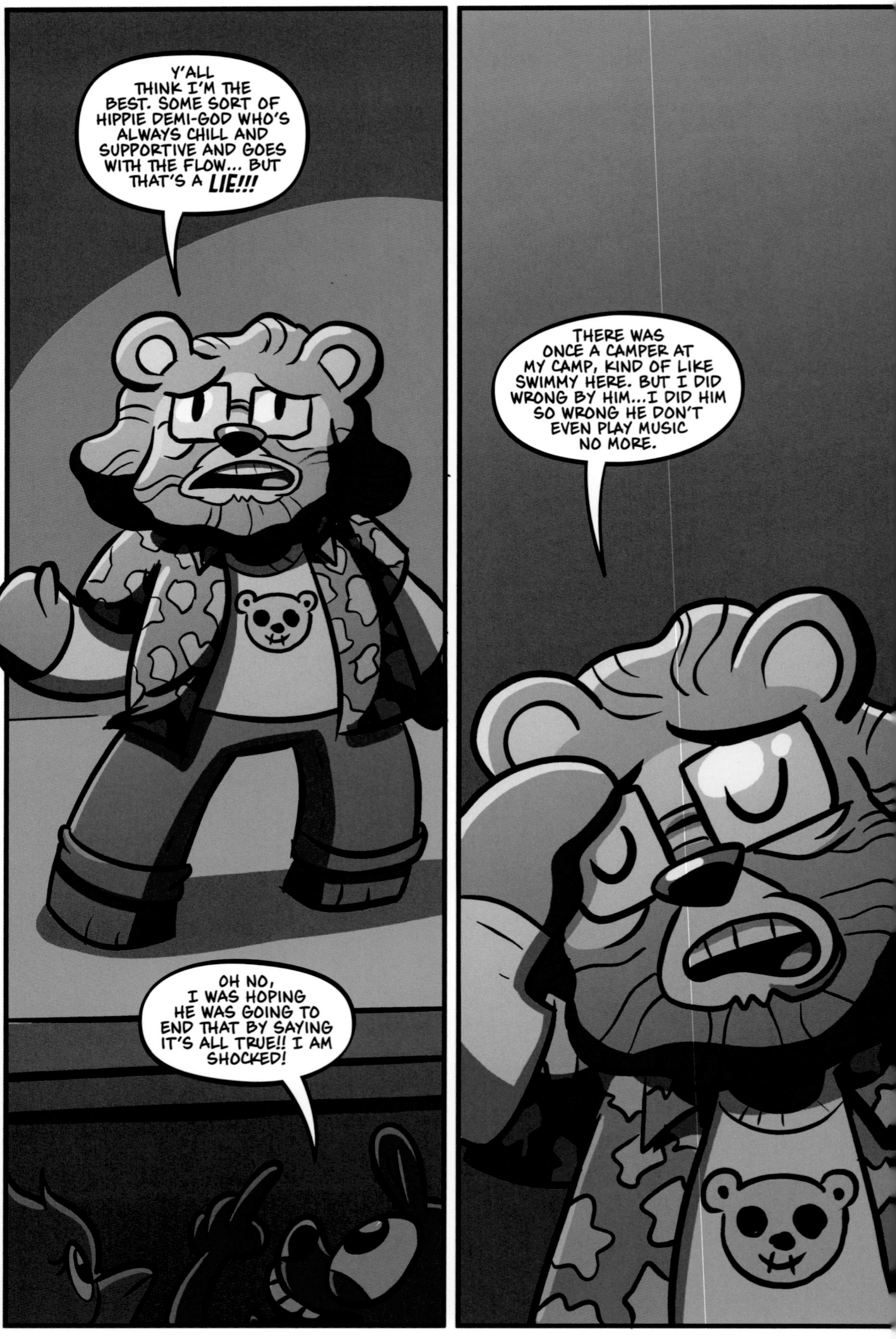
Y'ALL THINK I'M THE BEST. SOME SORT OF HIPPIE DEMI-GOD WHO'S ALWAYS CHILL AND SUPPORTIVE AND GOES WITH THE FLOW... BUT THAT'S A LIE!!!
OH NO, I WAS HOPING HE WAS GOING TO END THAT BY SAYING IT'S ALL TRUE!! I AM SHOCKED!
THERE WAS ONCE A CAMPER AT MY CAMP, KIND OF LIKE SWIMMY HERE. BUT I DID WRONG BY HIM...I DID HIM SO WRONG HE DON'T EVEN PLAY MUSIC NO MORE.

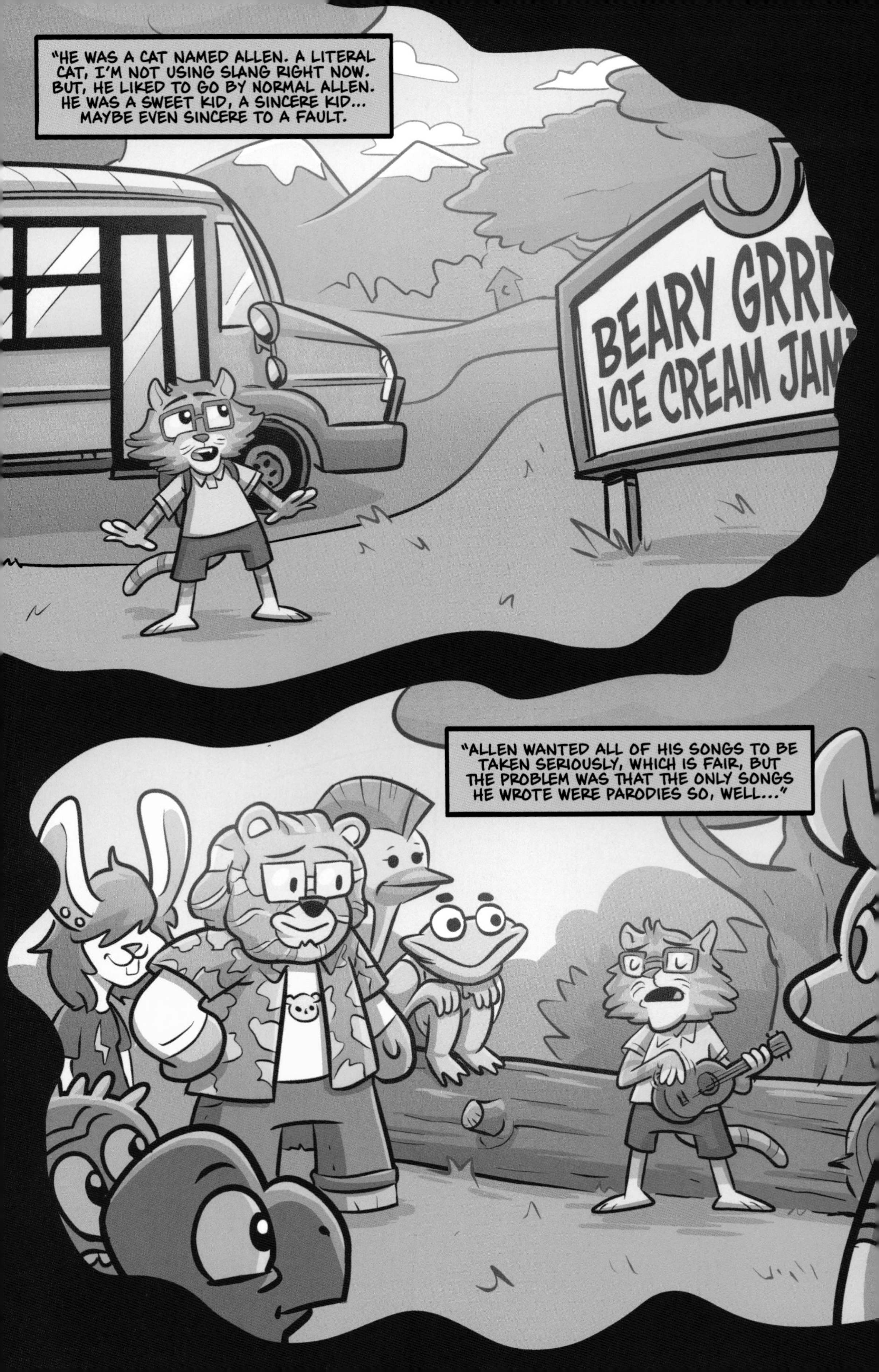
"HE WAS A CAT NAMED ALLEN. A LITERAL CAT, I'M NOT USING SLANG RIGHT NOW. BUT, HE LIKED TO GO BY NORMAL ALLEN. HE WAS A SWEET KID, A SINCERE KID... MAYBE EVEN SINCERE TO A FAULT.
BEARY GRRR
ICE CREAM JAM
"ALLEN WANTED ALL OF HIS SONGS TO BE TAKEN SERIOUSLY, WHICH IS FAIR, BUT THE PROBLEM WAS THAT THE ONLY SONGS HE WROTE WERE PARODIES SO, WELL..."

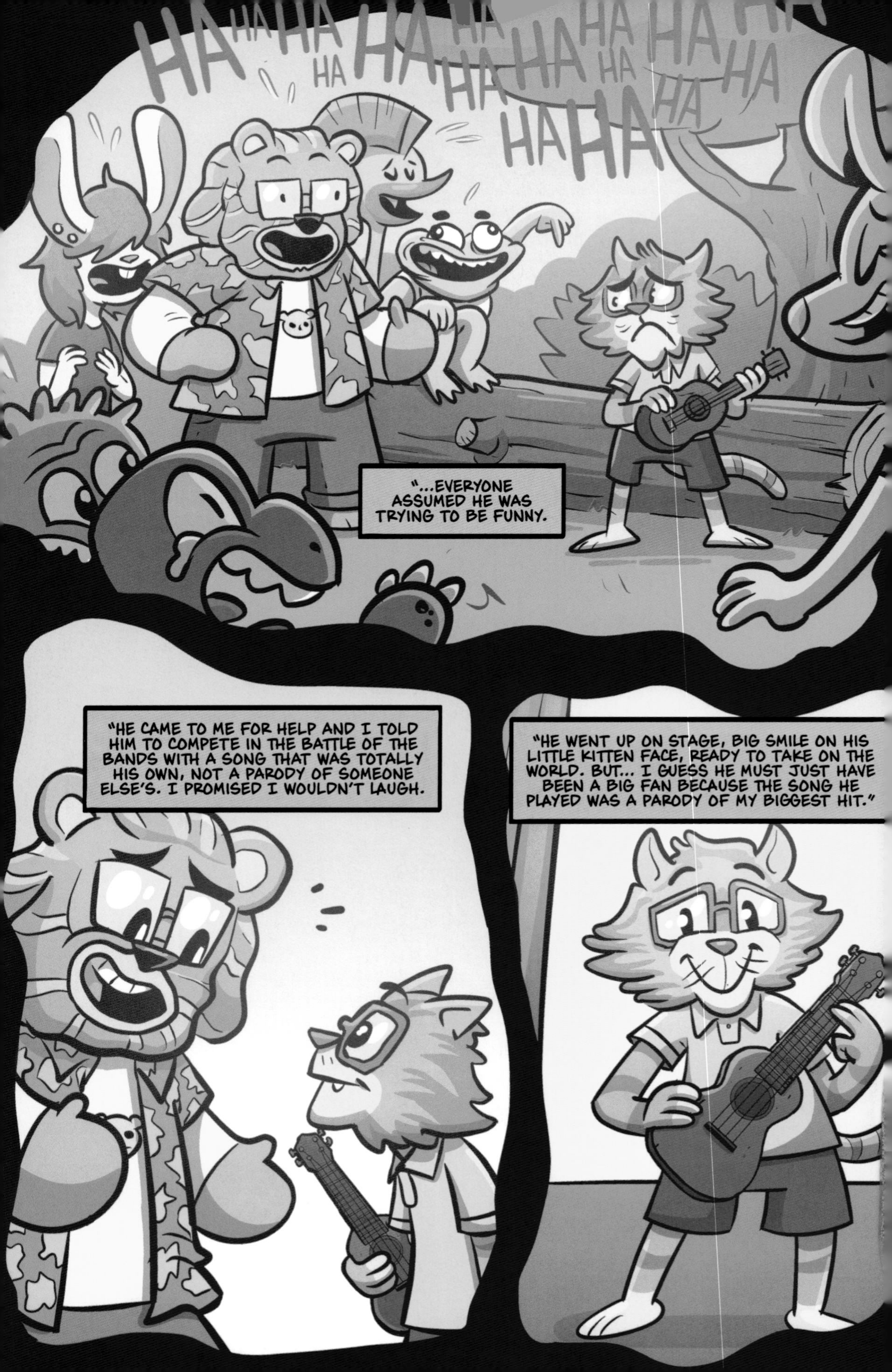
HA HA HA HA HA HA HA HA HA HA HA HA HA HA HA HA HA HA HA
"...EVERYONE ASSUMED HE WAS TRYING TO BE FUNNY.
"HE CAME TO ME FOR HELP AND I TOLD HIM TO COMPETE IN THE BATTLE OF THE BANDS WITH A SONG THAT WAS TOTALLY HIS OWN, NOT A PARODY OF SOMEONE ELSE'S. I PROMISED I WOULDN'T LAUGH.
"HE WENT UP ON STAGE, BIG SMILE ON HIS LITTLE KITTEN FACE, READY TO TAKE ON THE WORLD. BUT... I GUESS HE MUST JUST HAVE BEEN A BIG FAN BECAUSE THE SONG HE PLAYED WAS A PARODY OF MY BIGGEST HIT."

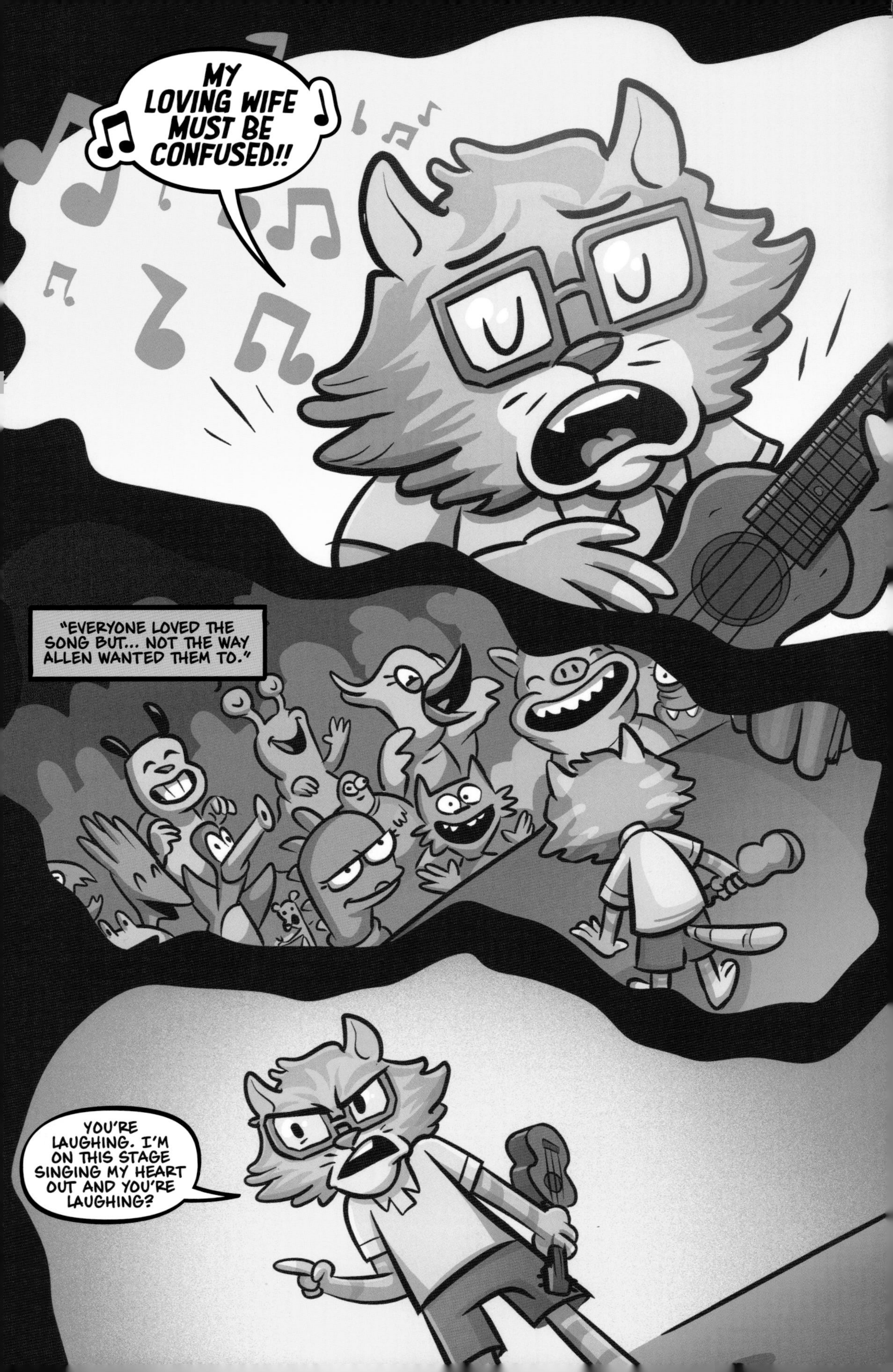
MY LOVING WIFE MUST BE CONFUSED!!
"EVERYONE LOVED THE SONG BUT... NOT THE WAY ALLEN WANTED THEM TO."
YOU'RE LAUGHING. I'M ON THIS STAGE SINGING MY HEART OUT AND YOU'RE LAUGHING?

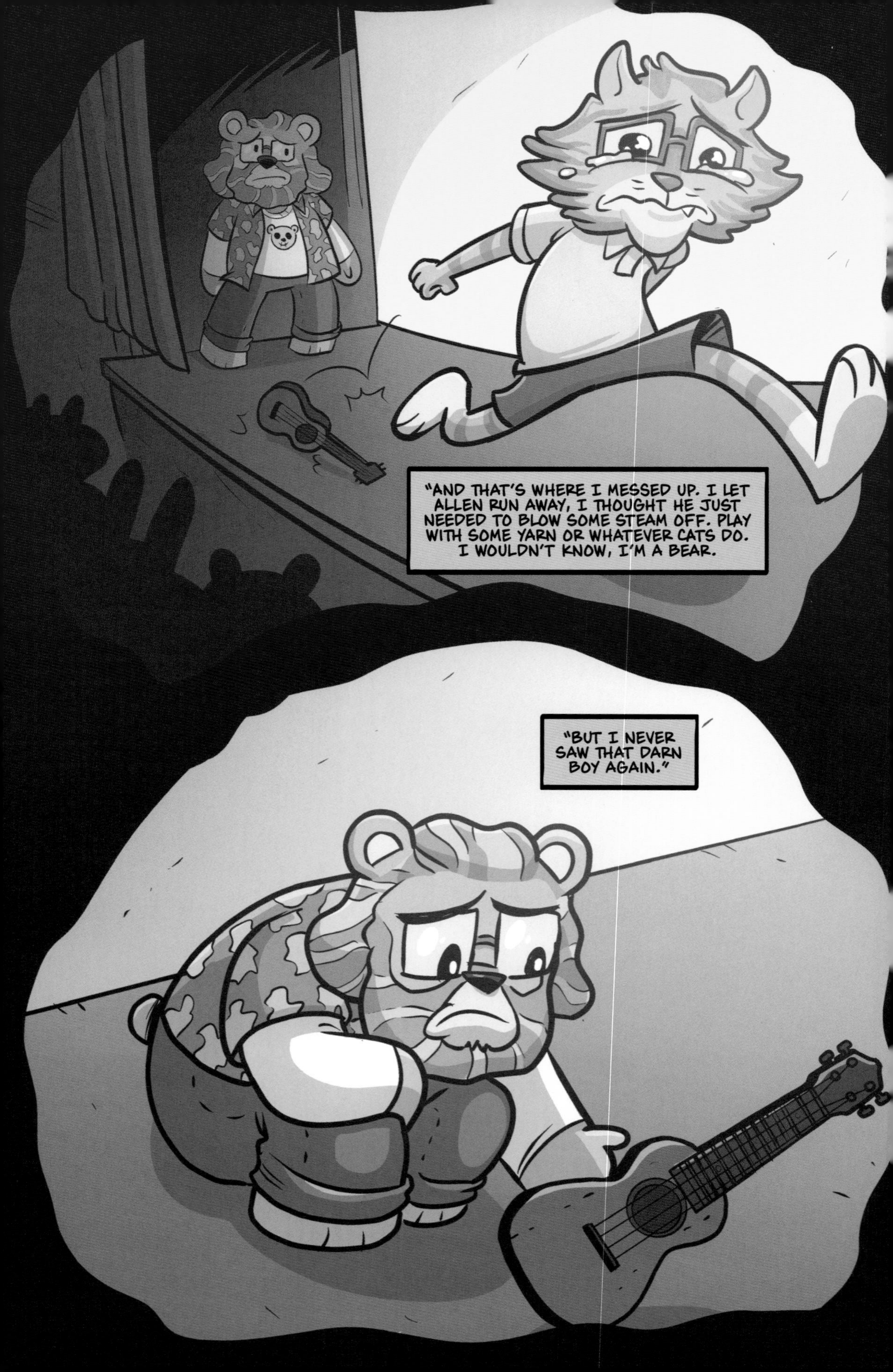
"AND THAT'S WHERE I MESSED UP. I LET ALLEN RUN AWAY, I THOUGHT HE JUST NEEDED TO BLOW SOME STEAM OFF. PLAY WITH SOME YARN OR WHATEVER CATS DO. I WOULDN'T KNOW, I'M A BEAR.
"BUT I NEVER SAW THAT DARN BOY AGAIN."

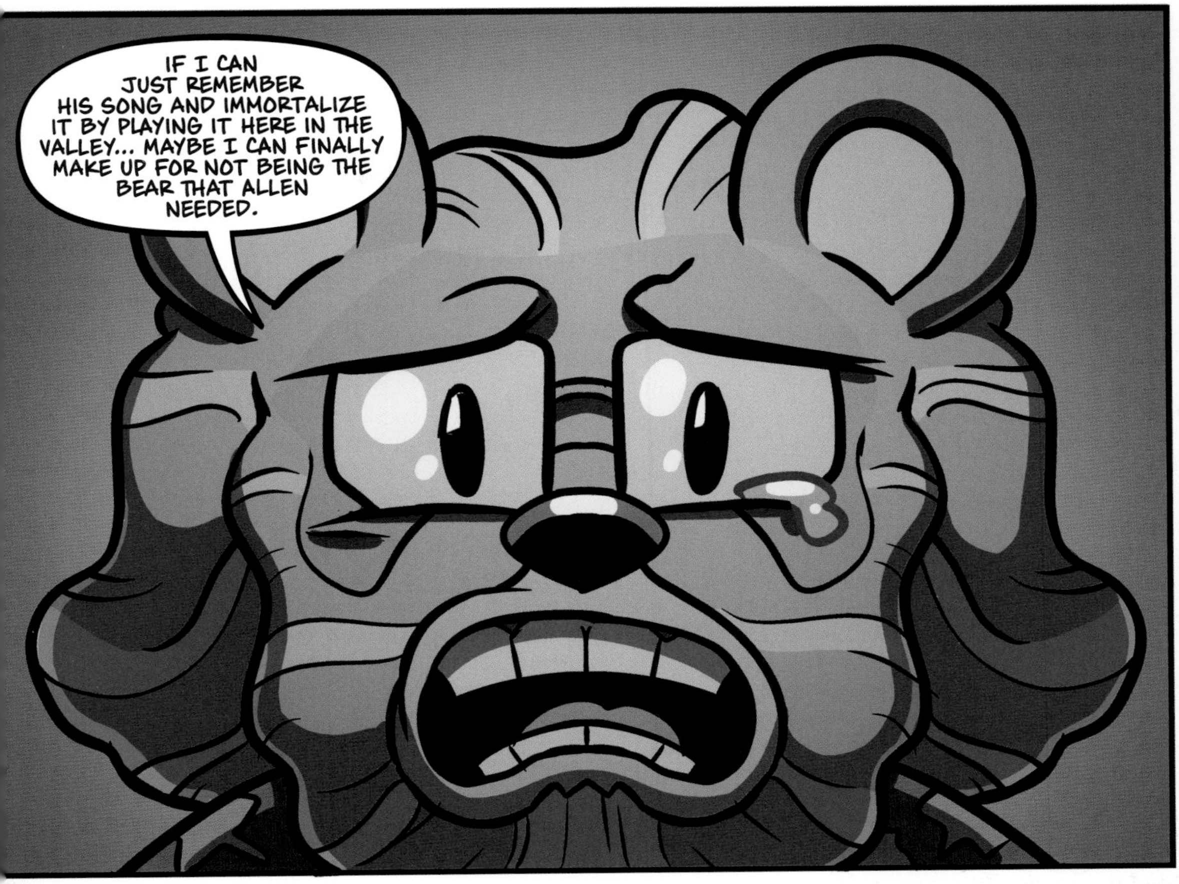
IF I CAN JUST REMEMBER HIS SONG AND IMMORTALIZE IT BY PLAYING IT HERE IN THE VALLEY... MAYBE I CAN FINALLY MAKE UP FOR NOT BEING THE BEAR THAT ALLEN NEEDED.

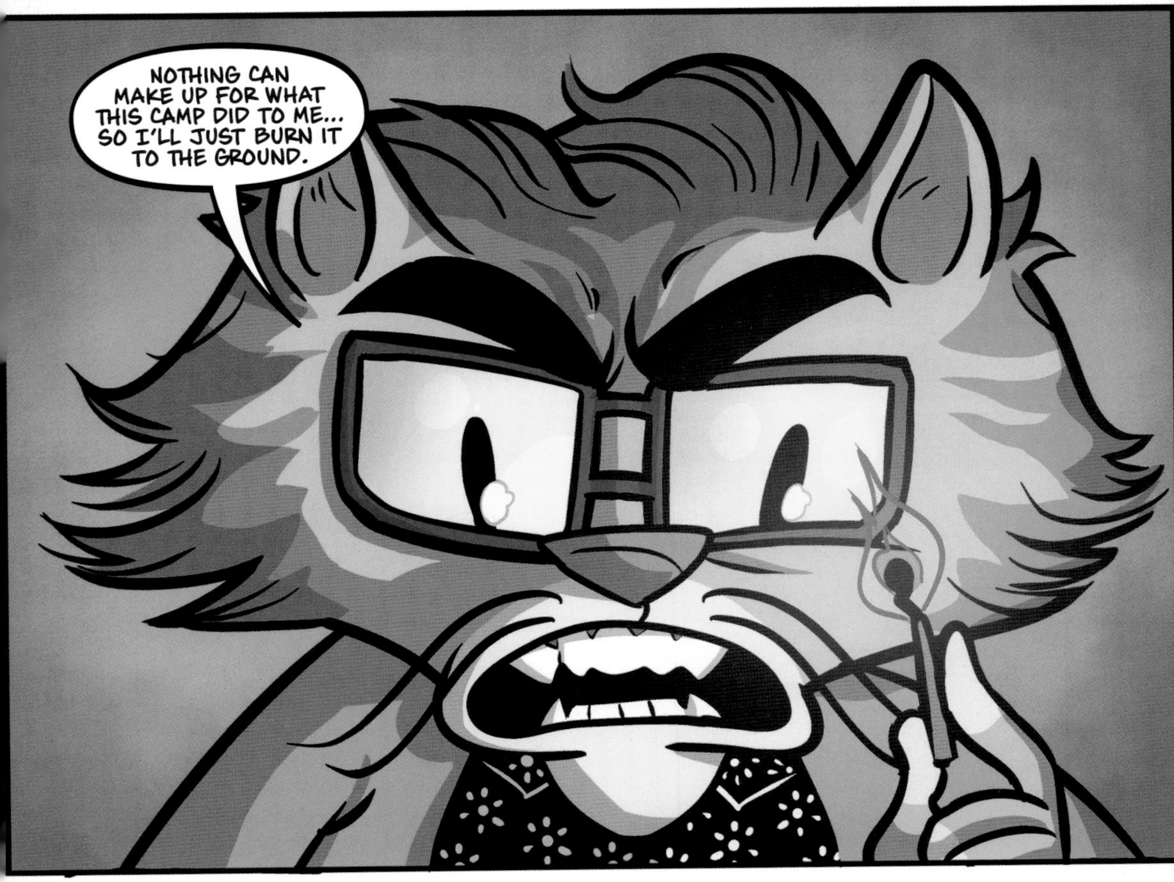
NOTHING CAN MAKE UP FOR WHAT THIS CAMP DID TO ME... SO I'LL JUST BURN IT TO THE GROUND.

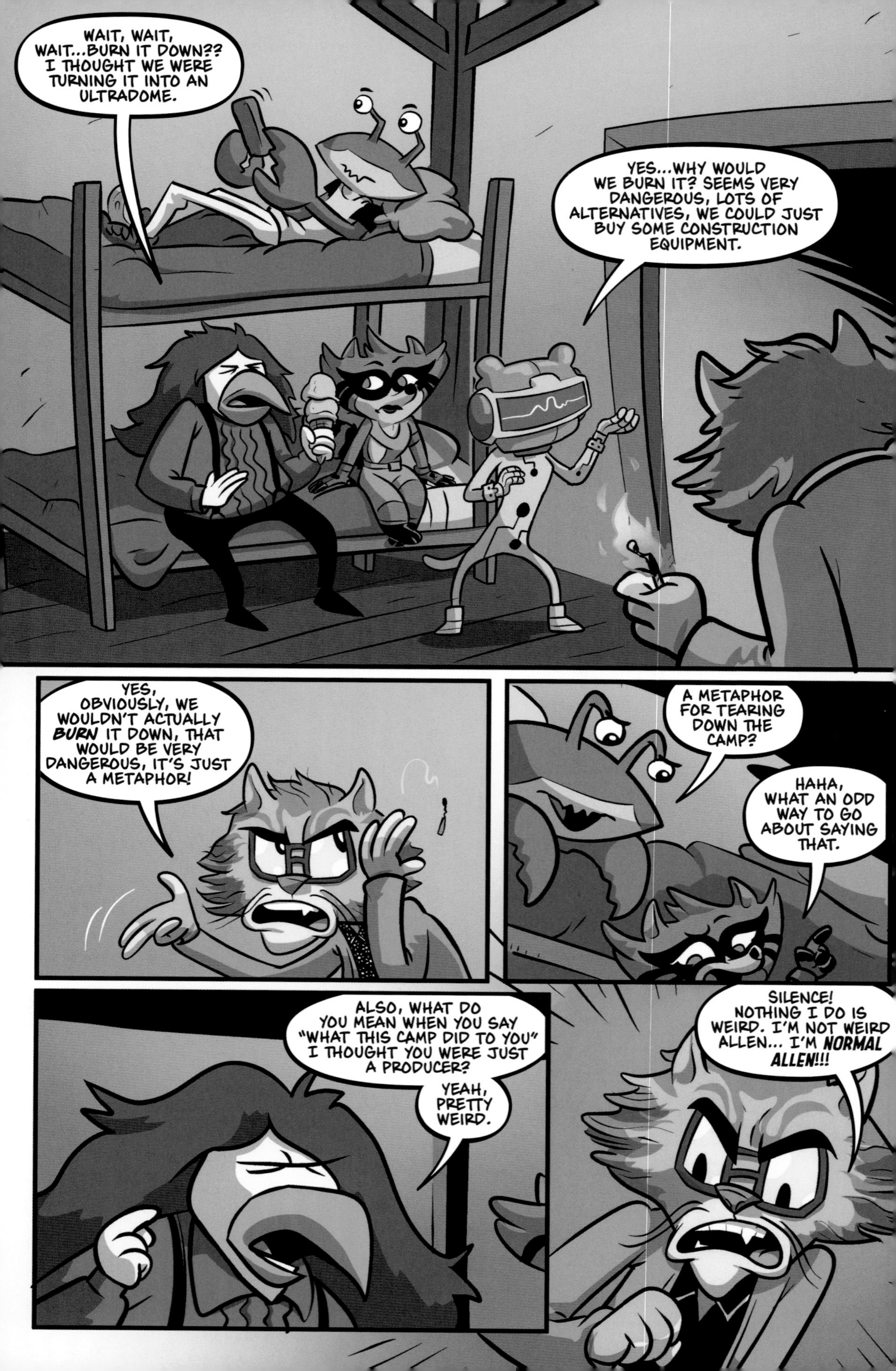
WAIT, WAIT, WAIT...BURN IT DOWN?? I THOUGHT WE WERE TURNING IT INTO AN ULTRADOME.
YES...WHY WOULD WE BURN IT? SEEMS VERY DANGEROUS, LOTS OF ALTERNATIVES, WE COULD JUST BUY SOME CONSTRUCTION EQUIPMENT.
YES, OBVIOUSLY, WE WOULDN'T ACTUALLY BURN IT DOWN, THAT WOULD BE VERY DANGEROUS, IT'S JUST A METAPHOR!
A METAPHOR FOR TEARING DOWN THE CAMP?
HAHA, WHAT AN ODD WAY TO GO ABOUT SAYING THAT.
ALSO, WHAT DO YOU MEAN WHEN YOU SAY "WHAT THIS CAMP DID TO YOU" I THOUGHT YOU WERE JUST A PRODUCER?
YEAH, PRETTY WEIRD.
SILENCE! NOTHING I DO IS WEIRD. I'M NOT WEIRD ALLEN... I'M NORMAL ALLEN!!!

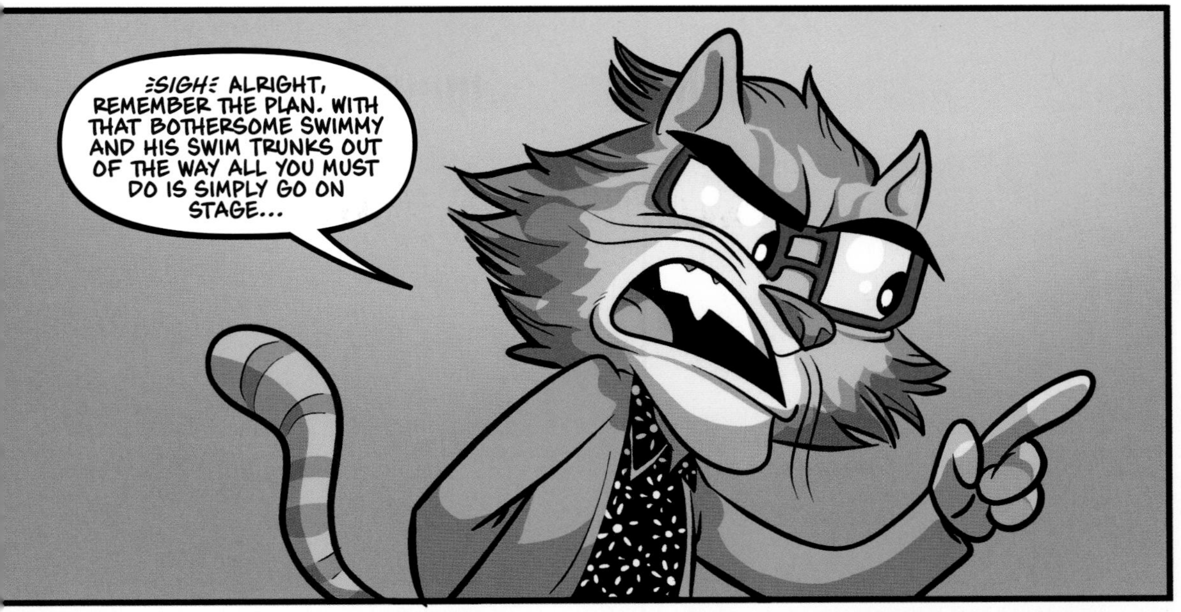
SIGH ALRIGHT, REMEMBER THE PLAN. WITH THAT BOTHERSOME SWIMMY AND HIS SWIM TRUNKS OUT OF THE WAY ALL YOU MUST DO IS SIMPLY GO ON STAGE...

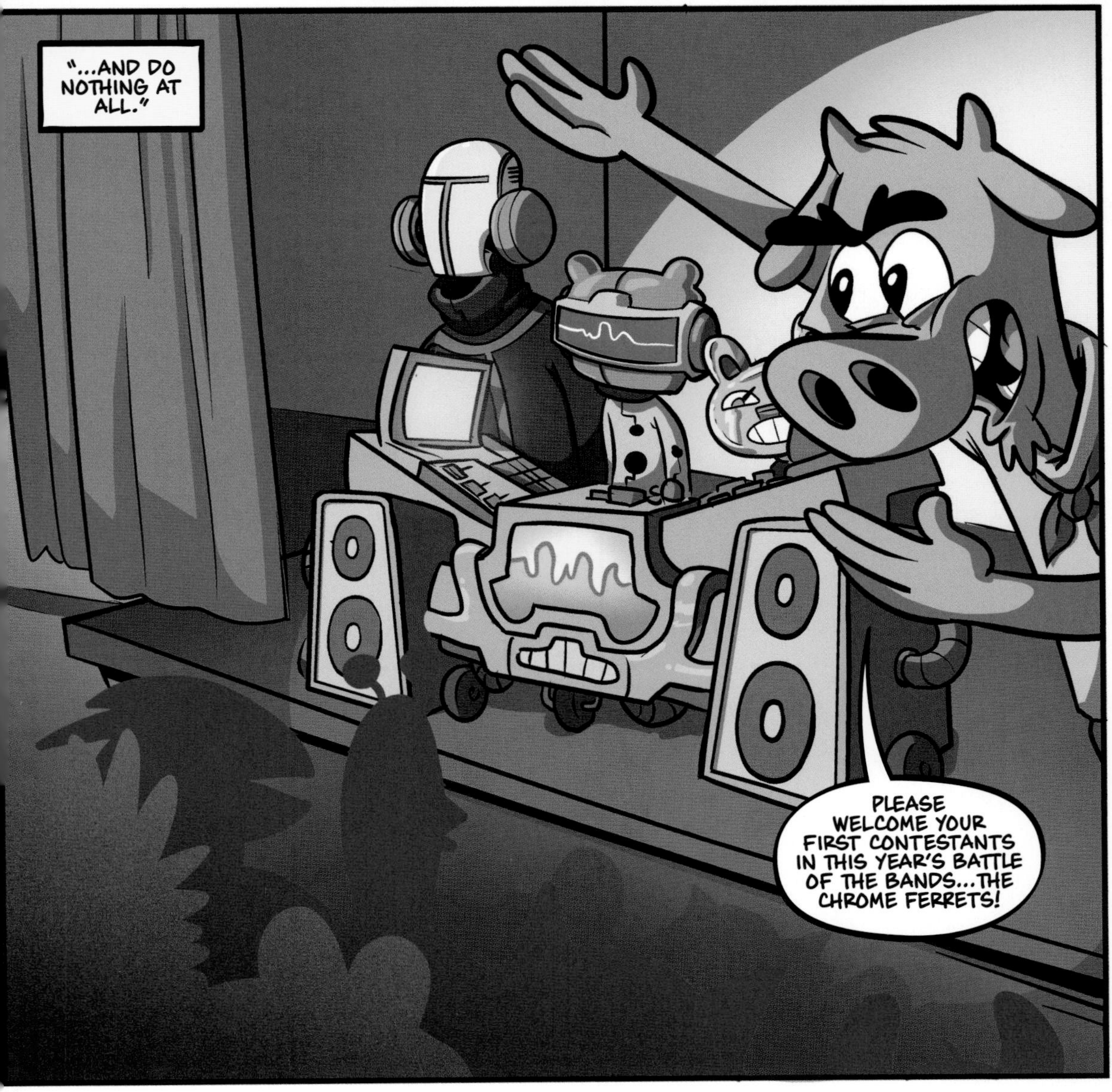
"...AND DO NOTHING AT ALL."
PLEASE WELCOME YOUR FIRST CONTESTANTS IN THIS YEAR'S BATTLE OF THE BANDS...THE CHROME FERRETS!

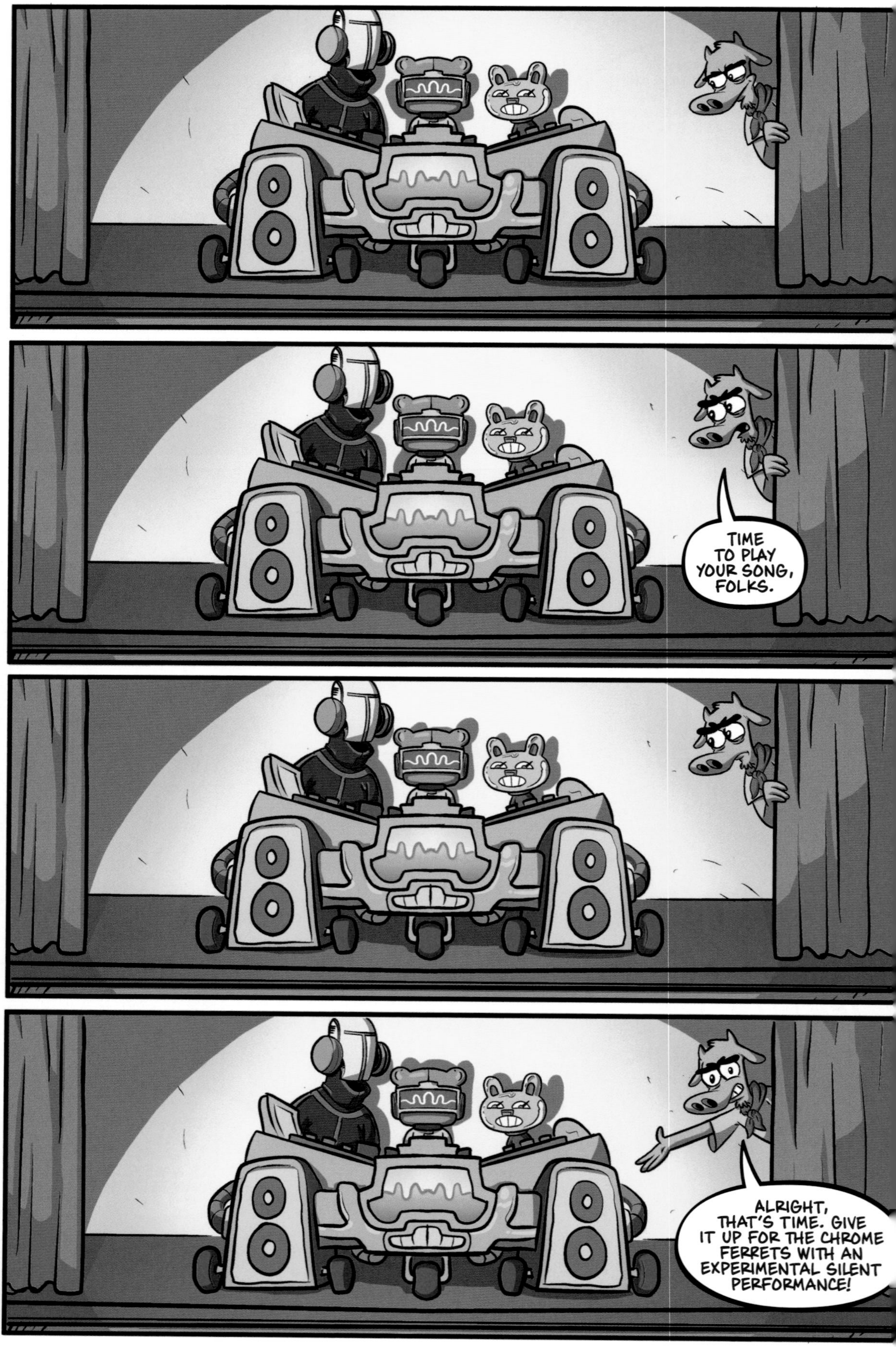
TIME TO PLAY YOUR SONG, FOLKS.
ALRIGHT, THAT'S TIME. GIVE IT UP FOR THE CHROME FERRETS WITH AN EXPERIMENTAL SILENT PERFORMANCE!

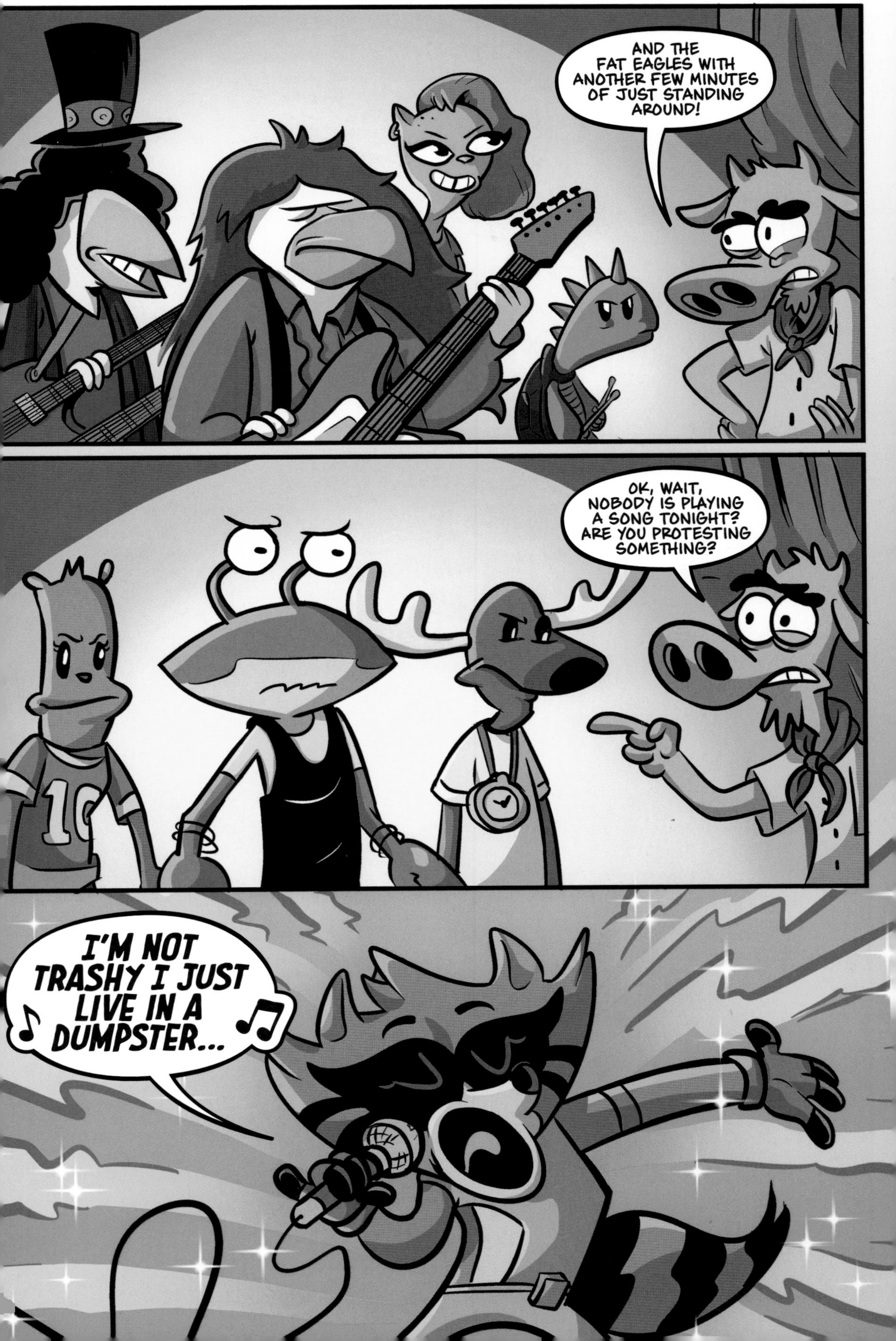
AND THE FAT EAGLES WITH ANOTHER FEW MINUTES OF JUST STANDING AROUND!
OK, WAIT, NOBODY IS PLAYING A SONG TONIGHT? ARE YOU PROTESTING SOMETHING?
10
I'M NOT TRASHY I JUST LIVE IN A DUMPSTER...

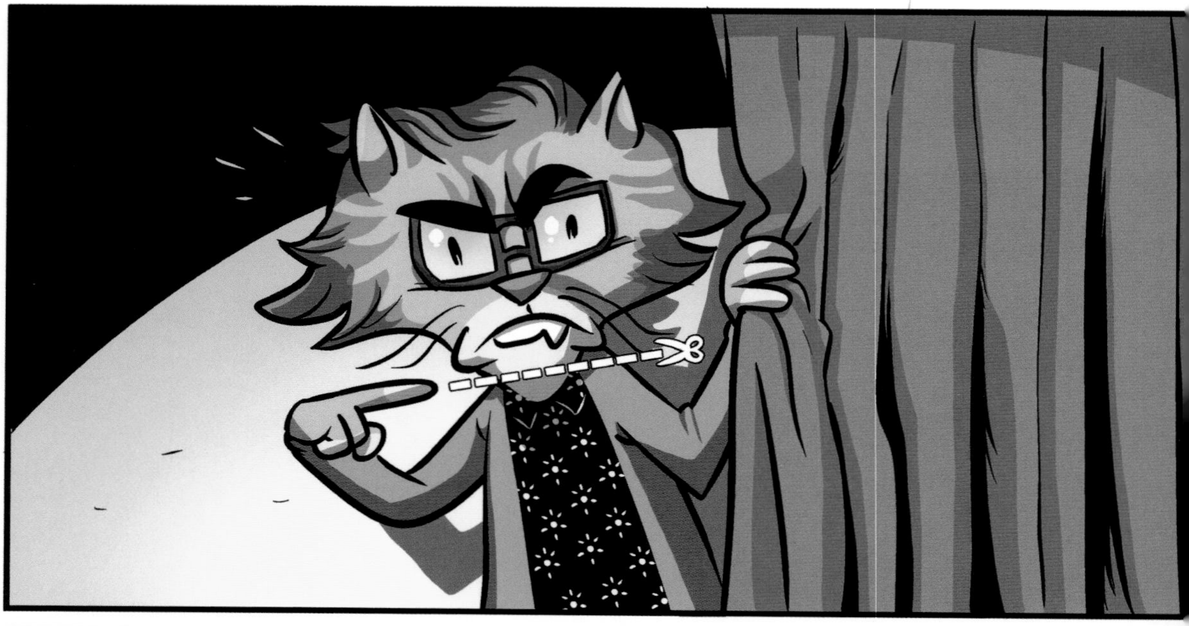

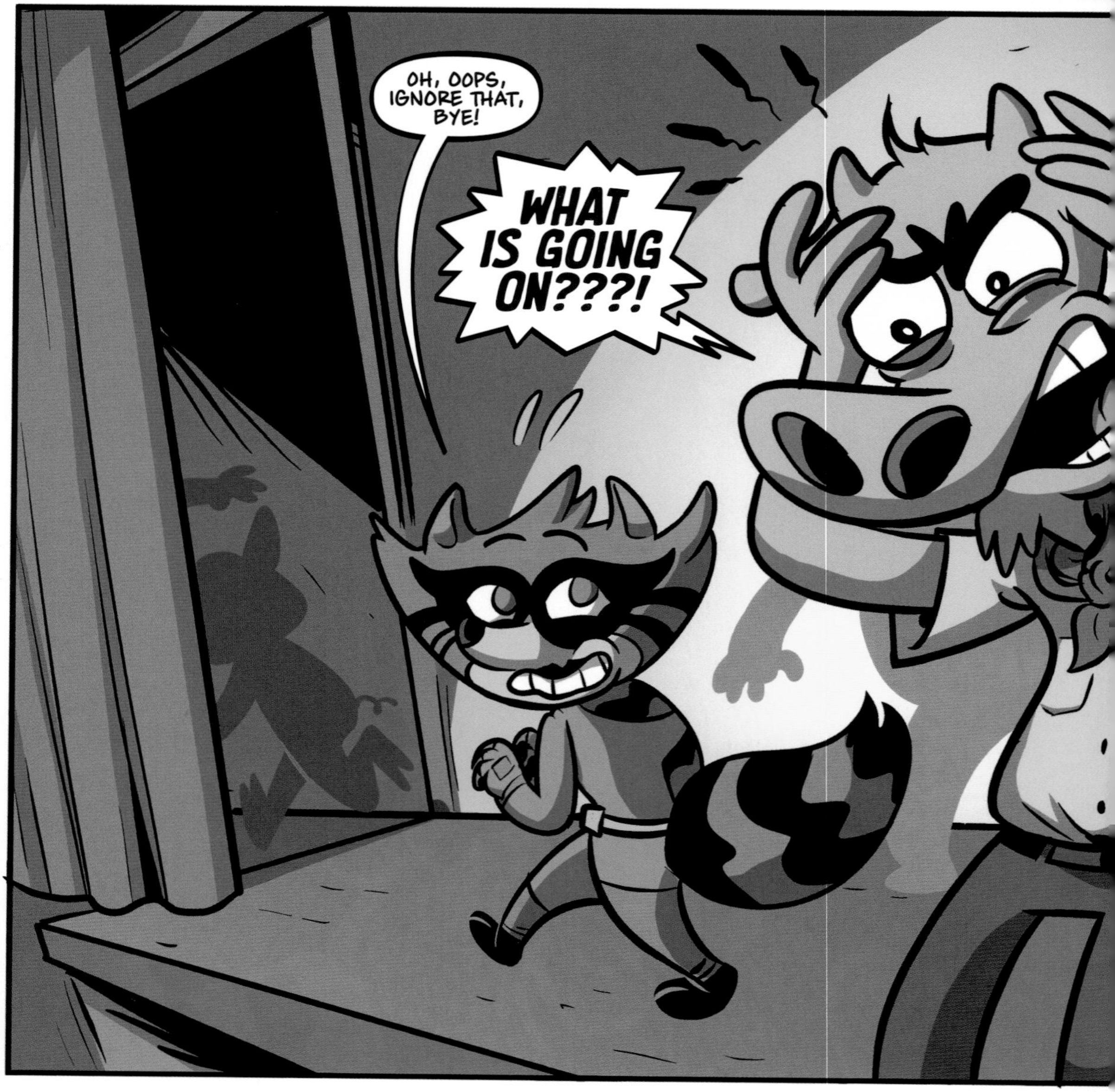
OH, OOPS, IGNORE THAT, BYE!
WHAT IS GOING ON???!

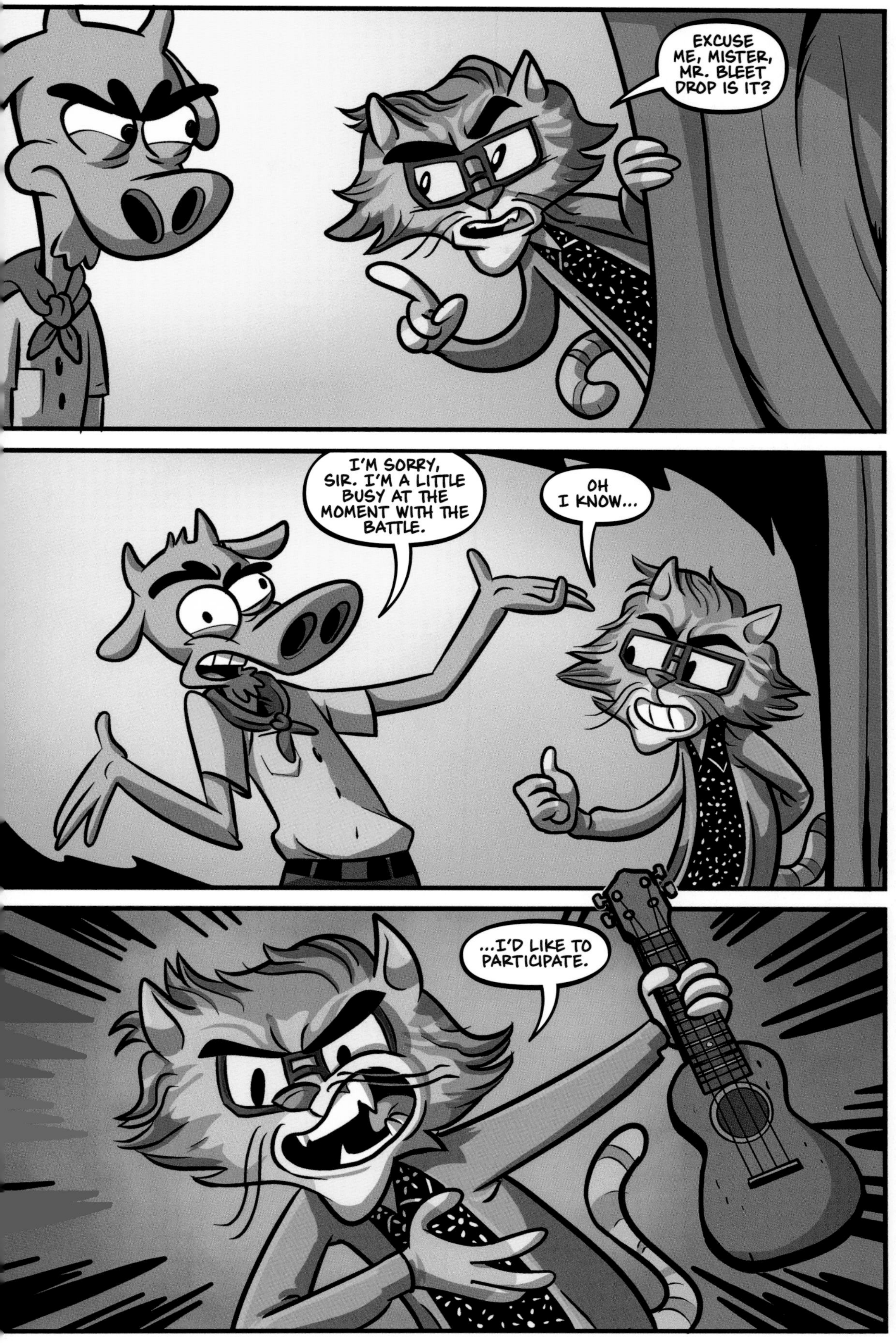
EXCUSE ME, MISTER, MR. BLEET DROP IS IT?
I'M SORRY, SIR. I'M A LITTLE BUSY AT THE MOMENT WITH THE BATTLE.
OH I KNOW...
...I'D LIKE TO PARTICIPATE.

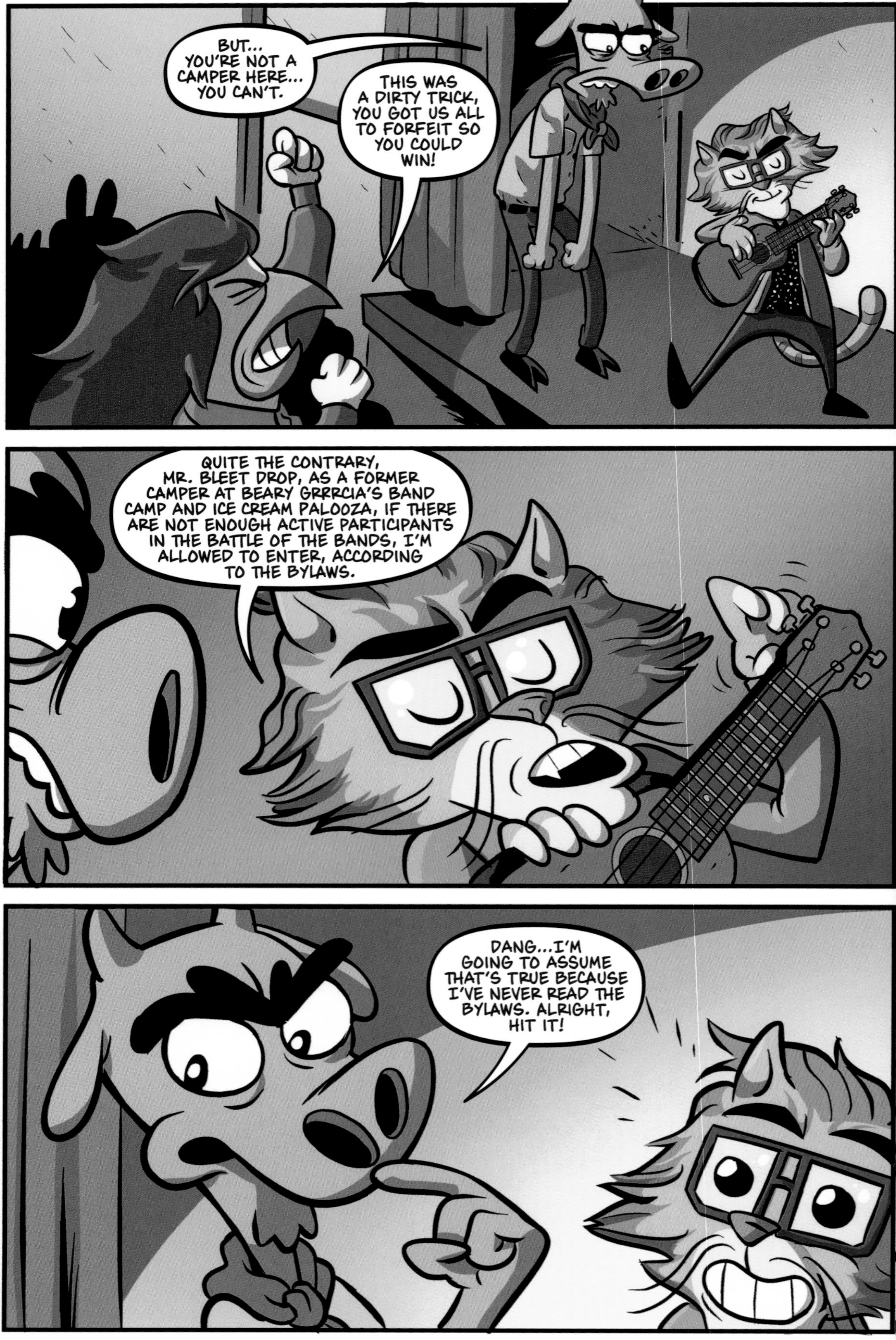
BUT... YOU'RE NOT A CAMPER HERE... YOU CAN'T.
THIS WAS A DIRTY TRICK, YOU GOT US ALL TO FORFEIT SO YOU COULD WIN!
QUITE THE CONTRARY, MR. BLEET DROP, AS A FORMER CAMPER AT BEARY GRRRCIA'S BAND CAMP AND ICE CREAM PALOOZA, IF THERE ARE NOT ENOUGH ACTIVE PARTICIPANTS IN THE BATTLE OF THE BANDS, I'M ALLOWED TO ENTER, ACCORDING TO THE BYLAWS.
DANG...I'M GOING TO ASSUME THAT'S TRUE BECAUSE I'VE NEVER READ THE BYLAWS. ALRIGHT, HIT IT!

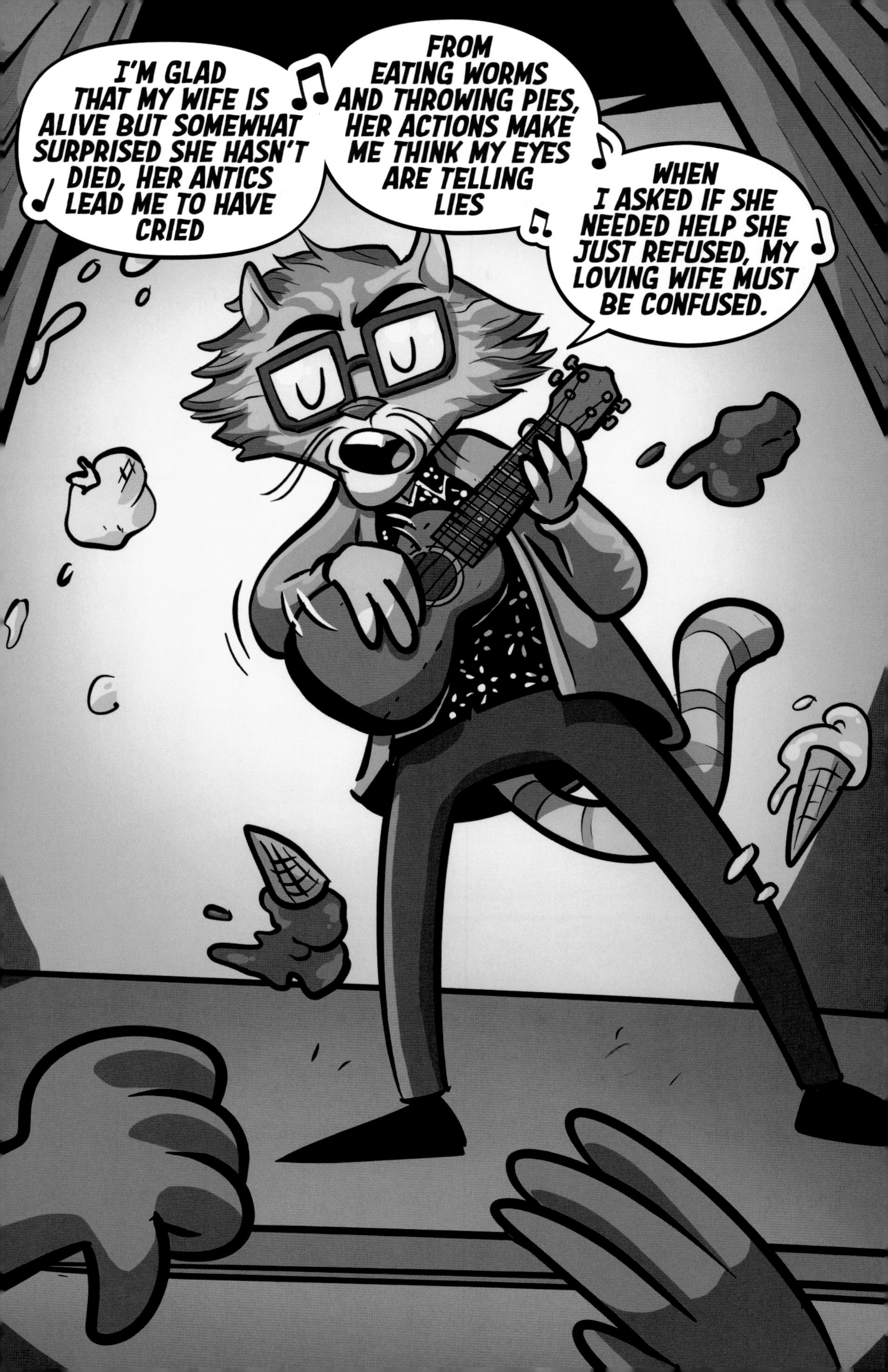
I'M GLAD THAT MY WIFE IS ALIVE BUT SOMEWHAT SURPRISED SHE HASN'T DIED, HER ANTICS LEAD ME TO HAVE CRIED
FROM EATING WORMS AND THROWING PIES, HER ACTIONS MAKE ME THINK MY EYES ARE TELLING LIES
WHEN I ASKED IF SHE NEEDED HELP SHE JUST REFUSED, MY LOVING WIFE MUST BE CONFUSED.

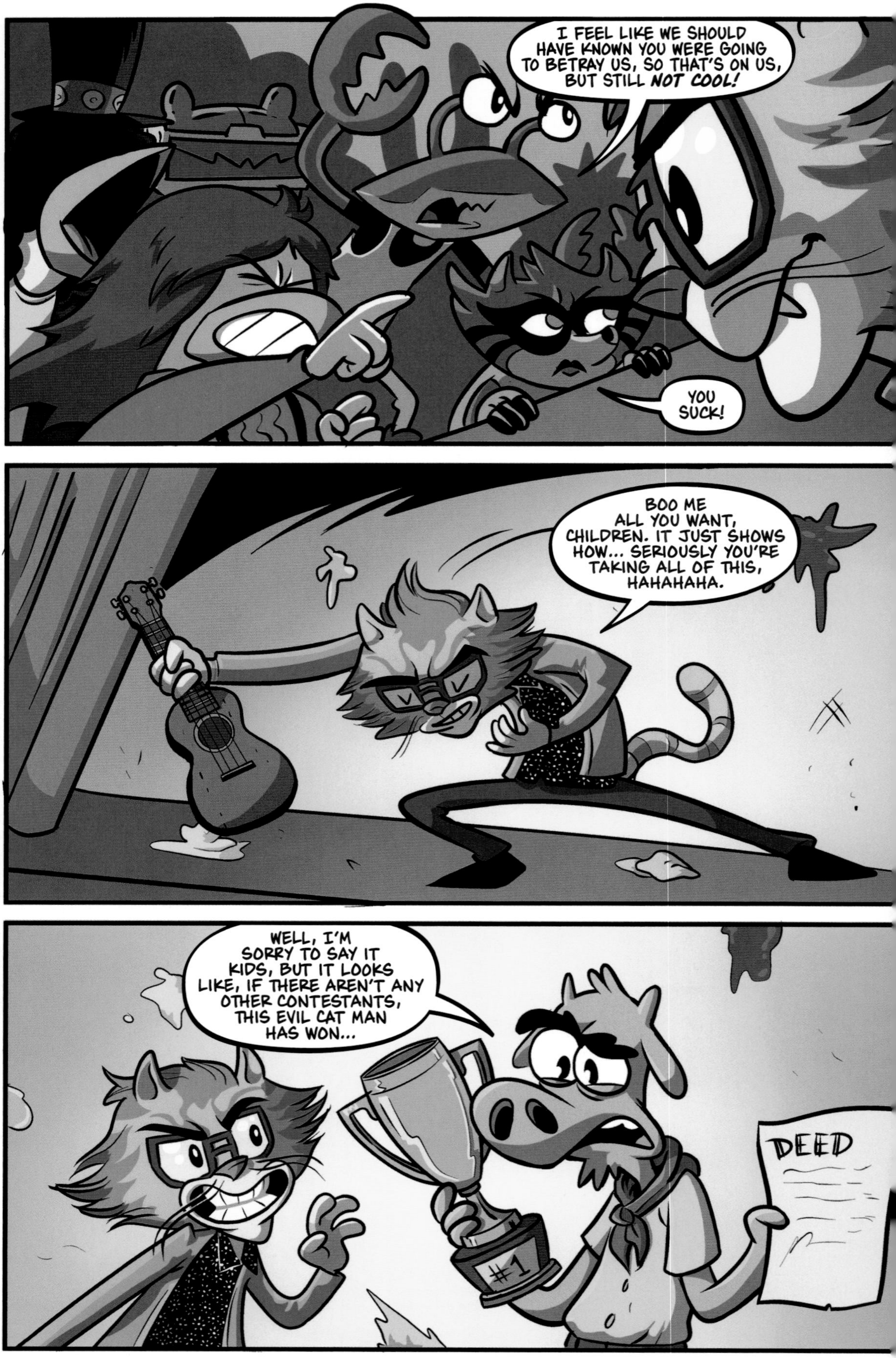
I FEEL LIKE WE SHOULD HAVE KNOWN YOU WERE GOING TO BETRAY US, SO THAT'S ON US, BUT STILL *NOT COOL!*
YOU SUCK!
BOO ME ALL YOU WANT, CHILDREN. IT JUST SHOWS HOW... SERIOUSLY YOU'RE TAKING ALL OF THIS, HAHAHAHA.
WELL, I'M SORRY TO SAY IT KIDS, BUT IT LOOKS LIKE, IF THERE AREN'T ANY OTHER CONTESTANTS, THIS EVIL CAT MAN HAS WON...
#1
DEED

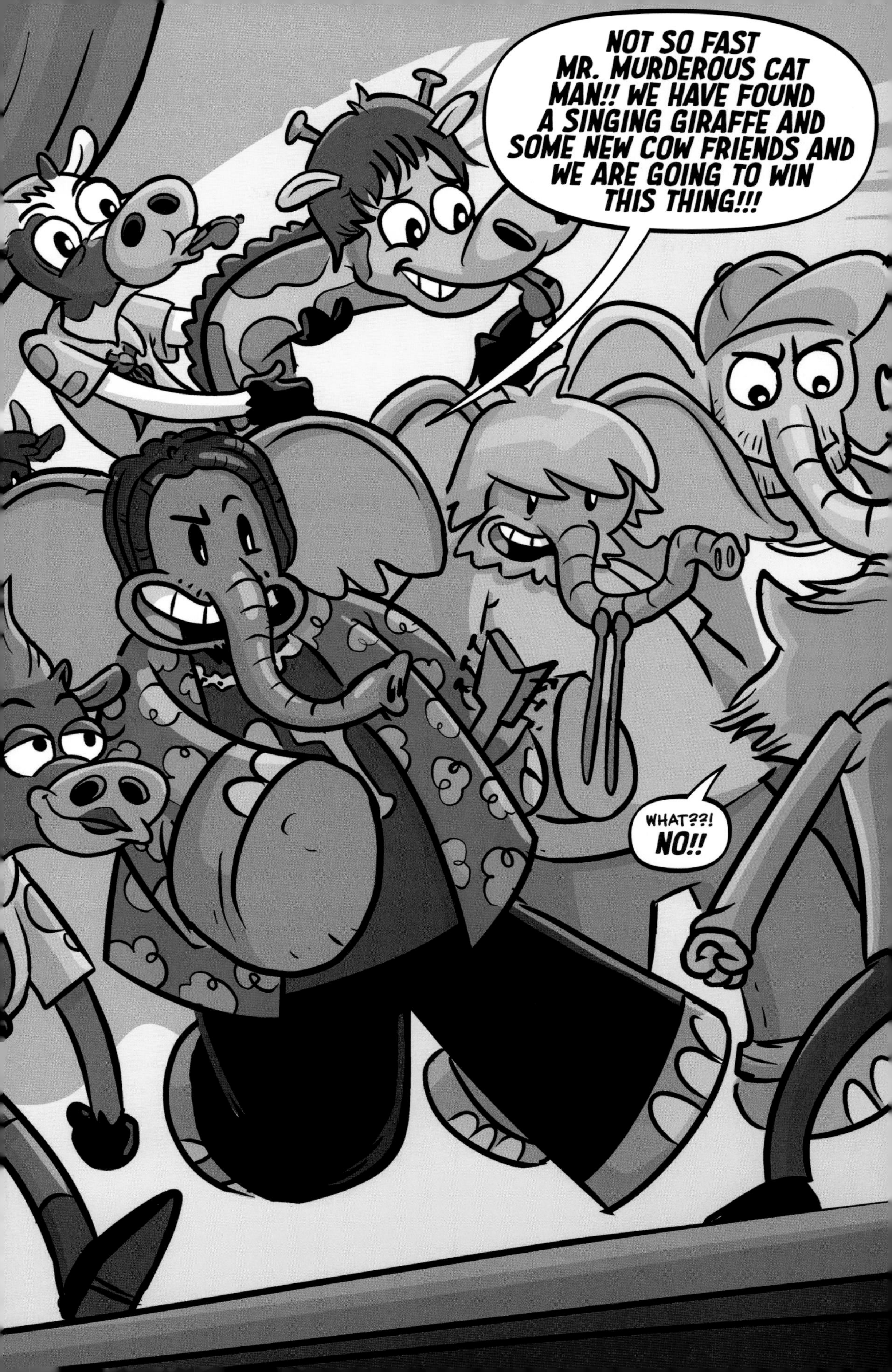
NOT SO FAST MR. MURDEROUS CAT MAN!! WE HAVE FOUND A SINGING GIRAFFE AND SOME NEW COW FRIENDS AND WE ARE GOING TO WIN THIS THING!!!
WHAT??! NO!!

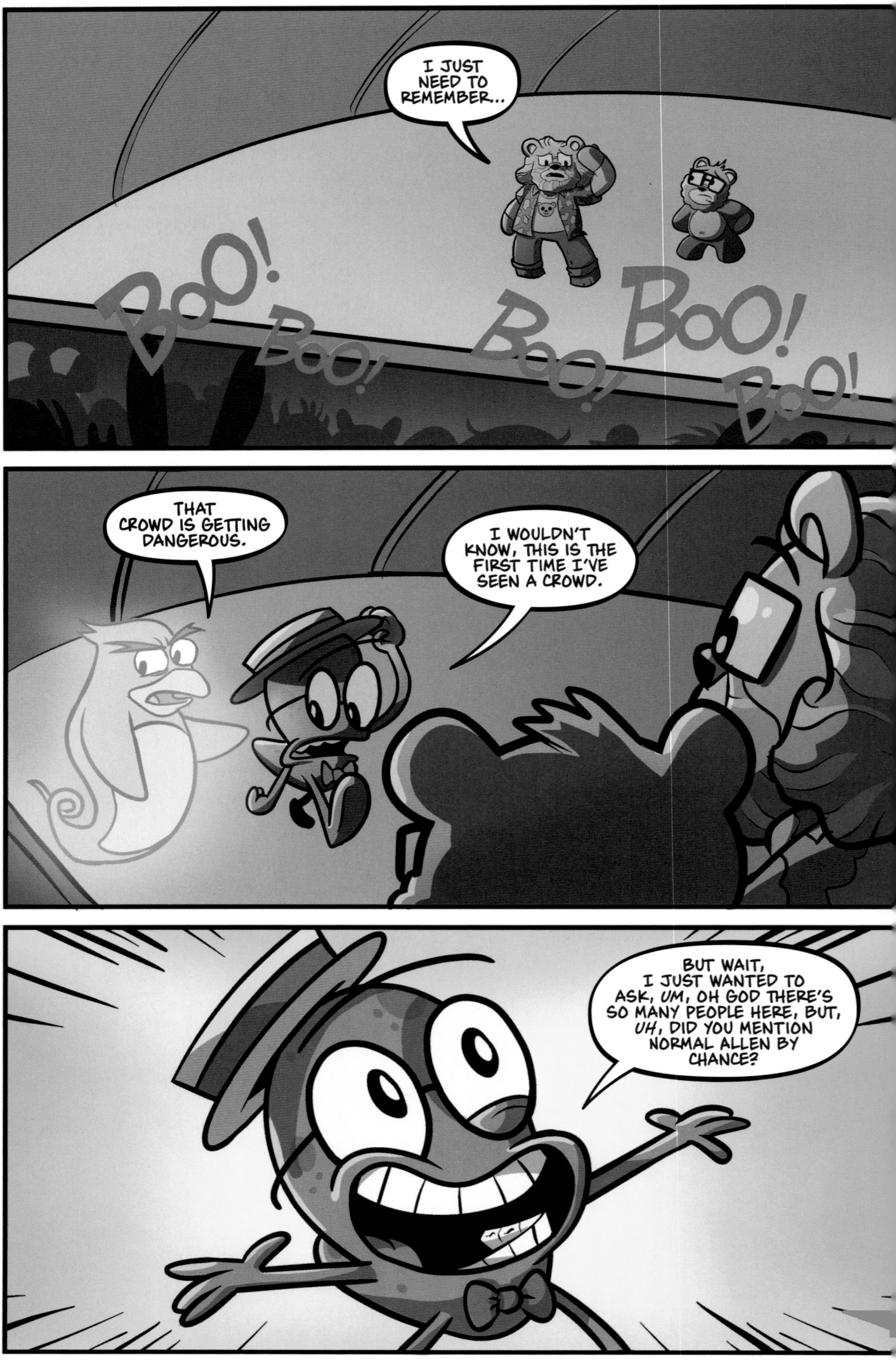
I JUST NEED TO REMEMBER...
BOO!
BOO!
BOO!
BOO!
BOO!
THAT CROWD IS GETTING DANGEROUS.
I WOULDN'T KNOW, THIS IS THE FIRST TIME I'VE SEEN A CROWD.
BUT WAIT, I JUST WANTED TO ASK, *UM*, OH GOD THERE'S SO MANY PEOPLE HERE, BUT, *UH*, DID YOU MENTION NORMAL ALLEN BY CHANCE?

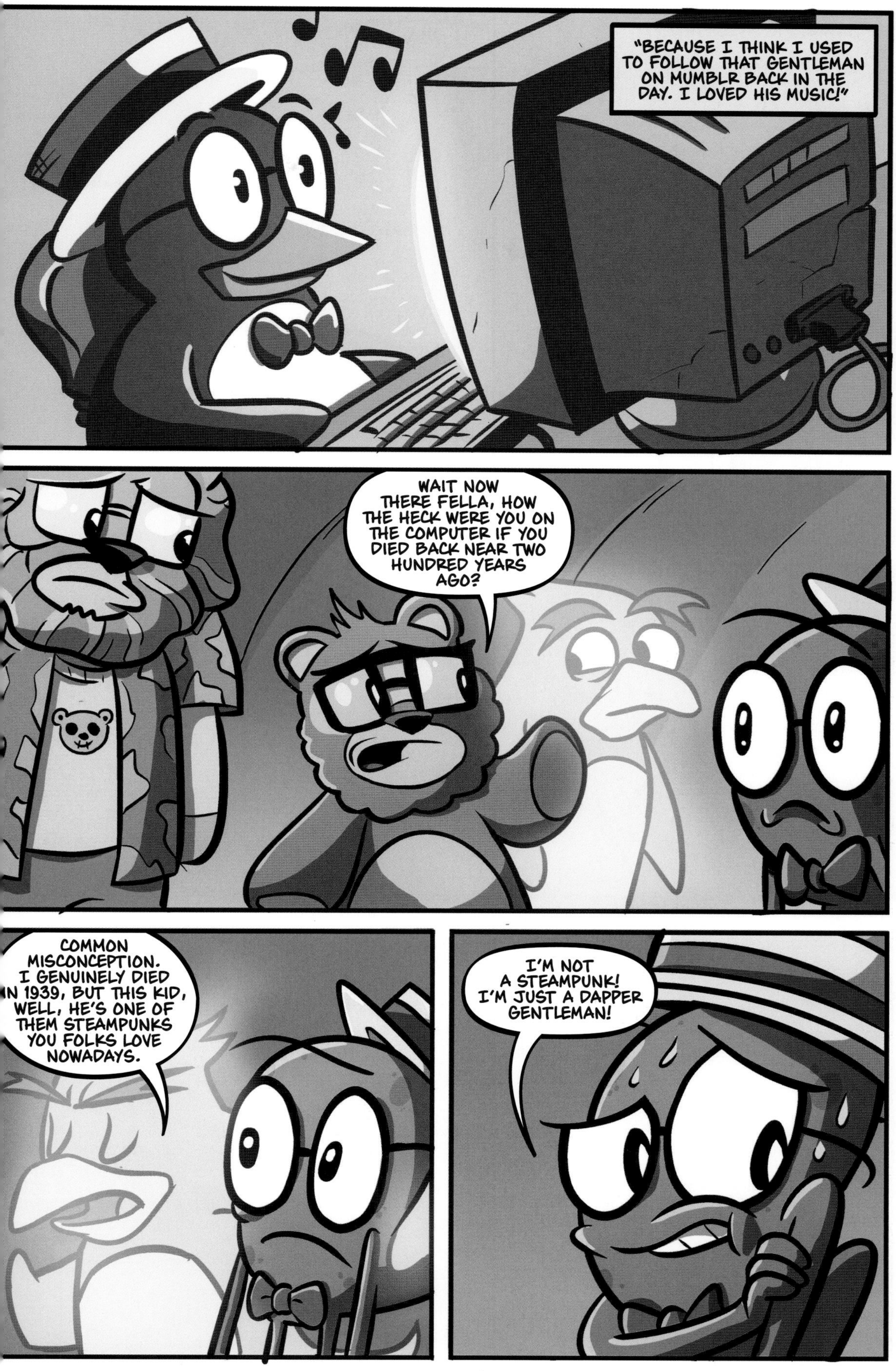
"BECAUSE I THINK I USED TO FOLLOW THAT GENTLEMAN ON MUMBLR BACK IN THE DAY. I LOVED HIS MUSIC!"
WAIT NOW THERE FELLA, HOW THE HECK WERE YOU ON THE COMPUTER IF YOU DIED BACK NEAR TWO HUNDRED YEARS AGO?
COMMON MISCONCEPTION. I GENUINELY DIED IN 1939, BUT THIS KID, WELL, HE'S ONE OF THEM STEAMPUNKS YOU FOLKS LOVE NOWADAYS.
I'M NOT A STEAMPUNK! I'M JUST A DAPPER GENTLEMAN!

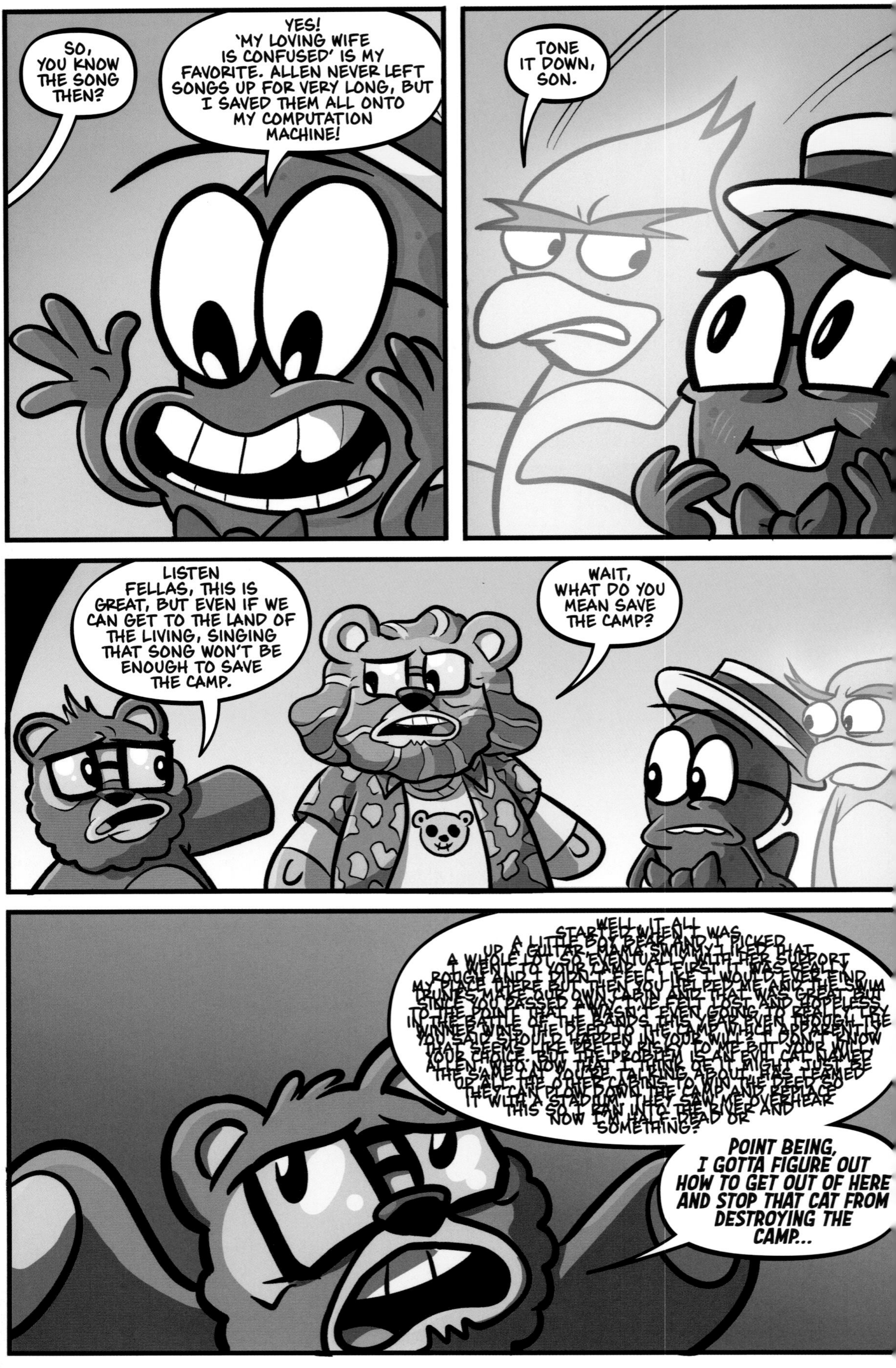
SO, YOU KNOW THE SONG THEN?
YES! 'MY LOVING WIFE IS CONFUSED' IS MY FAVORITE. ALLEN NEVER LEFT SONGS UP FOR VERY LONG, BUT I SAVED THEM ALL ONTO MY COMPUTATION MACHINE!
TONE IT DOWN, SON.
LISTEN FELLAS, THIS IS GREAT, BUT EVEN IF WE CAN GET TO THE LAND OF THE LIVING, SINGING THAT SONG WON'T BE ENOUGH TO SAVE THE CAMP.
WAIT, WHAT DO YOU MEAN SAVE THE CAMP?
WELL, IT ALL STARTED WHEN I WAS A LITTLE BOY BEAR AND I PICKED UP A GUITAR. MAMA SWIMMY LIKED THAT A WHOLE LOT, SO EVENTUALLY WITH HER SUPPORT I WENT TO YOUR CAMP. AT FIRST IT WAS REALLY ROUGE AND I DIDN'T FEEL LIKE I WOULD EVER FIND MY PLACE THERE BUT THEN YOU HELPED ME AND THE SWIM TRUNKS MAKE OUR OWN CABIN AND THAT WAS GREAT BUT SINCE YOU PASSED AWAY I'VE FELT LOST AND HOPELESS TO THE POINT THAT I WASN'T EVEN GOING TO REALLY TRY IN THE BATTLE OF THE BANDS THIS YEAR EVEN THOUGH THE WINNER WINS THE DEED TO THE CAMP WHICH APPARENTLY YOU SAID SHOULD HAPPEN IN YOUR WILL? I DON'T KNOW THAT SEEMS LIKE PRETTY RISKY TO ME BUT YOUR WILL YOUR CHOICE. BUT THE PROBLEM IS AN EVIL CAT NAMED ALLEN, WHO NOW THAT I THINK OF IT MIGHT JUST BE THE SAME CAT YOU'RE TALKING ABOUT, HAS TEAMED UP ALL THE OTHER CABINS TO WIN THE DEED SO THEY CAN PLOW DOWN THE CAMP AND REPLACE IT WITH A STADIUM. THEY SAW ME OVERHEAR THIS SO I RAN INTO THE RIVER AND NOW I'M HALF-DEAD OR SOMETHING?
POINT BEING, I GOTTA FIGURE OUT HOW TO GET OUT OF HERE AND STOP THAT CAT FROM DESTROYING THE CAMP...

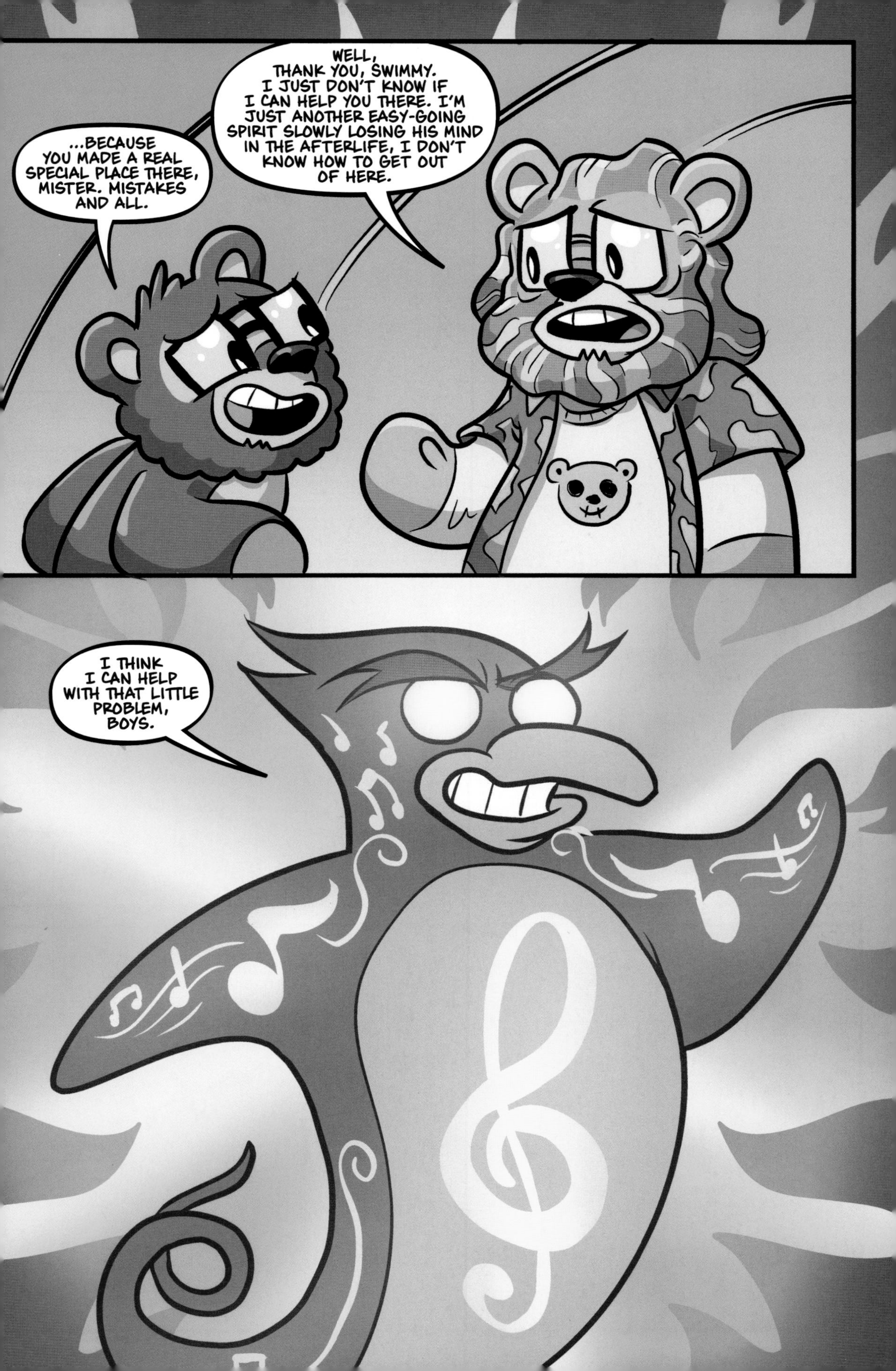
...BECAUSE YOU MADE A REAL SPECIAL PLACE THERE, MISTER. MISTAKES AND ALL.
WELL, THANK YOU, SWIMMY. I JUST DON'T KNOW IF I CAN HELP YOU THERE. I'M JUST ANOTHER EASY-GOING SPIRIT SLOWLY LOSING HIS MIND IN THE AFTERLIFE, I DON'T KNOW HOW TO GET OUT OF HERE.
I THINK I CAN HELP WITH THAT LITTLE PROBLEM, BOYS.

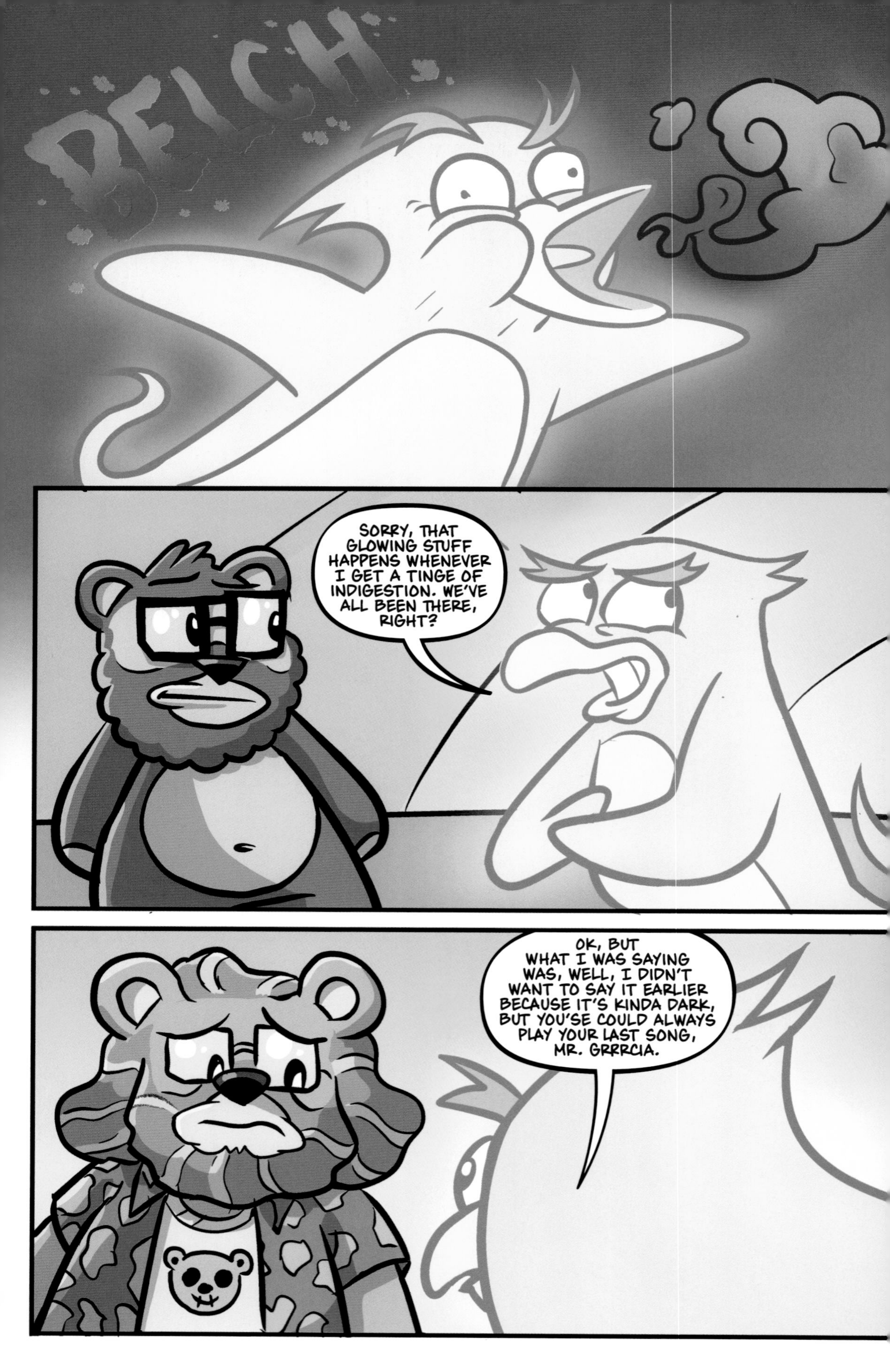
BELCH!
SORRY, THAT GLOWING STUFF HAPPENS WHENEVER I GET A TINGE OF INDIGESTION. WE'VE ALL BEEN THERE, RIGHT?
OK, BUT WHAT I WAS SAYING WAS, WELL, I DIDN'T WANT TO SAY IT EARLIER BECAUSE IT'S KINDA DARK, BUT YOU'SE COULD ALWAYS PLAY YOUR LAST SONG, MR. GRRRCIA.

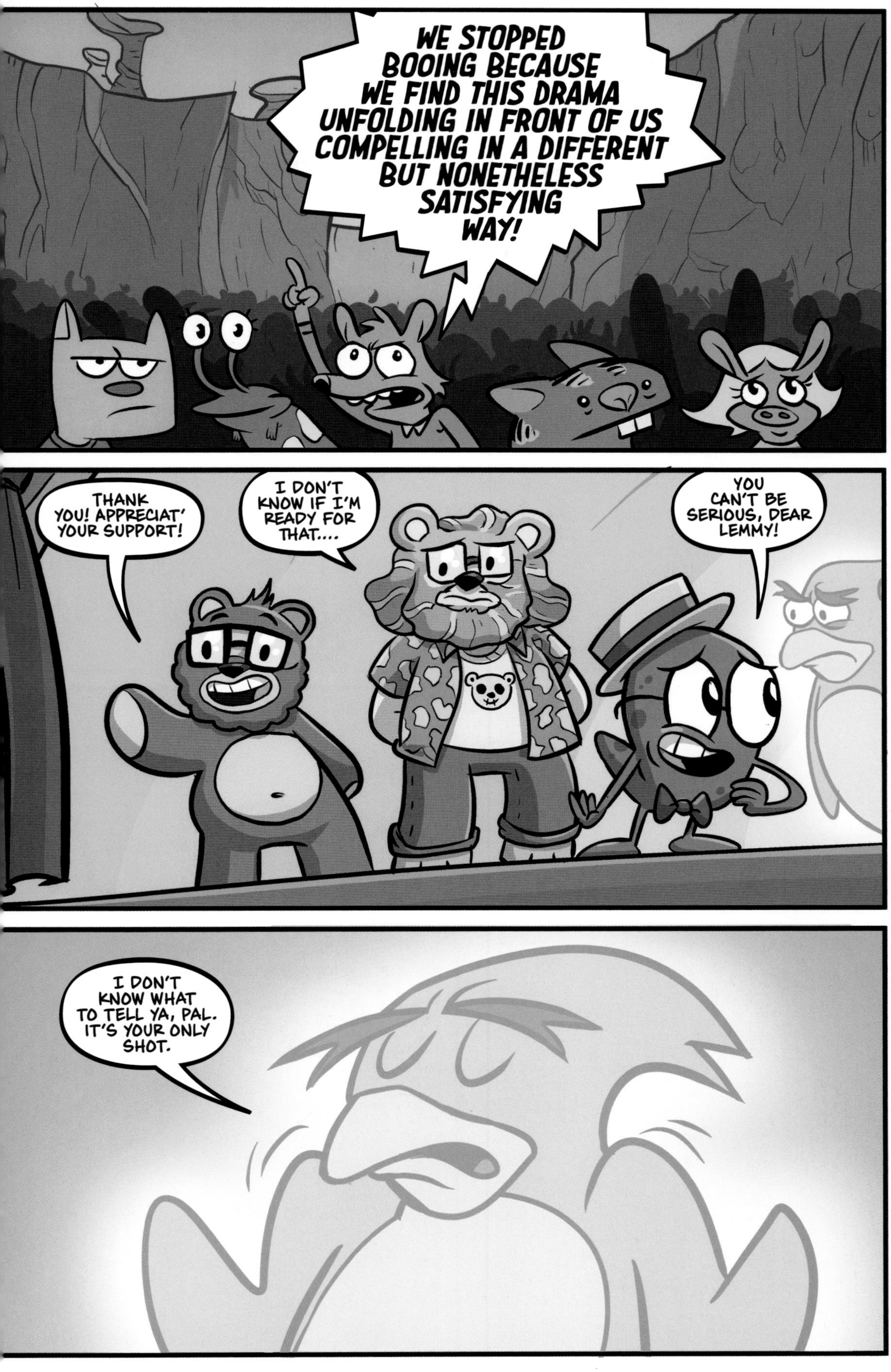
WE STOPPED BOOING BECAUSE WE FIND THIS DRAMA UNFOLDING IN FRONT OF US COMPELLING IN A DIFFERENT BUT NONETHELESS SATISFYING WAY!
THANK YOU! APPRECIAT' YOUR SUPPORT!
I DON'T KNOW IF I'M READY FOR THAT....
YOU CAN'T BE SERIOUS, DEAR LEMMY!
I DON'T KNOW WHAT TO TELL YA, PAL. IT'S YOUR ONLY SHOT.

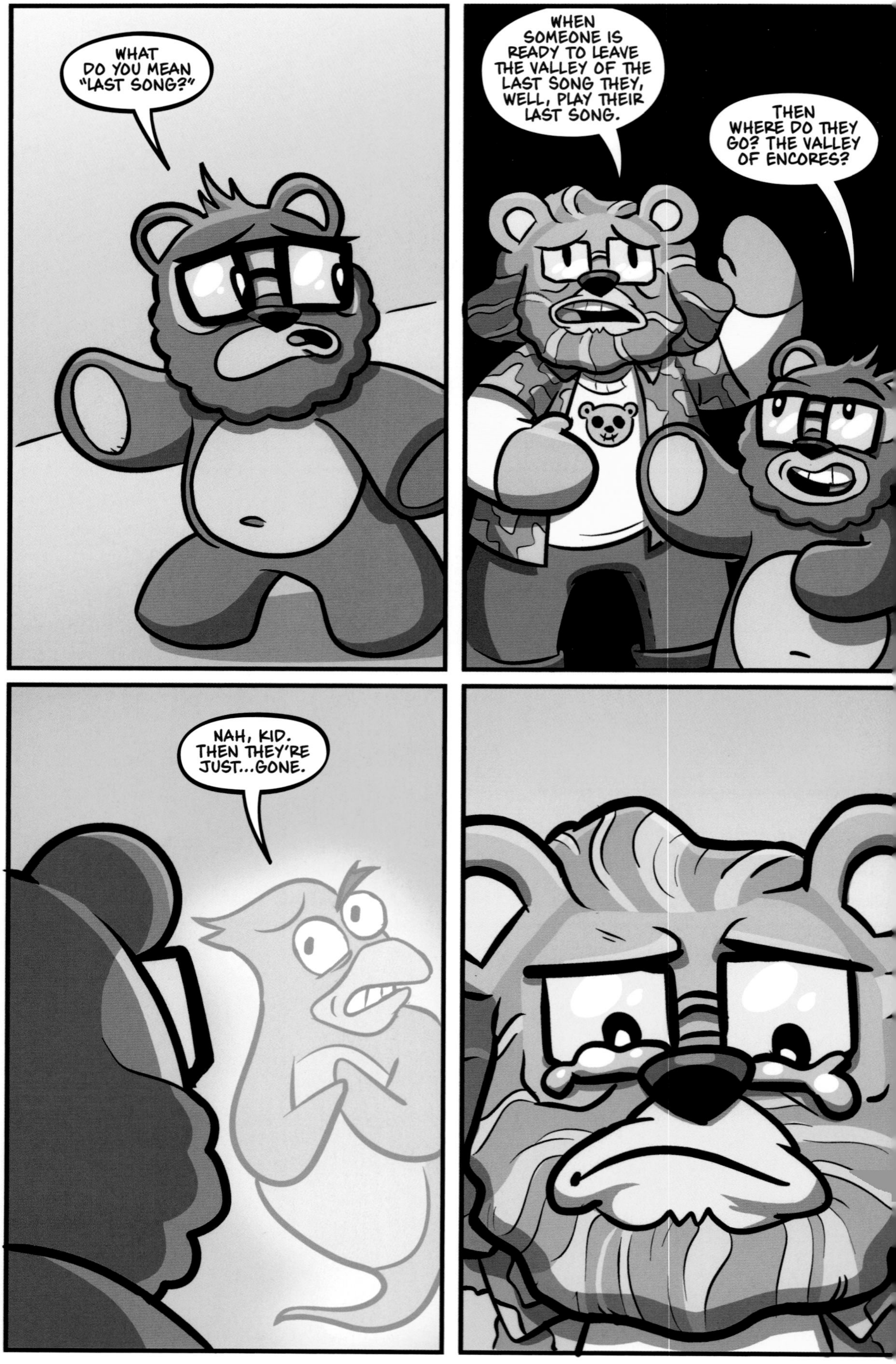
WHAT DO YOU MEAN "LAST SONG?"
WHEN SOMEONE IS READY TO LEAVE THE VALLEY OF THE LAST SONG THEY, WELL, PLAY THEIR LAST SONG.
THEN WHERE DO THEY GO? THE VALLEY OF ENCORES?
NAH, KID. THEN THEY'RE JUST...GONE.

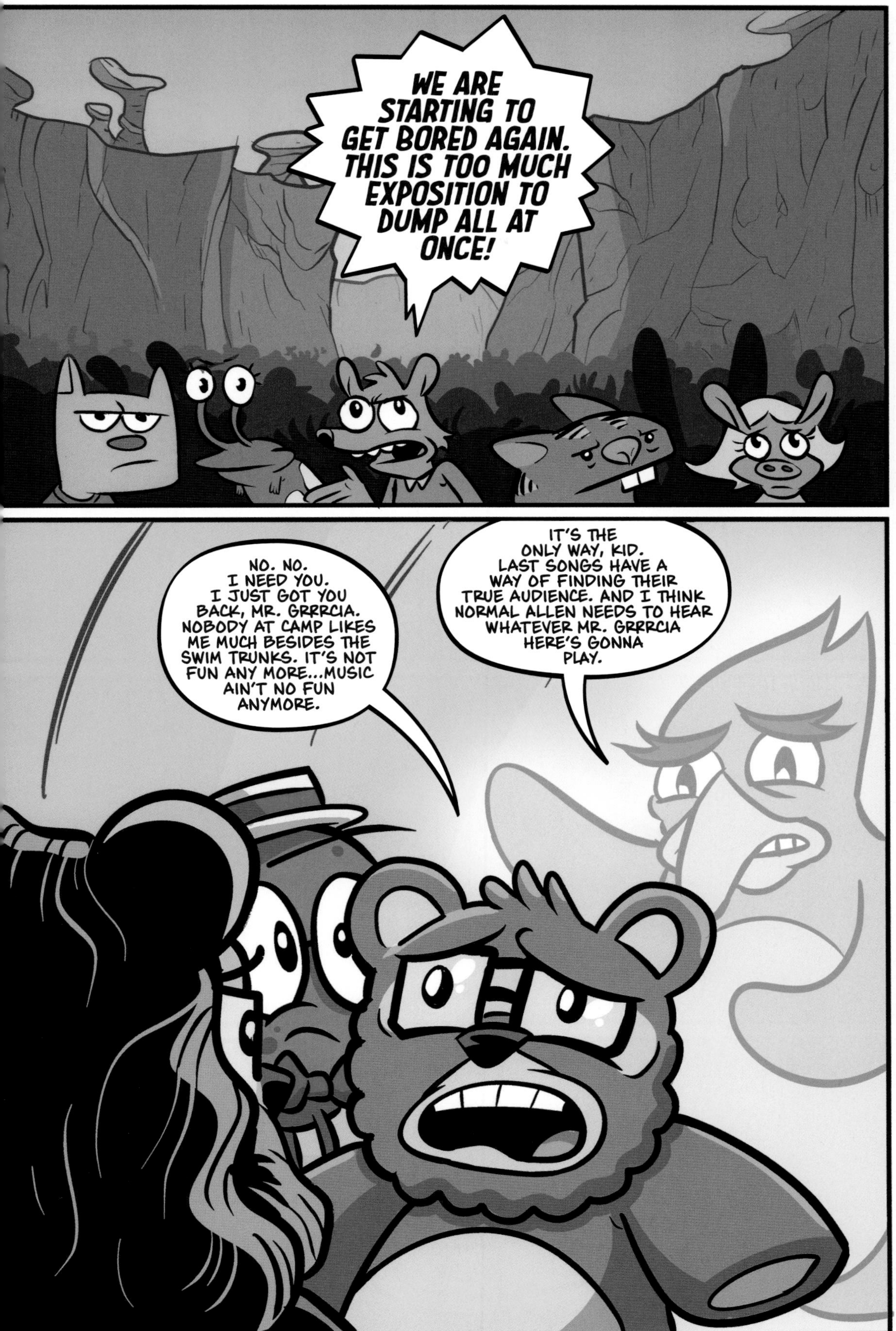
WE ARE STARTING TO GET BORED AGAIN. THIS IS TOO MUCH EXPOSITION TO DUMP ALL AT ONCE!
NO. NO. I NEED YOU. I JUST GOT YOU BACK, MR. GRRRCIA. NOBODY AT CAMP LIKES ME MUCH BESIDES THE SWIM TRUNKS. IT'S NOT FUN ANY MORE...MUSIC AIN'T NO FUN ANYMORE.
IT'S THE ONLY WAY, KID. LAST SONGS HAVE A WAY OF FINDING THEIR TRUE AUDIENCE. AND I THINK NORMAL ALLEN NEEDS TO HEAR WHATEVER MR. GRRRCIA HERE'S GONNA PLAY.

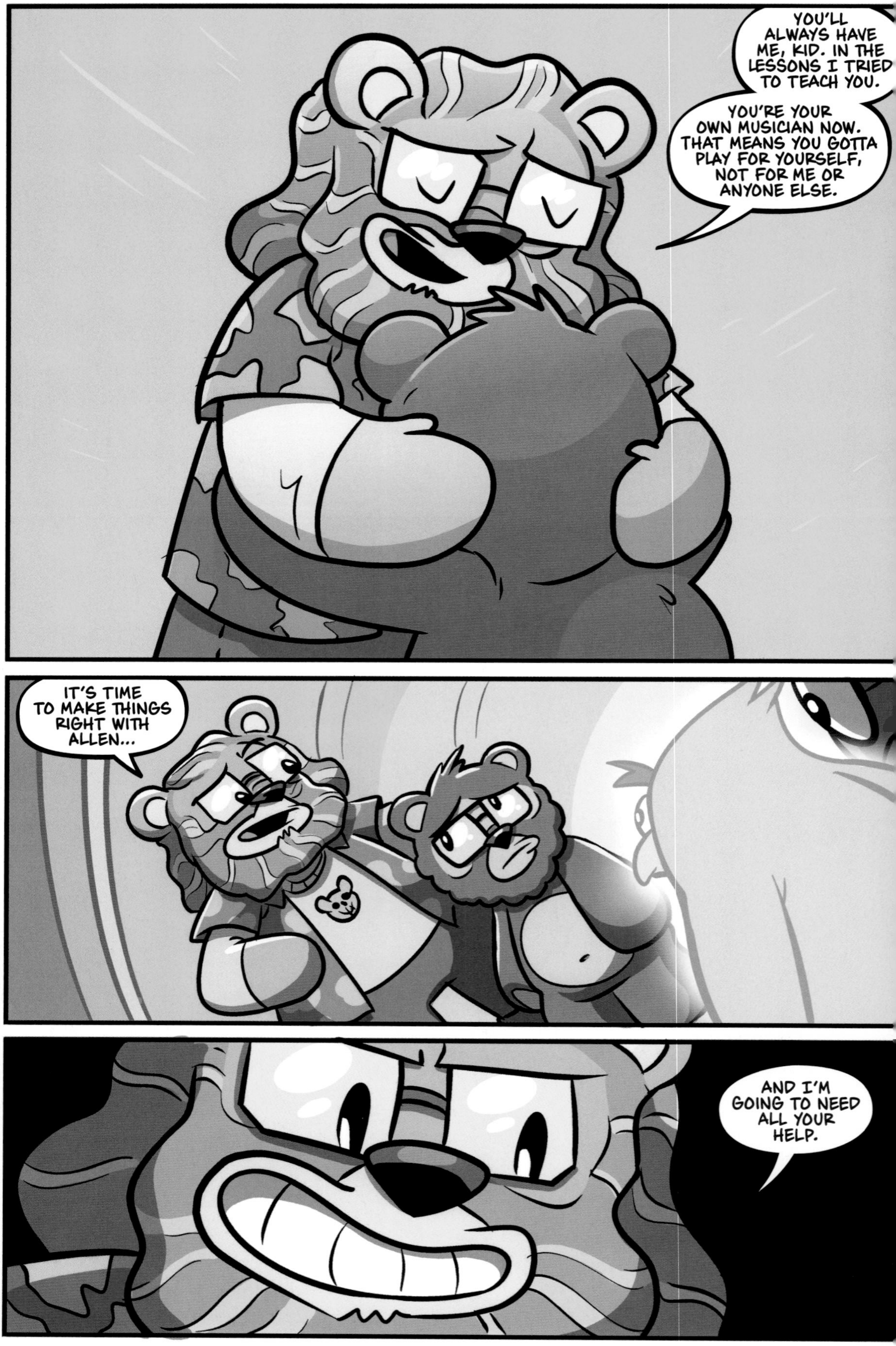
YOU'LL ALWAYS HAVE ME, KID. IN THE LESSONS I TRIED TO TEACH YOU.
YOU'RE YOUR OWN MUSICIAN NOW. THAT MEANS YOU GOTTA PLAY FOR YOURSELF, NOT FOR ME OR ANYONE ELSE.
IT'S TIME TO MAKE THINGS RIGHT WITH ALLEN...
AND I'M GOING TO NEED ALL YOUR HELP.

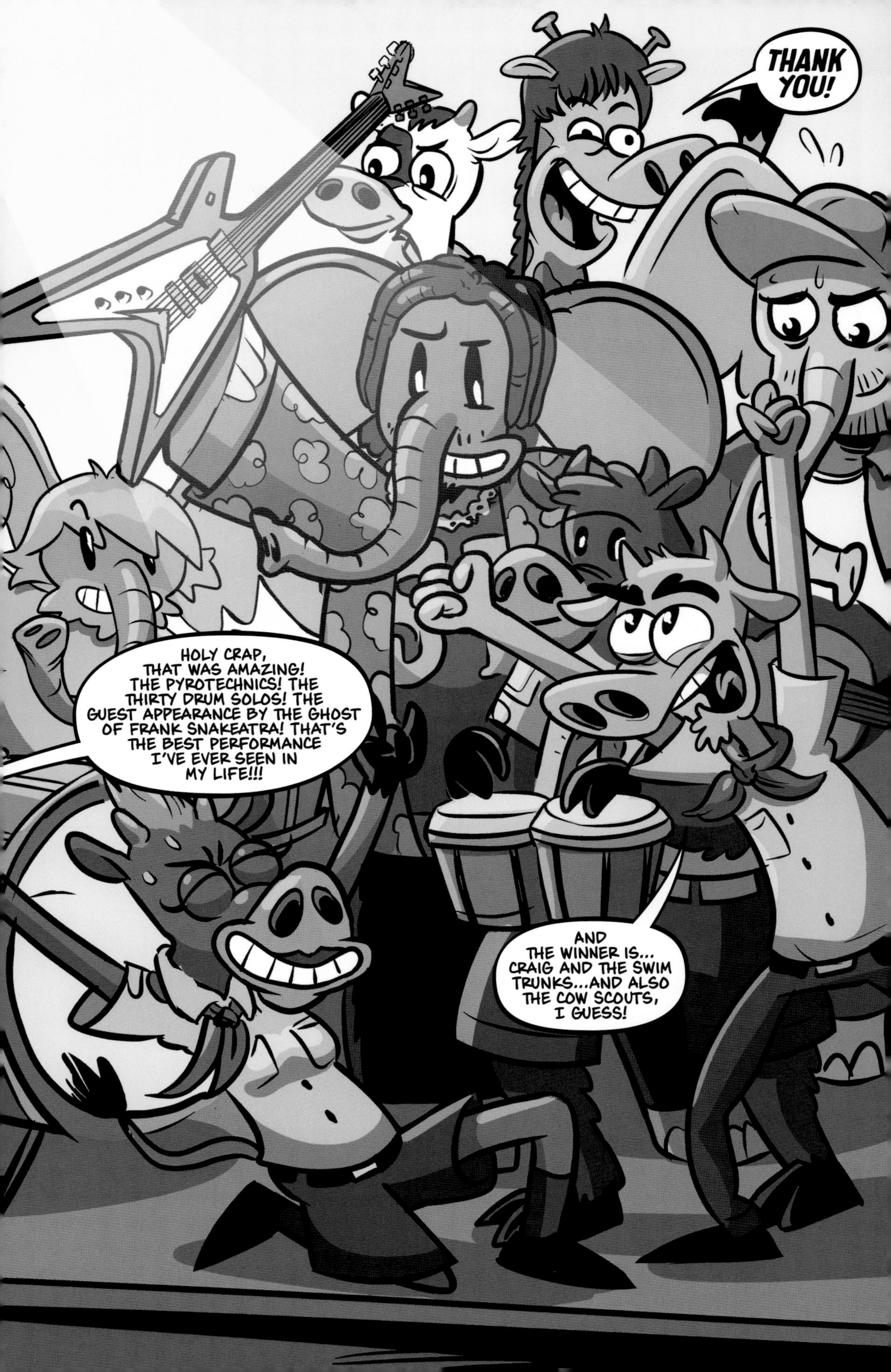
THANK YOU!
HOLY CRAP, THAT WAS AMAZING! THE PYROTECHNICS! THE THIRTY DRUM SOLOS! THE GUEST APPEARANCE BY THE GHOST OF FRANK SNAKEATRA! THAT'S THE BEST PERFORMANCE I'VE EVER SEEN IN MY LIFE!!!
AND THE WINNER IS... CRAIG AND THE SWIM TRUNKS...AND ALSO THE COW SCOUTS, I GUESS!

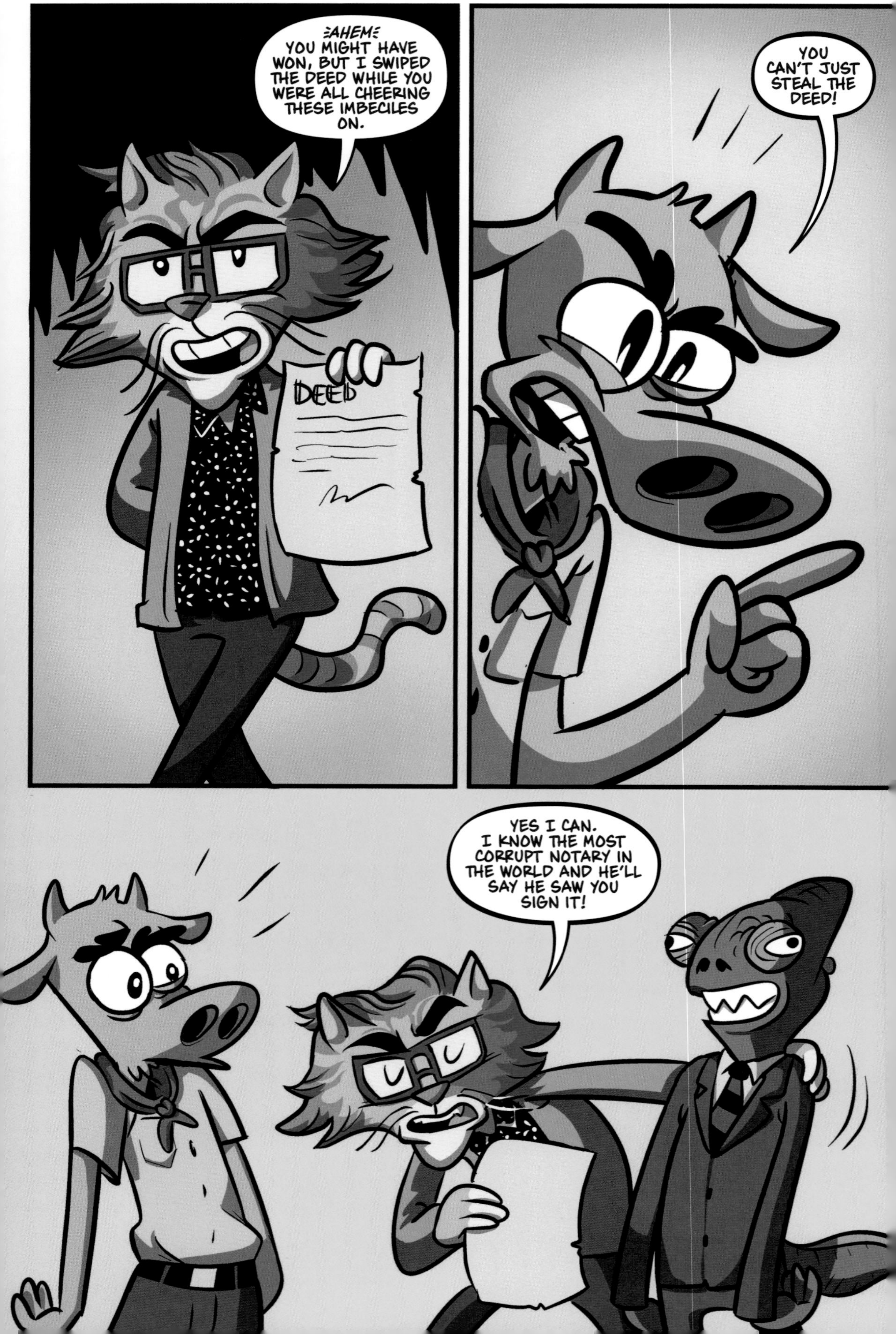
AHEM
YOU MIGHT HAVE WON, BUT I SWIPED THE DEED WHILE YOU WERE ALL CHEERING THESE IMBECILES ON.
DEED
YOU CAN'T JUST STEAL THE DEED!
YES I CAN. I KNOW THE MOST CORRUPT NOTARY IN THE WORLD AND HE'LL SAY HE SAW YOU SIGN IT!

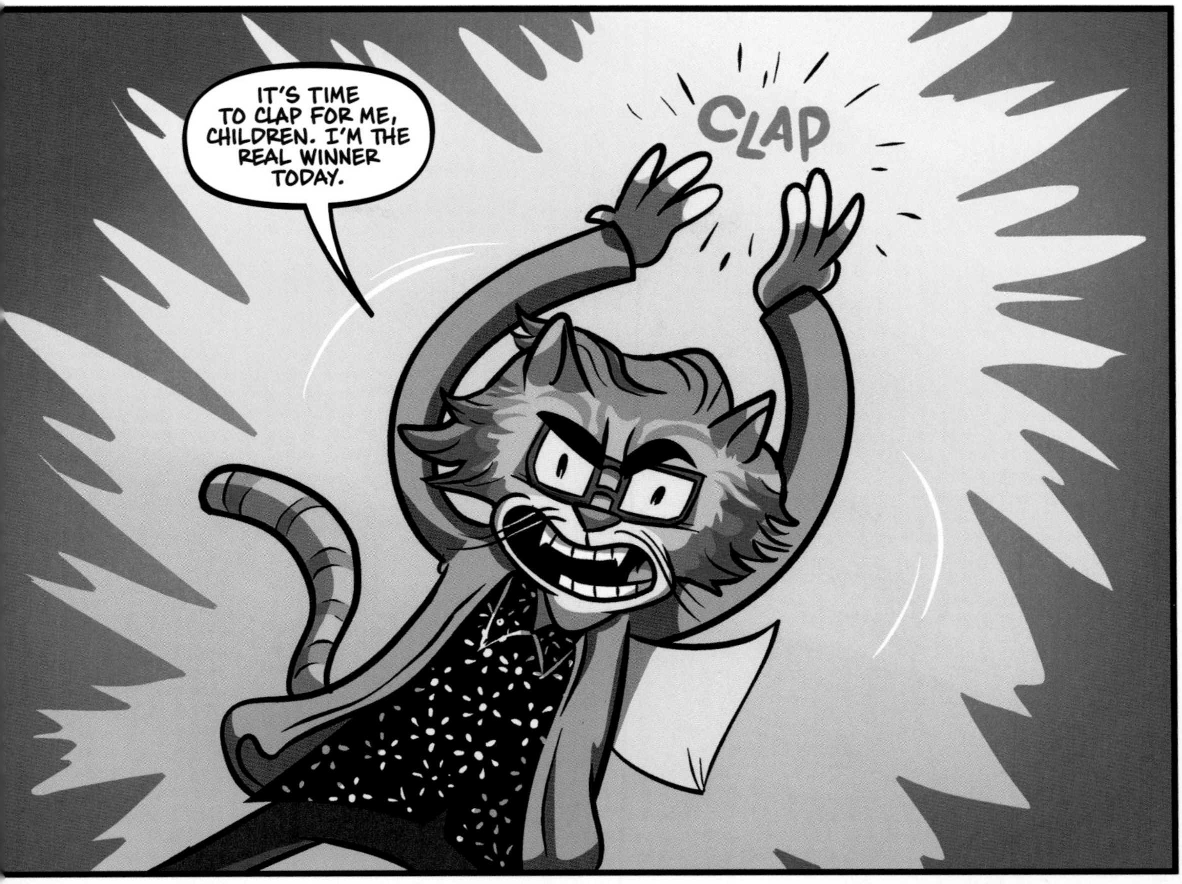
IT'S TIME TO CLAP FOR ME, CHILDREN. I'M THE REAL WINNER TODAY.
CLAP

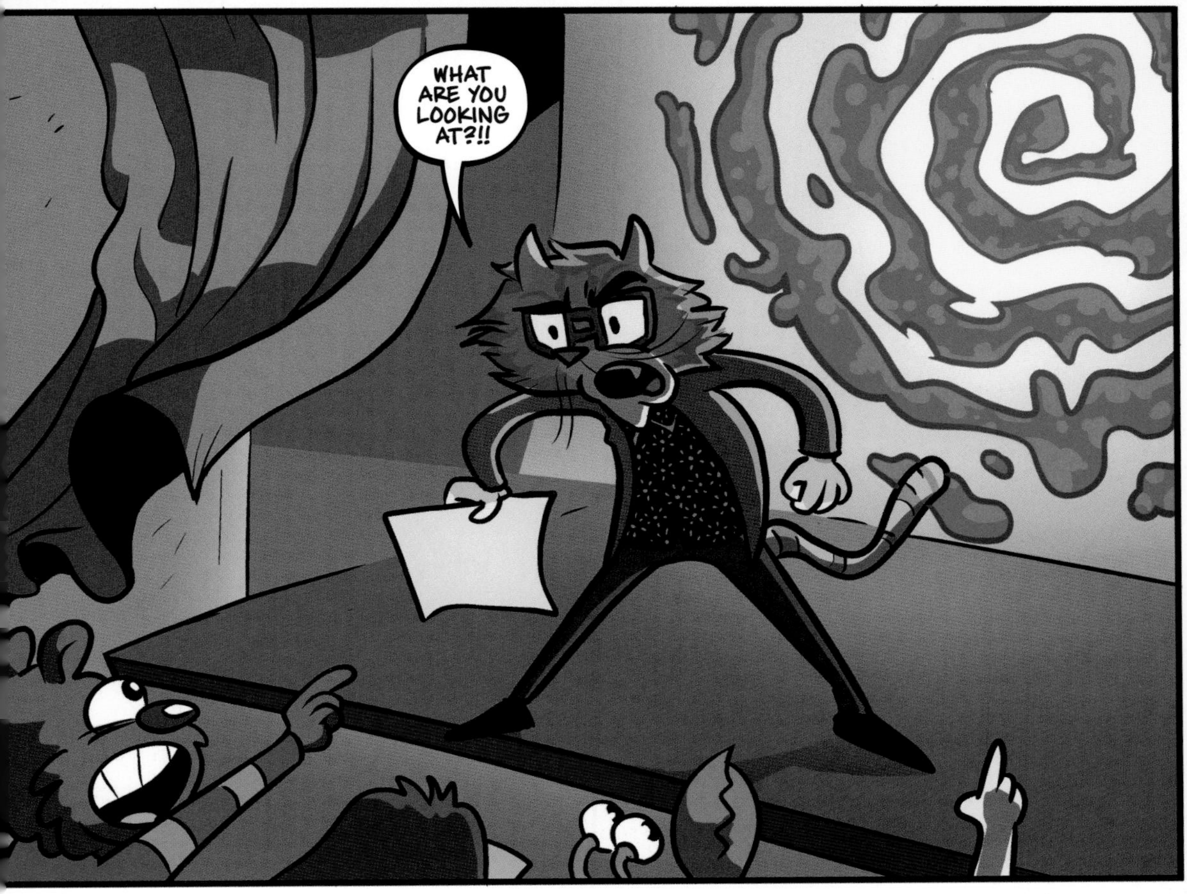
WHAT ARE YOU LOOKING AT?!!

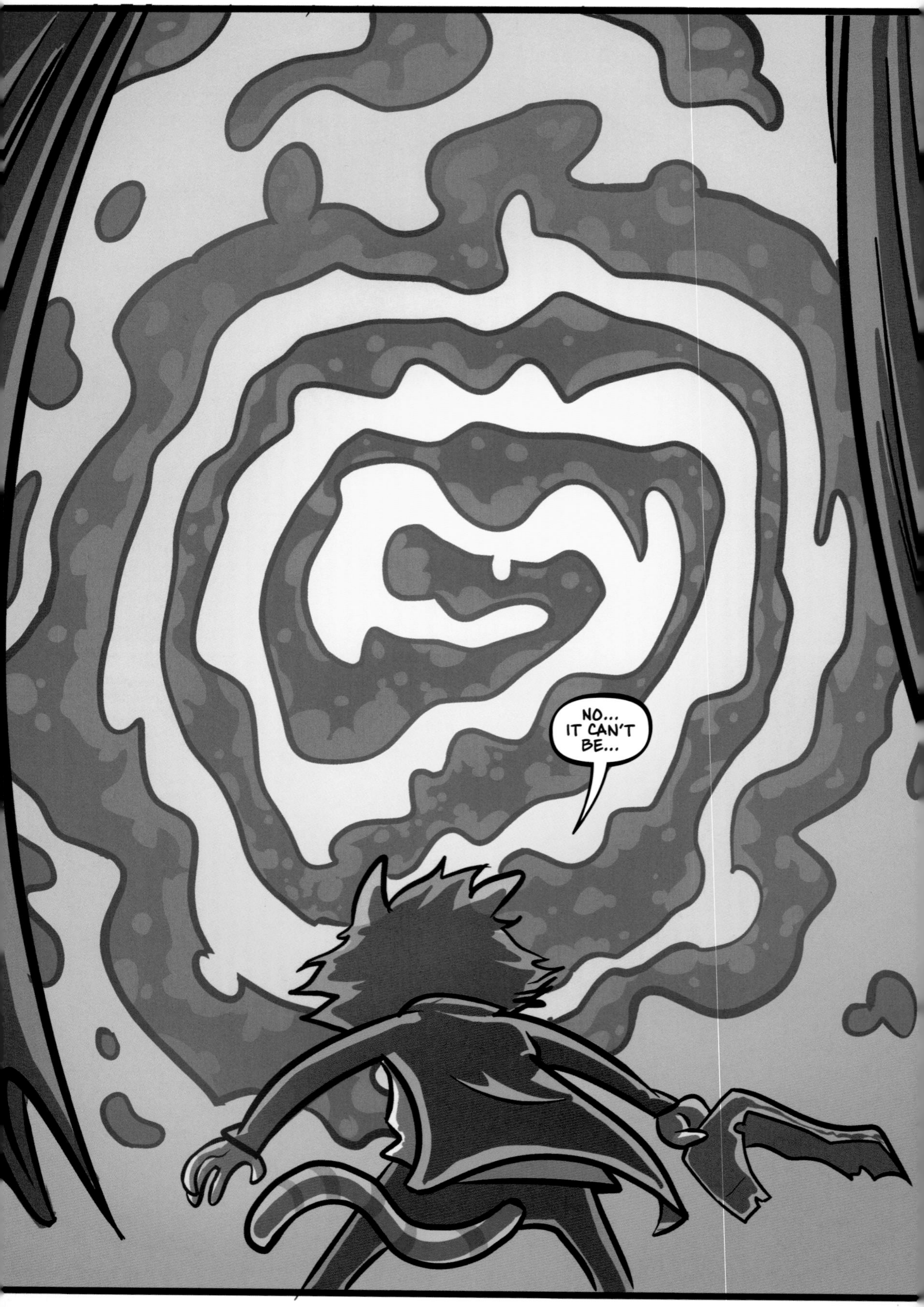
NO... IT CAN'T BE...

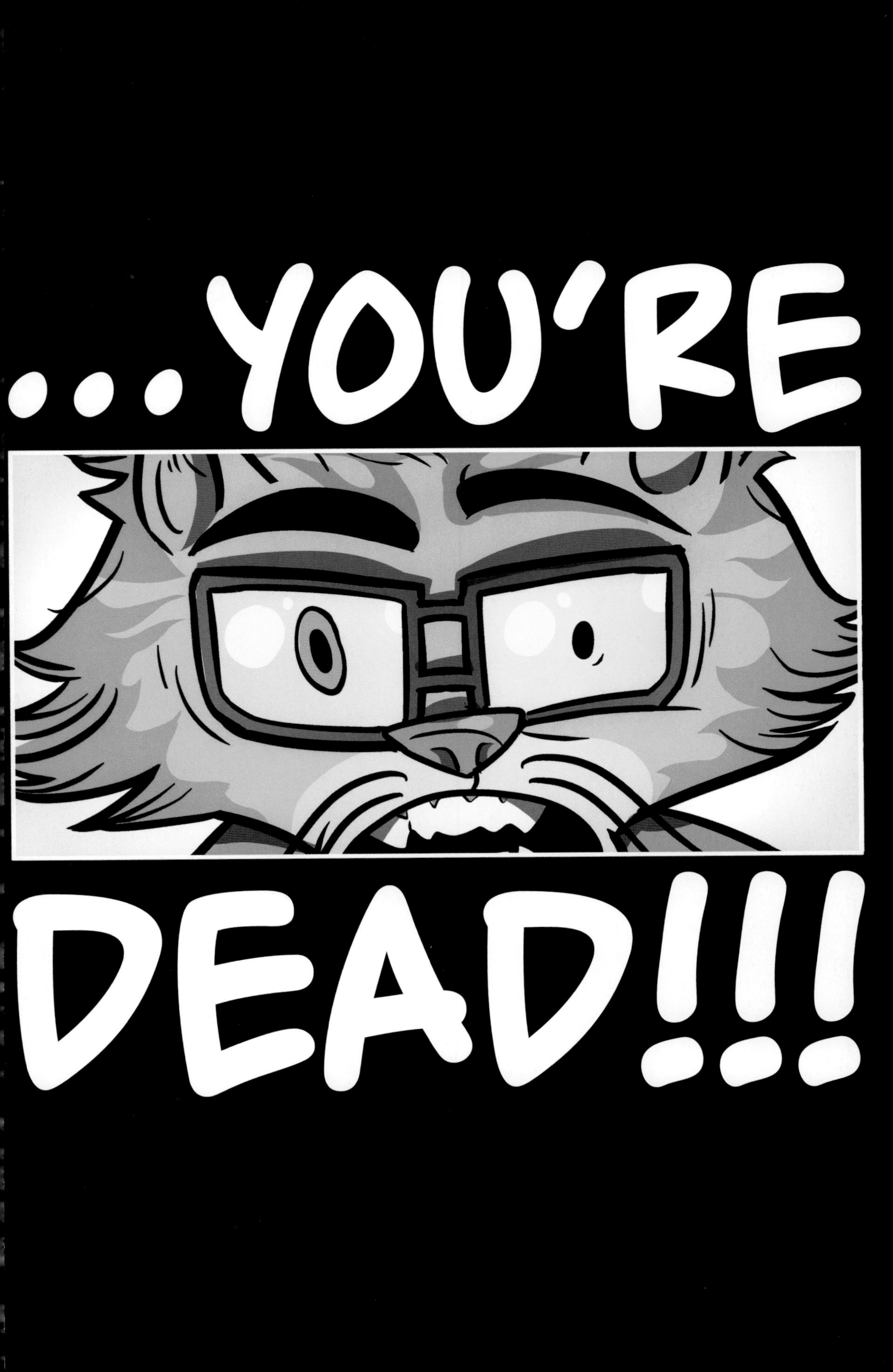
...YOU'RE
DEAD!!!

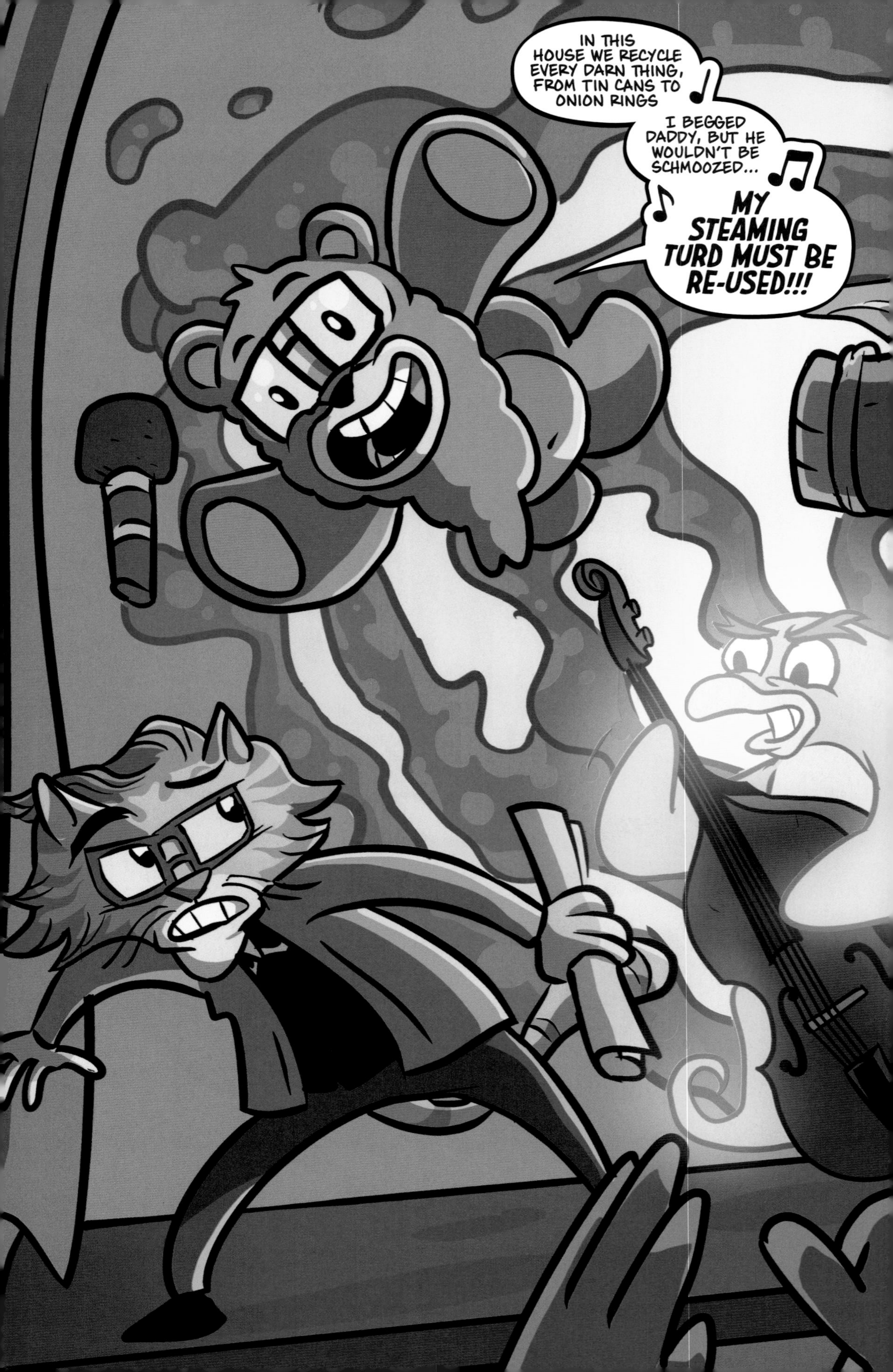
IN THIS HOUSE WE RECYCLE EVERY DARN THING, FROM TIN CANS TO ONION RINGS
I BEGGED DADDY, BUT HE WOULDN'T BE SCHMOOZED...
MY STEAMING TURD MUST BE RE-USED!!!

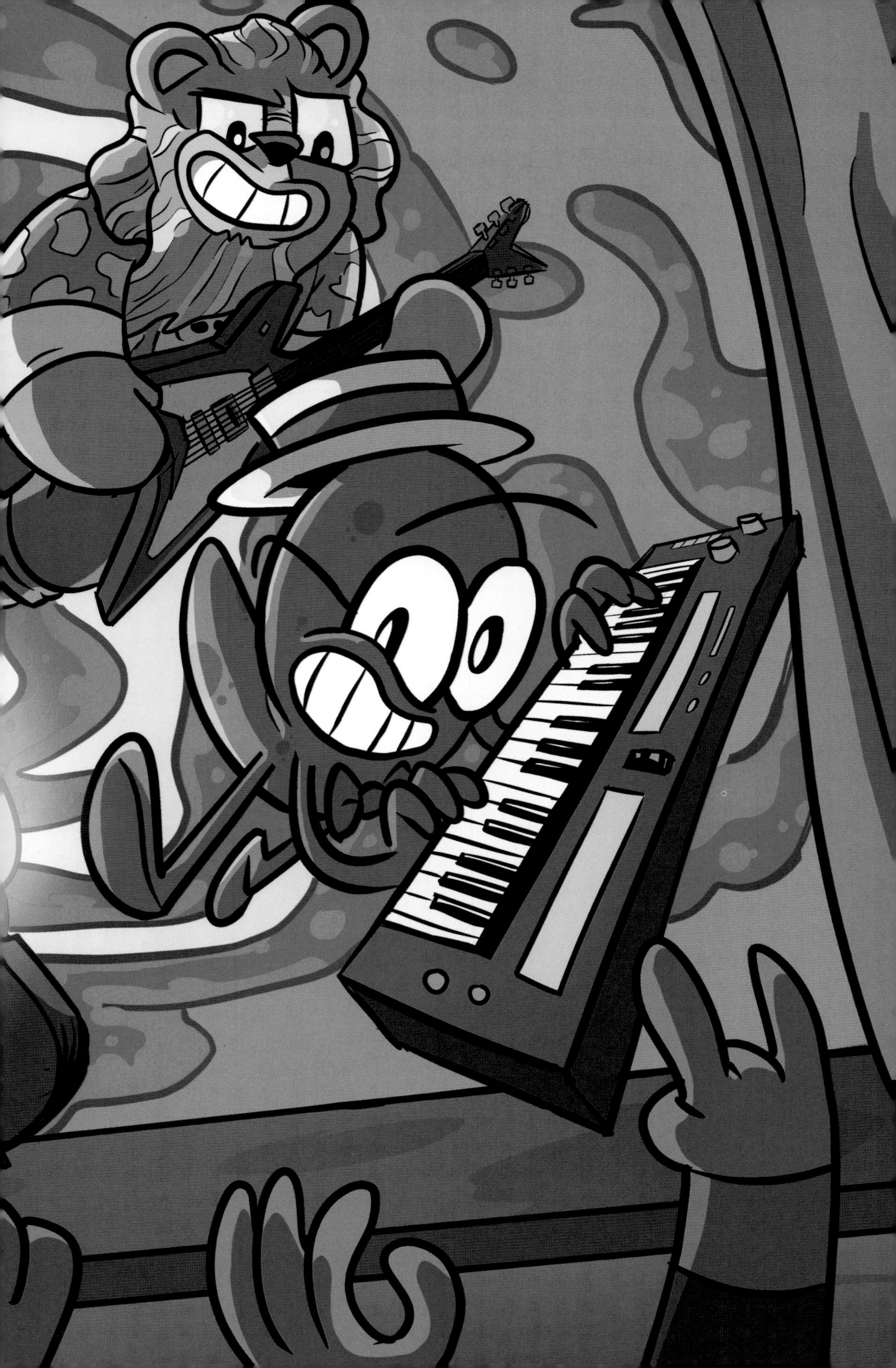

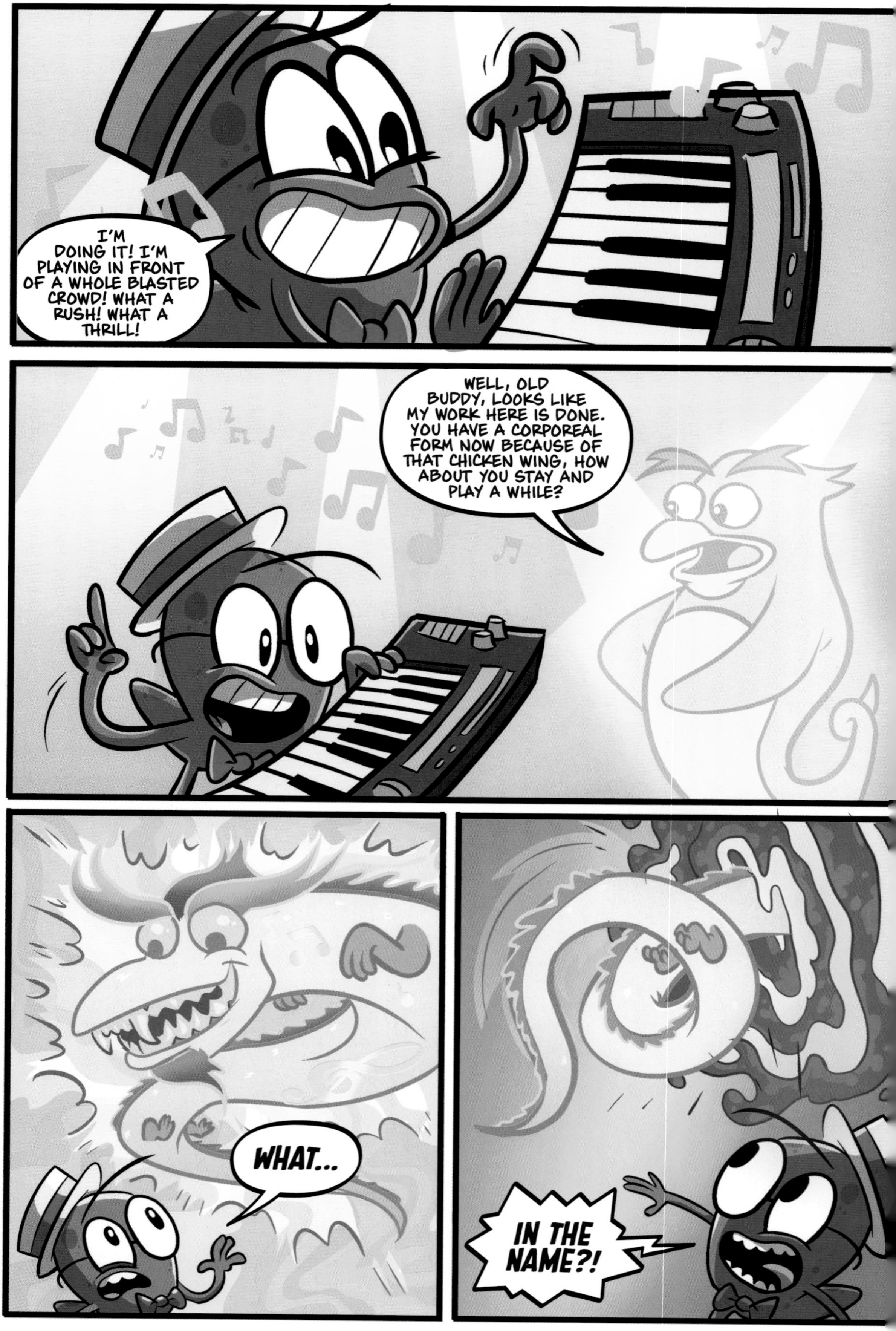
I'M DOING IT! I'M PLAYING IN FRONT OF A WHOLE BLASTED CROWD! WHAT A RUSH! WHAT A THRILL!
WELL, OLD BUDDY, LOOKS LIKE MY WORK HERE IS DONE. YOU HAVE A CORPOREAL FORM NOW BECAUSE OF THAT CHICKEN WING, HOW ABOUT YOU STAY AND PLAY A WHILE?
WHAT...
IN THE NAME?!

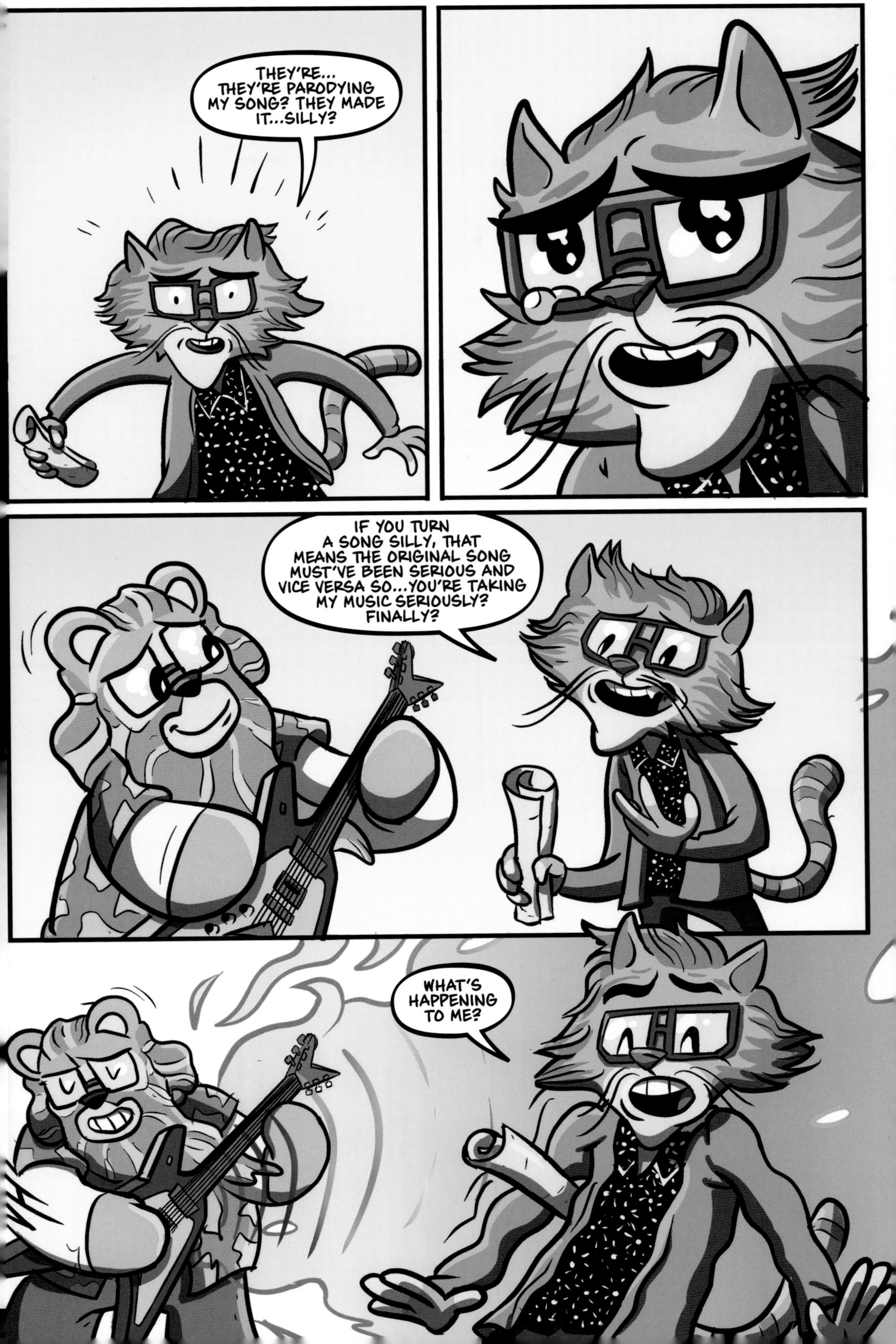
THEY'RE... THEY'RE PARODYING MY SONG? THEY MADE IT...SILLY?
IF YOU TURN A SONG SILLY, THAT MEANS THE ORIGINAL SONG MUST'VE BEEN SERIOUS AND VICE VERSA SO...YOU'RE TAKING MY MUSIC SERIOUSLY? FINALLY?
WHAT'S HAPPENING TO ME?

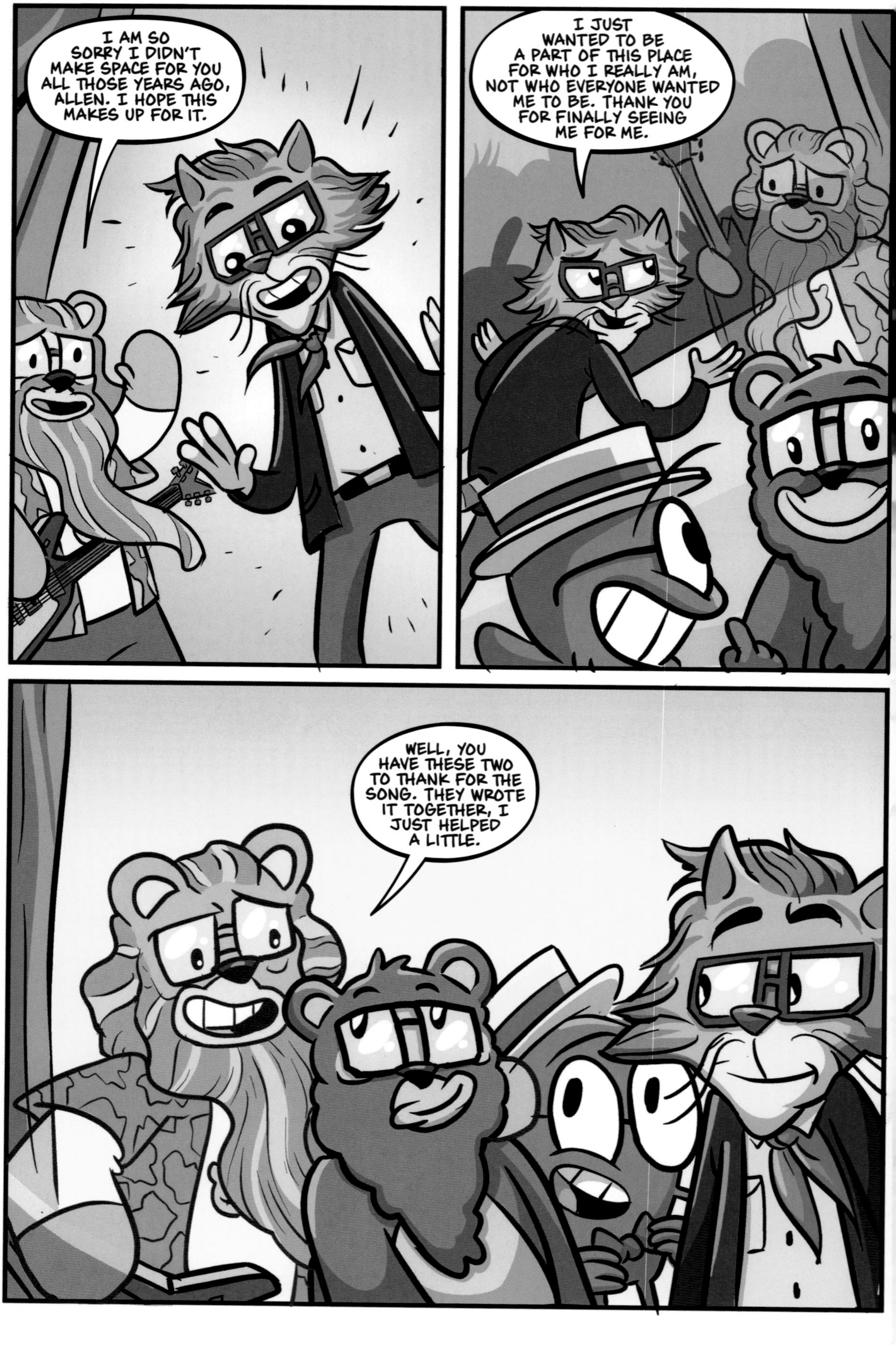
I AM SO SORRY I DIDN'T MAKE SPACE FOR YOU ALL THOSE YEARS AGO, ALLEN. I HOPE THIS MAKES UP FOR IT.
I JUST WANTED TO BE A PART OF THIS PLACE FOR WHO I REALLY AM, NOT WHO EVERYONE WANTED ME TO BE. THANK YOU FOR FINALLY SEEING ME FOR ME.
WELL, YOU HAVE THESE TWO TO THANK FOR THE SONG. THEY WROTE IT TOGETHER, I JUST HELPED A LITTLE.

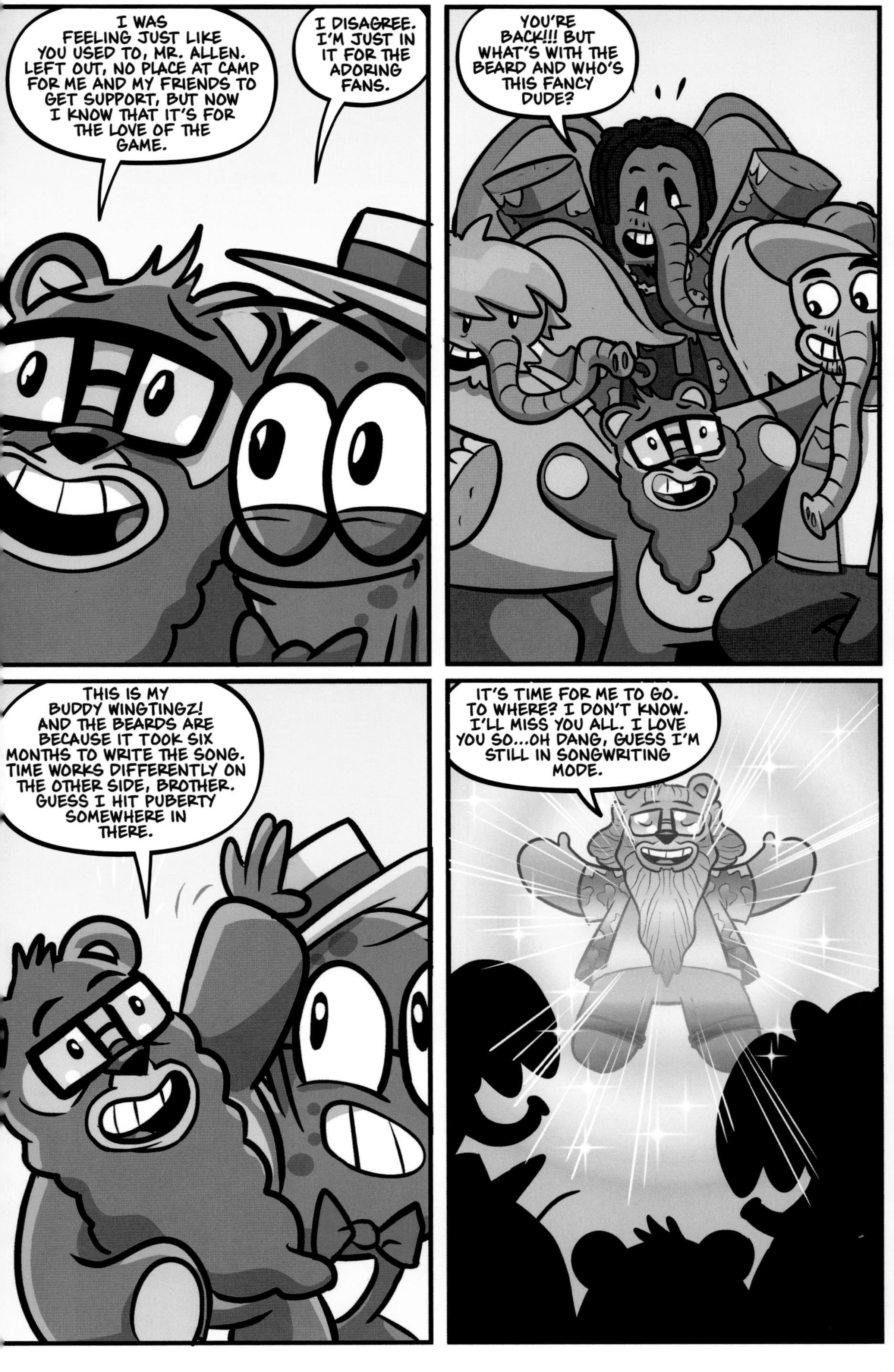
I WAS FEELING JUST LIKE YOU USED TO, MR. ALLEN. LEFT OUT, NO PLACE AT CAMP FOR ME AND MY FRIENDS TO GET SUPPORT, BUT NOW I KNOW THAT IT'S FOR THE LOVE OF THE GAME.
I DISAGREE. I'M JUST IN IT FOR THE ADORING FANS.
YOU'RE BACK!!! BUT WHAT'S WITH THE BEARD AND WHO'S THIS FANCY DUDE?
THIS IS MY BUDDY WINGTINGZ! AND THE BEARDS ARE BECAUSE IT TOOK SIX MONTHS TO WRITE THE SONG. TIME WORKS DIFFERENTLY ON THE OTHER SIDE, BROTHER. GUESS I HIT PUBERTY SOMEWHERE IN THERE.
IT'S TIME FOR ME TO GO. TO WHERE? I DON'T KNOW. I'LL MISS YOU ALL. I LOVE YOU SO...OH DANG, GUESS I'M STILL IN SONGWRITING MODE.

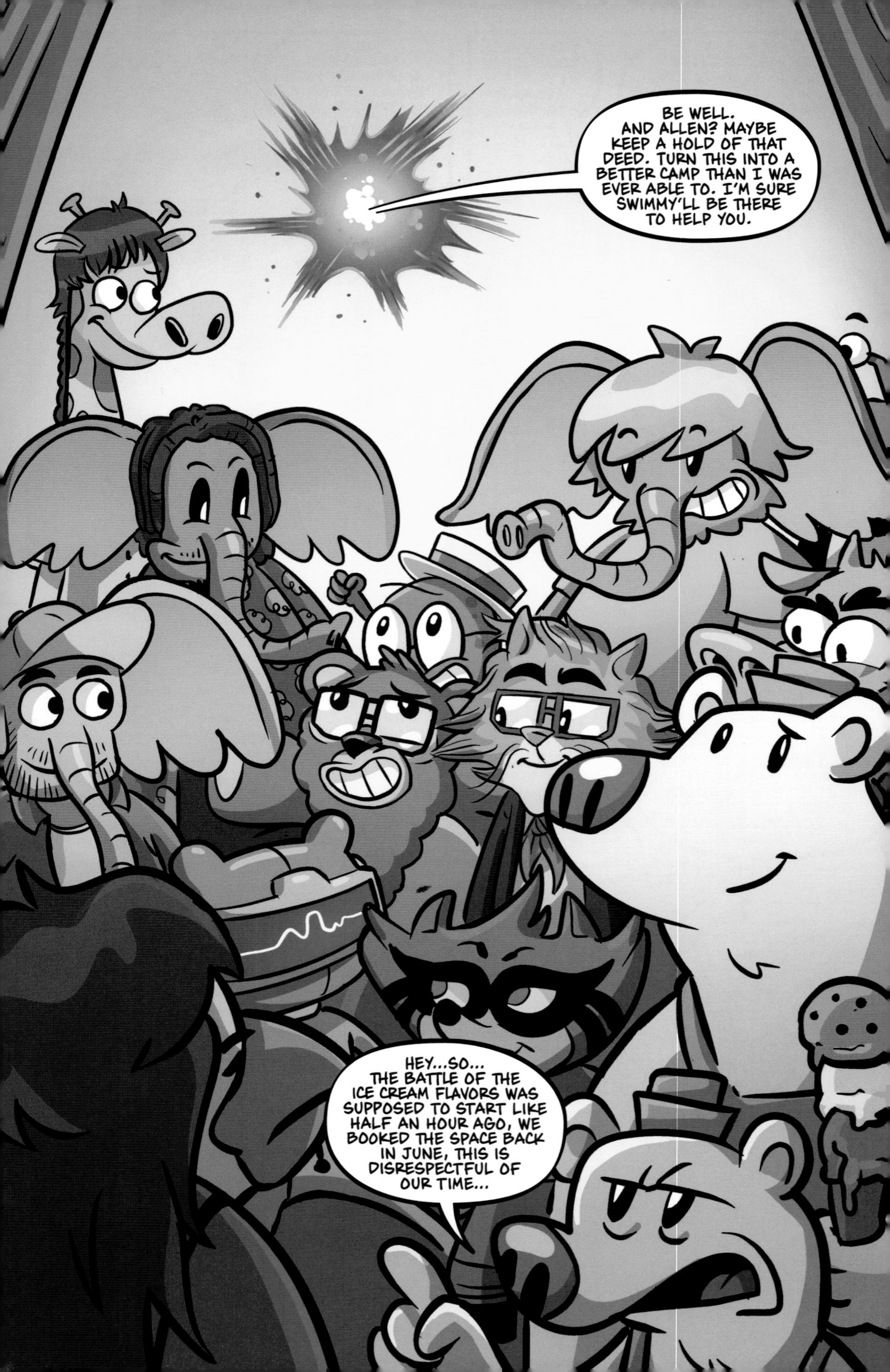
BE WELL. AND ALLEN? MAYBE KEEP A HOLD OF THAT DEED. TURN THIS INTO A BETTER CAMP THAN I WAS EVER ABLE TO. I'M SURE SWIMMY'LL BE THERE TO HELP YOU.
HEY...SO... THE BATTLE OF THE ICE CREAM FLAVORS WAS SUPPOSED TO START LIKE HALF AN HOUR AGO, WE BOOKED THE SPACE BACK IN JUNE, THIS IS DISRESPECTFUL OF OUR TIME...

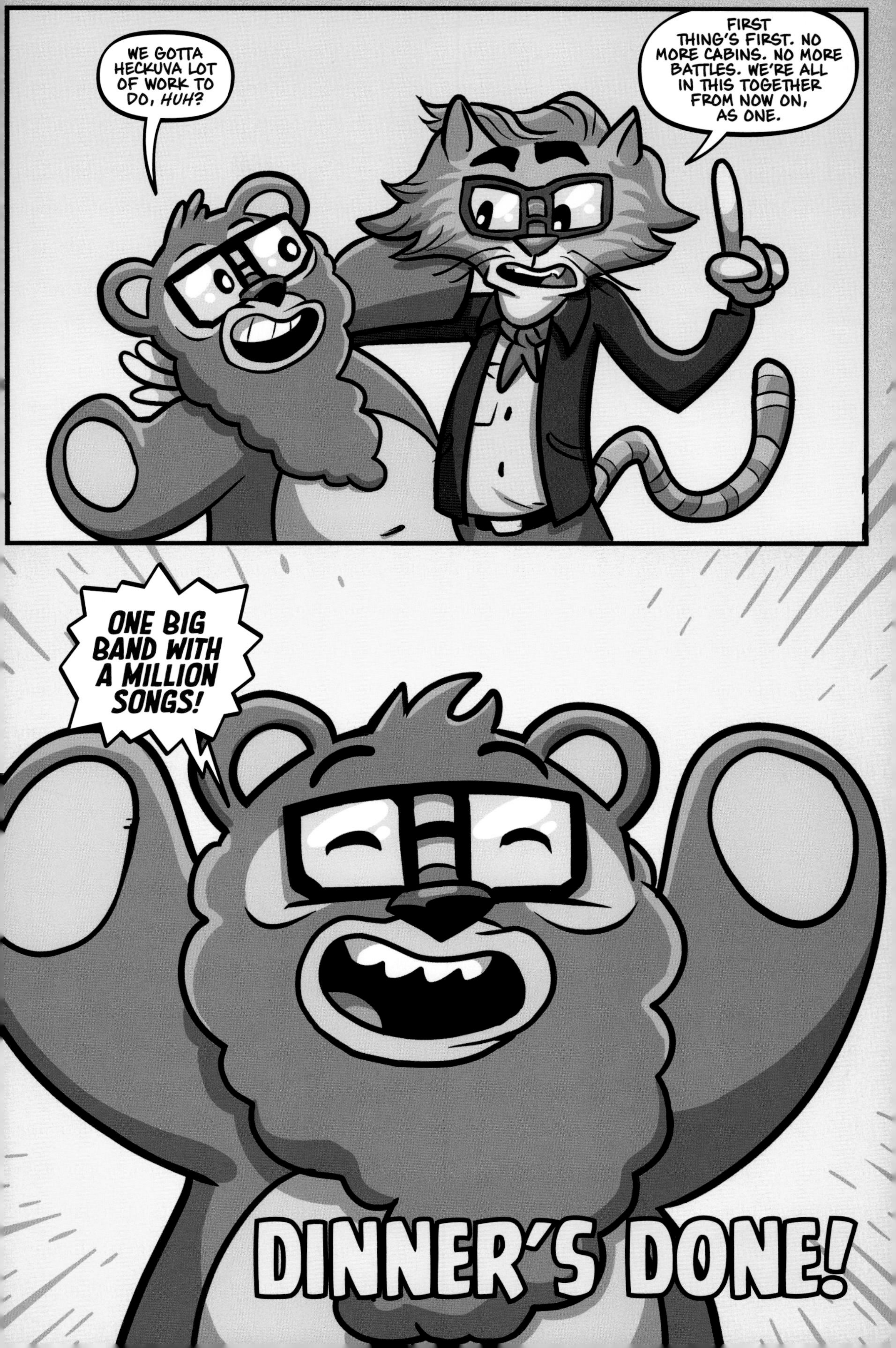
WE GOTTA HECKUVA LOT OF WORK TO DO, HUH?
FIRST THING'S FIRST. NO MORE CABINS. NO MORE BATTLES. WE'RE ALL IN THIS TOGETHER FROM NOW ON, AS ONE.
ONE BIG BAND WITH A MILLION SONGS!
DINNER'S DONE!

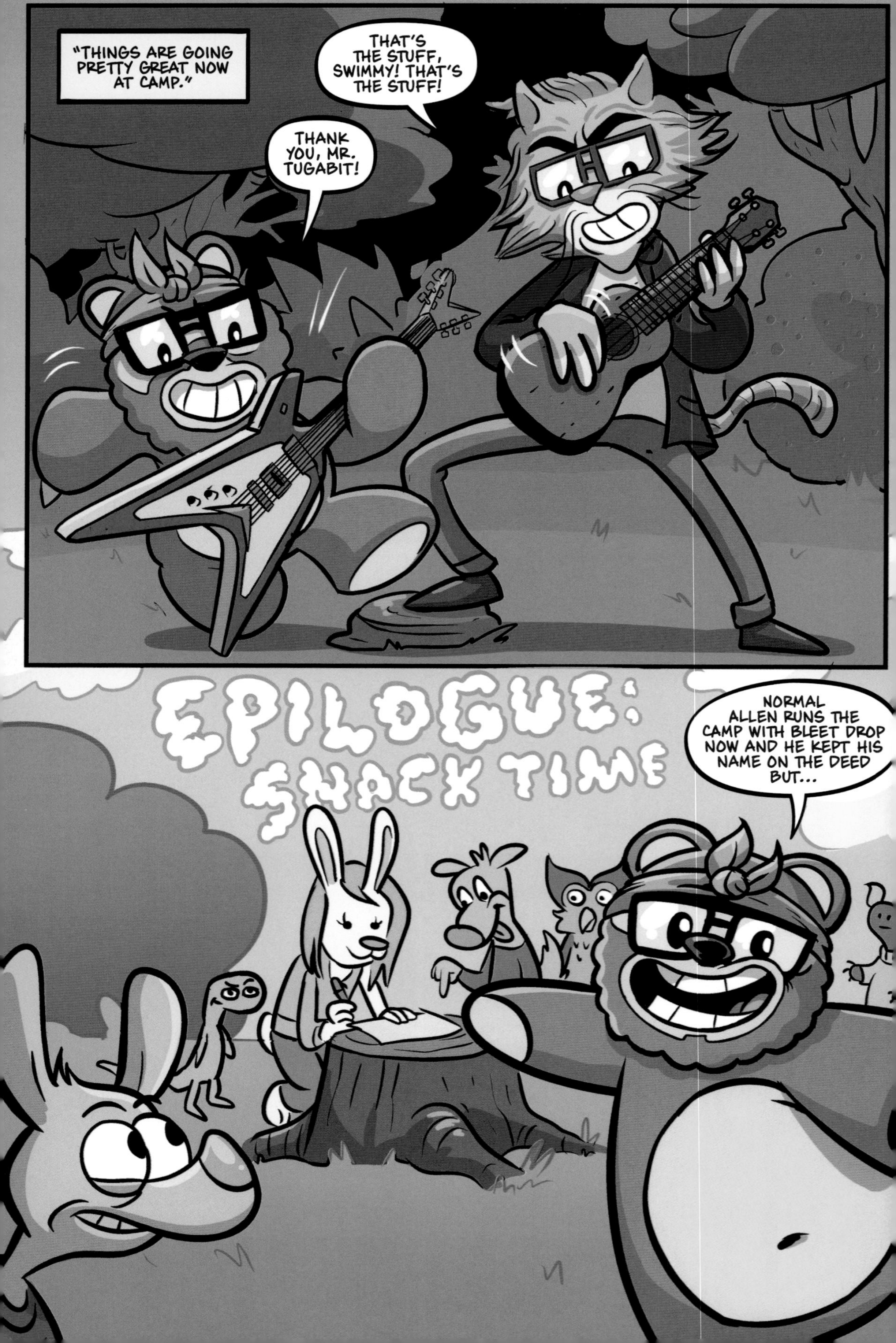
"THINGS ARE GOING PRETTY GREAT NOW AT CAMP."
THAT'S THE STUFF, SWIMMY! THAT'S THE STUFF!
THANK YOU, MR. TUGABIT!
EPILOGUE: SNACK TIME
NORMAL ALLEN RUNS THE CAMP WITH BLEET DROP NOW AND HE KEPT HIS NAME ON THE DEED BUT...

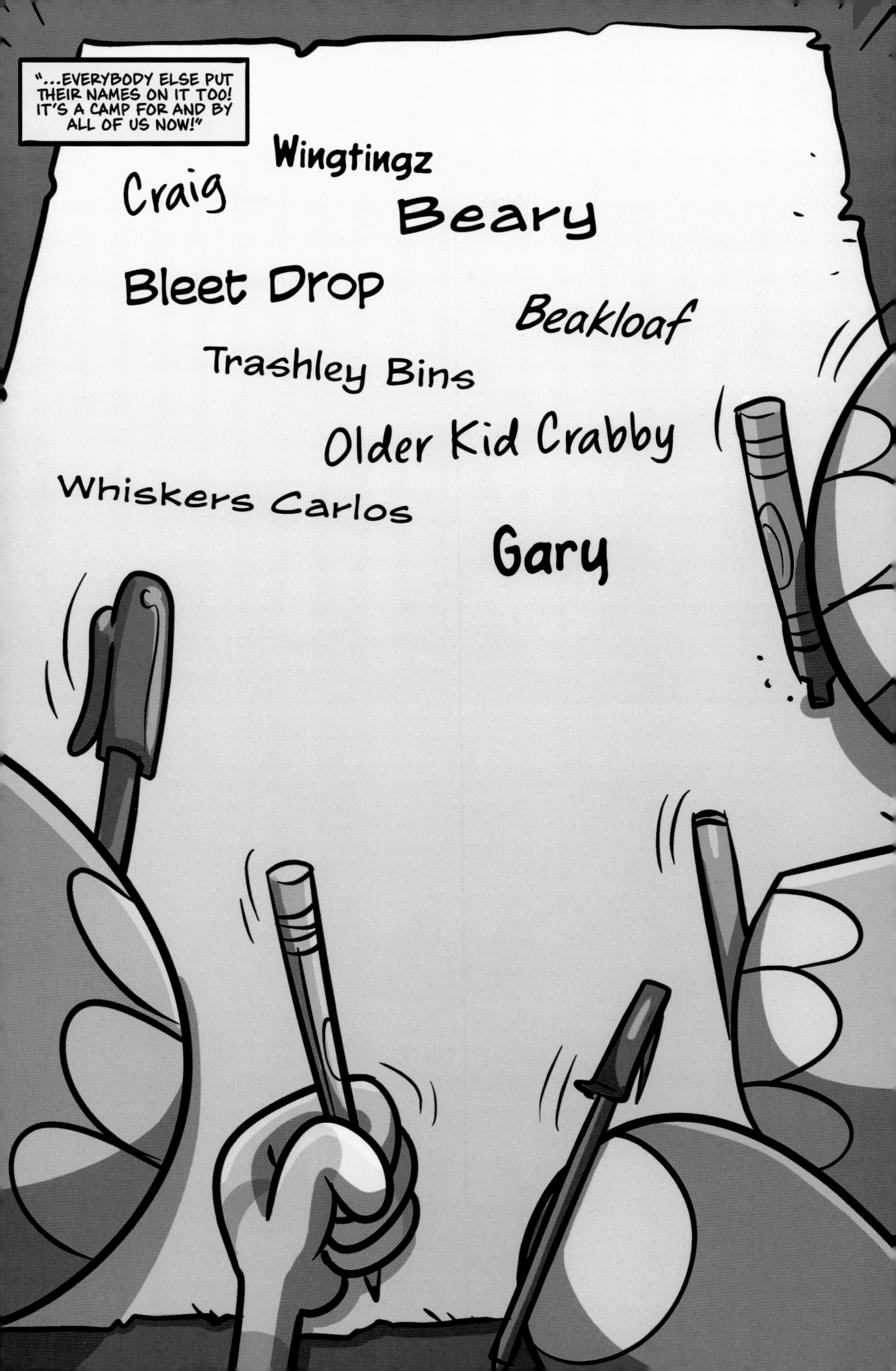
"...EVERYBODY ELSE PUT THEIR NAMES ON IT TOO! IT'S A CAMP FOR AND BY ALL OF US NOW!"
Wingtingz
Craig
Beary
Bleet Drop
Beakloaf
Trashley Bins
Older Kid Crabby
Whiskers Carlos
Gary

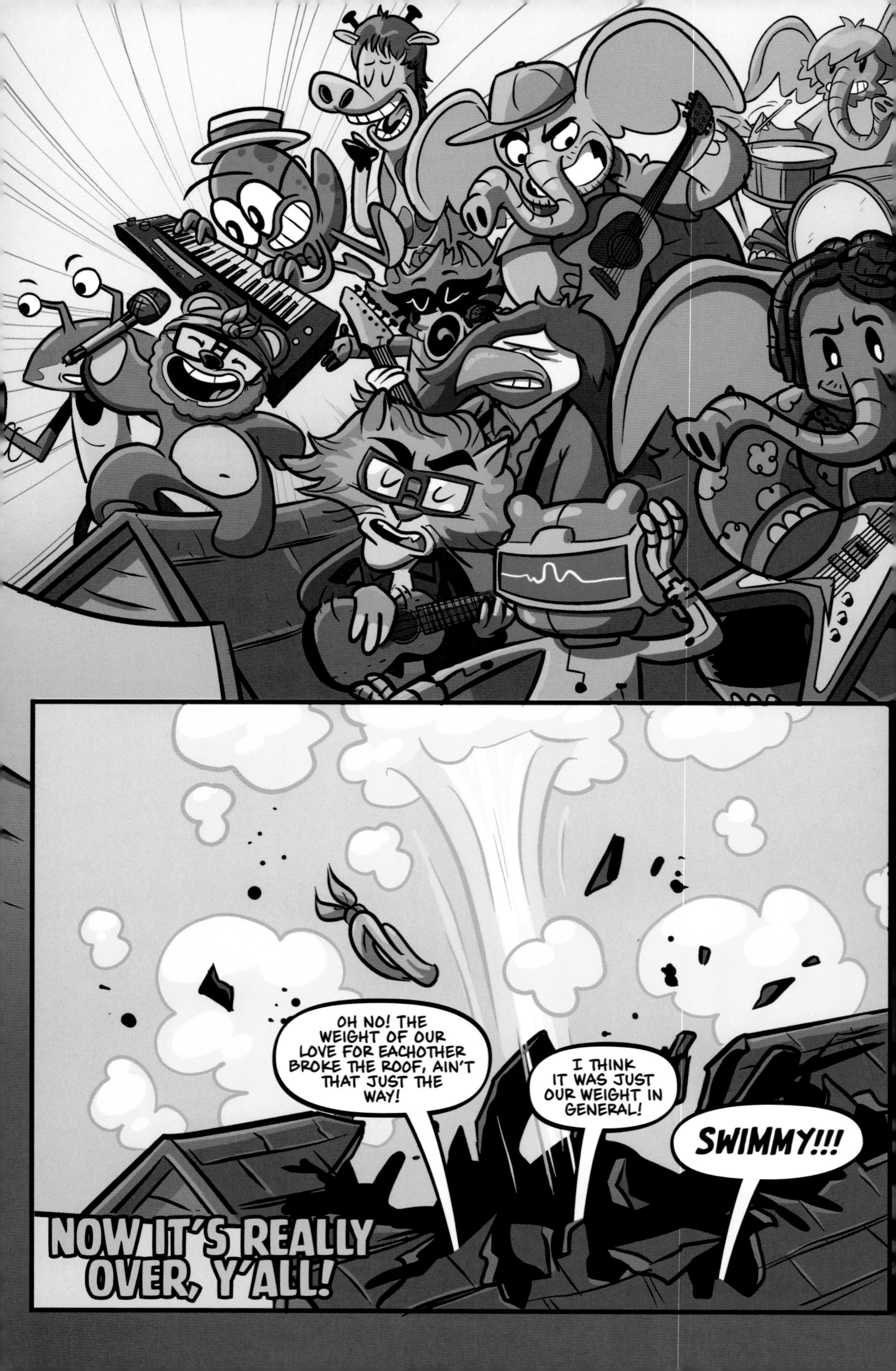

OH NO! THE WEIGHT OF OUR LOVE FOR EACHOTHER BROKE THE ROOF, AIN'T THAT JUST THE WAY!
I THINK IT WAS JUST OUR WEIGHT IN GENERAL!
SWIMMY!!!
NOW IT'S REALLY OVER, Y'ALL!

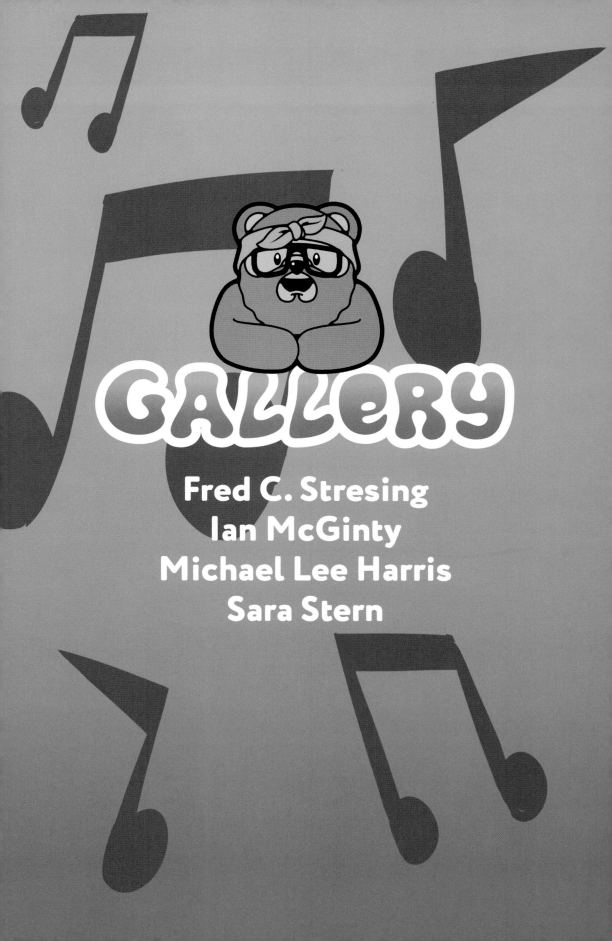

GALLERY

Fred C. Stresing

Ian McGinty

Michael Lee Harris

Sara Stern

"THE SWIM TRUNKS"

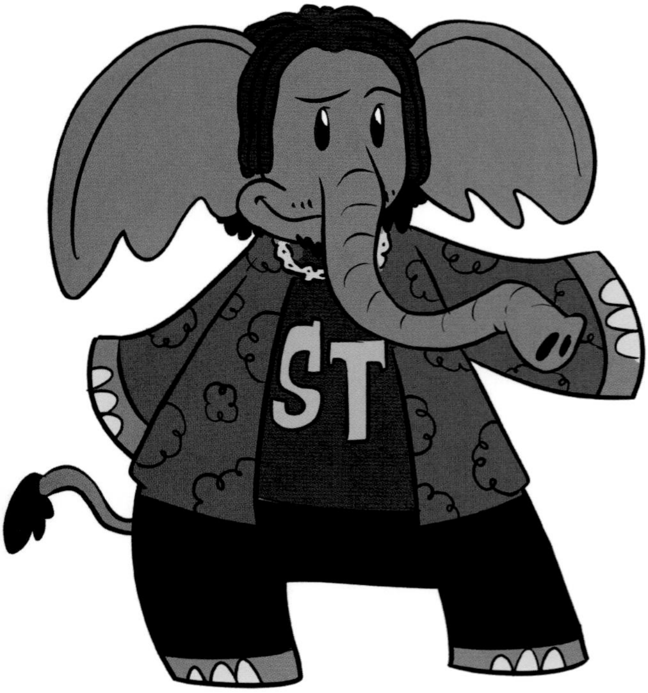
ST

"ADDY"

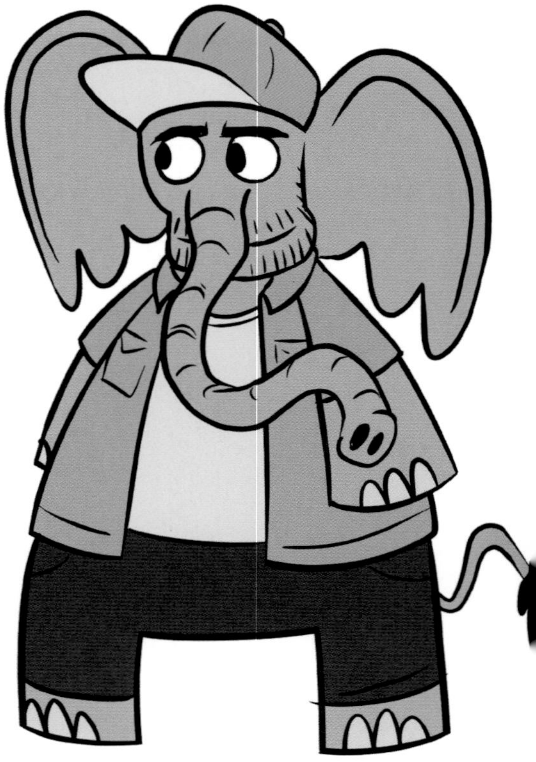

"JAMP"

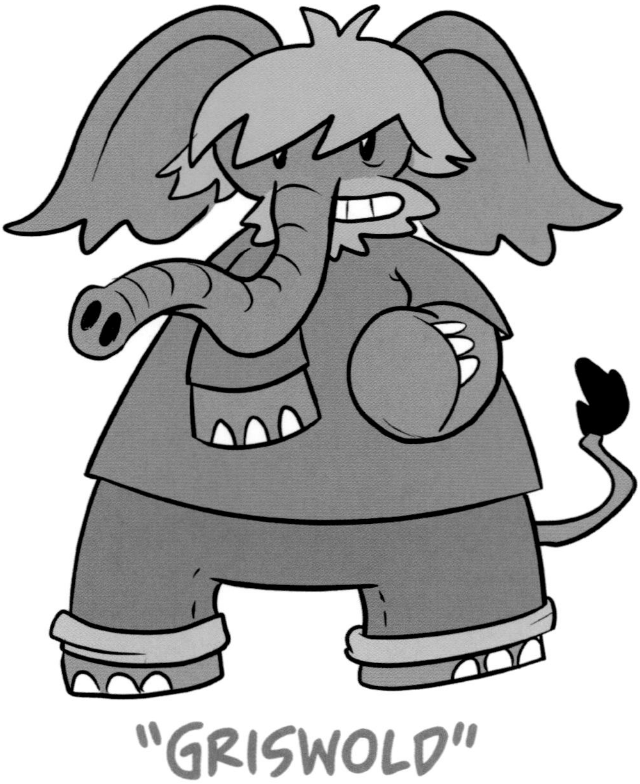

"GRISWOLD"

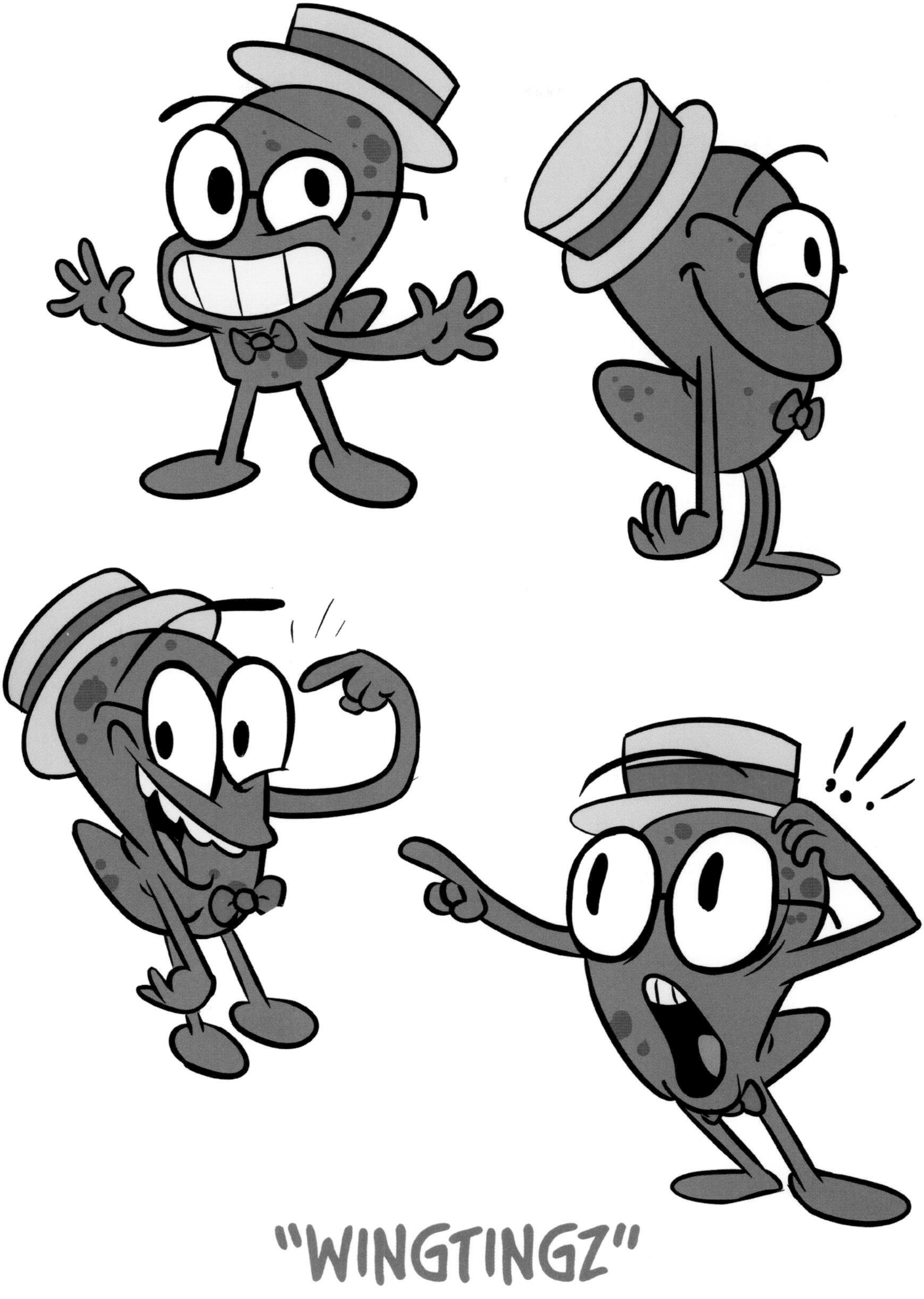

"WINGTINGZ"

"BEAKLOAF"

"TRASHLEY BINS"

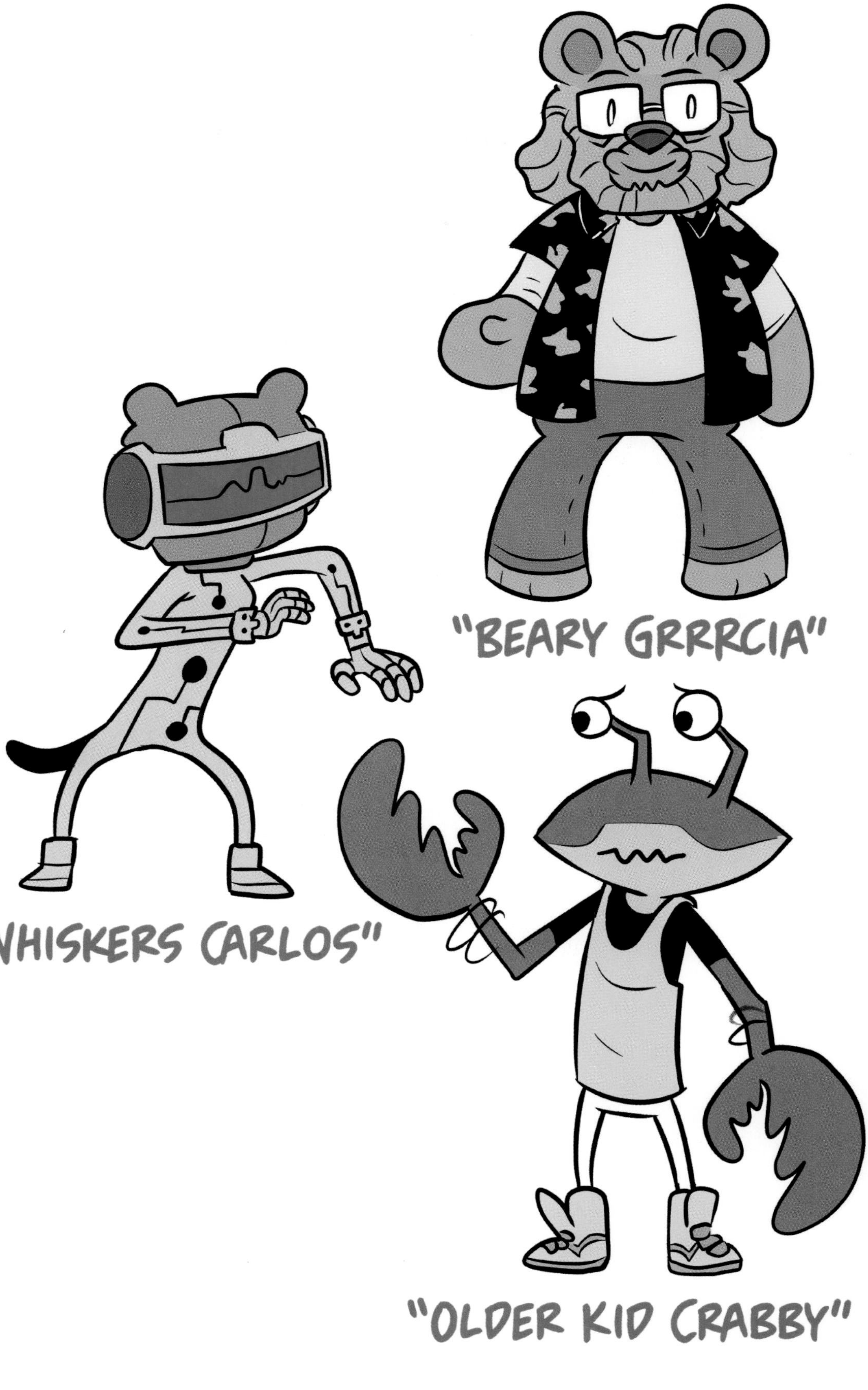
"BEARY GRRRCIA"
"WHISKERS CARLOS"
"OLDER KID CRABBY"

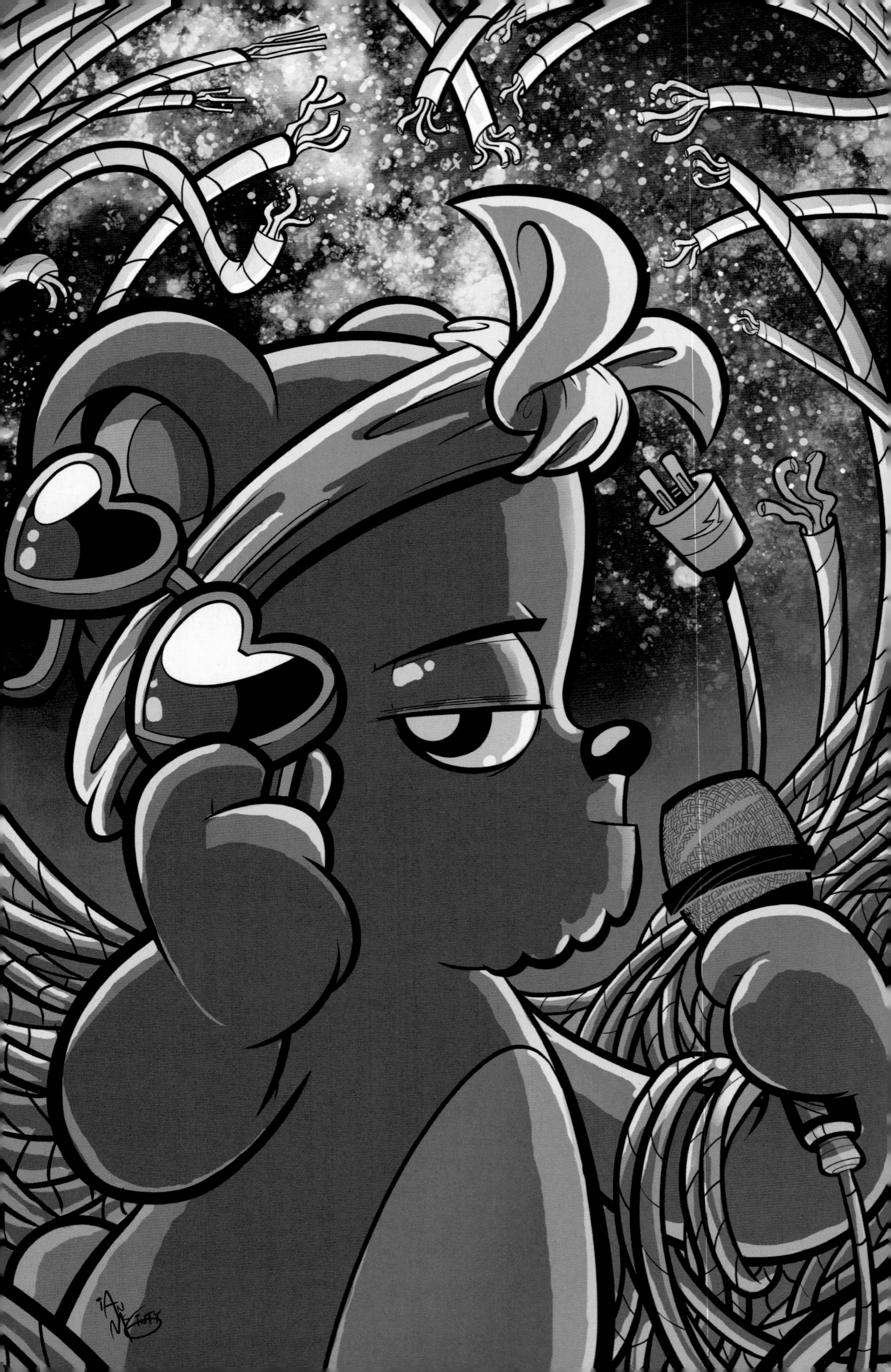

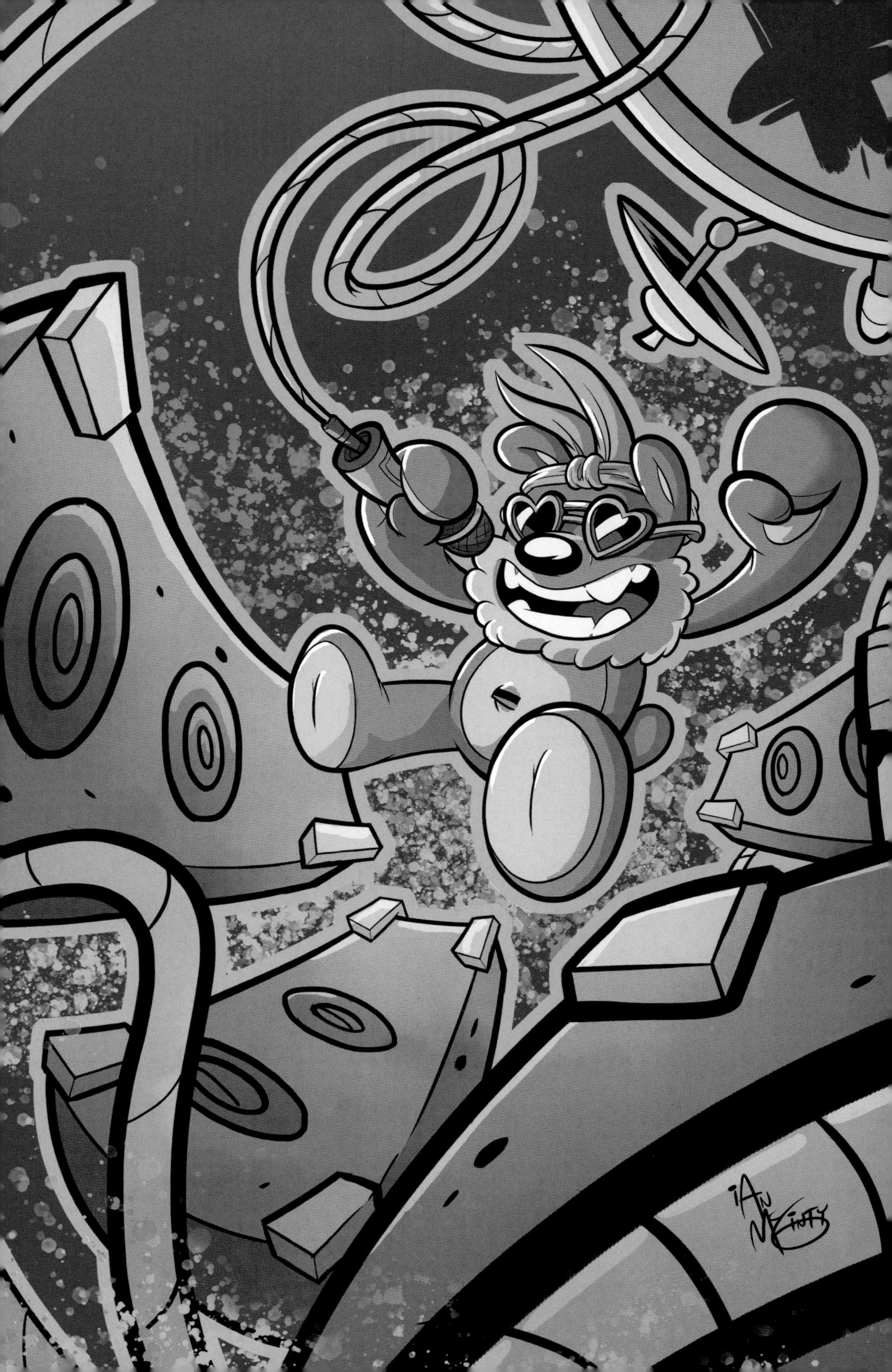

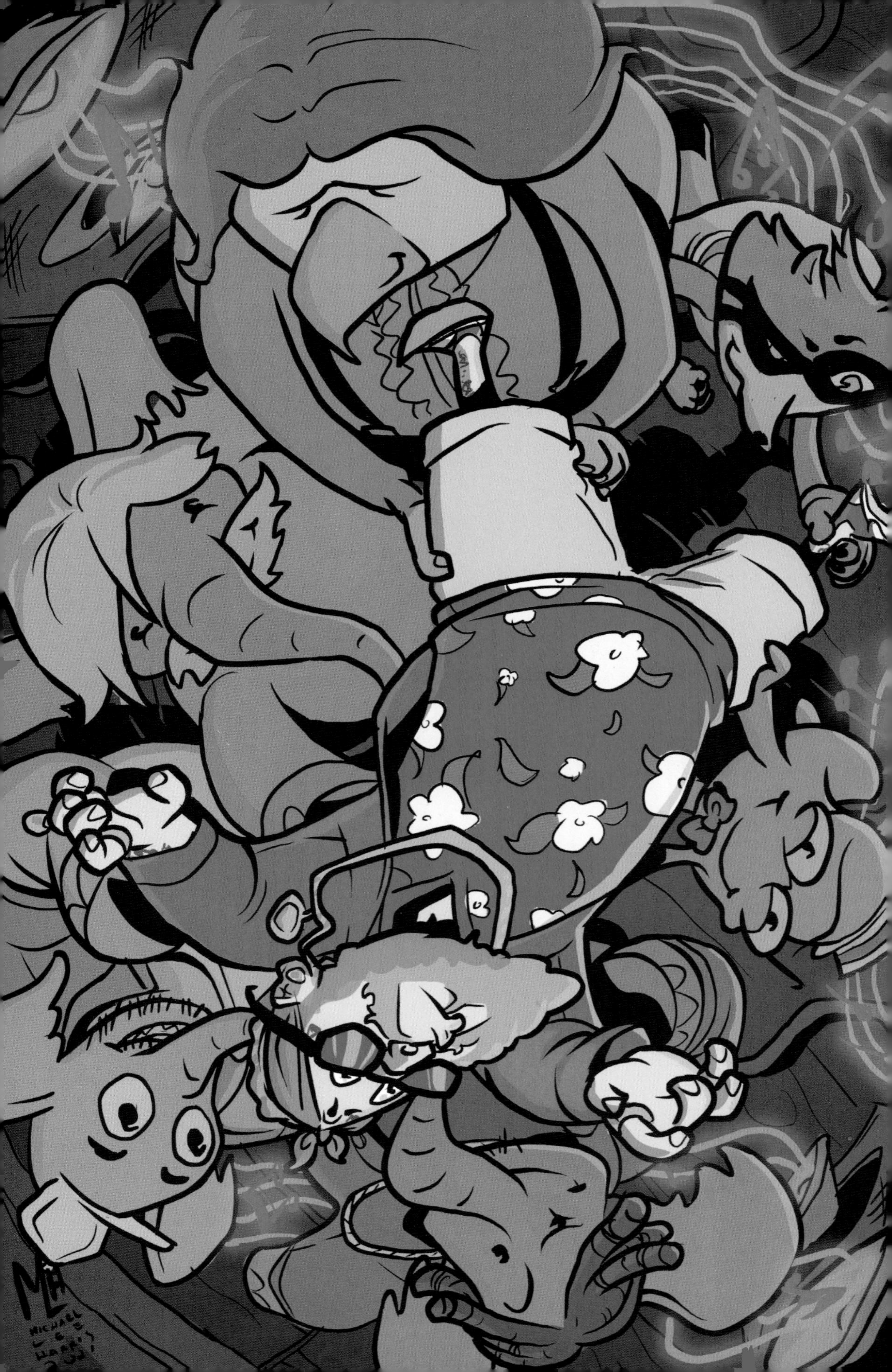
MLH
MICHAEL LEE HARRIS

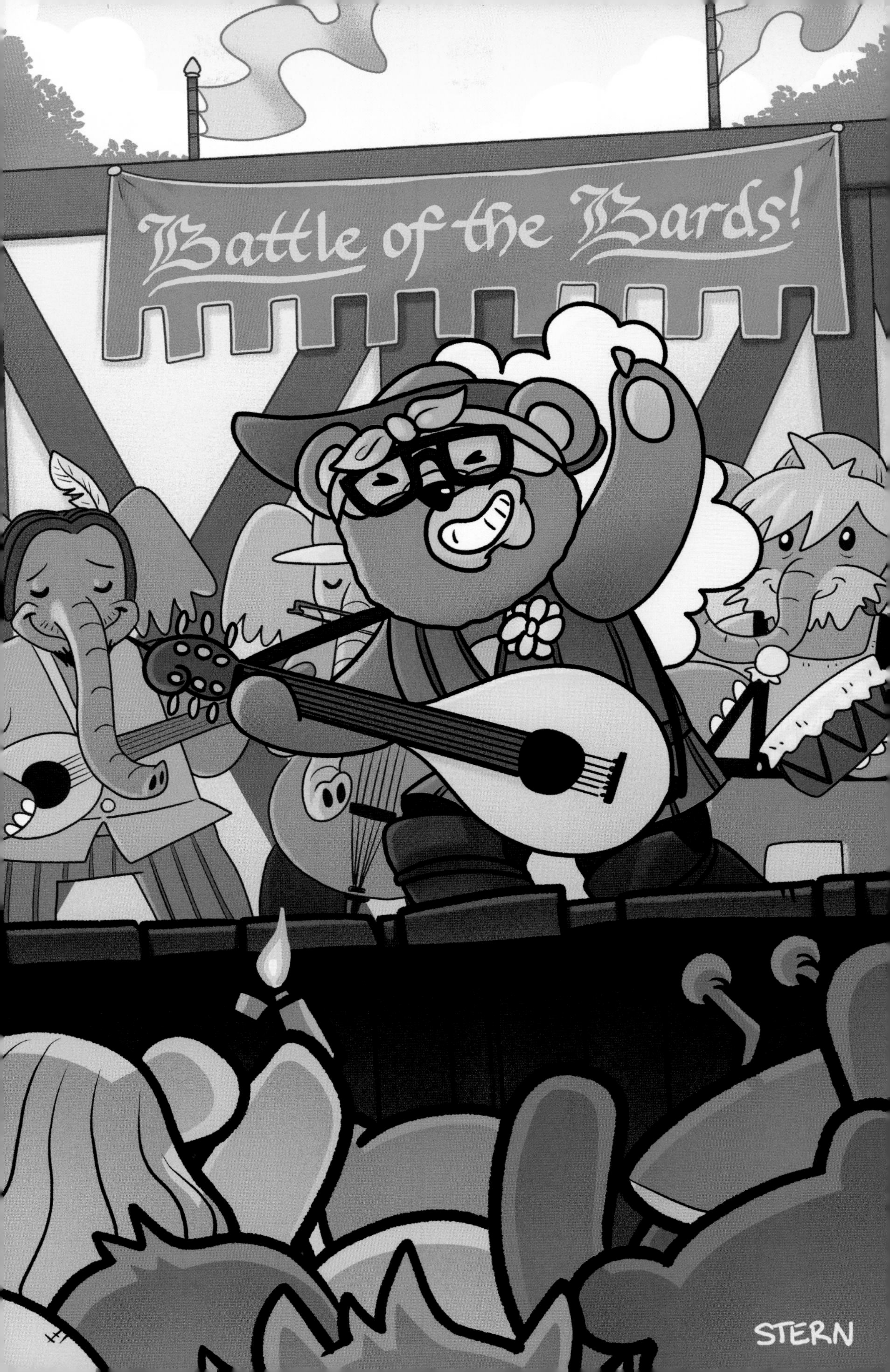
Battle of the Bards!
STERN

Be
Sweet